Desperate
Journeys

Advance Praise

"Vividly imagery-soaked, fast-paced with an upbeat of eventfulness from start to stop, Lola's *Desperate Journeys* surprises with justling suspense, raising your tingling hairs with startles of isolated and collective traumas. In focus is Kila, the central consciousness of the picaresque gallop from inferno to hell in the guise of emigration to an Eldorado of dream-Amerika. Some drown, others are auctioned into slavery, raped or sodomised in the excursion of many, all duped by Kaba. Highway brigands, self-serving forces of law and order, transborder insecurity, geographical inclemency, penury and economic improvidence are worsened by the COVID-19 world conditions. From a ravaged village, Kila makes rounds of encounters with crude cruelties and inhumanity in extremis before returning to a home she has wrecked by taboo pregnancy to face the wrath of tradition. "Messy shifts from a wrecked life to an unfulfilling dream that died in shame" approximates the description of *Desperate Journeys,* and the well-honed lesson is that *greener pastures* are fiercely fictive; be careful."

—**Ntangnyui Patrick Tata**, *editor and critic, PATAMAE Research and Editing Consultancy; Regional Inspector of Secondary Education, North West Region, Cameroon*

***

"Lola's *Desperate Journeys* questions the quest for greener pastures using the gruesome experiences of the protagonist, Kila, to show that illegal migration exposes the African youth to heart-wrecking perils. Lola advocates dialogue and reconciliation when faced with conflicts and humanitarian crises. Three compelling strengths define *Desperate Journeys*: a finely tuned command of imagery, an ability to sketch IDPs, refugees, and migrant characters with intricate accuracy, and an unrivalled understanding of issues and the challenges faced by African migrants, including scamming, identity crisis, trauma, conflict, ecological hazards, and gender-based violence. I strongly recommend Lola's *Desperate Journeys* for the United Nations Humanitarian and Refugee Commissions."

—**Sinyuy Geraldine, PhD**, *writer, editor, and critic; educator; Teacher of English and African Literature*

***

"A must-read poetic narrative, *Desperate Journeys* is aptly innovative and imaginative, full of suspense, apt imagery, metaphors of empire/trauma, vivid descriptions, pathos, humour, flashback, and symbolic in characters and settings, which are highly suggestive in treating themes like displacement, identity, migration, IDP/refugee crisis, disillusionment, and human trafficking. The novel will serve as a treasured resource handbook for High School and University students interested in Migration Studies, gender issues and Conflict and Peace Studies."

—**NYAA Hans Ndah**, *Associate Professor, American and English Literature*

Desperate Journeys

Pepertua K. Nkamanyang Lola

SPEARS BOOKS

Denver, Colorado

SPEARS BOOKS
AN IMPRINT OF SPEARS MEDIA PRESS LLC
7830 W. Alameda Ave, Suite 103-247
Denver, CO 80226
United States of America

First Published in the United States of America in 2025 by Spears Books
www.spearsbooks.org
info@spearsmedia.com
Information on this title: www.spearsbooks.org/desperate-journeys
© 2025 Pepertua K. Nkamanyang Lola
All rights reserved.

ISBN: 9781957296531 (Paperback)
ISBN: 9781957296548 (eBook)
Also available in Kindle format

Designed and typeset by Spears Media Press LLC
Cover designed by D. Kambem
Cover art by Toh Bright

Distributed globally by African Books Collective (ABC)
www.africanbookscollective.com

Contents

Foreword

Nforbin Gerald Niba

In many universities, degree courses in Cameroon Literature, African Literature, Postcolonial studies, sexuality discourses, and Gender and Feminist studies are often attracted to a wide range of subjects, including colonial legacies, slavery, gender, literary ecology, cultural identity, migrations, conflict resolution, peace-building, and the IDP/refugee scourge. Lola Perpetua Nkamanyang Kin-inla has emerged as a pacesetter on topical themes in Cameroon Literature in English. Her play, *The Lock On my Lips* (2014, 2023) extensively explored gender issues in an androcentric postcolonial African (Cameroonian) society while her novel, *Rustles on Naked Trees* (2015) took on the burning ecological issue of environmental degradation and climate change. Besides the subject of gender, her *Healing Stings* (2016) handles other current issues in contemporary Cameroon politics and social life. *Desperate Journeys*, the latest of Lola's intellectual ejaculations, takes on another topical issue: "bush-falling," the tragedy of Africa's (Cameroon's) youthful population. Lucid and shockingly candid about the plight of African youths who dare the challenges of the sea, deserts and jungles, in a quest for greener pastures, the work tracks the trajectory of the protagonist, Kila, from various trials and tribulations to her return in shame and dishonour rejected by her androcentric society that has no place for "fallen women." I consider *Desperate Journeys* an extensive refugee crisis workshop.

While African and Cameroon creative writers have contributed significantly to narratives of displacements, the forte of Lola's *Desperate Journeys* lies in its captivating use of narrative devices, indigenous proverbs, language of emotions, discourses of sexuality and rape, tragi-comic humour, symbolic imagery, metaphors, and thick descriptions to explore the global disturbing phenomena of migrations, humanitarian crisis, transborder insecurity, and crisis of belonging, among others. I consider *Desperate Journeys* an intensive IDP/refugee crisis theatre and find it an incredible encyclopaedia for students and researchers whose research interests include Cameroon/African literature, gender, migrations, Postcolonial and queer studies.

Preface

Desperate Journeys tells our story. Targeting lovers of fiction and students of Cameroon (African) literature, the narrative explores global subjects, including conflict and internal displacements, migrations, humanitarian crisis, disease and pandemics, refugee crisis, homelessness, trauma, sexual assault, human trafficking, hunger, culture shock, the place of children born out of wedlock, transborder challenges and identity crisis. A few excerpts on which the narrative hangs its major thematic trails are worthy of note.

> I was like an uprooted forest tree that began a new life in a farmland where it was deposited by the passing floods... I felt strange and different, somewhat like a plant violently plucked by rainstorms from the burrowing arms of a moulded ridge and hurled into the bush to wither and die... What does a woman know about rivers and land borders?...

The graphic sexual assaults which further depict the hazards of illegal migrations cannot be overlooked:

> The strangers soon launched an aggressive invasion of my lap, tearing down my domestic borders. The shocking demolition prompted a large-scale exodus of blood from my womanhood, leaving my domestic borders porous like a land without a title deed... I was not the only one that suffered invasion and occupation...

These are pricking lines from *Desperate Journeys*, which have gruesome pictures of the experiences of illegal migrations, involving a perilous desert journey and a sea passage that exposes the protagonist to physical and silent battles. On these hang the plot of *Desperate Journeys*, whose central consciousness is Kila, the protagonist victim of a scamming network. Upon losing everything in a communal clash over land ownership between farmers and herders, she plunges into the disorienting status of an Internally Displaced Person (IDP), undertaking the journey to the imaginary Amerika purpose-bound to change her narrative. Quite early in the journey, surmising from the unaccounted change in their itinerary, she realises that she and her companions have been duped by Kaba, who conveys them to a border country en route to Amerika across the desert, which climaxes the narrative with some migrants drowning, some being sold off into slavery, and others raped by the human traffickers of Kaba's network, while survivors grimly continue the journey. Lacking valid documentation and compounded by the sudden eruption of the COVID-19 pandemic with consequent travel restrictions, the journey is truncated, constraining the desperate travellers to sojourn in a transit country. The stranding circumstances make for a surge in immigration. Kila and her companions slip into the IDP camp and then to the refugee facility to evade arrest and deportation. But being undocumented exposes them to new forms of frustration and challenges. Life for them becomes a survival race of the fittest, and they devise strategies to beat its daunting hurdles, in the process nursing hope to raise enough money to continue their journey. Some do farm jobs, others steal yams and cassava from farms, and some pick spilt grains from the market grounds to cook or sell. Still others hunt crawlies from the bushes and eat wild fruits for survival. Even though they are not conscience-stricken by these affronts on social justice, they are soon head-on with the host community, which reports them to the immigration office. Eventually, Kila is fished out and deported, returning more frustrated than she left and with the lesson that "there is no place like home, illegal immigration is not good . . ., greener pastures are not as green as they seem from afar." For all the deadweight of suffering, Kila's achievements are the videos and recordings of her experiences. These she uses as evidence to denounce and incriminate human trafficking scammers in her novel. Her haunting terror, however, is the 'palm bush affair' consequence, which becomes the stinking blot on her, a taboo pregnancy that becomes an insurmountable barrier to her reunion with her husband or acceptance in her local community.

In an interactive exchange, Prof. Nforbin observed, "*Desperate Journeys* is an extensive refugee crisis workshop [that] explores the global refugee crisis … based firmly on facts, first-hand accounts and case studies." In his words, "Kila returns home with a little token – an unwanted pregnancy – the scar of her vain and reckless drifting from home." He captures the central concerns of the work, for conflicts, migrations, humanitarian crisis and resultant trauma, as well as the issue of indigenous identities caught between ethnicities, are major global concerns.

Written predominantly in the first-person narrative, the novel presents conflicts, displacements, and illegal immigration as recipes for humanitarian crisis and problems of identity and belonging. It poses questions for reflection: What are the causes of conflicts, illegal migrations, and humanitarian crisis? What is the role of the creative writer in addressing the global scourge with the power of the ink? Of course, a social problem requires a social intervention and the creative writer must address social problems.

Desperate Journeys certainly also exposes the negative cultural perceptions around both women and children (born out of wedlock) through the voices of Ability and Jeff's father.

I remember having a fruitful discussion on excerpts from *Desperate Journeys* during the course "Contemporary Critical Theories in Language and Literature," and some of my postgraduate students at the English Department of the Higher Teachers' Training College of the University of Bamenda asked about the themes or dissertation topics for which *Desperate Journeys* might provide suitable analytical data.

I hope that lovers of Cameroon (African) Literature, Comparative Literature, Post-colonial studies, identity, migration and conflict studies, and literary students at all levels of education would find *Desperate Journeys* relevant for perusal and exploitation.

Perpetua K. Nkamanyang Lola
Abuja, Nigeria

Acknowledgments

While the story features its own themes, character preferences, and linguistic vehicles, it is rightly rooted in familiarity with migration experiences, conflict-affected environments, and victim narratives, including discussions with various groups of my post-graduate students at the Universities of Douala and Bamenda.

The person who said, 'the reader is part of the production process,' must have had editors and proof-readers in mind. The origin, metamorphosis, and production of *Desperate Journeys* also devolves on experiences and people from whom I have tapped many forms of treasured ingenuity. In this regard, the genius of error-hunting, Ntangnyui Patrick Tata, returned a bleeding manuscript to me upon submitting it to the editorial expertise of the PATAMAE Research and Editing Consultancy. Leaving nothing to chance, he made insertions and deletions, arrowing structural adjustments and straining out linguistic impurities with suggestions of alternatives for sprightly readings. He also suggested that modifications relating to quality, skin colour, and mood be made to the picture illustration of the migrants. To Tata and the consultancy he heads, therefore, I remain indebted. I also owe a massive debt of gratitude to Dr Sinyuy Geraldine for proofreading the work. She perused the manuscript, checking for grammatical errors, and proposed relevant adjustments, which I incorporated into the work. Prof. Nforbin Gerald, Lola Vitalis Nyuy-dze and Prof. Nyaa Hans were also my proofreaders, each doing the marvellous job of picking out the slips of language and content that strayed unnoticed. The invaluable contribution of my son, Ngambam

Maclouski Nkamanyang, cannot be ignored. When the first draft of the picture illustration of the migrants drowning at sea was forwarded to me for appraisal and opinion, Ngambam, in his usual curiosity, analysed the picture and noted that the faces and body language of the migrants were more relaxed than tensed as would be expected, and didn't create the impression of panic and danger. I immediately forwarded his comments to my cover design artist, Toh Bright, who made the required changes.

I am deeply indebted to the world-class giant in publishing, Spears Media Press, for their rare professionalism in transforming my manuscript into readable print. Spears Media Press subjected my work to four vigorous phases of editing: initial proofreading by a subject-area expert, peer review, editing, and final checking of the edited work, much to the profit of my novel. In this regard, Prof Jude Fokwang, determined to eliminate gremlins ever lurking and attempting to ruin the work, performed the laborious task of editing the work. In his quest to ensure that the final product does not suffer from linguistic and structural impurities, he wrenched out the weeds of language, identifying clumsy narrative structures and interrogating imprecise usages with suggestions of substitutes for consideration, engaging me with productive phone calls for queries and clarifications, and followed up with final checking. Publishing with Spears Media Press not only gave my novel the visibility, marketing opportunities and potential royalties which remain significant challenges to Cameroon (African) authors but also introduced me to Zoom book launch events, subject-area experts, the WhatsApp platform for Spears Media authors, and above all, renowned authors from other cultures with whom we network and share ideas, relevant information on existing titles, and excellent tips on creative writing and publishing which the classroom does not provide.

1

The Desert Journey

Of all the things I have seen and done, my journey to Amerika is an experience analogous to a horror dream that gives shivers. Back then, I was forced by a protracted bloody crisis between the farmers and the herdsmen to leave home for greener pastures. The perilous journey was one of tiptoeing from border to border to enter Amerika from the backdoor. I do not, however, carry all the blame. When he came to harvest money from my hands for my travel documentation, Kaba did not say that the road to Amerika would pass through the desert. And that's what happened.

The things I saw still make me shudder with fear. Despite the strangling fear of facing the stings of tradition should the council of elders hear that a queue of reckless human tubers invaded my domestic borders and trod the path of my womanhood, leaving its boundary in shreds, I have decided to tell my story and serve aspiring migrants with words of caution. Yet, I know many will wonder why I should transform my own life into a novel. First, answer me: Who would urinate and drink and eat fresh soil and leaves and barks of trees while being smuggled from one border to another and not tell would-be 'Bush fallers' that it is dangerous to travel abroad through the backdoor? Who would sit quietly after suffering a mass invasion of the waist region and left to leak with drool like a broken water pipe? As I speak, scammers with fake profiles on internet walls, pose as liaison agents for foreign companies and academic institutions. They still storm the streets of social media with appetizing traps and promises of facilitating migrations to Amerika and Dubai. I hear some ask unsuspecting victims to pay 2,000,000frs CFA and get ready to travel to Amerika or Germany the next day to pick up juicy jobs. Many of you still fall for it. Allow me to be brutally honest with aspiring 'Bush Fallers,' as those who leave their country for better opportunities abroad are called. These aspirants I now invite to follow my story with its detailed look at the sneaky odyssey, destination— Amerika. The journey across the border town with its straggle of houses and squatting roadside huts, buzzing with currency-exchange merchants, was the last environment where I felt at ease.

Fear ripped through my heart, rattling it as our vehicle suddenly dug into the migrant flow pathway and began to jostle through the cloud-covered dwarf-like scattered trees. I wasn't the only one that looked scared. I still remember the reactions of the others when our vehicle turned into the desert pathway. Jawara, Aboki, Atang, Livinus, Savage, and Fola stood with their shoulders slightly lifted while their mouths hung open and the fringes of their upper eyelids were raised. We all stared at one another and then, from one end of the desert to another, all panicky.

From the start of the desert journey, I knew we were bound to face danger. Sitting on the top edge of the carriage, I had command of a broad range of sight and was at liberty to roam the unending stretches of land we passed. What looked like flakes of ashes drizzled continuously from the sky, falling from all sides like migratory termites. My ears droned continuously with the snore of storms while mournful voices of the roaming winds howled and rustled off to the skies. The desert trail itself looked thirsty and starved of attention. My heart galloped and shrank. The dry-hairy winds felt sandy on my skin, leaving it with a shrivelled and pale look. I could feel painful cracks on my lips. There was no sign of human presence. I remember seeing only lifeless sheets of collapsing clouds hanging frighteningly from the sky as we drove across the desert. The air was thick with both dust and fear.

"Is there a habitable place in this land?" I wondered aloud, staring across to the far ends, where trees and frowning clouds looked like the place where earth met the sky. There were empty lands everywhere. Only sand and trees could be seen. Questions kept pounding my heart.

I had duly paid for my international passport and flight ticket when Kaba collected the money to process my travel documents. My passport came with an Amerikan visa stamped on one of the pages. Why, then, weren't we travelling by air, and where was the driver taking us? Was there a route to Amerika through the desert?

Jawara muffled questions that showed that he too was terrified.

"Kila, where are we now? What's the name of this country? Are we safe?" He spoke through his teeth, staring at me, open-mouthed, but his questions broke the silence. In no particular order, Savage and Livinus started digging up stories they had heard from survivors who fled inhuman treatment in other lands and travelled back to Kibaaka through the same desert.

It is a land of trees and vast expanses of seas and less-known forests where human traffickers and slave merchants lurk in wait for prey. It is a migratory route for smuggling migrants from Africa to countries that are financially seductive to job seekers. It is the Agadez desert trail where clandestine vehicles and motorbikes smuggle migrants from Bamfada and Kibaaka into neighbouring countries for transit journeys to far-off lands like Dubai, Qatar, Spain, Italy, and Amerika. There is also the sea to be crossed. The giant sea smuggles travellers across Africa to the land of the white man. Thousands drown yearly while trying to cross the sea. People who sell arms, too, use the Agadez trail. Terrorists and human traffickers have bases in the desert strip. I closed my ears with the flaps of my hands to avoid hearing more of the dreadful stories.

We rode on, not noticing the time-lapse as we had all fallen asleep at some point.

The sound of crickets chirping from the sand reminded me that we were approaching a new day. I was now so weak and thirsty, my feet benumbed, and the joints disjointed. My arms also became loose at the joints. I felt the prick of the winds. My throat became too dry after eating some biscuits that were stored in my handbag. I felt warm sensations below my lower stomach. I wanted to urinate. God answered my prayers. The driver suddenly stopped briefly at a bend and stepped out to urinate. Like others, I quickly climbed down and slipped into a nearby bush. It's hard to believe that I did what I did. I carefully collected drizzles of my own urine into my cupped hand. Much of it ran over the edges, but a few drops reached my mouth. I returned to my seat, disappointed. Others, too, urinated and drank, not being as unsuccessful as me.

Something happened here. Two muscular motorbikes transporting bloated bags and large gallons with sticking-out stomachs approached and stopped. The thick smell of petrol hit my nostrils. Our driver and one of the riders drifted behind our vehicle to talk with the motorbike rider. Our driver squeezed something into his hands, collected a wrap, and opened it. I saw something like the lips of a gun and quickly turned away my face, afraid. Livinus must have noticed my prying gaze.

He said they were transporting fuel and arms in a muted voice, staring at me. The unguarded desert borders made it convenient for illicit activities. I didn't follow up on Livinus' details because I felt drowsy and soon fell asleep—I can't say for how long. I was still sleeping when a frail voice awakened me.

"Water! Water!" It was the voice of Savage. I quickly opened my eyes and trailed her pointing finger to a massive body of water across the land. It forked at the far end like exit branches. Precious water! I screamed with joy. The breeze must have wafted bad breath from my sticky mouth towards Livinus. He plastered his nostrils with his hands when I spoke. He acted as if his own breath wasn't stinking but that didn't matter to me. I felt happy seeing water for the first time since the start of the desert journey. Savage's face also blossomed with instant joy at the sight of water. Everyone looked excited at the river as we approached it. It wasn't only the sight of water that brought excitement. I could see a canoe spilling over with travellers. It glided frenziedly back and forth over the simmering waters. A vehicle was also offloading passengers at the sandy shore. A man who looked like an elephant grass stem at the top of a distant hill sat on the edge of another empty canoe, thrusting a long flat stick into the waters that were going and receding. By the time we were close enough, the vehicle had offloaded the passengers and was already returning. That is when it became clear to me that it was a sea, not just a river in front of us.

"Are we going to travel by sea?" I asked, staring at the waves leaping across and plunging into the canoe, swerving back and forth on the confused waters. Everybody now focused on the waves, staring open-mouthed and wide-eyed, not seeming to have heard my question. The joy of drinking water was suddenly killed by the waves' threatening activities, which took our attention for almost ten minutes.

The swelling waters agitated continuously, its waves leaping over and plunging, then fleeing and coming back in a confused spread. The water ran towards us and swallowed our legs as if it were a welcome ritual. But it instantly retreated. Afraid to go near and scoop up water with my hands and drink, I stood for a while, staring at the bully, frozen with fright. Then, the simmering waves suddenly went mad again, dancing, swiftly rushing back and forth, and swinging up towards the shore, swallowing our legs up to the knees and flapping their wings against our faces. The waves were too confrontational. My internal organs must have felt intimidated by the menacing waves. I felt warm sweat running down my cheeks. I struggled to hold the ridges of my buttocks into a tight squeeze. I hoped to transform into a whisper, the ballooning wobbling air that struggled to storm out. It didn't work. A thunderous blast struck the air that recklessly rushed out of confinement. Warm urine scurried down my legs as if craving more attention from Livinus, who had clamped his nostrils with his upper lips after the first of the chain of roaring sounds was loosed, spreading around a sticky, reeking stench.

"Let us move away from this area now," I suggested, but the terrified travellers were already shifting away before I did. We supportively held out our hands and waddled to a slightly raised surface away from the sprays of the waves. We stood about a hundred meters from the shore but I felt unsafe even there.

The waves charged across and up the raised surface, greedily engulfing stretches of land, at times leaping high and flapping their wings in the breeze in repeated back-and-forth movements. I felt like going back home even without knowing how. Others too hated the confronting waves and I could tell from the way Savage, Jawara, Fola, Atang, Ntumfon, Aboki, Yuka, Verdzekov, and Livinus shivered nearby, their teeth sticking out, and the fringes of their eyelids raised. A young man with food particles lodged between his teeth, held a Bible in his hands, shuddering convulsively as he prayed,

"Blood of Jesus! Blood of Jesus! Shababa! Ishabalaba, Ishabababa! Father, you said in the Holy Book that no weapon fashioned against your children shall prosper! By the strength of that declaration, Father, if there is an evil spirit hiding inside that water with the intention to promote the agenda of the devil, I command the Holy Spirit to descend now and create confusion in their camp!"

"Amen!" We chorused, instigated by dread.

We felt relieved when the waters ran back to the sea. My mouth was sticky. I looked around me, craving water and to wash my mouth. I made a little hole in the sand. Water soon collected into the bowl-shaped hole for me to scoop and drink. It was sticky and salty. After drinking, I moved the water in my mouth to my throat with the help of my tongue and then spat it out. I then cut a short, wet stem from a shrub and chewed it to form bristles. With this, I brushed my mouth thoroughly. Others followed my example.

"We may soon start going," Atang said, pointing at the withdrawing waves. It was evident that we would soon get on the canoe when I saw Kaba approaching.

"The waves are gone. Now, listen very well. We collect 25,000

CFA, or N35,000, or $70, per person! Go down to the shore and pay your transit fares and take your seats in the vessel, very fast," Kaba ordered, pointing at the canoe.

The canoe was a half-rounded wooden bowl, the size of a small lake, large, long, and deep in the middle, with pointed edges in front and rear. The furrow-shaped vessel was encircled by raised ridges that served as seats. The Graffi people of the North West Region of Kibaaka would see a similarity between the boat and the presentation of an achu meal with its deep cut in the middle. I was obsessed with taking pictures of the travellers trooping down the shore where the vessel was roped to a post.

"I need to take pictures and forward to Miranda. We need to keep tracking signals," I whispered in Savage's ears and then turned to take the last shots.

I directed my camera at the travellers filling in like ants into the canoe. I focused the tiny camera on my mobile telephone on the sagging heads of the travellers, drooping exactly like a congregation of miracle-seeking ailing worshippers bent double over church benches, praying and waiting for miracles to relieve them from poverty and disease. Loose legs, flabby arms, and sagging heads of travellers leaked over the edges of the vessel like calabashes or pumpkin gourds spilling over rows of pillars channelled across farmland ridges to serve as supports. A man that had looked from a distance like a withered corn stem before we reached the shore, sat at the front edge of the canoe. He was thrusting a wooden stick with a flat end into the waters, slowly pulling it back and forth, and screaming at travellers.

"Make all man come inside vessel make we go! I no go wait for anybody! Na last warning this!"

"Let's hurry, the boat is getting full. You can continue taking the pictures when we're seated," Savage said, pointing at the queue of travellers who were paying their fares and moving into the full canoe. When Savage and I reached the shore, the vessel was already spilling over.

I was the last person to climb up in the canoe. I sat wedged to the ridge. My left hand and left leg were inside, while my right hand and right leg dangled over the boat's edge, almost touching the water. I feared falling off into the water if the canoe jolted. So, I passed my left hand around the waist of the prayer warrior standing close to me. He held a Bible in his hand, calling us 'unbelievers' and bragging about how his prayers stopped the waves from swallowing us, how he predicted the victory of Obama during the American presidential elections, and it came to pass, and how he prophesied that his neighbour's daughter would marry at the end of the year and it happened. He urged us to give our lives to God and receive spiritual empowerment. I was, in no doubt, aware of the power of the Holy Spirit the young prayer warrior certainly possessed. I then gripped the edge of his trousers firmly, for his presence around me would save me from falling off into the water. The guy must have interpreted my safety measures as a body-language invitation to emotional affection. He quickly shot his eyes, partially allowing a lingering smile to form on his lips in a way that looked like a silent expression of reciprocity. Waking up to the embarrassment I had caused myself, I quickly released my shy hand.

My heart almost leaped out of my chest immediately the canoe lurched forward into the sea and started to glide along. Without realizing it, I grabbed and held tightly to my neighbour's trousers once more, my eyes firmly closed and my heart galloping faster than before. My lips twitched repeatedly while my hands and legs trembled. I felt like the boat was whirling in an eternal spin. When I opened my eyes, however, I saw that the boat was only gliding across and burrowing through the waves and not spinning. The waves were constantly confused, treacherous, and intimidating in their movements, running forth and back, leaping across and plunging in heaves. My heart suddenly danced a wild dance inside my chest when a ridge of waves unfolded swollen bodies gliding in large piles over the water's surface. The stiff bodies charged from side to side like the explorer or traveller who lost his way in a foreign land. Every now and then, our canoe rammed into the hedge of lengthened bodies, fleeing confusedly back and forth in long-range glides, causing my heart to dance like a skirt of leaves on the waist of a corn plant.

My fear increased with the slithering of the boat over the wavy waters. I closed my eyes firmly, hoping to stop being a spectator of the stiff, swollen bodies and confrontational waves that seemed to have no other agenda than to leap out and up occasionally and smack our cheeks. Before long, I felt my body whirl around once more as if I was performing a stunt of turning round and round. I was forced to open my eyes again. Waves had started surging higher up, fleeing away and returning in massive heaves, leaping and slapping our faces with larger flails. Panic heightened in my shivering heart. We were now unsteady and quirked to the jolting and swaying of our boat and from side to side. Then, the canoe suddenly started drifting along at a spiralling speed. We started screaming and pleading with the paddler to reduce the speed of the sail. But the canoe continued to move in swift glides and heaves and leaps. For all I knew, the paddler had no more control of the cantering sail, which went on for many hours. I turned to the prayer warrior, but he had grabbed my dress and was now shivering like a chick in the grip of a hawk, screaming for help.

At this moment, the sail suddenly rattled in a dreadful manner. The waters and the winds, too, started to enter the sail. The bashing waves elevated their violent sizes and came and went in heaves and surges. They unpredictably but progressively leaped higher, plunged deeper, and waters broke into the canoe. At this point, the paddler seemed to notice that danger was at our doorsteps. He started making rapid swerves with abrupt and sharp turns. He would thrust his wooden stick into the water and pull hard, forth and back, changing directions suddenly and kinkily. With a rapidity analogous only to the speed of a storm, he would veer across the surface of the water and swing from side to side as if he was avoiding a collision with something. The paddler attempted to burrow through the hedge of the furiously flaring waves but met with aggressive resistance. I gripped the leg of Savage's trouser, panting breathlessly, praying, thinking of my children as the paddler jostled through the wild sheets of water. I heard voices screaming, praying, and begging God to spare our lives but I was too distraught to pray or concentrate. The canoe was now almost half filled with water. Some travellers started scooping water from the canoe with their joined palms. Nothing could convince me that the paddler had not planned to commit mass suicide for us all.

The suicidal conviction was still settling when, suddenly, a rolling hedge of waves with the shape of a massive fleeing ridge leaped back and rammed itself in our faces. I heard a heavy sound that was like a gigantic scraping scoop. I didn't immediately know that the waves had swallowed us until I found myself submerging and resurfacing. Then, I felt the salty water entering my mouth. At the same time, I heard wild screams rending the air from above my head. They were the voices of other drowning victims crying for help. The swimming lessons and techniques I received in the rehabilitation facility back in my country came to the fore. The lessons were never meant for this wild monstrosity of seawater. But they were a handy save.

I barely managed to keep my body upright, my head above the water. I needed to regain balance. Then, I tried hard to pedal my legs up and down as if riding a bicycle while my arms moved in a rotatory motion. It was like double pedalling a bicycle without actual pedals or a handlebar. I paddled all the same while looking across the right and left flanks of the water to figure out which direction was safer to swim in. My eyes fell on a water trail meandering toward the beach, not too far from where our canoe had overturned. When I struggled to swim across, I felt utterly fenced off by the heaving waves. I could see heads popping up, hands thrusting forward, and then submerging and resurfacing. The waves were relentlessly agitating, pushing back and forth lengthened bodies, making movement infinitely difficult. My legs and shoulders became heavy. That is when I started praying to God to save my life and give me another chance to live. I cursed the day I met Kaba and regretted leaving my country. The teaspoon salary I earned every month, I now decided, was better than this wild hazard. It was better in the classrooms, I affirmed. When I thought my world was at an end, I felt a hand pushing me towards the shore from behind. It was Savage, as I later learned. I had no clue what happened to me immediately I was pushed to the shore, but I did eventually understand that I stayed long in that mood of unconsciousness.

What I saw upon coming back to life was Savage pressing hard on my stomach with her fingers and I was regurgitating water. For over twenty minutes, the water I had swallowed was welling up and pouring out from my mouth at each push she made.

"W-w-what h-happened to me?" I managed to mumble, coughing out more of the water.

"You can speak! She's alive! She's alive!" Savage screamed excitedly, attracting the attention of Kaba and the boy who had been propelling the canoe. They were kneeling and pressing the stomachs of other survivors with their knees and fingers. I was not the only one throwing up. The canoe man was pressing down on Jawara's stomach causing water to gush out of his mouth. Atang and Livinus also vomited water on the sand. I was thanking God and Savage for saving my life. I groped in my underwear and was excited to find my telephone well burrowed in the plastic paper I had used to wrap it round before entering the canoe, to keep it away from water. A thought struck me. I had not seen those with whom I left the village. Where could they be?

One after the other, my searching eyes fell on Aboki, Fola, Kitam, and Ntumfon. They lay scattered across the sandy beach, slightly squirming. My joy at seeing them alive was short-lived. Stiff bodies lay in a piled-up mass like discarded plastic bottles stacked on the banks of swamps along River Mairin. Bodies with bent limbs, looking exactly like athletes jumping over hurdles, lay in confused spatters stranded on different locations on the sandy shore. A tiny mountain of bodies in tangled piles lay on another bank of sand, just below my legs. I watched gawking mouths and wide-open eyes staring vaguely into the sky, some wearing frowns of agony. I could recognize many of the faces we had travelled together. While I was accommodating and trying to make sense of what was happening, three stretched-out figures heaved over to the shore, turning and swinging from side to side. Then, they started fleeing and coming back to the shore, repeating the action over and over. Tears welled up in my eyes when I discovered it was the bodies of Verdzekov and Yuka being hauled back and forth. It wasn't only the bodies that were coming and going. Bags had been hauled up onto the shore and were fleeing, returning, and floating on the water's surface near the bank. My bag was among the few that Savage had managed to rescue and pulled up to the shore. I changed my shoes and dress and put on a gown.

We eventually regained our strength to begin the next phase of the journey. The few lucky ones identified their bags among those washed up on the shore and lifted them to their backs. Livinus' bag was missing, but he carried one that nobody identified with. I bent forward, and Savage helped me lift my heavy bag to my back. Loaded bags jutted from our backs in all shapes, like babies, bundles of firewood, or overloaded baskets strapped to the backs of women returning home at the end of the day from banana and tea plantations. We trekked for days, led by Kaba and the canoe man. We limped, tired, bending double. We were like the tired heads of heavily loaded donkeys burdened with bags of food. We clambered over raised surfaces like pumpkin stems crawling over ridges in cultivated land. We jostled through the unfriendly desert flow way, staggering like overloaded donkeys scrambling up a stiff mountain. We sneaked from one border to another and wound our way between hanging boulders with slim passages. The difference between minutes and hours or night-time was lost to my sensitivities, given the dull continuum of it. I couldn't determine how far we had travelled; I had lost count of time. I only knew it was not night-time or daytime whenever darkness descended on us, or when I saw the moon and the stars above our heads, or when I saw the sun disappearing behind the far-off hills, or when I heard birds chirping.

Thankfully, the air in this part of the desert was only mildly hairy cold. Savage tapped my shoulder and pointed across to what looked like a country of trees way off. Have we crossed the desert? Or are we approaching another country from its suburbs? I wondered. Shrubs shelved into a settlement of trees stretching endlessly in the long spread. It was the first time we had seen such a village of trees since the start of the journey after the sea hazard. It felt refreshingly different trekking into the forest, but it would be another deadly adventure. It was the main passage the migrants used to reach transit countries to Amerika, we were told. It took us well over five days to cross the forest. Again, you easily lost count of time in the trudge through the shadowy ways. Glints of light through the branches of trees hinted when it was daytime. Otherwise, tired, we slept on leaves, got up, and continued following instructions. The forest had its own sights and wonders.

Obese trees in their menopausal stage, roofed with curls of leaves falling over their shoulders, swayed back and forth and from side to side. Long shadowy shapes stretched themselves along the surfaces. Excited monkeys swung across branches of trees, leaping from one tree to another on the rambling pathways. Immediately the animals sighted us, they paused their acrobatic displays and would howl in apparent surprise, some of them casting confrontational glances at us from the shoulders and branches of the trees as if it was a signal that human incursion wasn't allowed in the animal territory. We moved, bending over; sometimes, we used our hands and knees to crawl and avoid a head-on collision with branches of trees that stretched their arms to give us hard embraces. We crept across surfaces again. You felt like a creeping pumpkin stem in that lowly exercise. Head-swinging, confused trees kept swaying back and forth to the music of dry winds that howled above our heads and rustled off among the leafy undergrowth. They chafed and gnawed the cracked skin of my face and lips. Tangled stems smacked our arms and faces, leaving deep, bloody cuts and scars the size of woody roots as we groped through the dropping branches of trees. My skin looked like the mouldy bark of a kola nut trunk, with lacerated jabs that gaped at the sensitive penetration of the cold winds.

A particular incident is still fresh in my memory. We were

climbing a raised surface when Livinus suddenly sprang back, screaming at the top of his voice. We all reacted with animal instinct by running back, scared and stirred by his action. We staggered helter-skelter, rolling backward to the foot of the bumpy surface. Blood was dripping from my left knee, and I didn't know when it happened and that my dress had a cut on the knee. A severe backache worsened my plight. At first, I thought Livinus had bumped into a confronting snake, a human trafficker, or a jaguar. We had earlier spied a jaguar on a tree. We didn't wait long for him to recount what happened. He had bumped into the lifeless body of a woman; the breasts dug out from its chest. The eyes too were plucked off from the sockets. The legs were spread apart, and the macabre acts on the body gave it a horrifying look. He was scared. We quickly moved out of that area.

The undulating surfaces led through treacherously narrow passageways that wound their confused routes between boulders on the walls of a shelving hill. And there were no alternatives; it was the only visible trail along that stretch. It was anticipated that the track would lead us to the top of the mountain to descend to the valley and then cross over to the adjoining neighbourhood. Bent double and forward with bloated bags on our backs, we trudged, our arms hanging loosely down and swaying from side to side like head-swinging treetops, nodding and bowing to the passing wind. We clambered over the walls of the mountain, bumping into huge boulders, falling, and getting up. From some difficult raised surfaces, we crawled to the treacherous passageway, which only went up to the shoulders of the mountain. The other side of the mountain had crumbled, carrying debris of boulders and churned earth down the valley and leaving dangerously tottering edges pitted downward. We had no option but to descend back to the foot of the mountain from where we had climbed and thence take a deviation. Kaba and the canoe man did not seem to be sure of the deviation.

The mountain climbing and return journey drained me, especially since it was an irrelevant repeat. Like breasts that have become saggy after suckling twelve children, I lost steam and felt weak. My legs became heavy, and I felt as if needles were pricking the soles of my feet. Trees were whirling before me. At this point, I realised that a presence lying flat across my feet was trying to imitate my unsteady movements. It staggered a little ahead of me but constantly withdrew and returned to my body as if we lived in each other. It had a human shape with a body and a head. This second self seemed to know me better and had a lot of sympathy for me. It trusted me and kept withdrawing and returning into my body. It repeated every action I initiated. It staggered to a fall, stood up, and faltered with me. It did not leave me even when it was apparent from my gasping that I might not survive. I soon realised that it was but my shadow that trees had cast along the path. At the same time, thirst and hunger completely drained the crumbs of strength I was left with. I needed rest. I turned and whispered in Savage's ear, panting. Without uttering a word, Savage pointed at the muscular cane the canoe man held in his hand. The message was clear: I would be flogged for sitting down to rest or showing any signs of fatigue. I pulled off my bag and removed some of my clothes and shoes to throw away to reduce the load.

Savage was right. One girl who had joined our vehicle in Menda, whose name I have since forgotten, had been thrown off the vehicle earlier and abandoned in the desert. Her crime was that she shook violently, and watery stools crawled down her legs, attracting flies into the carriage. One woman too had slumped and died after receiving numerous strokes of cane from the canoe man on her buttocks and her back for complaining that she was feeling thirsty, hungry, and weak. She had swayed from side to side as she walked, then, all of a sudden, she had lurched forward with hands dangling by her side and stood like the drooping stem of a dying plant. Heavy thuds on her back sent her crumbling heavily to the ground. I watched a healthy branch wrenched from the limb of a nearby tree descending heavily on her face and buttocks. She wailed loudly before rolling over and over on her stomach. Then she took quick, loud, short breaths into her nostrils as we walked away. When we felt tired, branches of trees with muscles the size of obese ginger roots were used to beat us.

With thoughts like these in mind, I staggered along with the others. I felt slightly relieved when we came onto a narrow track, but my joy was short-lived. An assaulting stench hit the air. I leaned over, wondering where the smell was coming from. Two ridges of swarming flies across the field made matters clear. There were decomposing bodies of a young lady and a baby. Nearby, another swollen body lay on naked sands. It stared thoughtlessly into the sky, spreading fear and sticky reek that trailed us across the unfriendly paths. I could hear hearts pounding inside chest cavities immediately our eyes fell on them. The bodies were lodging jubilant birds, twerking maggots, and flies dancing, taking off and landing delightfully. We plugged our nostrils with our hands and moved fast past the grim company.

A few metres down the path, I heard something murmuring and chattering off like running water and tilted my head in the direction of the noise. It was like the melodious sound only water makes when moving between large rocks. The canoe man removed four plastic bottles from the small bag he hung over his shoulder and started tearing through the leaves, accompanied by Kaba. We all followed and drank water deeply from the brook and rested for a while before Kaba and the canoe man led the way forward. We followed until we entered what looked like a well-trodden pathway, still in the desert. I saw marks on the ground's surface that looked like car tire tracks. I felt relieved. We lumbered along for almost half a day. A prowl of houses could be seen in the distance far across the horizon. Seeing signs of life again warmed our hearts.

Just when I thought there were no more threats, something happened that left me wondering whether my revengeful hatred for my father or our mischievous childhood chase of Alhaji Kidado's cows onto the cliffs, was not haunting me. We had boarded a vehicle at the next locality and were moving toward the location of distant houses when our truck suddenly stopped along a stretch of sandy land overlooking a tiny forest. The driver, Kaba, and the canoe man jumped off onto the path and hurdled together. Their gaze was fixed on the tiny, unsociable forest down the path where shapes were burrowing vigorously through a hedge of trees. Were they expecting somebody from that forest? I wondered, my looks slithering across the forest. The urine I had managed to hold captive for so long was now threatening to storm out of detention. A sudden threatening shout from the road steered all eyes away from my wet legs.

"Make all man come out here and lie down!" The canoe man thundered, pulling a gun from the bag on his shoulders. He shot in the air twice. My heart resumed its wild dance as we speedily clambered down to the road. I lay flat on the ground and lowered my gaze, trailing the body language activities of Kaba, the driver, and the canoe man with the side of my eye.

I was not to be in doubt for long. Suddenly, a moving shiver of leaves began to falter energetically through the thickets that stretched right up to where we had parked, causing my heart to flutter violently. I grabbed the edge of Savage's jeans trousers, staring down the path. Heavily armed men, including two ladies, wiggled out of the shrubs and pointed guns at us. Was the gun-wielding parade a strategy to disarm the travellers from contemplating any form of resistance? I wondered, stealing glances at Kaba and the gang facing each other, exchanging nods.

"No movement! I go waste anybody who de try to act smart!" the driver shouted, wielding his gun before us. We did as he directed. He then snapped his fingers at Maigano and Baba, as he called them, and then at Kaba. They stepped aside to talk in low tones. I knew we were not safe. But I managed to roll my eyes around, ensuring I missed no signal or action, despite the menacing stares stalking us. Maigano and Baba shifted toward us, their eyes roving from one person to another. The fringes of my upper eyelids were raised, and my heart was pounding when they started lifting and allowing our arms and legs to drop heavily on the ground. After what appeared to be a fitness detection exercise, seven full-bodied young men, including Fola, Kitam, and Ntumfon, and three fair-skinned ladies with sticking-out buttocks, were selected and kept isolated. I watched them shivering like rams in a slaughterhouse from the corner of my eyes. Maigano then handed a bulging plastic bag to Kaba. There were wads of money. He poured them on the ground and began to count, frequently moving his head up and down like a lizard.

"Pa! Pa! Pa!" Came the sound of gunshots. Maigano had just riddled Fola's chest with bullets. Fola had tried to take advantage of their distraction by counting the money and crawling back to mingle with us. I watched Fola wiggle slowly to death.

It was not only the selected travellers that were in danger. I still shrug when I remember how I was subjected to a brutal invasion and occupation. The invaders soon launched an aggressive encroachment into my lap, tearing down my domestic borders. The shocking incursion and demolition prompted a large-scale exodus of blood from my womanhood, leaving my domestic borders porous like a land without a title deed. Even before Maigano shifted and stood entitled over my shivering body, I could already tell from his preying gaze that he was planning an invasion. I hated everything about him.

He was huge and looked untamed, with an overgrown nose shaped like a swollen Irish potato tuber. A chaotic bush of hair roofed his head and the entire width of his face. His chin was a spear-like bush. Streaks of hair shot out of his nostrils like grass from the decaying walls of an abandoned building and out of place. The scene of the brutal invasion is an engraving on my mind. I felt like a captive chicken in the clutch of a hawk when Maigano kicked my legs apart. A reckless cassava-size tuber, fenced by what looked like clustering bees, descended on me and began to invade my domestic hive, which at the time housed my precious seed. It was a wild graze comparable only to the front loader's claws bulldozing a road through a virgin forest. The place where my legs meet screamed with burning pains. I felt like my bareback was lying on pricking gravel. I groaned, writhed, and sniffled heavily, dreading to complain and be silenced. Two more bulldozers took turns, tearing through the borders under the stealthy gaze of Livinus as a spectator. The brutal incursion left me in shreds. I could feel a river of blood surging up and spilling over my screaming lap, accompanied by wild movements in my stomach. Some tiny legs were punching my stomach walls, in apparent protests. Fear gripped me and raised questions.

Was the ring on my finger, not a sign that I am a titled land with clearly demarcated borders and forbidden to invaders? Was the wild movement in my stomach some kind of resistance? Was my unborn baby protesting the invasion of its homeland? Was it wounded in the brutal encounter?

What was I to do now? The thought of what happened to Fola reminded me that I would face the gun if I dared resist. I gathered courage and prodded the invader on his arm with the ring on my finger. Unfortunately, this seemed to insinuate to him that I was asking for more, as he nodded his head like a lizard and continued harder.

I was not the only person who suffered encroachment and occupation. A man with broad shoulders violently plucked off Savage's jeans trousers together with her pants and pulled her legs apart but quickly leaned back, wide-eyed, open-mouthed. "Is this a man or a woman?" He asked, shaking his head as he shifted to the next prey. I wondered why Savage was disqualified and called a man. Atang was another victim of occupation. Maigano burrowed into Atang from the back like a stem clambering across ridges on farmland. The lady who came with the human traffickers lay flat on Savage. Agitating pain took away my attention from the invaders. My next occupier behaved more entitled than the invaders before him. Although it's hard to gauge how long the encroachment and occupation lasted, I indeed lost consciousness at some point. I have no idea what happened immediately after. I only recall lying in a pool of blood, feeling weak and tired and squirming, pondering in silent pain.

My dignity was violated. Livinus saw everything. The place where my legs meet was reduced to shreds! Was I still a woman, and was there any hope of being repaired? Was I going to survive after losing such a river of blood? What about the diseases the invaders may have buried in me? Was my baby still alive? This train of thought set me up for action, the first being to inform the world of the shame of the desert trail. Nobody needed to go through what we went through! The driver's voice soon distracted me.

"Wona return inside moto, now!" He shouted, and we all staggered into the vehicle. Kaba, his gang, and our driver stood apart to conspire. A muted jubilation swelled within me immediately the gang slotted themselves into the rigorously growing shrubs and began to burrow their way down the path. Bags hung suspended over the shoulders of Ntumfon and Kitam as they tore through the leaves under the guiding stare of their new masters, who followed from behind. I wept to see my brothers forcefully wrenched from the only family we had in the desert, taken away to a place none of us knew anything about.

I tried to sit on my buttocks, but the pain would not let me. I turned sideways, hoping to perch on the right ridge of my buttocks, but it felt as if my waist bone had been displaced from its joint. I could not kneel because my legs were too weak to carry me. To sit on my bag would be softer, I mused, trying to locate my bag. Savage must have read my mind. She tugged my bag out from among the pile of bags. Livinus must have noticed that I had difficulties sitting upright. He cast a pitiful glance at me, but I knew he would not throw such a pity party for nothing, not after what he had seen. I knew he wanted to say something before he even whispered in my ears.

"Next time, wear jeans trousers when you are travelling."

Whether or not, my outfit had made me the target of invasion, I didn't decide, but Livinus' remark was helpful. I pulled out a pair of hugging jeans from my bag and wore them to fortify security around the borders of my waist.

"Pim piiiiim, pim piiiiiim," the horn of the vehicle went and then we began to amble along. The rough pathways intensified my pains and anguish. My lap frantically seethed with peppery pain each time our vehicle danced and galloped wildly. Livinus snapped a finger before my face and said something.

"Kila, I saw what happened. But I hope this kind of news is buried alive. I know what I'm talking about. If the council of elders should hear that somebody other than Jeff gained access, you are finished! What happened to Regular will happen to you. Oh yes! You will go back to your father's house. And Jeff will miss his position as his father's successor if he doesn't send you back to your parents. It's not as if I am trying to make you feel bad, no, no. I feel for you, but I fear for you knowing the ways of Kibang land. Tradition does not have the word 'sympathy' in its dictionary. Don't be offended if I suggest something. If you cooperate with me, it will not go out."

Livinus was right. The ways of Kibang land are unsympathetic to the woman who falls victim to assault. The victim is punished. The culprit is not caught and so takes no blame. When a woman sleeps with her husband or his brother in the event of his death, it is called family communion. When she sleeps with a stranger, even if she is forced, it is called a foreign invasion. They say a stranger encroached into the family land. The action is treated with the same seriousness as land grabbing. The woman suffers doubly. Losing my marriage is what I couldn't bear.

Livinus suggested that I bury the story to save my marriage and husband from being dispossessed. The question was how I could hide what everybody saw. Besides, the brutal invasion left visible scars of porous borders, now leaking blood and requiring diapers. Blood keeps seeping out and creeping down my legs. The shame is hard to bear. I now place a thick cloth between my legs and fasten it around my waist to hold the faeces that come out unannounced. When I walk into the shop, Dzekashu brings out diapers before I even ask. He just brings it out and collects the money; we don't exchange words. Once, he quickly brought out two packages of sanitary towels and extended them to me before I said it was bread I wanted. The people around us were surprised, but Dzekashu and I understood each other. Now, Jeff can no longer perform his domestic duties with me. His family no longer wants me. Everybody avoids me. The only regular friends I have are flies. You will hear more about my present situation at the end of the story. Let me take you back to the desert journey.

Long before Dzekashu came into my picture, the last phase of the journey across the desert was intense and multiplied my pains and uncertainties. Hope and despair jostled for space amidst my total distrust of anyone and doubt about just anything. It took all my guts to decide what will be, will be. The drive was rough, and my buttocks were excruciatingly painful as if a thousand needles were continuously jabbed into them. I probably fell asleep at some point until we started inching towards the borders of another country and a finger prodded my shoulder.

"You have been sleeping for long," Livinus' voice announced.

The joy that had abandoned me for a long time immediately returned when my eyes fell on a towering signboard displaying the words: "Welcome to Bamfada." Here, four roads met and branched off to other places. I wiped my eyes repeatedly, desiring to ascertain that we were out of the desert, and that it was not a dream. We were back to the land of humans. I was actually excited to see people moving about freely. I saw a stream of cars across the road, dropping or picking up passengers. I stared at houses with overhead lanes of ropes springing up across the neighbourhood and tried to locate a restaurant in the sprawl of houses. Happy voices from our vehicle thanked God for bringing us out of the desert with our heads on our necks. Our truck pulled up slowly to the parking ground, where young boys and girls ran across the road to join those who had trailed our vehicle to the parking area. The urchins were selling maize, bananas, groundnuts, juice, water, biscuits, recharge cards, oranges, guavas, and other items, arranged in trays and wooden stands.

I climbed down from the vehicle, stood still, and looked around me before staggering to the rear of a nearby beer parlour. I hurriedly pushed down my trousers and bent over sprinkles of grass. I felt sharp pains. I knew why. Savage noticed the bloodstains on my pants and decided to save me from embarrassment. She gave me a scarf, underwear, and another pair of jeans pulled out from my bag when she noticed my condition. I tore the scarf into two parts and folded the bigger of the two pieces to look like a loaf of bread. I then put the cloth between my legs to keep the blood from leaking before I wore the underwear and the jeans Savage gave me. I felt shy as I murmured a thank you to Savage.

Everybody had gathered around our vehicle when Savage and I returned. The canoe man led us to a nearby eating place. A young girl smiling generously walked up to us to take our orders: "Welcome, Ma; welcome, Sir; we get roundabout, jollof rice, porridge yams, which one you want?" She also mentioned names of meals unfamiliar to me and many others. Everybody wanted rice. She served us rice with thick pieces of intestines, liver, and what looked like cuttings of towels. I also bought three sachets of 'pure water' from a hawker and drank. The salesgirl asked if I wanted to eat Kongo meat, and I simply shook my head as I didn't know what it was. While we ate, I plugged my charger into the socket on the wall. Before we left the restaurant, the telephone was almost half-full of black streaks.

Thoughts raced through my mind while we sat eating. I wanted to go back home. It was better back home. How was I to go home from here without meeting human traffickers on the way? They could kill me. Was there another road or deviation to return to my country? But I had lost my house to fire and with it everything else. Cattle had grazed on my crops, and the money my family received for rehabilitation was what we gave to Kaba to prepare my papers for travel abroad. No, no, I can't go back empty-handed. I need to work and raise money for my family, to change my story of tears.

Whether to continue or return to my country evoked memories of the conflict between the farmers and the herdsmen that had caused the immediate and premature exit from Kibaaka land.

2

Season of Food

Whether or not you will blame me for what happened during the desert journey, you need to know why I left home for greener pastures. The protracted conflict between the farmers and the herdsmen took away everything from me and left me with just one option: travel to Amerika, birthing a story whose scars I have tried in vain to erase. Telling the story of the said encounter without beginning with the 'season of food' is like building a house without a foundation. Prior to the bloody encounter and repeated cycles of violence, that 'planting season' was the best Kibang had ever witnessed. When they took off, the plants looked more winsome in shape and larger sizes than ever.

Fleshy corn cobs jutted from stomachs of maize stems in twins and triplets, causing the stems to lean backward like a pregnant woman climbing a hill. The maize stems looked like victims of under-age pregnancies in pain of parturition. They were, besides, so hefty that you would have even thought that corn cobs and pumpkin fruits were on a fattening course. Bernsah, my first son, apparently saw the farm as a birthing hospital with babies to be released from the pregnant plants.

"Mum, Mum, your plants are carrying babies on their stomachs. Your corn and pumpkins have babies in their stomachs. Mum, who put babies in their stomachs?" he asked, moving his excited finger from gigantic cucumber-sized corn cobs to melons and pumpkins that drew attention to themselves by their soft and thick skins, hanging down heavily from the shoulders of pillars like the tapper's calabashes dangling from a palm tree.

Bernsah had insisted on following me to the farm on that day as I used to do during non-working days. We spent over five hours stalking the farm for squirrels, goats, pigs, and cows that had started straying in to graze on corn cobs, onions, pumpkins, and melons. It was a common practice in Kibang land to see an effigy in the form of a slender upright object wearing a hat with large, rounded edges as well as trousers, erected in maize farms. Such scarecrows stood in farms in a stalking tilt and held out a long stick with pointed ends to scare off thieves, birds, and stray animals from coming around to feast on crops. The presence of stalking scarecrows on maize farms did not, however, stop the destruction of maize and other crops by cows, sheep, goats, and pigs. Open grazing was a common practice. Most farms thus served as charity restaurants where cattle walked in and out at will, feasting on crops, trampling on nurseries and sprouts. Stray cattle had a spread-out menu to select from: corn cobs, onions, corn stems with ravishing skirts of leaves, yam stems with gorgeous jackets of leaves, cabbage, bean sprouts, garden eggs, pepper, and pumpkin fruits with large flesh being their more staple choices. To save our crops and plants, Jeff and I started stalking the farm for stray animals whenever it was convenient. And that was what took Bernsah and I to the farm on that day.

Being Mama's son, he followed me almost everywhere when he wasn't in school; Bernsah was actively present the day the women's group planted corn, fodder sprouts and trees on their farm. He brought home some chunks of fodder sprouts to plant in my small vegetable garden, which he often insisted was his garden.

He got me thinking when he asked whether plants get pregnant and bear children. I struggled to explain that crops were not humans and that they had their own way of procreating. Before I was through, he asked an even more embarrassing question.

"Mum, is it Daddy who put babies in the stomachs of these plants?" He casually asked, pointing at the corn cobs and large pumpkin fruits across the farm and adding, "do plants have husbands; tell me na Mum…?"

"No, no, my son, it is not Daddy; it's not your father. Plants do not have wombs, so they cannot carry babies. What they are carrying aren't really babies." I fumbled for words, uncomfortable, because I lacked the right words to explain issues of human reproduction that his age and experience had not really equipped him to understand. He just turned thirteen and wouldn't have been expected to understand the notion of getting pregnant and giving birth. He didn't seem convinced by my explanation, however.

"Mum, what is this? What is this? Is that not two baby corns sleeping on the stomach of their mother? Mum, is that not long hair growing on the head of the corn? Mum, will Dr Jerry come to our farm to remove the babies from the stomachs of the corn and pumpkins? Mummy, I know the person who will remove the babies. It is Dr Jerry. I went to the hospital of Dr Jerry when Bame was in your stomach…"

"Plants do not have stomachs, they cannot carry a baby…, emmm, my son. Only a woman gets pregnant. And when a woman has a baby in her stomach, she goes to the hospital. Only the Doctor can remove the baby from a woman's stomach. It is a different thing with plants. When crops get fat like that pumpkin, or like the corn cobs you see, it means they are ripe, and we can now harvest them and cook and eat. You will know the difference when you are big,' I laboured to explain, still struggling to come to terms with the fact that at 13, Bernsah already knew that it is a man that impregnates a woman.

Bernsah had accompanied me many times to the Kibang Maternity Consultation Clinic for pregnant women when I was pregnant with his younger brother. He had seen many other women with big bellies. I guess he had that experience in mind when he inquired about crops getting pregnant and giving birth to children. The memory of pregnant women with bloated stomachs dancing riot-ously and aimlessly around or stamping their feet heavily on the ground while screaming was definitely in his mind when he saw the cultivated grounds.

But how would a child not think the plants were pregnant with babies? Pumpkins, gourds, and corn cobs looked extraordinarily large. It was as if an enhancement had been done to enlarge their buttocks, chests, and stomachs. Most pumpkins have side stomachs as large as that of freshly moulded ridges during planting seasons. Farms actually looked like plantation maternity centres where pregnant maize stems and pumpkin plants visit for the pre-birth medical fol-low-up to ensure the well-being of both the mother and her unborn baby. Corn cobs and other crops looked full-bodied and, more than ever, attracted cows, goats, and pigs to farmlands.

It was not only the cultivated grounds and farms that blossomed with crops. Valleys and fields bloomed with jackets and skirts of greenery that swirled around in the wind, like ballet dancers. Even bumpy rolling grounds swarmed with gorgeous vegetation, whose topsoil had constantly been eaten away and rendered barren by bush burning and floods. In the women's farm, fodder grass stood on ridges in ravishing queues like the raffia fibre pleated like skirts and tied upright around the heads of female masquerades to swing around when dancing.

Like maize, fodder grass was a huge source of income for the Bongkisheri Women's Group. It was introduced in Kibang as an alternative cattle feed by my group, the Bongkisheri Kibang Women's Empowerment Centre for Skills Training. Following the training we received, thanks to the partnership with women from other African countries experiencing farmers and herder conflicts, we trained Kibang Women to cultivate and preserve fodder grass for use as food reserves for cows. Fodder also had economic value as we sold the feed to cattle owners to serve them during seasons of prolonged dryness. The women's group planned to harvest and preserve their fodder pending when prices would rise in order to raise money for the torghu industrial sewing machines for the Women's Empowerment Centre. In another section of the women's farm, there were fully-fledged nurseries with different types of trees. Kibaaka had suffered periods of prolonged dryness and women and children often trekked long distances to fetch water from valleys. We had therefore, planted eucalyptus and raffia trees around the well in our farm to hold water in the soil that would serve us during periods of prolonged dryness. Where there is water, there is life. This was part of the reason behind the planting of trees. We also agreed to sell some of the trees to our partner, the Local Council, for landscaping of streets and, particularly, for fortifying security along the roads with adjoining crumbling surfaces and collapsing plunges.

My farm too flourished with yields. If one could assess its performance, it would be a loud excellent. The maize, banana, and plantain stems which Jeff and I planted that year had grown into fully developed drooping bunches. Like salary earners impatiently counting the remaining days to pay-day, farmers awaited the harvest season with excitement and impatience. Like the girl child betrothed, given in marriage before she was born, Jeff and I had taken a school fees loan of 500,000frs CFA from Bongkisheri Kibang Women's Cooperative Society. We had presented our growing crops as mortgage. Many farmers constructed additional barns, while others increased the size of the old ones in anticipation of copious harvests.

Ability planned to marry his second wife and take the highest red feather title in the land, hoping to raise money for both the coronation and bride price settlement, from selling his onions and maize. He had always wanted to be on the same rung in the traditional council as Wirkitum and Alhaji Kidado Musa. He had used his wife's little savings to buy corn and onion seedlings which he cultivated in a large spread, looking forward to raising money from the harvest to fund his coronation and marriage.

The conversation on every lip was about protecting the crops from cattle invasion. The only moment the people of Kibang community ever spoke in one voice, without drifting into opposing camps, was when the safety of their farms and crops was concerned, and that was the situation at that moment. The survival of the Kibang community depended entirely on land cultivation. The Kibang agric show was approaching. The farmers who would win prizes along with wheelbarrows, shovels, cutlasses, and other farm tools were already anticipated, given the healthy sizes of the crops. They looked forward to gathering their farm yields for exhibition and sales during the Kibang Agric Show, which the mayor would organize. The atmosphere was festive in anticipation.

Then, stray cattle started invading cultivated lands, grazing on crops and destroying some. Many of the farmlands were cattle routes. Soon, the expectation and excitement from the flourishing crops suddenly began to droop as fear of the invasion of farms by the cattle loomed large. The farmers were worried. The ban on open grazing was the word on every lip. All the farmers agreed it was the only way to protect the farms, maize, and other crops from cattle invasion. The mayor and Fon Fomu of Kibang were under pressure from the people to protect their crops and farmlands to justify their mandates.

Fon Fomu and members of the Kibang elders' council took measures to protect the crops. They created the Kibang vigilante group, which was mandated to go around the village and chase away stray cattle. Part of their mission was to report the presence of stray cattle in farmlands to the authorities of the Kibang municipal council. They held behind-the-scene consultations and meetings with all interested parties, including the governor, the Senior Divisional Officer of Kibang-Gidang, Bishop Kosimas, the MP, the mayor, the Alhaji of Gidang (as Alhaji Kidado was officially known), the president of the association of cattle breeders, the president of the association of farmers (Ability), and leaders of the different community groups that included the women, the herdsmen, the vigilante, and the guards. They scheduled an inclusive meeting in the palace to discuss security issues and seek lasting solutions to the problems related to the ownership of cattle routes, grazing land, water sources, and the constant invasion of farms by cattle.

As we trooped to the palace, we met and bypassed many people. Among these was the unforgettable encounter between Tav Kibari and Ability.

"Ability, Kinang, Shey Lukong, Atang, Livinus! Hrrrh, hmmm, this combination does not come together for nothing. Something is surely cooking up somewhere! My friend, Ability, when it comes to this that you and your soldier ants are jumping out of the bush path with suspicious looks in your eyes, holding empty gallons… hmmmm! I hope we will not hear again that cows ate grass on the hill and died of diarrhoea!" Tav Kibari, the former mayor of Kibang teased, his eyebrows raised. "Your trousers are even sweating like the face of someone who has just swallowed a bowl of pepper," he added, this time with a fixed stare at Ability, who, together with his boys tilted forward, looking at their feet.

"Tav Kibari, herrhh, emmm, we visited my farm this morning, to water the plants," Ability responded, unruffled, the corner of his eye winking at Atang, Livinus, Kinang and Shey Lukong, who immediately nodded in approval.

"I thought the crops were ripe already," countered Tav Kibari.

"The crops…, ripe, yes, no, no, w-w-we were fetching water and watering maize, herrh emmm, onions…," Ability gasped for words while stealing glances at the sweating surfaces on his trousers. Kinang, Shey Lukong, Atang, and Livinus nodded confusedly.

"Watering onions in the heart of the rainy season, Hmmm!" Tav Kibari was not the type to let a gaff go uncorrected. "Anyway, how are your crops doing?"

"The chests of my maize stems are sticking out with paw-paw-size breasts…"

"Paw-paw-size breasts!" Tav exclaimed, smiling.

"Go and see it for yourself. If my onions and maize plants were young ladies, all the young men in this village would queue into my compound! Ki ki ki ki ki," Ability joked and laughed with a chickening cackle. "Tav, if you visit my farm, you will understand why I have chosen to increase the size of my domestic map, ki ki ki ki ki ki ki."

"So, it is true that you want to increase the size of your problems?" Tav Kibari teased, releasing drizzles of laughter.

"When a real man is expecting abundant harvest, he must plan to increase the size of his domestic territory. My friend, get ready to follow me to see the family of Beti." Ability giggled.

"Ability, is that how you plan to enjoy your money when you sell your onions and corn?"

Tav asked, surprised, perhaps because Ability had a pending case to answer in the local council of elders brought on by his wife. He had broken her wooden bank and removed all her money, without her consent, to finance hunger-of-the loins-induced debts he owed Beti. She wanted all her money back. Ability's conversation was confirming the rumour.

"Tav, after lifting Beti off the streets, I will increase the size of my power. My enemies, like Alhaji Kidado, must feel the weight of my pockets, the weight of my manhood and the weight of my voice immediately after I sell my onions and corn! Ki ki ki ki ki ki ki," Tav Kibari stared strangely at Ability as he spoke.

We approached them from behind at a snail's pace, fascinated by their conversation.

Jaika, Dzekem, Regular, Beri, Berka, and I were all going to the town hall for an urgent meeting. We were gripped by Ba Ability's plans on how he would spend the money from the sale of crops whose harvest was yet to come. Ability would place his hand on the head or shoulder of another person and switch from one topic to another in order to feel superior. Exactly, that was what happened that morning when we approached the men and bent over to greet them. Ability's left hand rested comfortably on my head, and without uttering a word, he turned and continued his conversation with Tav Kibari whose left hand he had also grabbed and held in temporary detention.

"Tav, start planning to increase the size of your stomach because you will soon be dragging a goat behind me to see Beti's people as soon as I sell my onions...."

"That Beti you are talking about is not yet ripe. Or are you planning to eat her raw? Ability, do I need to remind you that your wife dragged you to the traditional council concerning this same Beti…."

"And so, what? Hurrh? What will the elders do to me? Is it the elders deciding who I should get married to?" Ability rattled on.

"Ability, I can see that you are determined to increase the size of your problems."

"I am the man here, and I am in charge!"

"How can the man be in charge when his wife is the husband?" Tav asked, laughing provocatively.

Ability must have felt insulted. He stood silent for a while before responding. "Tav Kibari, is it because I stopped patronising your sister, Regular, that you now think you can transform me into an object of ridicule in the presence of women?"

The jovial atmosphere turned sour; everyone left, one after another, beginning with the embarrassed Regular.

3

At the Community Hall

When we arrived at the community hall in the heart of the land as the palace was called, many people were already seated according to their positions on the social ladder. The common knowledge that the woman owed a lifetime of male worship was reflected in the seating arrangements. There were separate seating arrangements for the men and the women. Like hills jutting up from behind mountains, the women occupied the periphery of the hall. From there, we constantly stuck out our necks to glimpse what was happening at the front. The dignitaries were at the high table, facing the crowded hall of Kibang and Gidang people, including representatives of community groups, religious, and traditional groups. In the audience section, the men occupied the front seats. Representatives of the different groups and associations, including the women's group, non-governmental associations, the religious, farmers, herdsmen, and the vigilantes, were scattered all over the hall, some of them preferring proximity to their members.

Fon Fomu was the next personality to walk into the hall. The elders clapped their hands thrice, held their cupped hands below their chins, and droned as if a truckload of bees were singing. It was the customary manner of greeting the paramount ruler, chief of the clan. The Fon sat on the elevated stage facing the crowd. He was flanked by his traditional cabinet of red-capped chiefs. Alhaji

Kidado, Tav Kibari, Tata, Dr Jerry, and a few other men were among the members of the traditional cabinet. Ability sat on a separate chair, one step down from the right flank reserved for the council of elders and community leaders. He was yet to be initiated in the ladder of command.

All the mutterings ceased immediately the governor of the region, accompanied by two heavily armed security officers, and in the company of the SDO, the MP, and the mayor walked into the hall. Dr Jerry ushered them to the high table. The governor sat in the middle, flanked by the commissioner of police, 'Commandant,' including the mayor, the MP, Bishop Kosimas, and Alhaji Kidado. Some security officials stood outside the hall while the two who accompanied the governor stood alert and directly behind him. All eyes shot at the royal seat when the Fon cleared his throat to speak.

"The governor of Kibang and Gidang, we greet you, and we want to thank you for honouring our invitation to this meeting," Fon Fomu said, his eyes planted on the face of the governor as he greeted. The governor nodded, smiling.

"People of Kibang and Gidang, we greet you."

"*Mbeerrh. Nchang nchang. Bvere'eh,*" the elders, in the typical Kibang customary manner, acknowledged the royal greetings. In their Graffi native expressions, they denoted worship, lionising, tribute, praises, and honour of their King. Fon Fomu waited for the chorus of voices buzzing across the hall to die before he continued.

"People of our land, we are here today to seek ways of resolving the problems that are tearing us apart. This is not the first time we have gathered in the heart of the land to plead with the farmers and the herdsmen to bury their differences and embrace peace. I will go straight to the point so that we don't keep government waiting for too long. I will begin with what we can do at our level. As a group, we can take action to prevent old problems from coming back to face us; we can prevent new problems from being born; we can prepare ourselves so that even if the problems come visiting, they would not meet us in bed sleeping like women…"

"*Reng reng! Nchang nchang! Bvere'eh'!*"

"Number one, our crops are getting ripe and ready for harvesting. Our corn, onions, and pumpkins are tiptoeing towards the age that can attract a fatty bride price if they were young women. Cows have started loitering around the buttocks of farmlands the same way young men loiter around the family compound where a ripe girl lives. My people, we must protect our crops from cows like we protect ripe bananas from birds…"

"*Reng reng! Nchang nchang! Bvere'eh!*" The elders sang out. Fon Fomu continued. "My people, when a man plants a seed in his wife, he prepares for the safe arrival of the baby. He can only do so if he protects the woman who carries the unborn baby. Our big worry is how to protect our crops from cows, sheep, goats, and pigs. The vigilante boys need raincoats and rain boots. As you already know, rain mixed with stones is pouring from the sky these days, striking the boys on every part of their bodies. What that means is that they can no longer guard our farms and crops from stray cattle, especially when it is raining. The ladder of command has received complaints that cows entered the farm that belongs to the women's group. Had Lankar not gone out to check his traps, seen the cows on the farms, and run back to inform the villagers, we would have met naked stems and ridges as it happened many times in the past. The number of graves sticking out from behind compound yards because of farmers' and herdsmen's clashes would have been increased by now. My people, we need to raise money to buy raincoats and boots for the vigilante boys…"

"*Mbeeerrh! Nchang nchang! Bvere'eh!*"

"My people, we have heard about what we can do at our level to prevent problems. We know that some of the problems are bigger than us, but when a house has a roof over its head, the family is safe from rain and storms. For that reason, the father of the land is here," the Fon looked at the governor as he spoke. "Government is here to play two roles in the matter: as the father of the land, Government is for everybody and will listen to all. For that reason, we want to join the government in resolving the basket of problems our land is carrying on its shoulders." The Fon paused and then continued.

"Government, the passing wind has uprooted a big tree and cast it over our roof. Your children need you to lift it off and save the house from crumbling."

The governor, SDO, MP, and mayor nodded simultaneously, and the Fon continued. "There are four or five heavy problems sitting on the shoulders of our land. Let me name them. Number one, just like a woman who goes everywhere she wants because no bride price payment has roped her to the tether of the man's loins, cows, goats, sheep, and pigs have started grazing in open fields and people's farms." While the governor and some others convulsed with laughter at Fon Fomu's metaphor, Ability stretched out his head and glanced at Alhaji Kidado. It was as if the Alhaji's cows had similarities with the loose woman in the metaphor. Meanwhile, the Fon went on and on, listing the complaints brought to the council of elders by individuals, groups, and Alhaji Kidado.

"Number two, some people from Kibang attack and kill and break the legs of cows with cutlasses. Some have vowed that the cows will no longer drink water from Kibang streams. Some have said cows will not eat grass growing on the soils of Kibang land. Some stab and push objects into the anuses and stomachs of cows, pulling out intestines."

At this point, the Fon lifted pictures of cows with intestines hanging down heavily from their stomachs and continued, "Cattle owners have complained that Kibang people are farming and building houses on cattle routes and should stop and move to other locations. Kibang people have complained that cows destroy crops when they come down to Kibang to graze and drink water. They complain that cows sully the streams by churning them with splashings of mud and excrement. There are also complaints that some people in Kibang chase away Gidang women from carrying water or catching tadpoles from Kibang streams. Governor of Kibang and Gidang, the people of Kibang and Gidang are asking these questions: whether there are cattle routes in Kibang land, who owns them? Who owns River Kibang? They are asking where Kibang land begins and ends and where Gidang land begins and ends?"

"*Nchang nchang! Bvere'eh!*" voices chorused across the hall.

"The disagreement over ownership of cattle routes and River Kibang is the main problem tearing the two families apart." Graves stick out from the backyards of homesteads as if to listen to gossip, as a result of this disagreement. For a long time now, you cannot hear a baby's cry in many compounds that used to be beehives of children. Visit the house of Dr Jerry. Graveyards sit up like stones on the chest of a big river that has suddenly dried up."

Tears ran down my cheeks and the cheeks of those other women around me as Fon Fomu spoke.

"Government, we want a lasting solution to the problem between the farmers and herdsmen," he stated.

"*Nchang nchang! Bvere'eh!*" voices chorused across the hall. Then, suddenly, the hall went dead silent as the governor stood up and stretched out his hand to take the microphone Dr Jerry had bent forward to release to him. He wanted to respond to the issues raised by the Fon.

"People of Gidang and Kibang, accept greetings from the Government of Kibaaka, which my team and I here represent. Your Chief has spoken well. Kibang and Gidang want peace, and that is very important. Nothing can be done without peace. Since I took over office ten years ago as your governor, many complaints have come to my table. These complaints have the same subject matter: farmers are farming or building on cattle routes; farmers are encroaching into grazing reserves; cows or pigs or sheep or goats are straying into farms and destroying crops; cows are muddying the streams and people are drinking dirty water and falling sick or dying of cholera; this or that individual or community knows the people rustling cattle but has decided to protect them; some people in Kibang are trying to stop cattle from grazing on the fields and valleys; farmers have stabbed and killed cattle and fighting has started, leading to many people losing their lives; people have fled their homes to bushes where women and girls are defiled…"

The governor shook his head sadly as he enumerated the complaints. "We are deeply concerned about what is happening in this land. I was thrilled when the Chief of Kibang and the Alhaji of Gidang came to my office to invite me to this meeting. I directed them to ensure that everybody was represented. And I am happy they did. We must put our heads together and seek a peaceful and lasting solution to what is tearing Kibang and Gidang apart. We can do it with everybody's collaboration. Before I respond to the issues raised, I have something important to say: Report any action that can tear people apart, cause injury or death, to your chief, to your Alhaji, to the mayor, and the police. Don't wait for smoke to become a fire before you report that you saw smoke. There are better ways of addressing problems. Do not use knives, cutlasses, iron rods, sticks, stones, or divisive utterances to settle your differences. Do not take the law into your hands. Whatever you want to say, whatever action you want to take, always ask yourself this question: is it something I will be proud of when I look back at my life? Is it something that will bring people together or tear people apart?"

The governor's cautionary message received nods across the hall. He looked around and continued.

"I will now announce the ongoing measures initiated by the Government of Kibaaka to address your problems and bring lasting peace to the land. Some measures will produce immediate solutions; some will take a little time before we begin to see the fruits; some will depend on your collaboration with your community leaders and the Government. But not all will reflect your own views. It is important to note that whatever we decide will be in the interest of all. It is better to live with a broken heart than to live with broken limbs or in a grave. Regarding the protection of crops and farms from cattle, we have the following suggestions, which are not totally new: The government has signed a law to ban open grazing in Kibang and Gidang…"

"*Reng reng, abei!*" Exclamations rang, denoting consent, jubilation, and praises. Ability, Atang, Livinus and Shey Lukong dramatized their joy by staging a few dance steps. Even when the others had returned to their seats, Ability remained standing, peeping and searching across the hall, trying to locate the Alhaji as well as Wakilu, Jawara, Aboki, Musa, Yaaji, Dabari, and Kodume through his spread-out, see-through fingers planted on his face for that purpose. When the voices had died down, the governor continued.

"As another step, government has signed a book to create a 'Cattle Reserve' in Mbiame village in Kibang. You can call it Cattle Village...."

"*Ngomna, usoko, usoko Ngomna, madalla, madalla,*" were the words of joy, approval, and thanks that stumbled from the lips of Wakilu, Jawara, Aboki, Musa, Yaaji, Dabari, Kodume, and Gidang people scattered across the hall.

"According to the text creating the cattle village, part of the land owned by the Mbiame Municipality of Kibang is officially allocated for ranching. That is where cattle will be kept and raised."

The decision announcing the creation of the cattle reserve in Kibang elicited different reactions and emotions across the hall, some positive, some negative. Ability, Atang, Livinus and Shey Lukong did not hide their disappointment. Like an eruptive disease that suddenly springs up on the skin in small blistering bumps or pimples, Ability leaped over to the floor, wagging his fingers in the air in rage.

"Did I hear the governor saying government has decided to transform Kibang land into a cattle colony? Did the governor just say part of the land in Mbiame has become the cattle village? It will not happen! Not when Ability is breathing! It is now clean and clear that government is trying to give undue advantage to people whose only duty is moving from one place to another and babysitting their cows on people's farms."

Voices hailed Ability across the hall as he spoke, hitting his chest.

"When I told Tav Kibari and Fon Fomu that government is always lax when cattle destroy crops, nobody listened to me; nobody accepted my suggestion to stop the Come-no-go and their cows from drinking our water and grazing on our fields. Well, the fact that Government has seized our land and given to cattle owners indisputably takes away the presumption of neutrality in Government actions which Fon Fomu had made us believe in ...."

"Ability, calm down, the governor is still speaking."

"Fon Fomu, I am not in support of cattle colonialism," Ability barked again, inviting nods from many across the hall, the likes of activist Kaba, Atang, Shey Lukong, Livinus, and the MP lifting and dropping their fists in jubilation.

"Mr. Ability, calm down, calm down and listen, please," the governor pleaded, simultaneously gesturing to the two policemen who quickly stepped down to the floor to build a fence between the feverishly threatening Ability and the high table.

"People of Kibang and Gidang, government does not intend to create a cattle colony anywhere in Kibaaka land. The story about creating the cattle colony that I am aware of, did not start today. It was fabricated by people who want the conflict to continue for them to sell their arms. My good people, let me clarify again: the cattle reserve will be allocated where River Kibang twirls thrice like an injured massive snake, before dividing into two. That stretch of land belongs to the Mbiame municipal council. I want us to know that Municipal land is government property. That means the land we are talking about is council land and council land is government land. Now, back to what I was saying, we cannot allow cows to move freely because they will enter farmlands, eat crops, and destroy some. That would fuel the problem we are trying to solve. So, all cattle will stay in the cattle village. This will have a fence around it. Cattle must not be seen moving along the valleys, the fields or straying into farms. This is the main reason for creating the cattle ranch and the ban on open grazing. The decision is in the best interest of all. We are also aware that one of the legs of River Kibang flows through the cattle village, which means that cattle will no longer have the water problem. You may ask questions on what you don't understand," the governor ended.

Eyes trooped toward Bishop Kosimas immediately he raised his hand to react to the governor's explanation. "Mr Governor, nomadic cattle rearing is our main problem in this land. So, the government of Kibaaka should enact laws to ban open grazing of livestock in Kibang. Promises will not solve the problem. Laws and strict implementation will do."

The bishop applauded the measures to bring peace between the Kibang and Gidang communities, pledging to work with the stakeholders to resolve the disunity between the farmers and the herdsmen. He encouraged the enactment and implementation of anti-open grazing law, a suggestion that attracted cheers from many across the hall who raised thumbs and fists. Particularly, Ability, Shey Lukong, Kinang, Atang, and Livinus pointed up to the sky. Bishop Kosimas didn't support creating a cattle ranch in Mbiame. He considered the decision one-sided and not in the interest of the farmers and the Kibang people. He proposed that part of the council land should also be carved out and allocated to the farmers to cultivate crops. He left immediately after his intervention to attend to his other episcopal duties.

Alhaji Kidado reacted before lifting his hand to speak. "*Usoko, usoko, Ngomna* (Government). We have heard from *Ngomna* that the place where River Kibang bends its buttocks three times and builds a half fence with a body of water before stretching its left arm to the far end where it swallows a small river is council land. We have also heard that council land is *Gommen* land. Baba Bility, we hope you now know it is the lips of *Ngomna* that created the village for cattle."

Alhaji Gidado nodded to the verbal applause from his Gidang people across the hall and continued.

"I have question to ask *Ngomna*. Now that *Ngomna* has created a cattle village in Mbiame, will *Ngomna* also send *sikirity* to the cattle village?" Alhaji Kidado asked, pointing at the two policemen in the hall, a gesture to suggest what he meant by 'sikirity.'

"*Yowaaaaaaarrrh, madalla,*" the herdsmen encouraged in unison.

"Alhaji Kidado, when a man gives out his daughter to another man for wife, it does not mean that he has decided to cut off his daughter from his family. No, no. It does not mean he has sold off his daughter like a goat. This also applies to the creation of the cattle ranch. It remains under Mbiame municipality and will enjoy the benefits, protection, and obligations under the security structures in Mbiame and Kibaaka."

Conflicting reactions and emotions arose across the hall. What was expected to be a peaceful, inclusive meeting soon morphed into a heated debate. Blames, retorts, and insults were hauled back and forth. Ability's bitterness and dissent were heard in his voice.

"Alhaji Kidado, if government tells the people of Gidang to give part of their land to the people of Kibang for farming activities, would the Gidang people also accept? Tell me, will they?" Ability asked, shrugged, and continued, "People of Kibang land, there is some conspiracy to transform our land into a cattle colony. And for that reason, any cow I will set my eyes on in the so-called cattle village will walk on crutches!"

"*Reng reng!*" was the total agreement from several voices. I could see the fists of Atang, Livinus, Kaba, Shey Lukong, and some others sticking up across the hall. Perhaps encouraged by the chorused approval, Ability reasserted:

"Any cow that will be seen loitering around just anywhere along the fields or plains in Kibang will sit on wheelchairs…" He liked the rhythmic falls of his voice and its predictable response.

"*Reng reng*"

"Baba Bility, farmers should build fences around their farms," Wakilu shouted. He had been more of an observer to this moment.

"The Come-No-Go should create cattle reserves in Gidang and raise fences around them before educating farmers on how to build fences around their farms!" A murmur from voices scattered across the hall greeted Ability's reaction.

"Giraffi man, my father told me before he died that the land on which Kibang people are farming in Mbiame used to be cattle routes. So, who is the Come-no-go between Giraffi and Fulani?" Wakilu retorted. He was becoming more and more worked up and involved.

"No part of Kibang land will be used for ranching!" Ability reiterated.

The hall became calm when the governor, to end the tense atmosphere, asked if the SDO, the mayor, or any other person had something to say.

"As the governor has said, the decision to create an isolation reserve for cattle would be in the best interest of all; it is the best we can do for now to stop cows and stray animals from entering into farms and grazing on crops…" The SDO was saying.

"I said it, I said it, and I am now convinced that the SDO has also taken bribes! Yes, cows and pregnant envelopes have exchanged hands as usual! The governor has photocopied his heart and given Gidang the original and given Kibang the photocopy without know-ing the hidden intentions of the herdsmen. Very well then," Ability said and then turned to face the governor.

"Mr. Governor, Mr. Senior Divisional Officer, keeping cattle is personal business, just like farming is personal business! What that means is that if anybody needs grazing land, he should buy it! I do not support land grabbing!" Ability barked in an uncompromising tone.

Atang, Livinus, Shey Lukong, and Kinang cheered Ability as he spoke: "A Come-no-go comes to our land to connive with the big people to seize our land, and nobody is saying anything! We only know how to grumble behind the scenes! Mr. SDO, I am disappointed in you! Where is the MP?" Asked Ability, shuffling insinuating stares from the SDO to the MP and eventually to Shey Lukong and Kinang. He lumped them into one basket of accusations: "Mr. SDO and the Honourable MP, I am surprised with this level of silent complicity! When the two of you came to this land, you had no fowl. But today, each of you has a village of cows on the hills and stretches of land for the cows in your names…"

The governor stared at the SDO and then at Honourable, open-mouthed.

"Well, no one talks when there is food in their mouth," Ability said. Then, he turned to confront his friends.

"Shey Lukong, Kinang, when I was flushed from the military service, I joined you in this village. We became friends. You told me many things. Is it not from the two of you that I learned that each time cattle destroy or graze on crops, the herd boys and their cattle masters would prefer to rush to the SDO and the MP with cows instead of compensating the farmers? Were you not the one who dug up the secret? Hurrh? And did we not agree to expose all of them here today? Was that not our plan? Kinang, Shey Lukong, you came here and decided to play the drums for me to sing and dance all alone on the stage, right? You want to look good in the eyes of the same people you vehemently condemn and even wish dead behind their backs! No problem." Ability exploded, foaming in the mouth and constantly shifting his gaze from Shey Lukong to Kinang and back. The two accused fellows stood with their heads hanging heavily and awkwardly.

"Ability, it's enough! We are here for solutions!" The fon ventured but was cut in:

"Fon Fomu, what I am saying is also part of the solution. I have rights to what I consider the solution no less than you! Fon Fomu and the governor find it convenient educating Kibang people on what they should consider as solutions in a meeting that is supposed to be inclusive…"

"Ability, have you considered the fact that you could be the problem? You cannot always act like you know everything! No! You cannot always act like you are in control of everything! You fling comments here and there, even saying things that can raise doubts about your integrity!" The Fon barked and continued.

"Abili…, Abili…, the tortoise that ran faster than was expected and reached Heaven before the dog! The anteater that attended the election day of all animals on the back of the lion and became the king of the animals! We respect your opinion. Calm down, please; calm down."

The tributes and praises calculatedly showered on Ability were like potent healing herbs that soothed his effusively aggressive and windy reactions. Thus, the Fon watered down the tension.

"My people, this is the time to build bridges; we are here to look for ways to be close to each other; we are here for solutions. Let us focus on the way forward. History has recorded that we are great warriors. But the same history will surely record that what we always brought back from war was nothing but corpses, hacked arms, and heads…."

Tav Kibari and Tata nodded repeatedly as the Fon spoke.

"My people, there is no compound or homestead in Kibang and Gidang that is not heavily guarded by graves. Every day, we watch rivers of blood flowing from the chests and the backs of children we thought would grow up to bury us. Every day, we bury our hands, legs, or fingers. Brothers cannot take up arms to fight each other. A child who says his mother will not sleep stays awake with the mother!"

"*Reng reng, Abei!*" Came the response from the entire hall, and the Fon waited for murmurs to die down.

"Farmers, herdsmen, you need each other. You need food and meat. Our crops need cow dung to grow well. A complete Kibang dish brings the farmer's and breeder's products to the table. A complete Gidang dish brings the farmer's and breeder's products to the table. Breeding is not done by the Fulani only. Graffi people also keep cows. Would it not be a good idea to go to any restaurant in Kibang or Gidang and get yams and meat on your plate?" The hall applauded as the Fon concluded his speech. Even the governor spontaneously gave the Fon a handshake.

One important member of the council of elders who had not spoken was Tav Kibari, adviser number one of the Fon. The hall was silent when he got up to speak, and he spoke at length.

"Farmers and herdsmen," he began, "our people say that the hunter should not set a trap that will spring on his own legs when he is returning from checking his other traps. What am I saying? If we say we will not allow the piece of land in Mbiame for grazing

45

activities, what we mean is that we don't want a solution to the problem. It is even as good as saying that we want war. Trying to oppose the decision of government to ban open grazing too is as good as saying that we want war." Tav shrugged and went on, "What we should be saying is that Government should tell us what they intend to do for people whose lands are seized and transformed into the grazing village." Tav Kibari's words received positive but subdued reactions across the hall. The governor nodded repeatedly, bending over a sheet of paper to take down notes.

Tata was a representative of the farmers. He kept nodding repeatedly like a lizard to express consent when the Fon and Tav Kibari spoke. Tata was the oldest member of the traditional cabinet and council of elders. He had lost one of his sons in a previous round of violence between the farmers and the herdsmen. This made him rather sensitive each time the land issue came up at a meeting. Whenever he spoke, the tiny ridges and furrows around his lips pulled inside, giving his lips the shape of the bark of a tree healing from injured tissue. Although he jerked violently and stooped forward when he walked as a sign of advanced age, he was, like Tav Kibari, always rational and restrained in his choice of words.

"Our Fon has spoken well. Tav Kibari, you have spoken well and like someone willing to clear the bush around his yard to keep his house safe from bush fire. When an owl perches at the edge of the rooftop and begins to cry in the night, a child looks for his catapult to shoot it. What he thinks is that the gods of the land have answered his prayers and sent him the bird for his evening meal. What he does not know is whether the bird was singing a dirge. What I have said needs to be removed from the sheath of words for the women and those without grey hairs to understand better," Tata said. "We should not cut parts of the story and keep them in our belly. We know the root cause of what brought us here. The problem between the herders and the farmers was born before many of you saw the sun. I was there when it was born, and it has grown up right before my eyes. It swallowed one fruit of my loins and the mother of my

46

children. Many seasons ago, some people from Kibang decided that cows from Gidang would no longer come down to Kibang to eat grass and drink water from the streams of Kibang. The reason was that the cows destroyed crops when they came down to the valleys to eat grass and drink water. The people were right to be angry at their crops always being destroyed. But our fathers used the wrong herbs to heal the itching buttocks. They looked for a stick to scratch the itching instead of digging out the scabies, whose roots were firmly planted in the seat of the body. Today, the disease is spreading its roots to other parts of the body. People of our land, we will not make the mistake that our fathers made. If *Ngomna* wants to turn Mbiame to the village for cattle, *Ngomna* should tell us whose name will be written on the land book as the owner of that land."

Voices hailed Tata as he spoke.

"*Simall Gomen*," Tata turned toward the governor who was still taking notes: "When you go back, tell Big *Ngomna* that we have said that the name on the land Book should remain Kibang!"

"*Reng reng!*" Loud voices of applause tore through the hall. This reaction to the speech invited a mixture of emotions; farmers like Ability stared confusedly into space. Of all the interventions that could be described as on a tie, Tata seemed to have dug out the tail of the antagonism, tearing the two brothers apart. The governor clarified again that the land remains the property of the State and continued to take down notes.

When the turn of the women's group came, I stood up and walked to the middle, stooping. Then, I straightened up and stood sideways, careful not to have my back facing the elders.

"The women appreciate the work that the governor, MP, mayor, our Fon, the council of elders, groups, the association of herdsmen and the vigilante group, as well as individuals are doing at their various levels to resolve the conflict between the farmers and the herdsmen. Let me start with suggestions and questions; after, I will talk about what the women think we can do to end the problems concerning cattle routes and water sources.

"Your Excellency, the conflict over ownership of water sources and cattle routes keeps coming up because we lack alternative sources of income. We depend largely on cattle breeding and farming. That means if there are no cattle or no possibility of going to farms, as it usually happens when the fighting starts between the farmers and the herders, we will all die of hunger. Your Excellency, we need alternative sources of income and support. We need to reduce over-dependence on crops and cattle so that people will have other choices. If the Kibaaka government can set up alternative economic facilities, it will empower people. Opening farm-to-market roads would generate some alternatives. Commercial vehicles and bike riders will easily transport passengers, goods, and food from Kibang to Gidang, from Gidang to Kibang, from farms to markets. The problem of unemployment affecting the youths will be reduced, and families will be happier. Incidents of food getting rotten in bushes and valleys will be minimized. Vehicles transporting food items from farms to markets would not tumble on the way due to bad roads. The Ministry of Agriculture or Fishery can organise training workshops for the youths in piggery, raising chickens or fish, or any farming activity, and assist with loans or implements. Once you can identify and develop an economic activity, you can also control it. Another suggestion is that the Fulani should not only do grazing; the farmers should be more involved. Some Fulani people too should do farming. There is a need for a peace agreement. The farmers and herdsmen can sign an agreement to give peace a chance by avoiding violence, intolerance, hate speech, and harassment, as well as conduct and utterances that may instigate violence or cause division. That done, a forum for farmers and the herdsmen to discuss their problems and seek common solutions can be created. We need to partner with farmers and cattle owners from other lands, we need to find out how they are managing the problem of grazing land."

The governor nodded and smiled, taking down notes amidst the applause rending the air across the hall. My ego rose, and I continued.

"Your Excellency, permit me to ask questions now. Who are the people who will be allocated land or will live in the cattle ranch? Is it the herdsmen and the cattle, or can anybody live there? If the land is for the herders and their cattle, does that mean anybody with cattle can settle there?"

I could see heads nodding in approval across the hall.

"Will the cattle owners and their families move to the Ranch or only their cattle? Who is the head of the cattle village? Who will decide who owns what proportion of the land or space in the cattle village? What will be the criteria for sharing space in the cattle village? Who will determine the criteria? What will the government do to ensure that the cattle village will not be used for any other purpose besides the one assigned? Your Excellency, perhaps cattle owners should also be free to build and stay in that village. All we need to know is that the land should be used in our own interest and that Government should make that clear."

"*Reng reng, abei!*" was the shout intermingled with showers of voices that greeted my intervention.

When the murmurs died down, I continued. "Your Excellency, you said the land allocated for ranching is the property of Mbiame council. I work for the council as assistant mayor and know where the council land begins and ends. What if the cattle breeder gets a portion of land and later becomes so ambitious as to start pinching and crossing the boundary?"

I could see that I was quite impressive from the repeated nods while I spoke.

"And what happens if some people decide to sell their own portion of the land in the future? Will that not take us back to where we started?"

"Ohooorrr!" The hall roared, while the governor kept writing, a smile on his lips.

"The women's group met and agreed before coming here, and what I will say now reflects our collective voice. We are happy with the suggestions made so far, especially those encouraging tolerance, love, living together, and harmonious living. We have some suggestions to make. Let me start with what we consider to be homemade solutions. The conflict over land and water resources is happening in many other places. We are in contact with one women's group in a neighbouring country, Benin, facing a similar challenge. The activities of their NGO are similar to that of the Bongkisheri Kibang Women's Group. We joined hands with them. We visited them to find out how they were going about resolving their communal, land, and tribal conflicts. We learned a lot from them. One of the things that can be helpful to us is planting trees and fodder grass. That is what the women have been doing for two years now. Fodder grass is good feed for cattle. Fodder can be harvested and preserved in heaps and large pits. It can be sold to cattle owners during the season when there is no rain and no vegetation, the season of prolonged dryness. Besides, cattle owners can also be trained to plant and preserve the grass, in addition to farmers cultivating it for sale to cattle owners during periods of prolonged dryness. This is one way we can solve the problem of grazing land between farmers and herdsmen…"

Voices hailed, and the governor nodded approvingly, seeming to be very edified. Naturally, I picked up the cue of approval and continued rather loquaciously.

"We have noticed that Gidang has stones and sand which Kibang does not have but needs to construct houses, roads, bridges, and other types of infrastructure. On the other hand, Gidang needs vegetation and grazing land. If Gidang could give part of their land where stones and sand are found to Kibang, it would be a good deal for Kibang to offer back the cattle village, which has vegetation almost all year round…"

"*Reng reng*, hililililililililililili, eh woman errrh, herrrh, eh woman eh, herrh…", the hall vibrated with rowdy exclamations of consent and endorsement.

Your Excellency, the women also dug a well in the women's land and planted trees around the well to ensure regular water retention in the well. That well has never lacked water. Kibang and Gidang villages carry water from that well even during periods of prolonged dryness. Bricklayers no longer trek long distances to buy water or fetch water from valleys to make bricks. Women and children no longer trek to distant villages and valleys, looking for water to buy or carry. This is our humble suggestion."

The hall rang continuously with applause. The Fon, Tav Kibari, Tata, and other elders nodded approvingly. The governor continued taking down notes after clapping for me.

"Kibang people can come and carry sand and stones from Gidang to build in their own land," Alhaji Kidado said promptly.

"Usoko, usoko, Madanlah," the herd boys expressed their grateful compliance with the suggestion from Alhaji Kidado. This ushered in Alhaji Wakilu, leader of the cattle breeders' association. The MC announced him, but he visibly shocked everyone, asking all the cattle breeders and herd boys not to sign the attendance sheet. To him, putting their signatures on that paper would mean that they endorsed the ban on open grazing.

Like the governor, the mayor thanked everybody, particularly the women whose suggestions were very relevant to him. After a muffled discussion with Tav Kibari, the fon again thanked each speaker and all who participated in the discussion.

"I want to thank particularly the governor for his attention. He was writing down everything we said and did not allow any crumbs to drop on the floor. My understanding is that he will take up the problems that cannot find immediate solutions to big government. My people, on our part and for the sake of peace, let us forgive each other for our mistakes in the past. Let us accept what the governor has said and respect the decisions we have taken or will take today. If we choose to empty dirt on the floor of our minds instead of casting it away in the garbage heap, we will continue to live with filth."

"Bve'reh! Nchang Nchang! Reng reng'!" were echoed, denoting the fon's attributes of courage in the lion image, his royalty, and the people's respect, and other forms of praise. The governor reached for the microphone from Dr Jerry. It was time to round up. No disagreeing voices were again heard.

"Chief Fomu, Alhaji Kidado, the leadership of the cattle breeders' association, the council of elders, representative of the Women's Group, leader of the Vigilante group, people of Kibang and Gidang, I thank you so much for participating in this important meeting. I have taken note of all your worries. I have already mentioned the two important steps big government has taken to resolve the problem of grazing land and bring lasting peace to the land. I mentioned the ban on open grazing and also that part of government land in Mbiame village has been allocated for cattle ranching. So, some of the problems can be addressed here, but those we cannot address will be carried to Big Government. Your voices will be heard..."

Exclamations of excitement flustered across the hall.

He continued, "We have agreed on many things, and we have disagreed on a few: the issue of ownership of cattle routes, the lack of consensus on allocating the council land for ranching, and the question of ownership of water resources. On that note, I have the following: If cattle destroy your corn or plants in a demarcated area, you don't have a case. But if cattle destroy your crops in non-cattle demarcated areas, report the matter to the competent authorities. Report to your mayor immediately if you find cows, sheep, goats, or pigs grazing on your crops. It is the duty of the municipal council to impound or arrest stray animals and keep them in confinement until a solution is reached between the parties concerned."

The mayor nodded to this.

Point 2. River Kibang belongs to everybody. Nobody should try to stop another from fetching water from the streams, no matter where the stream is found; cows must be guided by herdsmen to the streams to drink water or to graze. In any event, no one is to take the laws into their hands. If you are unsure what to do, meet the Chief, Alhaji, or your mayor and speak to them. They are our eyes and ears. They will guide you. If you are unsatisfied with their intervention, go to the official security service like the police and report the matter. We will follow up to ensure justice for the victim. Learn to love and tolerate each other. We are humans and bound to make mistakes, but these mistakes should not tear us apart. They should not be deliberate or purposeful, though. We need and will always need each other. Work very closely with your traditional and religious leaders. They are the link between the people and government. They are closer to you than we are; they know everybody; they know when a stranger comes in or goes out; they know every hideout in the land. In the days ahead, government will release a book saying that the land in Mbiame village is officially reserved for cattle ranching. There will also be another book to enforce the ban on open grazing. We will also consider the important suggestions from the women."

No opposing voices were raised. Ability, Atang, Livinus, activist Kaba, Kinang, and Shey Lukong, whose protesting fingers could still be seen wagging in the air, were not as vigorous as earlier. Almost everybody seemed contented with the governor's conclusions. The day was placidly drawing to a close, but it did not. Something unexpected happened.

"*Nkom, nkom, nkom, kutu…*" heavy footsteps, accompanied by a desperate scream, suddenly came from the backyard of the hall. All eyes trooped towards the main entrance to the Palace. It was Lankar. He charged across the courtyard and staggered into the hall, panting and pointing across the neighbourhood.

"*B-b-bve'reh, B-bve'reh*, it-it-it has happened…"

"Lankar, what is it?" Asked the Fon, staring through the door.

"C-c-c-cows, cows, cows, c-c-c-crops…"

"Lankar, what has happened to cows and crops? Speak!"

"Cows have eaten crops and grass and died!"

"*Hei! Mbarang! Kai!*" Was the interjections to express the overwhelming situation that simultaneously came from several lips.

"Lankar, what do you mean by cows have eaten the crops and grass and died?" asked Fon Fomu.

"And what were cows doing in somebody's farm?" asked Ability.

"*Bvere'eh*, I was checking my traps in the bush when I saw dead bodies of cows lying here and there. I then decided to run back to the village and inform the Fon. On my way to the council hall, I saw more dead bodies of cows scattered in the maize farms and in the bushes." Lankar said, bending forward and pointing across the yard toward the farmlands. "I did not see any plant standing up. I am not even sure that the soul of any of the cows I met lying in the hills, farms, and valleys is still around! Cows ate the crops and grass and died. Go and see for yourselves."

"People of Kidang-Gidang, calm down. The commandant and the commissioner of police are here, and they know what to do. They will move to the farmlands and bushes to commence an investigation. We will fish out the bad people and their sponsors to face the full wrath of the law."

It is possible that hardly anyone heard what the governor said. For, before he could open his mouth to speak, many people had already stormed out. The women trailed the men, stampeding toward the path that meandered across the neighbourhood to reach the site where some of the village farms were located.

4

Double Tragedy

We experienced a mixture of different emotions and reactions when we arrived at the scene of the tragedy. The smacking of hands and buttocks, stamping of feet on the ground, rending of clothes, and crossing of hands over the heads were accompanied by questions, exclamations, wild screams, and lamentations. Beheaded stems and crushed trunks were sweating and weeping like the limbs of chopped trees. It was not only the women who transformed the scene into a corpse-removal scene. The men stood frozen, their mouths hanging open in a half-wide-eyed yawn. Some stood staring absent-mindedly into space; some shook their heads while others held their lips firmly gathered as if stitched into a fold with a needle as they glided their eyes over the farms from one end to another. Repeated shrugs of their shoulders accentuated the question, "Who did this?"

Alhaji Kidado and his Ganakos, as Musa, Yaaji, Kodume, Dabari, and other herd boys were called, did not hide their frustration. While others held their arms crossed over their heads, Musa burst out,

"*Kai, kai, kai,* my cow dem don die! Somebody don killam all; no job for me agen, I don finis *kwata kwata* (completely), I don finis, no cow, no work."

Tears trickled down my cheeks as I moved toward my farm. Naked ridges crawled along the entire rows. A few headless maize stems with deep gorges on their chests that had formerly been sheaths for corn cobs stood here and there as the only surviving descendants of the once gorgeous farms. Fodder grass that I watched some days back, jutting on ridges and swaying back and forth like skirts of leaves, had all been uprooted. Onion shoots and bean sprouts with long ears lay lengthened and wilted on the ridges with bruises all over their leaves. Cattle had trampled heavily on them.

On the ravaged beds and furrows were littered cows, sheep, goats, and pigs with stiff limbs and bloated stomachs. Each of the dead animals seemed to have been in their last term of pregnancy before death suddenly paid them a visit. I immediately sensed what had happened.

The animals had died after destructive grazing on the farm. What caused their deaths?

"Someone seemed to have sprayed the crops with something poisonous. Who could have done this? And how did the person know cattle would invade the farms at the same time the meeting was taking place in the palace? Could it be…? Hmmm."

I still remember Tav Kibari's discreet remarks as he stood beside me, wondering, tapping his forehead, and throwing probing glances at Ability.

Ability's dramatic reaction soon invited all attention to his farm. It was pathetic watching the naked ridges in the section of the farm where he had cultivated corn and onions. His onions had all been dug up from the root and eaten. Watching Ability's farm, I knew he would confront the cattle owners even before he started.

"I saw it coming, and I told Kibang people that Alhaji Kidado's cows should be stopped from coming down to Kibang to drink water from our streams, but nobody listened to me. I knew the cows would not rest until they transformed our farms into a charity organisation. I knew that Gidang cows would complete the work that the likes of World Wars and the Come-no-go virus started, and I told Fon Fomu to ban cows from drinking our water. See what has happened now!" Ability lamented, pointing at the empty ridges and decapitated maize stems across his farm and shaking his head, moving back and forth.

"*Wallahi tallahi* (I swear to my God), the sun will never shine on the head of anybody who has a hand in the death of my cows, and his household will never know peace!" Alhaji Kidado threatened, pointing at the bloated bodies of cattle scattered in the vicinity, his chest rising and falling.

"Alhaji Kidado, when your cows transform people's farms into a charity organisation, you should not complain when the same cows are transformed into charity gifts!" Ability snapped. Alhaji Kidado looked fixedly at Ability with wide-open eyes.

"You heard me. Tell your cows to stay away from our streams and farms or be ready to see more of what has happened."

"Baba Bility, let it not be what I am *tinking*!" Alhaji Kidado fumed.

"Alhaji Kidado, you heard Baa Ability!" Atang quipped.

Then, Musa, Aboki, Kodume, Wakilu, Yaaji, and Dabari, who had, before now, been trying to count the dead bodies of their cattle, returned and stood beside Alhaji Kidado and Jawara, with hands crossed over their heads.

As Ability and Alhaji exchanged words, I caught Livinus' stealthy actions. He leaned slightly back, closing and opening his left eye rapidly while pressing down his toes on the surface of Atang's foot as if to stop Atang from completing the sentence. That action was sufficient to make the three men the objects of suspicion. Jawara also seemed to have noticed what Livinus was trying to do.

"Baba Ability, you are provoking somebody whose cows are found dead in your farmland under suspicious circumstances!" Jawara cautioned, panting.

"Do not be an oppressor if you cannot manage resistance!" Ability dared, Atang nods.

"We shall see!" Thundered Alhaji Kidado.

"What can a Come-no-go do to a son of the soil?" Asked Ability.

"Revenge has no expiry date!" Jawara said to Ability, puffing.

"I should be the one planning to revenge the destruction of my onions and corn!" Ability snapped.

"The grave is dug! Someone must occupy it, and that person would not be the Come-no-go!" Jawara said in a voice masked with threats, which Alhaji Kidado confirmed.

The heartbroken villagers drifted into smaller groups of frustrations expressed in talking, lamenting, uncoordinated movements, hauling across accusations and threats at each other. The tense atmosphere soon focused on two groups. Ability, Kinang, Shey Lukong, Atang, and Livinus, on the one hand, faced Alhaji Kidado, Wakilu, Musa, Yaaji, Kodume, Jawara, Aboki, and Dabari on the other.

"Alhaji Kidado, Jawara, you said the grave is dug, and somebody must occupy it. I have something to say. My crops are as important to me as your cows are important to you! I lost my job, and the only thing I had left was my crops! But where are the crops now? I have lost the only thing my survival depended on...all because of your cattle! And you are here threatening the people who should threaten you! Come-no-go! Strangers! Go back to your land, or else the rest of your cattle will leave this land limping!" Ability threatened.

"Baba Bility, your fipur killi my cow dem and you talk say we be *tringers*? Baba Bility, if you open mop (mouth) call my fipur Come-no-go agen, I am going to *tich* you what Come-no-go can do!" Musa fumed, and Jawara, Aboki, Yaaji, Kodume, and Dabari saluted his words with continued nodding.

"Musa, did you just threaten my father? Have you forgotten who I am?" Atang threatened with inciting gestures from Kinang, Shey Lukong and Livinus.

"Atang, don't worry; I can handle them," Ability said before turning toward the herders. "Listen very well! I am a son of the soil! I can swallow an insult, but not from someone whose occupation is babysitting cows!"

A fight was brewing in the pot of provocation and divisive language. Ability had dared the herd boys. Musa, Kodume, Yaaji, and Dabari were among the herd boys feared by almost everybody in Kibang because of their intolerance, thirst for vengeance, and fiery temper. Everybody quickly fell behind before Musa, Kodume, Yaaji, and Dabari pulled thirsty knives from the sheaths around their waists. Then, they stood alert, facing the camp of Ability, Atang, and Livinus, who also were on alert, each with one knee and one arm bent forward.

The verbal confrontation had attracted the attention of the Fon, the Alhaji, the mayor, and the police, who were still in the yard counting the damaged farms and the dead animals. The police, acting as mediators, soon stood in the middle of the two camps.

"People of Kibang and Gidang, calm down. We are all affected in one way or another; we are all hurt, but we will not allow you to take the law into your hands."

One of the two police officers gave this advisory language to calm down the flaring tempers. After whispering with the Fon, the Alhaji, and the mayor, the police officers stepped aside for the Fon to address the crowd.

"People of Kibang and Gidang, our hearts are bleeding, but as government has said, we will not take the law into our hands. The women should go back home and take care of the children. Elders of our land, let us all move to the palace now. Kila, you can join the elders."

The meeting in the palace was brief. Only the Fon spoke. "Alhaji Kidado, talk to your people to stay calm. I will talk to my people too. Government will help us to fish out the bad seed and punish accordingly. We will allow the police to do their work. They followed us to the farm. They saw everything. My people, go home now and rest until you hear from us."

It was unanimously agreed that the matter should be reported to the police for proper investigation and action. After the brief meeting at the palace and then with the mayor, my next stop was the MP's backyard.

I was actually on my way to the MP's house following his text message requesting me to come over and brief him on what happened at the disaster site when I saw his car parked at a bend a few metres away from his compound. Ability, Kinang and Shey Lukong were also there. What separated me from them was a cluster of plantain stems at the bend. The drooping branches had covered the entire road, shielding any approaching person from view. I didn't trust this company. I tiptoed into the farm and bent behind the clustering plantain stems from where I peered across through the armpits of leaves, listening carefully to the conversation between Ability and the honourable member of parliament.

"…Honourable, what else do you want to hear? We have just told you what you need to know. So, it is left for you now to take the necessary action."

"Ability, what do you want me to do at this particular moment?" the MP asked.

"Alhaji Kidado's cows destroyed my crops, leaving me financially barren and irrelevant! And the MP, a lawmaker and son of the soil, does not know what to do? Honourable, Honourable, with all the power and money you wield, you still don't know what to do?" Ability shook his head repeatedly. "Alhaji Kidado's bank accounts are suffering from financial obesity, thanks to our streams, grass and crops that feed the very cattle that destroyed my crops! And me, a son of the soil, my pockets are in perpetual financial starvation. I cultivated onions and maize in large quantities. I planned to sell my crops and raise money to reverse this financial affliction in order to become a man again. See what has happened. The same crops have been destroyed by cattle belonging to the very stranger who talks to me anyhow simply because his bank accounts and waist pockets are in a state of constant financial constipation. Honourable, Alhaji Kidado and his herd boys should immediately be arrested and dragged to the police! They should stay behind bars until they pay ten million for the damage their cattle have done to my only source of livelihood! If the police collect money and release them as usual, I will do what I know how to do best. Yes! The evidence of the shocking and malicious destruction of my maize and onions is alive! Go to my farm and see what I'm talking about in order to understand how I feel right now! That's not all. The so-called decision to create the cattle reserve in Mbiame-Kibang must remain only on paper! That land is Kibang land! My boys and I will make Kibang and Gidang ungovernable if an inch of that land is given to strangers! I know you can do something. That cattle reserve project should remain a miscarriage; it must die in the womb of the decision that created it! Honourable, ensure that the farmers get compensated; that the herd boys are arrested and put behind bars for life."

"*Reng reng,*" Kinang and Banadzem echoed Ability in an exclamation that denoted approval in their native Lamnso.

"Ability, this same intolerant, impatient, divisive, and incendiary attitude is the reason you lost your prestigious job in the military. I don't need to remind you!" cautioned the MP.

"Honourable, when I plotted with you and the SDO to arrest and detain the villagers of Nsengong village who protested when you seized their ancestral lands for your cattle, I was not impatient, intolerant, divisive, and incendiary. When I persuaded the Fulani people to offer ten cows and sheep to you in exchange for favours and protection, I was not impatient and divisive! Ha, ha, ha, ha, ha. Honourable, this is my turn. If you do not use the weight of your pockets to support my boys to frustrate the creation of the cattle reserve project; if you do not use the strength of your pockets to facilitate the arrest of Kidado and his herd boys; and if you do not use the power of your pockets to ensure that the farmers get compensated, I am no longer your campaign manager! And when I go, I take my family, connections, Kinang, boys, and Shey Lukong with me. You know what that means." Ability threatened.

"*Reng reng!*" chorused Kinang and Shey Lukong.

"Are you threatening me?" Honourable barked.

"Consider it a big threat!" Ability fumed.

"Nobody fights government. Ability, it is not every time that bullying tactics work! I have said this to you several times. I can't do what you're asking me to do. I can't. I cannot fight Government! I cannot force Alhaji Kidado and the herd boys to pay for any crop damage! You told me they equally lost their cattle! The outcome of investigations will do that job for us. Police will soon swing into action, I know. By the way, what you said in the hall was not necessary. I have told you that we can't be hard on Alhaji Kidado and the herd boys now, even if they are guilty. I need their votes; I need everybody now more than ever before! You know my ambitions. The governorship elections are approaching. You know the Governor will not contest the elections because he wants to join the Senate. I want to take over as the governor of Kibang-Gidang. Ability, try to reason with me. I need everybody in Kibang and Gidang if I must win this election. I am not happy about what happened to your crops. But we cannot be hard on whoever is responsible now."

"Honourable, the mayor wants to compete for the governorship elections; everyone knows. He is grooming Kila to succeed him as mayor. He is your political rival, and he is very powerful. He has done a lot for the people, and everybody likes him; every household in Kibang has pipe-borne water thanks to him. He has carried the water project to parts of Gidang, and there are plans to construct farm-to-market roads here and there. All the markets have good toilets; all the Government schools have good toilets; he pays school fees for many orphans from Kibang as well as from Gidang; he has bought benches for schools; he is building classrooms in many schools; he bought sewing equipment, tables, chairs, and trees for the Bongk-isheri Women's Centre for Peace, and assisted them with ten bags of cement to construct a second borehole. I attended the ceremony. He has drafted a road project linking Kibang and Gidang; he has bought water pipes to channel water from Kibang to Gidang through the mountain; that young man is just everywhere; we need a village of people behind us to get what we want."

"And that's another reason we cannot be hard on anyone now. Ability, I have told you everything. If I win the governorship elections, you will become my private secretary. I have already told you about my plans for you."

"Honourable, you don't speak like somebody who wants to win an election!" Ability replied.

"Now, considering everything the mayor has done for the two

communities, and bearing in mind the water project he promised the Gidang people, do you think Gidang people will give me their votes if I lock up their leader and his herd boys? That's not all. The herdsmen are born warriors. I am told they can fight for ten years without getting tired...." The MP was still talking when Ability cut in.

"Honourable, if your problem is numbers and physical force, then you have no problem. The greatest warrior in Kibang is Atang. That boy is the product of the sweat of my anthill; I am talking about this edifice," Ability boasted, tapping his manhood. "Have you heard about Livinus before? He is short, but no storm is strong enough to uproot his legs from the ground. Even if you succeed in putting the backs of Atang and Livinus on the ground, don't take a step anywhere closer to them; make sure the distance between you and them is the length of a river."

Kinang and Shey Lukong nodded in corroboration. Ability bragged on about the unrivalled strength of Atang and Livinus. "We can also count on Shey Lukong, Kinang, and Banadzem. They have big boys," he added. "Honourable, what are you saying concerning my crops? We need compensation. I've done a lot for you. This is your turn to help me." Ability reminded.

"Very well then, emmer, you said earlier that the grass and the crops that the cattle ate and died were sprayed with a powerful poison. Who do you think might have sprayed poison on the grass and the crops? Do you have any suspects in mind so that we can start from there?" the MP asked.

Ability bent over and looked across the vicinity from the right to the left-hand sides as if to ensure that nobody was around and spoke, "Something is telling me that our political rival sponsored people to spray poison on the crops and grass..."

"Hurh! The mayor! Why would he do that?"

"Honourable, a rival can do anything to have his way. Trust any politician at your own risk. Honourable, you jumped into politics because you were repatriated from Amerika. You are just three years old in the political game. Allow those who know every corner of the political field to tell you how the game is played. The mayor wants to tear the community apart to ruin your chances of winning the upcoming governorship elections. He already has people behind him. He predicted that the cattle would consume the poisoned crops and herbs and die. He anticipated that the people of Gidang and Kibang will use the recent happenings to determine where your loyalty belongs," Ability elaborated to convince the MP. "Honourable, you need Kibang more than you need Alhaji Kidado and his herd boys. What's the population of Gidang compared to that of Kibang? Hurh! I have a forest of boys behind me. With just a snap of my fingers, they will fight and seize the political wrestling belt from the Governor. Honourable, when it comes to planting, watering, and harvesting political disciples, Kibang is a more fertile catchment site. Oh yes! Just make sure that the ranching project is frustrated. Ensure that the Governor pushes for an anti-open grazing law and that the farmers get compensated for the damage done to their crops, and the whole of Kibang will rally behind you. The vigilante boys and the guards listen to me," Ability bragged.

Honourable removed a healthy brown envelope from his car and handed it to Ability, stating that it was the first consignment of the campaign materials. I sat on my hind and leaned back. The three walked past by, discussing in Lamnso, grinning. I knew they wanted to hide their conversation from Honourable, who, as a result of being born and raised in the city by a Kibang father and an educated Gidang mother, was very distant from what many would call 'mother tongue'. I watched Kinang and Banadzem staring suspiciously at Ability's greedy fingers as he counted the wads of money he had just pulled from the brown envelope. He carefully glided his thumb back and forth without lifting it as if to hide the figures on the notes. As they moved away, I overheard Ability talking about the sharing formula, although I didn't really get the details. They disappeared at the bend before I stepped out.

A confused and unresponsive stare remained on Honourable's face even after Ability and his friends had left. When they were physically out of reach, Honourable mumbled, "Ability is a necessary danger. I will play along with him for the moment. I will load his pockets with money. I will play along with him until the elections are over. Once the results are proclaimed, I will never take a telephone call from him again." So, saying, he abruptly looked at his watch and exclaimed, "Hurh, hurh, bull shit! I almost forgot I needed to see Kila. The women listen to her. I need to see her. She was supposed to come and see me. She should be on her way now!"

When I later joined the MP in his sitting room, he asked me what had happened and who the suspects behind the spraying of poison on the grass and crops were. He wanted to know what was discussed in the Palace, too, as well as the people's reaction to the tragic events. He asked what he could do to win the approaching governorship elections. On who might have sprayed poison on the fields and the farms, I told him the police had commenced investigations to determine the culprits. On the question of how best to prepare to win the elections, I simply said the ballot box should decide. He offered to assist the Women's Centre with 2,000,000 CFA francs in exchange for votes from the women and held out a swollen brown envelope to me. I thanked him and, without intending to sound rude, suggested that he keep the money and make arrangements, with my assistance, to share it with the farmers and the cattle owners who lost their crops and cattle. Before I left, he invited me to another meeting, adding that he would send a message with details of the date and time.

5

Three Days Later

The atmosphere in Kibang and Gidang resulting from the destruction of crops and the mass death of over five hundred cattle, as reported by the media, was toxic, divisive, frustrating, and strained. It was characterised by distrust and antagonism. It was frustrating because both the Gidang and the Kibang communities had lost the sources of their livelihood; the survival of the majority of the Kibang community depended entirely on crop farming in the same way that the Gidang people depended on cattle rearing as a source of their welfare. The farmers and the herd boys were mad at each other, accusing each other of the losses incurred. Mistrust was brewing war. Gidang blamed Kibang for the killing of their cows; Kibang blamed Gidang for the destruction of their crops. Rumours went around that both communities were gearing up for reprisals against each other. Gidang herdsmen were planning a payback attack, while Kibang farmers were mobilizing for retaliation. That was the talk on every lip. People started escaping to the cities and distant villages as they did not want to become casualties of the impending war. But before the cutlasses, knives, and spears could leave their sheaths to rip open stomachs and slit throats, something happened and delayed the anticipated attack.

First was a thick, disgusting smell that hung in the air. People started coughing, hissing, suffering from stomach aches and severe runny stomachs. A wave of death erupted. Many dropped dead after developing diarrhoea and vomiting. Cough and cholera-affected patients in the health centres and hospitals swelled each passing day. Within three days, stiff bodies lay in homes and Kibang medical centres. Birds, too, dropped dead on rooftops and everywhere. Stiff bodies of dogs, pigs, sheep, goats, fowls, rats, cats, wall geckos, donkeys, and horses with rigid bent limbs lay across courtyards and pathways. Ants, insects, and crawlies in general littered surfaces. The beds in medical centres were full. Patients lay on the naked floors and across verandas and balconies.

People reacted to the eruption of the epidemic in different ways. Interpretations of the erupted calamity were many. The world was coming to an end. *Ashoh*, the god of the land, was angry. It was a sign of the end times, a famous man of God called Barnabas told his congregation, selling them anointing oil and water at the Fountain of Grace Ministry. Other religious leaders alleged their prophecies were being fulfilled. A half-litre bottle of anointing oil rose from 2000 CFA francs to 5000 CFA francs, and the price of palm oil tripled. While many resorted to heavy consumption of anointing oil, water, and palm oil, others visited native doctors to reverse what they believed was a curse from *Ashoh*.

The outer layer of Fonyuy's skin became pale and whitish. It began to peel off the same day we ate the contaminated beef. We lost Fonyuy that same day. Mbiame, my second son, and Bernsah, Jeff and I also developed symptoms, our skin, and hair shedding off. New growths kept coming on and peeling off, leaving what looked like pale white segments and gaping cracks on our lips, cheeks, and arms. I lost my voice and could barely pant and hiss.

Many did not realise that the cough, diarrhoea, cholera, skin-shedding disease, and sudden deaths resulted from the consumption of contaminated meat or contact with the foetid air. The beef from the poisoned cattle was toxic. Ability, Atang, Livinus, Faya, Kinang, and Shey Lukong had slaughtered the dead cattle and sold the meat to many. Rumour later spread around the village like a wandering storm before the rains.

The epidemic and sudden deaths invited prompt interventions. The Minister of Health declared it an epidemic, cautioning that any further consumption of the poisoned beef would lead to more deaths. Fon Fomu recommended licking palm oil. The price of palm oil shot up, but what was the high cost measured against the devastation of death? My family bought and drank significant quantities of it. Other families did the same. Before long, palm oil had run out in the local markets and shops. People from the neighbouring villages in Menda drove into Kibang with truckloads of palm oil and anointing water.

We also took other things to combat the epidemic. We harvested and scraped aloe vera leaves, squeezed other herbs, and drank. Bernsah had harvested the herbs from Yaya's herbal garden when he last visited and had planted them in the garden behind our house. We now found them useful, although we had always scolded him for planting many things in the garden. Yaya had herbs, plants, and trees on the hillside where she lived. With them, she treated people suffering from prolonged coughs, mental disorders, rashes, and diseases in general. Some of the herbs we had already started taking were potently curative, harvested from her herbal garden. Yaya had taught us to use herbal extraction remedies for runny stomachs, stubborn coughs, stomach aches, body pains, and other ailments.

The government also intervened with remedial measures. By the second day of the epidemic's eruption, the Mbiame village of Kibang and its vicinities had lost about 30 people. The medical team organised by the health ministry went from house to house to provide assistance and ensure that sanitation measures were followed. Severe cases were rushed to nearby medical facilities.

Immediately the Kibaaka Minister of Health declared the eruption of the deadly epidemic, protocols for proper sanitation were prescribed for households and public facilities. The people of Kibang and the adjoining Gidang communities were prescribed a four-week lockdown. The medical team and Mrs. Comfort, the leader of the community-based organisation, did proper fumigation of churches, mosques, households, markets, public offices, classrooms, and school environments. Hand washing facilities, sanitizers and face masks were provided to households within the affected vicinities. All out-door activities were suspended except for defined essential services. All public gatherings were also suspended during the lockdown. Media platforms, including the state television and radio networks, ran daily programs on proper hygiene. Compulsory wearing of face masks at home and in public was instituted. Everybody was given at least two face masks. We stayed indoors observing pollution-induced lockdown measures prescribed by the government of Kabaaka land. Palliatives and other relief items poured in from the government, elites, groups, cultural associations, and human rights groups. The lockdown measures and wearing face masks that covered the mouth to the nose helped reduce the number of pollution-related deaths in Kibang.

The epidemic left sad memories in Kibang and its neighbouring communities, one of which was the death of a whole family. This was not known until a frightening increase in clusters of flies started peering through the edges of the door and the windowpanes of my neighbour's house like gossipers. A thick, reeking stench was waft-ing towards my house from the same direction. Jeff and I became worried. Our other neighbours were still in the hospital. When we could stand it no more, Jeff and I agreed to break the neighbour's door. We did, but it was late. Five bloated bodies lay on the floor.

Jaika was a single lady living with her four children. They were now all gone. We wrapped the bodies in blankets and pulled them to the rear, directly behind the house, where we dumped them in a shallow grave and covered with soil. It was a frightening experience. I shovelled the soil and poured it on the bodies. We stepped into the half-filled hole and started stamping heavily on the soil. We stopped, put in more soil, and stamped, repeating the process until the pit was fully refilled. It was my first time digging a grave and my first time burying a corpse. It was the first time in Kibang land that a woman was digging a grave and stepping into an excavation to stamp on the soil over the corpse. I had been told that grave digging and burial activities were for men only. Well, I bungled through, learning on the job. Even long after the burial, the stench from my neighbour's house and the disturbing memories lingered on, causing me to have sleepless nights. I saw Jaika and her children in my dreams each time I slept. I loathed being alone in any environment.

Once I rushed out of the house to join Jeff and the kids in the courtyard. We were skimming through the newspaper Jeff had just bought from the market, a stone's throw from our house. We wanted more information on easing the lockdown measures, a news item published on national television the previous day. A muffled cough drew my attention to Yaya approaching from across the yard. She clamped her mouth and nostrils with her hand because the stench was still in the air. I ran across the yard with my children to receive her. Her joy of seeing us was short-lived. When I took her straight behind the house and showed her the spot where Fonyuy was buried, she was inconsolable, crying and rolling over and over on the spot. She eventually wore herself out, and we returned to the house.

Yaya immediately announced the reason for her brief visit, as she called it. She had heard about the government's decision to lift the ban on movements. She had heard that people were now free to move about. Therefore, she came to give us herbs. She wanted to take the entire family to her house in the suburbs of Mbiame until the tension was over. It wasn't safe to nose around the village during that period. She had also heard that I dug the grave and stepped into the excavation to stamp on the soil over the corpse. It was an abomination. Burying corpses was for men. She would cleanse me of a possible curse. She had heard about the invasion of farmlands by cattle and the poisoning of the cows. She had lived long enough with the herd boys and understood their unquenchable urge for vengeance. They were going to come down to Kibang to avenge the killing of their cattle. She warned that the epidemic might only have delayed their reprisal, reiterating that she had lived with the herders long enough to understand their thirst for revenge.

Jeff disliked the village. River Kibang lay too close to Yaya's house, Jeff argued, making the environment unsafe for children. He had to find a polite way to decline Yaya's offer.

"Yaya, we will be fine, and the children will be too. We had a brief meeting in the palace. Alhaji Kidado was present. The Fon appealed to everybody to avoid revenge and allow the police to do their job. Alhaji Kidado accepted. So, there is no reason to be afraid," I reiterated. Yaya was still uncomfortable and insisted she would not leave if the children would not go with her.

"Kila, when mother hen sits on her chicks, it is not because she wants to feel big but because she wants to spread her wings over them and keep them safe from the rains. When it happens, do not say I did not warn you!" Yaya said and went to bed, where she grumbled the whole night.

It happened as Yaya had predicted. It was about 10 pm, the third day of Yaya's visit. Jeff and I had returned from an evaluation meeting with the government representatives, to which all who had lost their crops or cattle were invited. We had gone to bed immediately after eating dinner, feeling exhausted. Unknown to us, the herd boys had planned a reprisal attack on Mbiame Upper Kibang village and were apparently waiting for the air pollution to subside and for the lockdown to be lifted.

That night, sharp, agonizing cries and screams began to inch in like soft raindrops in every direction, awakening us from a deep sleep.

"Fire! Fire! Fire! Somebody he-e-e-elp! Somebody heeeeelp!"

"What's happening?" I asked with a violent shudder. I quickly panicked out of bed but found myself in a hazy, smoke-invaded room. Confused, I grabbed the blanket and then my telephone to light my way to the nearby room, where the screaming voices of Yaya and my children could now be heard loudly. Their room was already invaded by smoke.

I groped for their hands immediately to drag them out of the sweltering room. Jeff grabbed the bag containing our certificates and necessary credentials and rushed to the sitting room to break open the main door to ease our exit. Following my advice, Yaya and Bernsah held my dress from behind. I had already carried Mbiame on my back and grabbed the blanket with one hand. With Yaya and Bernsah holding me from behind, I stretched my hand forward to feel the way as we tore through the thick darkness along the corridor. Before we approached the sitting room, excited tongues of flames were already consuming the window near the exit door. Jeff was still trying to kick out the hinges of the door. We struggled to tear through the hedge of flames and the smoke surging across the room but drifted back immediately, screaming for help. I felt like I was in the heart of hell. I threw the blanket over our heads to reduce contact with the roasting flames and heat. I was screaming and calling God to come to our rescue, and it seemed God had answered my prayers. A sudden loud sound indicated that Jeff had unleashed a heavy kick and wrenched off the door with its hinges. His impact hauled him together with the door off across the yard. Choking smoke dug into our eyes, throats, and nostrils. We hissed and coughed repeatedly, unable to determine the direction of the door. I became very weak and unable to move my legs. Yaya fell heavily to the floor, and I felt a hand around me. It was Jeff. Bernsah had seized his hand from mine and ran outside with Mbiame. Jeff grabbed my hand and dragged us in a bunch through the hedge of smoke interspersed with tongues of leaping flames. He succeeded in flinging us across the yard before we collapsed in a heap. After a lingering time-lapse, I woke up and found myself lying alongside many others on a bush nearby. Yaya and the children were lying beside me, gasping, hissing, and coughing. Jeff was happy when I opened my eyes and spoke. After speaking briefly with the children and Yaya to be sure they were okay, Jeff told me it was thanks to the blanket he had flung over his head that he was protected along with us from fire burns.

The rest of the night was long and looked like a year. I sat with my back on a coffee tree, fighting mosquitoes, constantly changing positions but staring across the vicinity. As the moon cast its rays on surfaces, I could see tongues, sheets of feverish flames, and dark smoke shooting up toward the sky from the tops of many nearby buildings. There were women with children on their backs scampering in every direction and screaming. Some people might have been trapped in flames. A mass of hairy black smoke, mixed with tongues of flames, was dancing quickly and volcano-like through rooftops across the living quarters of Upper Kibang. While we watched, a heavy blast of fire, like the sound of a gunshot, came from one of the burning houses. The blasts were repeated and soon became rhythmically frequent. Houses puffed out more smoke into the air from the direction of the fuelling station, stretching towards the market centre.

Upper Kibang was the only emerging town in the municipality of Mbiame and had more buildings than any other neighbourhood in the entire Division. Fires were still leaping high and huge in some areas of Upper Kibang towards the early morning hours. When morning came, I was eager to visit my house, hoping I could still recover the books and pots or anything that could help. First, Jeff and I lingered for a while to ensure that the children were relaxed and safe on the leaves where they lay, sleeping as only innocence can, before we followed the other residents to the living quarters.

Everything had been burnt down. The fire had consumed the houses that used to spill over across my neighbourhood like cars streaming along the road during moments of heavy traffic. I could barely recognise the few signs that people had once lived in the vicinity from the glowing stumps of buildings still attached to surfaces on the ground. Like an animal whose internal organs have been removed, leaving only ribs and bones, smoke-coated iron bars jutted up from the stumps. They were held out at the chests by a few shredded blocks. You could see the ribs on the chests of gutted buildings.

A cold welcome gripped me immediately I walked into my yard. A headless stump measuring about half a yard, with sparse butchered concrete blocks sticking out from the chests of smoke-coated iron rods, stood staring at me, forcing a stream of tears down my cheeks. For the first time, Jeff's eyes had the colour of blood. I could tell that we were thinking about the same thing. This is what remains of my home, only skeletal walls. We had lost everything, all that we had laboured for. Questions queued in my mind. What were we going to do now? Where were we to start from? Where were we to relocate to? What about food to eat? What about clothes and shoes to wear? My laptop with all the data, everything was gone! All was gone, leaving me with nothing.

I decided to make a report to the police as evidence that I had lost my house and everything in it. I pulled out my telephone from my pocket and took pictures, moving from one point to another. A heap of broken blocks sat in the middle of the living room like a tiny mountain, causing more pain. It was the same in the other rooms. The fire had eaten up everything, leaving only charred and gaping walls.

I took pictures of the neighbouring buildings too. In three houses from mine, the lower parts of two bodies with bent limbs were sticking out. The victims' faces were burnt beyond recognition—some of the bodies I took pictures of looked like roasted goats with kinked limbs. One of the bodies looked like a galloping horse that had met death while in motion.

I was a mush of many messy colours and jarring turns and intents. A man approached me and others, asking questions and bringing a microphone close to my mouth. He wanted to know my name, my relationship to Kibang, and the nature of the damages I had suffered. He was digging about where we passed the night and who the people who set fire to the houses were. He looked like a reporter with Kibaaka National Television because he was taking pictures with a big camera and, at the same time, constantly speaking into the microphone. He ended each conversation with: "Over to you, Ngambam Emmanuel," or simply, "This is Verdzekov Basil Venkika, reporting from Upper Kibang." He was with another reporter.

Pieces of what the journalist said after talking with some of us were clear: "…some of the Kibang residents survived the fire; some sustained burns, minor and major; many are feared trapped inside the buildings; so far, ten stiff bodies have been identified; many survivors have fled to the bushes. One resident who identified himself simply as Ability spoke to me, and this is what he said: "Upper Kibang residents have fled into bushes and to distant villages for fear of reprisals; the herd boys are behind the burning of the houses and property… A few villagers are seen around; some are sitting on surfaces with their children and crying; some are moving about, taking pictures of the destruction. Houses, food items, shops, motorbikes, the Kibang credit union, the fuelling station, the Salvation Embassy Church, the Upper Kibang main market, and cars parked along the road are burnt in the fire disaster. As of now, it is impossible to determine how many people lost their lives or to ascertain the level of damage; over to you, Basil Venkika." I took pictures of the wreckage, and we returned to the bush with heavy hearts.

The children were already awake, and Yaya was still grumbling when Jeff and I joined them. Yaya was angry that we hadn't listened to her. She asked whether we could recover anything, and the tears running down my cheeks were my answer to her question.

Yaya suggested that it was better for us to join the others in the bushes; it was safer there. She said it was better for us to think together. So, we staggered across the neighbourhood alongside the trail of residents we joined on the way until we got to our new home in the bush. We sat on surfaces in a spread of grass, mostly under shrubs from where we stared across the vicinity, often watching the towering Kibaaka Mountain with its shelving hills, wondering what would happen next.

Meanwhile, billows of black smoke started shooting up into the sky from behind the hills across Gidang, attracting our attention to the scary sight. "What is happening in Gidang?" everyone was asking. Rumours started filtering in of how Ability, Atang, Livinus, Kinang, Shey Lukong, Faya and Taiga had led Kibang boys to Gidang to avenge the burning of their homes. Speculations of a cycle of reprisals loomed large and led to fear and uncertainty. We drifted into smaller groups, and on our lips was a discussion about the possibility of cycles of retaliation. For the moment, there was little for us to do. We sat in the bush, staring at the smoke across the hills, shuddering at the slightest rustle, creak, or quiver of a leaf around us.

Yaya added to our incertitude by saying that we were not safe from the reach of bullets, stones, arrows, or spears. We therefore, needed to proceed to the outskirts of Mbiame Village. She was still talking when we sighted a group of men charging wildly down the winding ways, on the walls of the Kibaaka Mountain chased by a second group. They were fleeing through narrow surfaces. The fleeing men were chased down to the foot of the mountain, close to the adjoining neighbourhood in Kibang. Some of the fleeing men soon joined us. It was easy to guess; herdsmen were coming for a reprisal. Before long, sounds of gunshots started tearing across the neighbourhood from every direction.

Nobody needed to remind anyone that we were not safe at our location. I slung Mbiame on my back. Bernsah refused to climb on Yaya's back, instead holding his father's hand. While the men charged back to the neighbourhood to confront the herd boys, the confused mass exodus of women and children screamed, staggering further into the bushes. It was not easy to tear through the bush in that disruption. Women dragged their younger children. Some had blankets; some carried pots and light belongings, while others had babies on their backs. Countless times, we stumbled to the ground, sometimes rolling over, at times crawling on our knees. Moving on my hands and knees to avoid stray bullets was exhausting. That is also how I kept the pace of Yaya, whose legs were not strong enough to carry her through long distances. We needed rest. I lay on my stomach, and Yaya did the same. But it was not yet safe to lie around, so I started to creep toward the interior of the bush. Soon, Yaya could no longer move. She wasn't the only one who was exhausted. The women were now moving forward by twisting from side to side, reminding one of a winding river. The hairy grass had stabbed and pricked my legs as I crawled, wiggling through the tangled bush. Yaya had kept pace as I was carrying Mbiame on my back. I sustained some cuts, and blood was dripping from my legs. Beri soon crumbled to the ground, her stomach drooping heavily, a sign that she was pregnant. Other women and children were panting. We lay on the grass, the stinging grass. I kept listening to the stream of fear flowing along the banks of my body. That is how we went into the night of nature's embrace, and the hours went by.

On the morning of our second day in the bush, the battle raged on. It started very early in the morning. I raised my head slightly, looked around, and then across where I located a group of men popping up from the middle of the overgrown grass and thrusting arrows and spears toward their enemies. They would do so and then rush back into obscurity to re-strategise and target, resurfacing for another strike. Repeated sounds of gunshots grumbled from every direction across the village.

"*Cha Vum, chaka vum; chaka vum; cha vum; cha vum, pah, pah, pah, pah, pah!* Ku ku ku ku ku ku ku ku cha vum!" It was a close shot, a narrow miss. A thirsty bullet wheezed past my head. I could feel the heat of the frenzied bullet rustling past. It did hit a target, the head of a little girl. We flattened on the ground, shivering while furious bullets from the hill coughed, roared, rumbled, grumbled, or whizzed past our heads. My heart was the battleground. Even Jeff's heart was galloping inside his chest.

"It is not safe here," Jeff whispered. The scene of the battle was shifting toward our location. Guns belched and coughed out bullets that zinged across our hideout in quick successions of knocking, tapping, or cracking sounds. Our pounding hearts gave us shivers as we twisted from side to side while the erratic sounds of gunshots drew closer. I stole a glance at Yaya and my kids. Bernsah clung to his father like a tick on the scalp, and Mbiame hugged me, my right arm wrapped around him. Nearby, Yaya was shivering and grumbling to herself. Smoke from exploding guns dispersed across the neighbourhood.

The bullets and arrows continued to tear through the air above our heads, causing different reactions and emotions. I tried to move backward, sliding my whole body back and forth like a snake, but I was rammed by a hedge of bodies. For five hours, I lay on my stomach, not knowing what else to do but nodding toward the right from a left-handed jolt or toward the left from a right-handed swing. Automatically, I tried to dodge the hurdling spears and zapping bullets above our heads. Shivering bodies twisted back and forth and from side to side. I shrugged off my arms or legs to haul off vermin. You imagined that there was actually a rat, a millipede, or a snake slithering down or up your legs as if they were also fleeing from the erratic gunshots.

When Jeff pointed at a group of boys charging frenziedly toward our shelter from the left chest of the neighbourhood, holding blood-thirsty guns, flaring knives, and spears, I immediately understood why continuous rounds and sounds of gunshots had been drifting towards us. The boys were being chased by fighters who were shooting sporadically across the yard.

Some of the targets of the hurdling spears and hissing bullets that continued to tear through the air had started fleeing toward our location. One arrow tore through the back of a fleeing young girl who before now lay adjacent to Yaya. I watched the waterfall of blood spewing from the tear on the wall of her back as she staggered and stumbled to the ground. Before long, she breathed her last, and she was not the only one. My face was hugging the surface of the ground when another spear stabbed a fleeing kid. I heard a loud groan, and a heavy fall followed the sound of gunshots that intensified.

"Ku ku ku ku ku ku ku ku ku, shweep! Shwsssssssp, Shwssssssssp!" A mixture of coughing, gunshots, hooting, and repeated hisses from charging spears rattled my nerves and stirred my head to tremble. A long scream came from a manly voice,

"Somebody he-e-e-elp." The next thing we knew, someone was crumbling heavily to the ground. I relocated my ears to the direction of the horror, knowing for sure that another person had been shot dead. I feared opening my eyes even after thumping legs had stopped running across our bodies. A thought crossed my mind that they might have shot and killed Jeff or one of my sons, who might have been trying to escape. My heart started pounding again. I was still musing when a hand shoved me on the leg. I opened my eyes cautiously and then exploded joyfully when I saw Jeff, Yaya, Mbiame, and Bernsah lying around me. They were all okay, but we lay on quietly until we no longer heard the gunshots or approaching footsteps for a while. We got up one after the other and started looking off into the bushes and around us to ensure the fighters had retreated. What we saw was abominable.

Dying persons lay groaning and writhing in slow death. From the galloping postures and the position of wounds on the bodies of the victims, one could deduce how they came about. A charging spear had pierced through the back of the fleeing girl and had come out through the walls of her stomach, carrying with it her intestines. Another spear that ripped through the back of a fleeing woman had come out through her chest with a chunk of meat from her left breast. Blood pumped out from the dying woman's chest as she lay twisting like the tail of a wounded snake. She was watched in tears by her baby of about three years, who was fending off anybody from touching her. Jeff joined others to pull out the arrow from the woman's chest.

I recognised one of the bodies as that of the KRTV journalist I had met some days earlier, trying to record events. He had undoubtedly been trying to take pictures of the battle when the battle scene shifted to our location. I remembered how he had knelt beside me, his eyes half-closed, looking across the neighbourhood through the rounded eye of the Camera, which he held close to his right eye. He wore an armless jacket with four baggy pockets, two on his right and left breasts and two below. A tag hung on one of his chest pockets bearing the inscription KRTV. A black cable with two round edges on both ends descended from what looked like eyeglasses worn around his forehead. One of the extensions was stuck in his right ear while the other, with a round black edge, was pulled toward his lips. Even before the battle proper started, he had been talking into the microphone, ending each conversation with the words: "This is Jared Dzekewong, reporting from Upper Kibang." At the same time, he had filmed the events unfolding. No one was there now to film his own fate.

A young girl of about eight years old lay dead. She had fallen to the ground when a stray spear stabbed her on the back while she was trying to escape to a nearby bush. A neighbour who watched the action detailed it to us. The spear stuck out from her stomach as she lay in her own pool of blood, already stiff. Fear stung me. It could have been my son. I imagined it and crossed my arms over my head, not knowing what to do. There was too much trauma for me to respond immediately.

I did not hear a scream or footsteps toward our refuge for almost an hour. But we were not sure of anything until later, we learned that there had been an intervention by the military that had stopped the fight. Two heavily loaded water-spewing military trucks had stormed the village, chasing and hurling water at the antagonists, dispersing them and ending the bloody battle. Arrests followed and included Kinang, Shey Lukong, Atang, Livinus, Musa, Yaaji, Kodume, Jawara, Aboki, and many others. They were all taken to the Upper Kibang police station for investigations, and some were later released.

During our third night in the bush, I realised I had not seen Kiven, Bandin, Kongnyuy, and Nyuydzesi. They were my siblings, but they were in the fray. I had almost forgotten about them. I had been preoccupied with the happenings right before me. Yaya also asked me to check on them; she was anxious to see them. My children grew tired of staying in the bush.

"Mum, mosquitoes are biting me. My body is burning and itching. I am hungry. When are we going back home?" Mbiame complained, scratching his arm with a stick and sweating profusely. I touched his forehead, and it was hot. I fetched water in a folded leaf and poured it on him, not knowing what to do.

Our problems soon multiplied as we became more aware of our circumstances. These included fear, hunger, attacks from insects, and health challenges. The men harvested guavas and some green berries from nearby bushes and distributed them to everyone. It was the first time we had eaten something in three days. We folded in large leaves with which we scooped water from the nearby branch of River Kibang and drank. We were eating the fruits when Beri suddenly pressed her lower belly and gave a long, shrill sound. That was the beginning of labour pains. She became restless, crying and pushing in her stomach with her fingers. Yaya requested that some items be brought or improvised. She asked us to harvest large leaves and spread them on a flat surface. She asked Jeff to extract the hard, slim bark from the bamboo stem. For many hours, Beri twisted her body in pain, crying. Yaya and Mrs. Comfort held her hand and helped her to walk back and forth to induce delivery.

Towards the evening of that day, water suddenly burst out of her lap. The women helped her lie down on the leaves, and Yaya requested that the men drift backward and away from the scene. It was the first time I watched the live experience of childbirth. Yaya and Mrs. Comfort pulled Beri's legs apart and asked her to push hard. She was unable to push, being exhausted. She failed to galvanize enough physical action with her body. Soon, she could not talk any longer. So, Yaya thrust her hands into her lap, and after moving the hands around, she skilfully pulled out the baby and cut its umbilical cord with the bamboo blade, which she cut from the bamboo stem. But a second baby was there too, lying sideways, making it difficult to remove it. One of the baby's hands was sticking out. Yaya struggled in vain to remove the second baby. She beckoned Jeff and the men over and gave directives. Jeff and some men wrenched off long bamboo stems with their hands and tied them around to form a rack using raffia fibres, which they had also extracted from raffia leaves. I wrapped the first baby round in my blanket to keep it warm. Beri and the baby were then laid on the bamboo rack. Jeff and the men lifted and bore it on their shoulders. They were unsure of the situation in the village but needed to save a life. It was an emergency, Jeff said, and they immediately left in an urgent rush for the hospital.

The scenes played before me, making it a horrible night. I couldn't sleep that night. I was awake, getting up and lying on the grass beside Yaya and my children, constantly groping my way down the valley to scoop water and pour on Mbiame, whose skin was oppressively hot. I worried about Mbiame, Jeff, Beri, and her babies, especially the one still in the womb.

The moon shone brightly, lighting up everything around me. I could see and hear the men and young boys snoring and changing gears from treetops where they sat on the limbs and shoulders of branches, their legs straddled. Some leaned back, supporting their backs on the trunks. Others sat with their heads slightly tilted forward and kept jolting in their sleep. The women and the children lay on leaves spread across the grass. I understood why many preferred sleeping on treetops. Millipedes and tiger ants were biting or pecking my toes and legs. A choir of mosquitoes hovered above my ears, humming continuously and biting my face, arms and legs. The activities of flying insects biting us as they whistled, hummed, and sang in mournfully annoying rhythms kept Yaya awake all night long. We kept smacking Bernsah and Mbiame on their jaws, legs, and arms to chase away mosquitoes. I soon became tired of scratching every surface on their skin. The bit of time I slept, Mbiame woke me with a long scream.

"What's happening? Are you okay?" I asked before realizing that I didn't need the answer. What smelt like urine was still drizzling from the treetop directly into my son's face as he lay on his back. I pushed him aside just in time. Then, following the urine and like a bag of potatoes, Tata crashed from the tree under which Mbiame had been lying. He had been the one who released urine on our faces. He didn't incur any serious injuries from the fall, as the distance from the tree branch where he lay was only about two yards. The Tata incident awakened almost everyone from sleep.

Sleep suddenly disrupted, we kept awake, wondering about the situation of Beri and the babies, as well as others who conveyed them to the village. But our worry was cut short as Jeff and three others came tearing out of the bush. We jumped up from the surfaces with some scurrying down from treetops to gather around them. They were all looking down at the ground, their lips pursed together tightly. They shook their heads repeatedly, lifting and relaxing their shoulders as if rehearsing. Bad news was sure to tumble from their lips. Beri stopped breathing before they got to the village. Dr Jerry confirmed her dead. He and others were trying to sneak into the village from their refuge in the bush. Beri and her unborn baby were buried in a shallow grave, and Dr Jerry proceeded to the residence of the governor with the surviving baby. Jeff said that the governor's wife took the baby and left immediately for Menda General Hospital, promising to give her proper care.

They also brought good news from the governor. He had asked everybody in the bushes to move to the classrooms of GBHS Upper Kibang in Mbiame village. It was exciting to return to the village, and it took a whole day to relocate. The government of the Republic of Kibaaka had directed the governor, the SDO, and the mayor to prepare Government Bilingual High School Kibang to serve as the rehabilitation centre for both the fighters and the displaced victims, the mayor explained during the reception on the first day of our arrival.

6

At the Rehabilitation Centre

Most of GBHS Mbiame-Kibang soon served as the host and rehabilitation centre for the internally displaced victims of the conflict between farmers and herdsmen. Due to the bloody conflict and the possibility of reprisal attacks by the parties concerned, physical academic activities were temporarily suspended and online learning was recommended by the government of Kibaaka in the affected areas. The school was built with shelving arrangements, and the Administrative Block was a three-storey building sitting on a raised surface as you approached the school campus. Below the Administrative Block, a little down the yard were buildings that served as the classrooms for the Sciences and the Arts sections. The extended buildings hosted the Sciences and the Arts sections. They stood facing each other from opposite ends and were separated by a large football field that stretched across the yard. The school buildings, from a distance, looked like giant coffins.

You could have thought that the Kibang and the Gidang communities had carried their hatred for each other right to the school compound. For Graffi IDPs, as the displaced farmers were referred to vis-a-vis the Fulani or Bororo IDPs, refused to live in the same buildings. Gidang IDPs of Fulani extraction lived in the rectangular buildings at the upper section of the school compound, while the IDPs of Kibang extraction lived in the Arts section far down the field. Clearly, the two communities did not want to share the same facilities even in their misery.

When we moved to stay in the school compound, the SDO, the mayor, and some officials came to see us. They collected our finger-prints and took photographs of us to make our identification cards, which were later distributed.

The issue of living in segregated spaces intensified immediately Ability, Kinang, Shey Lukong, Livinus, Atang, Musa, Yaaji, Aboki, Kodume, Dabari, and others arrested in connection with the poi-soning of animals or burning of houses and property were released from jail on bail, thanks to interventions from the MP and Kaba's Human Rights Group.

Each time I came out of a bad situation, I found myself in another. So, fresh antagonism began to brew in the school compound between the Gidang and the Kibang people. The two communities lived in separate classrooms and did not visit each other. The decision to live in segregated settlements seemed intentional. Some unknown individuals had sneaked out in the night and dug a long, narrow ridge across the edge of the football field separating the buildings housing the two groups with the words "No Crossing" and "Border Line" boldly carved out along the edges of the dug field. Blood marks were sprinkled across the demarcation ridge.

The fight over ownership of land and water resources was ignited by hate and divisive language, producing fresh bitterness. Children of Graffi extraction fought with those of the Fulani Bororo clan each time they met at the stream or on the football field. It was worse when someone of either a Gidang or Kibang origin crossed over the demarcated borderline separating the living quarters of the two communities. This is precisely what happened one evening between Livinus and Aboki. The MP brought a football for the children, and Livinus kicked it around. He kicked the ball across the field. It wafted through the air and crossed the border, hitting against the shirt Aboki had washed and spread over a rope in front of their building. I could see a smear of mud on the shirt when we rushed to the borders of the field and joined others in trying to separate the fight, which had started before we arrived at the scene.

Livinus' head was buried between Aboki's legs, his back bent double to almost breaking point. Aboki, who had the upper hand, sat on Livinus' neck, punching heavily on his back. All attempts by Jeff and some elderly people to wrench Livinus from the grip of Aboki met with stiff resistance. Their bodies were woven, turning over and over like a stone carrying a mixture of grass and plant roots and rolling down a hill. The security officers guarding the school charged into the scene and separated the fighters. They raised and lowered their hands as if to say, 'Calm down, calm down.' The crowd soon dispersed, afraid of arrests and detention.

Living as a displaced person in a classroom was very challenging, especially during the first months of our arrival. The classrooms were already overcrowded when we arrived at the school compound. Before the government of Kibaaka donated food and other relief items like mattresses, our beds were mats and matted palm leaves made from raffia palm fibres. These were placed in adjoining rows on the cold floors. Our fireside consisted of three stones arranged to form a tripod at one corner of the classroom.

Yaya and I worried about Mbiame, who was constantly vomiting and having abnormally high body heat. Yaya and I worried about the absence of my siblings from this camp. I had expected to find Kiven, Bandin, and Nyuydzesi, but they were not with us. Where could they be? Why are they not here with us? And why has nobody seen them anywhere? There is nobody in Upper Kibang village, so where could they be? These questions left me restless all the time. Jeff tried to convince us they might have taken refuge in Buwala, Bakissam, Fumban, or Mawunde, where many displaced victims were. They will return after the war; Jeff kept giving us reasons to be hopeful. I wrote to the relevant authorities, declaring my siblings missing. The mayor also repeated Jeff's words, assuring me and other families that the missing ones were fine.

Problems multiplied with each passing day. I was restless, going around and around the schoolyard every day. I looked over the hills and other surfaces across the neighbourhood, hoping to see Kiven, Bandin, and Nyuydzesi. As if the disappearance of my siblings had not caused enough mental havoc, another jolt came.

I found Yaya and my children sobbing and went nearer to find out what the matter was. Yaya said she would not eat until she saw Kiven, Bandin, and Nyuydzesi. My children were hungry and wanted to eat, but I couldn't help them because there was no food. I also missed my siblings, feeling the emptiness in my life from their absence. I have lost my house and property. I couldn't help my children. I had no life of my own, no clothes, shoes, sanitary towels, food, private pots, or kitchen utensils. I started getting worried every passing day and couldn't sleep but stared outside through the open door and the windows. I would gaze at the thick darkness and the moving shapes across the yard, counting my fingers to rush the minutes, seconds, and hours while winking the flaps of my eyes. At times, I sat up and leaned back, staring across the dark room, listening to babies screaming like crickets, watching shadowy figures of women dragging their children across the floor, talking to children off the rear of the building, urging or begging them to urinate and return to the room. It soon became habitual thinking and staring at places. It soon became a kind of hobby. Sunny moments and darkness whirled and glided past my staring eyes. My head throbbed, and I screamed with pain. Some violent headaches pounded repeatedly and inter-mittently. I started feeling a burning sensation inside my head. It was like needles pricking the walls of my chest and head, making me nervous all the time. I started hating everything around me, and bread or rice in my mouth tasted like sawdust.

Things got worse the day I started losing blood. It came much earlier than I expected, taking me unawares. I was passing through the playground when the young boys burst into unusual laughter, staring at my buttocks. "What's the matter?" I turned and asked the boys. In response, one of them ran forward and pointed at the surface of my dress from the rear. I pulled the edge of my dress forward and turned my head sideways to notice the cluster of matted flies hugging my dress around my buttocks. The boy pointed at my legs to indicate the blood crawling down my legs. I felt embarrassed, uncomfortable, and ashamed; the young man's body language attracted laughter from other young boys and girls who were jumping around the playground.

What was I to do? I had no sanitary towels, nothing to manage with. I recoiled from the crowd, went behind the classroom, sat on a stone, and awaited nightfall. The sun went down behind the hills. Then, I walked down to the stream below the school compound and bathed, washed my dress, and wore it wet before returning to the classroom. However, I couldn't sit or lie on the mattress because the flow had become too heavy. It was like a waterfall of blood streaming down my legs. So, I went behind the classroom and sat on a stone again to avoid further embarrassment. That is when Jeff came around, and we both spent the night sitting outside. Mosquitoes were pecking our legs and arms. He pulled off his shirt and gave it to me to tear up into six partitions and use as sanitary cloths. It was a horrible experience for me. For five days, I kept going down to the stream to change and wash the used cloth and spread it on the grass to get dry.

I was not the only one in that situation. When the buttocks of a woman on menses were not trailed by flies, she was trailed by the eyes and comments of the men, young boys, and girls. For the first time, I felt I was different. I felt terrible that I couldn't help myself. I started thinking of returning to my house. I strongly desired to return to my house, the burnt house, and an incredible feeling of loss overwhelmed me. I had lost everything I had laboured for.

The torment arising from this sense of loss and frustration was sickening, and the pain in my head intensified and spread to other parts of my body. The bread and sardines that were shared to us had no taste in my mouth. Jollof rice, the regular meal, had no taste, and I didn't feel like eating it. I was not feeling hungry. I detested everyone and everything around me. I hated crossing the yard when children were on the playground.

The burning sensation in my forehead persisted. Whenever it

started, I would forget everything. I started feeling a lot of other changes. I started forgetting, not always remembering everything. My speech coordination became poor, and I mixed up the connections between the concepts. camp life was deadening. My conversation with Jeff two years after I started speaking logically shaped my recall of my life after that. He told me what my behaviour was like when I was going through a mental crisis.

I was always going around, asking if anyone had seen Kiven, Bandin, and Nyuydzesi. There were moments when I got up and started shouting their names. There was a day I forgot that I was cooking jollof rice. The pot was on fire, cooking when I went from one end of the yard to another, accompanied by Yaya, asking if anyone had seen my siblings. The smell of burnt food and sheets of brown smoke from the fireside drew attention to the burnt food. Each time someone asked me a question or said something while I was in a conversation, I would start the story afresh or stop to ask what I was saying before I was interrupted. I sometimes searched for the same mobile phone or matchbox I held in my hand. I sometimes jumped in the air, moving my head forth and back as if trying to dodge a bullet. I was always complaining of headaches, bullets belching, whistling and coughing above my head.

Jeff was right about the things I did unconsciously. I did not always remember what I was doing, thinking, or saying before someone interrupted me. I didn't always remember the things I planned to do. There was a day I left the fireside and walked over to my sleeping space to collect a lighter to make a fire, but I did not remember what I went there to collect. Another day, Jeff and Yaya found me at the stream and brought me home. They had become worried when they did not see me. I had left the schoolyard without telling anybody. Strangely, I had been looking for myself, and when I saw Jeff, I stopped to ask if he had seen me. I cannot remember what happened when they brought me home that day. I remember joining Yaya and Jeff to look for the telephone I held in my hand, using it to light up the room. Jeff later noticed that I had the phone we were looking for. Another time, I vowed to stop listening to conversations. That was after I had followed two young girls to the stream, listening to their discussion about missing people. When I did not hear them mention the names of Kiven, Bandin, and Nyuydzesi, I decided to return to the camp. But I lost my way back to the school compound. And it wasn't only forgetfulness that I suffered from. Among other physical manifestations, my shoulders would shudder violently and then stop suddenly.

The social welfare workers and leaders of the community-based organisations must have noticed through their constant tour of the camp that many of the displaced victims of the fire incident and attendant confrontations were going through severe stress and needed attention. In that respect, a mobile swimming tarpaulin with rounded edges was set up in the yard for swimming exercises by officials sent by the Kibaaka government working in partner-ship with the World Bank. Sewing machines, too, were brought into one of the classrooms. Other facilities included fabric, cane stems, fibre woven from raffia trees, musical instruments including xylophone, and thread for shoemaking. These kept us busy. We were always doing one thing or another. The experts and Social Welfare Counsellors had come from Menda town. Mme Comfort and a few women were selected and trained to assist in health activities. Their work was to continue after the crisis. They would go from door to door and group to group, distributing essential drugs for cholera and malaria and educating women and the community on health issues. The trained community workers taught us how to swim and to use the facilities. We also listened to music, sang, and danced, besides practical demonstrations on bead-making, shoemaking, shoe-mending, weaving of mats and baskets, shoe-shining, cutting and sewing, packaging of clothes, bakery, preparation of puff puff, doughs, and door-to-door contact sales. We learned to play drums as well as the piano. We did swimming and physical exercises every morning, after which we folded our hands behind our necks and sat back for about thirty minutes before relaxing and walking around.

We had storytelling sessions too. Afoni or Madame Life Story, or Madame Food, or Madame ST, as she loved to be addressed, called her program 'Life Stories.' The program was about sharing personal experiences and explaining how to overcome or deal with challenges. Each session was usually allocated generous time for questions and answers. Volunteers were often invited to speak about their emotional, health, psychological and physical challenges and coping strategies. One of the life stories that touched me the most, inspired and gave me hope was that of Madame ST herself.

Madame ST had one leg and moved around, supporting her two hands on crutches. She told us how she coped growing up as a one-legged orphan. Her early childhood was spent with her uncle, and she had no idea what her parents looked like. She didn't even know whether she had siblings. She had lost her parents in a ghastly car crash when she was only a baby. Her leg was severely injured and had to be cut off. She was always indoors doing domestic chores for her uncle's wife, mostly laundry, cooking, cleaning, and plaiting the hair of the three little girls she cared for. She was never allowed to visit, so the only place she knew outside the home was the Catholic church. She didn't know she was living with her uncle until the day he tore her legs apart and descended on her. That was the moment he told her who she was. She was only ten then, and thereafter, she was constantly sexually abused by her uncle. He threatened to throw her into the streets if she ever informed anybody. Her lap was always screaming with pain. Matters became worse when she confided in her uncle's wife, hoping she would find a better way to stop the abuse. The couple threatened to kill her if she said anything to anybody that could tarnish their family image. One day, she escaped from the home and trailed her way to the Catholic church, the only place she knew. She recounted her ordeal to the bishop, who moved her to a distant village to live with his mother. The old woman soon died, leaving her alone. She cultivated the late woman's farm and sold the farm produce for her basic needs. That is how she sponsored herself from primary school through secondary school to university. She also made proceeds from working in people's farms and homes, selling pure water, and plaiting during holidays. While at university, she studied counselling and community welfare and learned a lot about food processing and baking. Two years after graduation, she was fortunate to join the public service when a special recruitment of counsellors was launched for qualified but physically challenged persons.

It was during a specific life story event that the whereabouts of my siblings were revealed. Madame ST had been in Buwala to take statistics of the IDPs from Upper Kibang, and in her records were the names of Kiven and Nyuydzesi. She added that Kiven narrated the story of his kidnapping and escape to Buwala, promising to tell me more later. The revelation brought peace and joy to my family.

My favourite moment was during cooking and food processing training, which took place twice every week. We learned to prepare many things, including cake, yogurt, bread, puff puff, ndole, egusi pudding, stews, sauce, jollof rice, fried rice, soya, and different local and continental meals. At the end of the training, I could cook better than before and with additional dishes like fried rice, jollof rice, and local and continental dishes.

I don't know how long my state of forgetfulness lasted. I can't even remember how long we had the cookery training and storytelling sessions. It might have taken over four years. I am pretty sure the life story sessions, particularly the cookery training, accelerated my healing. I started to heal without even knowing. If Madame ST could survive by herself, I also could, I told myself one day. Perhaps that is when I started taking the initiative to do things independently. I remember preparing jollof rice without any assistance from anybody and without forgetting my pot to burn. I gradually remembered things and then made plans for myself, going into the bushes to harvest edible crawlies. One of those adventures almost took away my life, however.

Our food was insufficient, so Buri and her daughter Bandin, Berka, and I went fishing for tadpoles, mushrooms and snails. Kibang forest and Lake Kibang were all catchments for these delicacies. The forest that straddled the foot of the Gidang shelving hills and the borders of Upper Kibang Lake stretched in a widening sprawl through the border communities of Mbiame to the distant land, where it disappeared behind the hills. A distant look cast Lake Kibang in the shape of a massive body with two exit legs in the middle of the forest. The surrounding forest was a home for snails, while the lake was home to fish and tadpoles. Before the crisis, people trekked there to harvest snails, crickets, tadpoles, and fish. Although the lake and its bordering forest were quite difficult to access, snails, crickets, tadpoles, mushrooms and fish made the sites attractive grounds for the internally displaced.

On that ill-fated day, we left the camp immediately we heard the crow of the first cock and started treading the tangled pathways to the lake in the heart of Upper Kibang forest. We harvested mushrooms, snails, and crickets from the roots of grass and trees and proceeded to the lake to catch tadpoles. I stood thrusting a long stick into the banks of the lake and pushing it forward and back. Berka scooped the muddled waters with a deep basket and poured over the grass while Buri and Bandin picked the tadpoles and put them in one of the baskets.

I didn't notice when Bandin crept into the forest to harvest guavas and blackberries. I only recall that she suddenly ran back to us with fruits folded in the edge of her dress, screaming wildly and pointing to the top of a nearby tree.

"What's on that tree?" I asked, trailing her shivering finger to a big tree across. Yaaji sat wedged between two branches, holding a slanted spear. Suddenly, grass began to rustle wildly from every direction. We were still confused, not knowing what to do when a furious spear charged down from the top of the tree and stabbed Bandin on the shoulder. She staggered and tumbled to the ground, screaming and bleeding from the wound. Nobody needed to tell us that we were not safe. Either the herd boys or Kibang fighters had seen us from their hideouts and apparently thought we were enemies. Another spear almost got me on the stomach but brushed past. Buri carried Bandin on her shoulder as we wound through twisted stems. We crawled on our knees at times to dodge the spears and bullets that were now tearing through the air. It wasn't easy to locate someone inside the thick forest. Tangled stems and branches of trees stretched unending, often crossing one over the other, and helped to shield us as we moved in twists. It was like a player dribbling a ball from one side of the field to another. As soon as we reached the camp, our heads still on our necks, we recounted our tragic encounter with Yaaji. Bandin had stopped breathing even before we reached the camp. The men took the body of Bandin to a nearby bush for burial. Meanwhile, the women took Buri to the classroom, where we sat crying.

Hostilities between Kibang boys and the herders soon intensified anew around the Gidang shelving forest following the killing of Bandin. The area had become the hideout and headquarters of both Gidang and Kibang fighters. Within the obscurity of the border forest, too, the herd boys and Kibang fighters would hide to ambush each other. People said the Gidang fighters hid on the steep walls of Gidang Mountain and its rocky hills, where they would crawl down to the border forest to attack the Kibang fighters. Others said Kibang fighters hid in the body of the forest between the Kibang borders and below the Upper Kibang plunge. Kidnappers would hide in the forest and kidnap women and children, tearing through the tangled stems in search of food. They often attacked and seized the raw food items from the women. Whenever the two groups of fighters sneaked out from their different hideouts, they stayed at opposite ends of the border forest, the gateway to their villages. They would wield cutlasses, guns, spears, and knives, allowing no stranger into Gidang or Kibang. Everyone going in or out of the two communities was subjected to vigorous checks by the fighters. They would collect money from people before allowing them to go. Kidnapping for ransom became common.

The killing of Bandin and the new wave of hostilities attracted different reactions. Yaaji was found hiding in the school compound and taken into police custody, where he confessed to the crime. Kibang fighters threatened an open war with Fulani indigenes living in the school compound, which caused the Fon to summon an inclusive meeting to stem the looming war immediately.

"They will say we are weak; Gidang Fulani must pay compensation to Kibang the same way Kibang returned ten big cows to them when our children went up the mountain and killed Alhaji Kidado's cows," Ability argued. We sat across the football field, waiting for the meeting to start. It was the first and the only time the displaced people of Gidang and Kibang had crossed into each other's territory and sat almost close to each other. Fon Fomu, Alhaji Kidado, and members of the council of elders' cabinet sat on the benches brought from the classrooms. The rest sat on the grass. The meeting had only one point on the agenda.

"Alhaji Kidado, as you are already aware, one of your herd boys, Yaaji Gado, shot and killed the daughter of Tav Kibari with a spear. Following the ways of our land, Yaaji must give his daughter, Halima, to the family of Tav Kibari in replacement for their daughter. Tav Kibari will marry Halima to his son Kesaya, and she will give that family children," the Fon said, pointing to the last son of Tav Kibari. The young man stood up, lowered his cupped hands below his chin, and released a series of heavy hums as if his throat were lodging a million bees. It was a hum of acceptance accompanied by a lingering smile on his face. "This is the decision of the council of elders," Fon Fomu concluded and was greeted by nods across the yard.

When the Fon spoke, Halima's face was smeared with surprise, and her lips stared wide open. Then, all eyes shifted to Alhaji Kidado, who stood up to respond to the council of elders' judgment.

"I am *veli* sorry that we lost our daughter. But as you know, our ways are different. Halima says her *pirayer* in Fulfude language. Kesaya says his *pirayer* in Lamnso, the language of Giraffi land. Kesaya is the man here, and Halima is the woman. Fipur of Kibang, can two dumb fipur speak to each other and understand themselves?

Will the language of the man not swallow the language of the woman if they join? Will the ways of one land not swallow the ways of the other land?" He shook his head disapprovingly and continued, "No, no, one cannot speak to his *kiriyetor* in the language of another land. A woman cannot speak to her God in the language of another land. The rewards that every *pirayer* brings will go to Giraffi land if Halima *pirays* in Lamnso. God will not forgive Halima if she throws her ways to catch the ways of Giraffi land. Can Kesaya also be asked to throw away the ways of Giraffi land and follow the ways of Gidang land? People of Kibang, Gidang is ready to repair the damage but not with the soul of Halima. Yaaji has worked for me for seven years and should be graduating from cattle guarding next year with eight cows. I will give part of his pay to Tav Kibari."

Alhaji Kidado's response leaned heavily on the difficulties of communication and ignited another wave of reactions. While the Gidang people supported his position, Ability sprang up from his seat to speak.

"Our people say that if you turn yourself into grass, goats and sheep will feed on you, but I am not grass. Alhaji Kidado, Bandin was not shot on the battlefront. The ways of Kibang land are clear in cases like this particular one. The family of the deceased girl must receive, as compensation, a daughter from the family that caused the death of their daughter. Yaaji is your son. That is how we know him. Do the right thing…!"

"Reng reng," I could hear exclamations of approval across the yard.

Yaya spoke after Ability. "Fon Fomu, Alhaji Kidado, elders of our land, there is already a sprain on the legs of the marriage, and it is limping. Heal the sprain before it festers and subjects the marriage to amputation."

Yaya's cautionary words touched the decision-making body of the land. Fon Fomu retreated behind his seat and beckoned Alhaji Kidado and the elders to come over to him. After opening and closing their lips rapidly, at times wagging their fingers in the air for over an hour, Fon Fomu, Alhaji Kidado and the elders returned to their seats. The yard was dead silent when Fon Fomu cleared his throat to speak.

"People of Kibang and Gidang, this is our conclusion following what Alhaji Kidado has explained to us: A Fulani male can get married to a Christian female, but the Fulani female is not encouraged to get married to a Christian male. The creator made the man the head of the house. With that authority, the man can convert his wife to his religion. A non-Fulani male will not encourage the Fulani woman to pray in the Fulani language and to practice her religion if they get married. We cannot force the ways of one land down the throat of another land. We cannot impose the ways of one land on another land. No tradition is superior to another. We have lost so many people. Therefore, for the sake of peace, we have decided that Yaaji will hear from government," the Fon concluded.

The crowd dispersed to their different living quarters, some smiling, some grumbling, but insecurity intensified. The farmers and the herd boys soon made life unbearable for everybody in the school compound and around the adjoining communities. Thus, the fight between the farmers and the herd boys took unforeseen dimensions, throwing people into confusion. News about the atrocities committed by the fighters was nasty. They broke into the remaining homes and shops, looted food items, carted away stray animals, invaded cultivated lands, and harvested crops to sell in neighbouring communities. Livinus, Atang, Musa, Kodume, and Dabari were arrested in different locations in Menda, trying to sell off cattle they had rustled. In the night, the big boys pinned the women and young girls who went behind the buildings to urinate on the walls or the ground and clawed into them. We lived in constant and greater fear, especially when Yaaji, Livinus, Atang, Musa, Kodume, and Dabari returned from detention through the intervention of human rights activists to join us in the school compound. Some said they had served their jail terms of seven months each. Others believed they had escaped prison to infiltrate the IDPs. Prison escapees had also infiltrated the IDPs.

Unknown persons invaded even the school compound at night. They carried away all the rice, sardines, garri, and bread that Government, NGOs, groups, and individuals brought to us. Villagers were constantly being arrested by masked individuals who would detain them in bushes or abandoned buildings for weeks or even months until a ransom was paid for their release. Some were judged in the bushes by their kidnappers and tortured or even killed. Death was sometimes induced by hacking. Kidnapping for a ransom was the new way of life. Information leaked to state security regarding the perpetrators of the crimes, was considered criminal. Phones were seized on suspicion and inspected by the fighters and state security agents. Information in phones could mean life or death for the owners. People avoided keeping incriminating information.

Kidnappers masked their faces before invading targeted locations. There were no boundaries for criminal activities. A boarding college was invaded in Kibang at night, from which some 100 girls were abducted to an unknown location. Some seventy were located and released by the military a few days later. It was rumoured that a ransom was paid for their release, although the military and the bishop denied it. Nothing is known about the remaining abductees. One incident involved some members of the council of elders. Tav Kibari, Dr Jerry, and Tata had led a heavy military team in the night to different suspected hideouts of the fighters from both camps. It was said that the simultaneous attacks yielded an abundant harvest. The surprise silent mission to Gidang Hills led to the arrest of thirty fighters. In addition, ten AK-47s, a pile of spears, knives, hard drugs, empty gas bottles, locally made explosives, and two bags of live ammunition were recovered. A hoard of arms, cutlasses, spears, and empty bottles of gas were discovered buried in the ground during the second ambush inside the border forest. The military recovered the weapons, thanks to the collaboration of the locals. During the simultaneous attacks launched by the military, there was a heavy exchange of fire, leading to casualties. Heavily armed boys were arrested and taken to detention facilities in Kibang. The military lost two of their colleagues, and one sustained a serious injury; the Hawks and the guards lost five members, and many fled with severe injuries, too.

Two days after the invasion of the hideouts, the body of Tata was found with knife wounds in a bush not far from the school compound. His killers were never discovered. Within the same period, Fon Fomu, Alhaji Kidado, Tav Kibari, and Dr Jerry received death threats from unknown persons. They were all accused of assisting government forces to recover arms from the herd boys and Kibang armed groups. The death threats created more panic in the communities, leading to Dr Jerry and many others escaping to the cities.

Although no gunshots were heard from the forests and bushes and the neighbourhoods following the mass arrests of armed groups from Gidang and Kibang during the military offensives, the spate of kidnappings for ransom and looting of property continued. People stopped attending worship services, afraid of being kidnapped by unknown gunmen. Farming, too, was abandoned. One could no longer stroll on the road freely. We stopped going to farms, bushes, and forests to forage for food or fetch firewood. Pupils and students stopped attending classes for fear of being kidnapped. Bushes grew up and swallowed the premises of markets, schools, and places of worship. Everything changed completely, requiring women and children to be accompanied by the vigilantes and men everywhere.

The atmosphere of insecurity attracted more intervention from the government and other sources. Truckloads of State Security forces had been deployed to many affected villages to restore calm since the fire outbreak and attendant hostilities. Two more security officers were deployed to the IDP camp for security. We only received supplies of food items that would finish the same week they were shared, leaving us to forage for crickets, snails, and tadpoles that crawled on bush trails. At different moments, the governor, accompanied by the mayor, Madame Story, the MP, and Kaba, brought us bags of rice, garri, palm oil, groundnut oil, onions, salt, bread, cubes of savon soap, and clothing items.

Kaba, a human rights activist, was the President of the Kibang Human Rights and Justice and Peace Movement (Human Rights), which he said was helping youths to travel abroad for greener pastures. The first time Human Rights visited us in the camp, Kaba came with a beautiful lady whom he introduced as a journalist. He had brought an envelope containing ten million francs CFA to share with the internally displaced. The money would assist some of us in starting a trade when we eventually returned to our communities, Kaba announced after gathering us together. Before the snapshots and interview sessions, Kaba gave us strict instructions on how to compose ourselves. The journalist held the camera close to her eyes, recording every event. Kaba held one edge of the heavy brown envelope, and I had the other edge, casting a guided smile as if I were the happy recipient of some award or certificate of recognition. All the women and children stood behind us like statues, smiling for the pictures. When the journalist took pictures of Kaba and the women, Kaba did not release the envelope to me. He said, "Wait for me here," and moved from one group to another, holding the same envelope in pairs and posing for pictures. At the end of his tour of the school campus, we didn't know in whose pockets the envelope ended. Kaba himself had no idea, he said, and suspected that one of the elders must have hidden it in his pocket. Even the last person with whom Kaba took pictures was confused. The council of elders was surprised when the other team leaders and I told them the envelope was not released to us after each photo session. Many suspected that either Livinus or Atang played a fast one with the envelope. It ended in confusion, with the visibly angry Kaba blaming us for dishonesty and lack of attention.

Although insecurity continued after the secret invasion of the hideouts, leading to arrests and detention of the fighters by the State Forces, Atang, Livinus, Yaaji, Kodume, Musa, Dabari, along with others, returned their weapons to the mayor and the SDO at different times, after a series of mediation meetings, persuasion and threats of arrests. It was said that some came in person and dropped their weapons in front of the mayor's residence, while some dropped theirs in the night. It was a sign that many of the fighters had chosen peace, many said. But, creating a military camp in Upper Kibang contributed to the relative calm.

As life gradually returned to the communities, women, girls, and children could go to the streams and bushes again, unaccompanied. Government officials came to collect information about the damage we suffered from the cattle invasion, fire incident, and attendant hostilities ahead of rumoured compensation.

Jeff and I stood at the edge of the football field that sunny afternoon of the visit, staring with impatient excitement across the neighbourhood for signs of approaching cars. Many people were already in the yard to receive the guests whose visit had been announced the previous day by Fon Fomu. I dressed differently from the other regular days for the first time since we came to stay in school. I wore a big, twisted gown that dropped right to my feet; it was the only good dress I had at the time. It had been given to me by Madame ST the day she brought us food and clothing items.

People stood in their new attire across the football field like small clusters of plantain stems, chatting and staring across the vicinity and then at the sun's position.

"The big people will be here any moment now," I told Jeff, who acknowledged this with a nod while staring at my shadow on the ground. My shadow fell between my legs, a few inches to my right toes, announcing the time to be about 1 pm. I was still trying to locate the exact position of my shadow when cars started blaring repeatedly, a little way off. There was jubilation when two Toyota Hilux cars stopped in the yard, and the governor stepped out. The mayor, two police officers, Madame Afoni, and other dignitaries followed and were ushered to their seats, arranged around two tables from the classrooms. When we sang the national anthem, the governor explained the reason for the visit. The visiting team was the Ministerial Commission of Inquiry, Assessment, Rehabilitation and Peacebuilding (MINCOMAREP), created by the government of Kibaaka following the insecurity and hostilities that led to the destruction of crops, cattle, homes, property, and the loss of lives. The team had to find the perpetrators of the destruction and submit their report and recommendations to the relevant service for attention. The team would not succeed without everyone's collaboration, including the farmers and the herders. They needed collaboration, especially with Alhaji Kidado, Fon Fomu, Bishop Kosimas, the council of elders, the women's group, the vigilante group, and the NGOs. The governor also explained the obligations and responsibilities of the community as he spoke. The farmers and the herders were to volunteer information to security operatives regarding the identity of individuals behind the poisoning of plants and grass, the people rustling cattle, fabricating weapons, burning homes, private or public property, or behind the kidnappings, violence, and assault. Even before the visit, I was already aware that security operatives had infiltrated the villagers and were working with trusted individuals who did not want the conflict to continue.

The governor spent much time explaining why collaboration with the community was necessary. "Traditional rulers know their people very well. They know all the strange faces around. They are aware of all the activities in their communities. They know the herdsmen who allow their cattle to enter farmlands and eat crops. They also know those who rustle cattle. They know the farmers who spray poison on the crops and grass for cattle to die after grazing on the poisoned crops and grass. Come to us and tell us in confidence who the bad people are. You can call and give us information to help us fish out the bad seeds. The rotten tooth must be pulled out of the mouth! We will give Fon Fomu and Alhaji Gidado our telephone numbers at the end of the meeting. Don't be afraid. We do not disclose the identity of our informants when we do our work because we know what can happen to them. We need your collaboration to end this conflict and to end the kidnappings and cattle rustling. We need the collaboration of traditional rulers, the women's group, religious leaders, civil society organisations, the vigilant group, and all of you to bring peace to this great family. My fellow people, some people think that the conflict will only affect other people and so it doesn't matter. Some of you are even benefiting from the conflict and do not want it to end. That is not a good mindset. Don't wait until you are affected before you realize the need to join the peace crusade." The governor's message was greeted with applause and nods across the yard.

The committee then moved in to say what everybody wanted to hear, but the governor delivered the juicy message. The Head of State of the Republic of Kibaaka has organised an inclusive national dialogue for the recovery, reintegration, reconstruction, and development of Upper and Lower Kibang. The leaders of the Farmers Association, the Cattle Breeders Association, Community-Based Groups, the women's group, the youths, NGOs, religious leaders, all relevant stakeholders, and the chiefs are invited. The president has also directed that all the former fighters and the displaced victims of the farmers-herders hostilities will continue to live at the premises of Government High School Upper Kibang until further notice. The classrooms would continue to serve as a temporary shelter until it is safer to return to the communities. MINCOMAREP would work with the Government to ensure the safe return of the IDPs and former fighters to their villages when it is judged convenient. MINCOMAREP was to assess the damages. Individuals, groups and agencies that would present credible and verified evidence of loss of life or damage to property would receive compensation.

Thus, we were requested to submit details of the loss with evidence. People immediately rushed to their spaces and brought picture evidence of destruction.

We had prepared for evaluation day well ahead of time immediately word had gone round that we would receive compensation from government. Kaba and his photographer had rushed to the school, taken us to our homes and farmlands, and assisted us with photo shoots. Many people had used their telephones to take pictures of their burnt homes, including other damaged property and farmlands. Kaba uploaded and produced the hard copies of the images and distributed them to the concerned before the governor came. He did the same for Jeff and I, helping us produce the pictures I had snapped when Jeff and I visited our fire-gutted house and the farmland.

The queue of people walking up to the table and submitting picture evidence of damage to life and property was longer than expected. I stood directly behind Ability, who was discussing this with Atang and Livinus. I had chosen to go right behind to avoid the pushing.

When my turn came, I gave my pictures and bent over the table to provide the spelling of my surname. Madame ST's look was not friendly when she received the pictures of my burnt house. I was confused, wondering what I had done wrong. I soon realised she was making a visual comparison between the image before her and the one I had just extended to her.

"Mrs. Kila Tantan Nyuyfokem Jeff, who owns the half building in this picture? This same picture has already been presented to us by... hmmm, Ability, Atang, and Livinus," she said, searching her records.

I felt embarrassed. Ability, Atang, and Livinus were immediately located in the crowd and called over to the table for questioning. I could hear the crowd hissing as Jeff, Buri and Berka stepped forward to confirm that the skeletal building on the picture belonged to Jeff and I. Livinus, who showed up alone, hung his head in shame, staring at the ground when he was questioned. He was like someone raised on milk from the breast of a sheep, Yaya said, inviting laughter from the crowd. More fake declarations came to the fore. One of the pictures Ability had presented, claiming to be that of his late son who died during the battle, was actually the journalist who had been stabbed to death by a stray spear. I could still recognize him. I couldn't say anything at that moment because I feared for my life and that of the members of my family. They could be targeted and killed by unknown individuals, as was the order of the day.

Ability, Atang, and Livinus were not the only individuals who made false claims to lifeless bodies and property to get compensation from Government. Yaaji also presented pictures of some seventy bloated bodies of cows. He had just returned from detention on bail. Everybody knew Yaaji was still serving as a herd boy pending settlement and that he had no cattle of his own yet. Alhaji Kidado disclosed this, and like that of Ability, Atang and Livinus, the evidence presented by Yaaji was rejected. However, the picture of Ability's farmland with damaged crops was retained.

Someone must have reported all those who made false claims. I still remember how Shey Lukong, Ability, Atang, Musa, Yaaji, and Aboki were later arrested from the school compound by the State Security Forces and kept in detention for making false claims of corpses and property by bringing pictures of bodies and damaged property that had already been identified and presented by some families. They were later released on bail, thanks to pressure from the MP and Barrister Kaba's NGO, whose members staged a two-day sitting strike to protest their arrest and using their IDP status as an excuse.

After their release, some people were tagged as 'blacklegs' and targeted as State secret informants. The end of bloodshed was not the end of war. Intimidation, bullying, and propaganda were weapons to silence informants. Truth became a casualty. Testimonies and evidence that would have expedited a rapid mediation and solution to the crisis were thus buried. Fear of being labelled a 'blackleg' did the trick. Facts were buried alive. Trust deficit heightened the moment the Governor promised protection and shielding of the identity of individuals who volunteered information to the Security agents. Some people were reported mainly to settle scores.

Every action, every posture, every image that someone used to describe a situation, every telephone call, and every movement around was usually viewed with suspicion: "you are an enabler, she is an enabler, he is an enabler, he was seen in town, or returning from town, he or she went to retail secrets; I saw you making a telephone call, who were you talking to? You are a 'black leg!' You will hear from us very soon; he will hear from us soon!" These were the words on the lips of many, not least Ability, Livinus, Atang, Musa, Yaaji, Faya, and Taiga.

The accusations were not always unfounded, for individuals sneaked into security facilities and gave information when they saw someone with cattle. The same happened if someone did something terrible. Ability, Atang and Livinus once informed the police that Faya and Taiga were the ones who burnt down the schools and homes in Gidang. This led to their arrest and detention, although many said their quarrel was associated with the sharing formula of the money they got through devious and dubious activities.

7

The Compensation Package

The day Kaba came from Menda holding a newspaper in his hand, he assembled us to break the good news: "The SDO and the mayor and Madame Afoni will be here tomorrow to share compensation packages from government to you. The names of the beneficiaries are on the pages of this paper," he announced, waving *The People's Voice* newspaper above our heads.

My eyes shot to the headlines on the front page of *The People's Voice* and read: "Kibaaka Government to grant financial compensation to Victims of the Farmers and the Herdsmen crisis... Insecurity threatens to disrupt Planned Gubernatorial and Municipal Elections..."

The news was greeted with wild jubilation. The women bent forward, moving their bodies rhythmically back and forth. Ability rocked as he hummed. The men danced to the beat of the pulsating native song wafting across the yard like the sound of droning bees.

There was jubilation when we received financial compensation from the government of Kibaaka through the team comprising the SDO, the mayor, Madame Afoni, and Madame Comfort. Government had also sent transport buses to facilitate and ensure a safe return to our villages in the days ahead, the SDO said, pointing to a queue of vehicles streaming into the yard, as they distributed the envelopes to the beneficiaries. Jeff and I received two million frs CFA, a bag of rice, and five litres of vegetable oil.

"Jeff, very soon, we will return to the village to start a new life. We need a house. We need to send our children back to school. Two million frs cannot solve these problems," I began.

"You are right. What do we do now?" asked Jeff.

I stared into space as if searching for an answer. We were not the only family that had lost their home and had nowhere to go. Many villagers who had received their compensation and relief packages stood in groups, making plans. We were still trying to figure out what to do and where to go when Kaba approached us from behind and directed us to meet him in the school's backyard.

"I am here to help you." He began. "My NGO is helping to prepare documents for interested displaced persons who can afford to finance their trip to Amerika. There are job vacancies in Amerika. There are nursing and teaching jobs. Babysitting jobs are available. I have been helping people to travel abroad even before the crisis started. Right now, a company in Amerika has written to me announcing job vacancies. You will be paid the equivalent of 900,000frs CFA per month. Hurry and secure a place. They need 50 people, and I have 45 already." He pointed to the crowd of other IDPs he had convinced and who were trailing him around the yard to pay for their travel documents.

Who would see the opportunity of travelling to Amerika staring them in the face and not clutch at it? Who could hear the phrase 'travelling to Amerika' and not forget the pot of soup cooking on the fire to burn to char? Who could hear a job offer of 900,000frs CFA per month and not sell their only family land to prepare travel documentation? Jeff and I were overwhelmed by the prospect of travelling to the world's financial capital. We were even ready to sell our only family land to travel to Amerika.

"Thank you so much, sir. You are our saviour; may God bless you, sir. We are really interested, sir," I said effusively, nodding and glancing at Jeff and others, who also greedily nodded consent and approval.

"Now, listen; I need five million frs CFA for travel papers, and the payment has to be made today!"

My hope and mood shrank when Kaba mentioned the heavy amount.

"We just received two million frs CFA from government, sir. That's all we have. We need to leave Yaya and the kids with some amount. But we can sell our land to top up the money," I pleaded. Jeff and I went into a serious bargain plea with Kaba, who eventually agreed to collect three million frs CFA for one person to travel, while the rest would be paid later.

"Well, I run a charity association. My NGO will complete the money to process your travel documents. But you need to sign a contract that you agree to complete the rest of the money when you get to Amerika and start working," Kaba said. "Now, who among you is travelling? I will allow you to decide on that one. I'll leave you for now. I will return with the forms you need to fill out in the evening." Before he left, Kaba warned that we could not disclose our travel plans to anybody, adding that evil-minded persons could do anything to frustrate our plans.

As soon as Kaba left us, Jeff and I discussed who to travel with.

"Kila, I suggest you should travel. You are pregnant. If you give birth to a child in Amerika, that child will automatically be recognised as a national of that country. That's what they say. While there, you will see how you can bring us over."

Miranda had also told me that birth tourism was the easiest means of securing foreign nationality.

Everything went as planned when Kaba returned two days later to begin the passport application process. Buri had offered us temporary accommodation in her moss-covered house. We had to sell part of our land to prepare for the trip. Kaba gave prospective travellers one month to get their passports ready. I didn't have to travel to Mawunde for a passport. The one I had was still valid, so I handed it to Kaba for the visa, as requested.

Three weeks had passed since we returned to the village. A lot was happening, too, in terms of reconstruction and development. The Presidential Plan for Reconstruction, the community-based organisation funded by the Kibaaka Government in collaboration with the World Bank and the United States Department of Agriculture, and also the "Kibang Give Back," an elite-funded group, were doing a lot at different levels. "Kibang Give Back" contributed huge sums of money, bought exercise books, and also provided partial school fees for all the students and pupils in schools in Mbiame-Kibang. Following the commission's recommendations for the Recovery, Reintegration, Reconstruction, and Development of the Upper and Lower Kibang communities, the recovery and reintegration phases started immediately. The first phase was launched in Lower Kibang. It was *Wailun* market day. The villagers gathered at the market square for training and to collect relief items and agricultural tools. Each household received five bags of cement, a 20-kg bag of rice, a five-litre gallon of vegetable oil, a five-litre gallon of palm oil, three cubes of 'savon' soap, two shovels, two buckets, two pots, a cutlass, 25 metal sheets, and different kinds of seedlings as could be seen from the labels. After distributing the items, Mrs. Comfort Gohfen and her team announced the program for the subsequent months. The youths will have a training session on piggery, fish farming, and raising chickens with Mrs. Comfort. Fingerlings would be distributed after the training. Another training session would be on peace, living together, and strengthening the skills of women and community leaders in conflict prevention and promoting dialogue. Madame Comfort concluded and left.

Kaba returned to the village the following day and distributed our passports and air tickets. You can imagine the excitement that gripped us when we received our passports with Amerikan Visas. Kaba told us there were no straight flights for Amerika from Kibaaka. The air tickets Kaba gave us a week before our departure had our travel itinerary, and our departure point was the Douala International Airport.

Before my trip, I spent sleepless nights thinking about the

conversation Madame ST and I had concerning my siblings. They had escaped the confrontations in the village and taken refuge in Buwala. I wondered about Berla. He had been hacked and his fingers dismembered. He was dragged into an unknown destination for two months running as the abductors awaited a juicy negotiation. His phone lines were still dead. I had no idea if Berla would ever tell me who did it. Nyuydzesi was smuggled out of the village at night and taken to Buwala. There, they swell the endless queues of other IDPs, groping the fertile lap of River Burri for snails, crayfish, earthworms, shrimps, fish, and tadpoles. There, they picked discarded food and fruits from rubbish heaps and ate. I regretted that I could not immediately establish contact with them. I thought of Jeff, my kids, and Yaya, who had moved to stay at Yaya's compound in the suburbs of Mbiame. We had only returned to our communities after many seasons in the classrooms of GBHS Mbiame-Kibang.

Before we left for Amerika, I handed over the leadership of the women's group to Berka and Buri. We then held a brief and restricted meeting with the other members of the decision-making board.

"My dear sisters, as you already know, I will travel to Amerika in the days ahead. You will always have my full support. I will learn what other women are doing in their communities and share it with you. I have created a WhatsApp platform where we can always share ideas. It will help us to hold online meetings. Berka and Buri will find time later to explain how to join the Zoom and WhatsApp rooms. This is my e-mail address and my WhatsApp number." I thrust the piece of paper into Berka's fingers and continued. "I will always share relevant information in our WhatsApp platform. I will continue to work with you from abroad. Women must play a role in ending the conflict between the farmers and the herdsmen in our land."

We hugged one another as the women, exuding emotions and tears of separation, wished me a safe journey to Amerika.

8

The Showy Escape

At about six o'clock in the morning, we left Mbiame on a jam-packed truck. Being the last to get on the lorry as Jeff and Yaya had difficulty tearing my children and I from each other's tearful good-bye grips, I joined the squashed crowd inside the long, four-sided, roofless extension. An iron-wall backseat compartment was raised above the wheels with spaces between the vertical bars. We stood leaning heavily over the iron bars like droopy bunches of plantains hanging down from their pulpy trees in the coastal farms along the Douala-Mutengene stretch of the Kibaaka Highway. I was excited but exhausted. I did not get enough sleep the previous night, during which, all night long, I listened to the endless wise counsel of Yaya, my mum. My children, Bernsah and Mbiame, had started missing me even as I packed my snacks, clothes, and dried foodstuffs like okra, bitter leaves, garri, eru, crayfish, and smoked fish, as well as my personal belongings in the bag I would travel with. The weight of fatigue plunged me into the momentary limbo of sleep just as our vehicle left the scene of departure. I dreamed I stood before my father, who was seated on his high-back cane chair. In his usual authoritative and menacing pose, he informed me that he saw a mountain collapse and block the road to Amerika. I was still listening to my father when our vehicle danced a wild dance, snapping me to wake up with a jolt. That was when I knew it was just a dream.

I immediately knew why I had such a dream at the start of the journey. I did not travel to meet my father for blessings for journey mercies, something we often did when we had to travel out of the village. Although the villagers had escaped to the major cities of Kibaaka since the start of the just-ended bloody conflict, making it challenging to trace displaced blood relations, my reason for not visiting my father was due to some discriminatory treatment in the past. He had not always remembered my name unless someone or myself reminded him that I was Kila, his daughter from his first wife. Yaya had always pleaded with me to forgive my father, but I found it hard to discard into the garbage can of forgiveness what had lived on in me since childhood. He never loved my mother and told me while I was in primary school that he was no longer responsible for my school needs. I tried hard to tear my thoughts away from the possibility of his curse and to focus on the journey.

The jolt had resulted from the driver wheeling the car over a broken waterway into the fuelling station. He returned to the main road jerkily. It was a fresh morning.

The hairy fingers of the breeze harassed my ears as our truck drove along the regional ring road that tore through Mbiame-Kibang and continued to the major town of Menda. There, it gave birth to many exit roads, one of which was the Kibaaka-Trans-African Highway.

The scars of the just-ended war were visible across the land. The Mbiame-Kibang stretch of the road was near-impassable right from the departure scene. Holes yawned wide-mouthed, capable of gulping the tires of vehicles and motorbikes and holding them captive. Our heads and hands hung heavily over the edges of the iron bars, swaying back and forth from upright to leaning over positions as the vehicle tried to dodge yawning potholes. At one sudden swerve from trying to dodge a fleeing motorbike rider, our front tires planted themselves into a furrow of thick and deep mud, causing my breasts to leap out of the bra. I had just unbuttoned my heavy jacket to catch some fresh air, not knowing I was freeing my milk catchment to leak out of the bras.

Before I could grab and push them back in the bras, Livinus had spread the fingers of his left hand across his face. He was pointing to my shy breasts and winking at Atang, with whom they thwacked the palms of their hands, laughing. I ignored them and began to button up my jacket to avoid another embarrassment caused by the gaping holes that sat everywhere along the road. To doubly secure them, I wrapped my hands over my chest to keep them firm. The vehicle kept swaying, dancing, and jumping into potholes as if exchanging fisticuffs with the road.

It was my first trip out of Mbiame since the just-ended battle between the farmers and the herders, a lingering battle that had displaced hundreds of villagers to Buwala, Bakissam, Mawunde, and neighbouring communities. My village was emptied and starved of life for a long time. About two months after the war ended, people hesitantly started trickling back there.

I kept staring across the village from the carriage. It looked like the Mbiame back in the days of my primary school. The first set of returnees had recently farmed some portions of the land, but there were visible signs that Mbiame had suffered protracted abandonment. A chaotic growth of trees with large umbrella-shaped tops of heavily drooping branches furiously grew across the village. You didn't need monkey dexterity to range from one tree to another and get to the next village without touching the ground. Trees and houses hugged each other intimately. But many of the few surviving buildings had suffered prolonged abandonment. Trees tilted forward like a woman in the weathering of menopause. I could not take my eyes off the houses and half-burnt buildings along this stretch. One of the buildings had fallen into a jumbled mass, some leaned forward. The walls and rooftops of surviving buildings wore mouldy green jackets. I remember seeing overhead grass and gorgeous treetops feverishly swaying and nodding at us. Rooftops of thick, head-swinging grass stood to the road's left and right-hand sides. Layers of grass and roots were growing furiously on the roofs of Mbiame-Kibang Health

Care Maternity Centre, too. My eyes fell on Baa Lankar, with one knee planted on the ground and pointing a long gun at two monkeys swinging excitedly from one tree branch to another. The once bustling Mbven Division now looked like an abandoned ancestral homestead whose survivors were only trees and smoke-coated houses with grass growing through their cracked walls. The moss-grown buildings could barely raise their heads from the heart of wild cola nut and raffia trees.

The Mbiame-Kumbo stretch of the Kibang ring road was a rough ride in and out of broken tar with yawning holes in the middle. Grass had grown forward from the sides and covered the entire width of most stretches of the road. From time to time, the grass slapped our faces, leaving bleeding spots on our cut skin. There were nonetheless visible signs that life was crawling back to the land after the farmers and herders' crisis that virtually made it the headquarters of chaos. I could hardly take my eyes off the beehive of activities across the village and the neighbourhoods. Courageous banners fluttered in the wind in front of schools and administrative buildings. People kept trickling onto the highway from side roads. They looked excited. Men and women were here and there, trimming low the grass that had roofed the width of the main road. Some were trying to scoop or clear away the charred tires and tiny hills of dirt that sat conspicuously on most stretches of the road. They carried diggers, shovels, and buckets on their heads and hands and sang as they filled some gaping holes on the road with ground and gravel dug from raised surfaces nearby.

Unannounced, our vehicle swerved into a deviation on the left wing of the village, only to join the main road later. This narrow path served as a cross-cut, an alternative track for pedestrians crossing from one village to another. The villagers called the pathway *konshot*, that is, a shortcut. Motorists, dealers and suppliers of marijuana and bush animals used it to evade the financial harassment by security men. Being less used as a driveway, the pathway was less pockmarked, enabling the user to avoid the men in uniform who checked ID cards while feeding fat from travellers and motorists that did not have their complete car documents.

This section of the village was busy too. People were repairing the roads as well as their houses. My eyes fell on the roofs of my father's compound, a stone's throw from the pathway. A part of the building was burnt down. The remaining trunk jutted up from among kola nut trees as our vehicle drove past. The 'big compound,' as we called my childhood home, had an imposing building that stood like a guard behind the single-room buildings reserved for my father's five wives. He had inherited three of them from his late father. I lifted my head to look at the home where I had started my life as a child. Grey-black smoke rose from the women's quarters and drifted to the surrounding trees. Lean elephant grass stems inclined from the upper walls of the building. Our vehicle kept dancing on the same spot, trying to pull out of a deep gutter created by fighters.

The sight of my father's compound reminded me of my struggles growing up. Yaya told me the story of why she left her marital home: "Kila, when a man hates his wife, he transfers the hatred to her children. That is not the only reason why I left your father's house. When a man is sick, and the elders take the wife behind the house and whisper in her ears: 'is he still eating?' they are not talking about food. They want to find out if his urine can still hit the ceiling. If you tell them that your husband does not eat from your dish again, you are saying that he can no longer plant the seed. You are saying that he is the reason why the family tree will no longer bear fruit. You are saying that he is two fingers away from the grave. They will simply put a fence around your kitchen and give the door keys to his brother. I am happy he did not join his ancestors. Kila, when the bag of corn is opened and the bad seeds are separated and thrown away, I will drop my own edge of the rope I am dragging with your father's people and return to my marriage." I hated anything that reminded me of my father's biased treatment. My eyes soon shifted to the buildings along the road. The walls had holes and noticeable cracks.

"The cracks on the walls must be lodging bullets," Livinus said, prodding me on the arm. He must have been observing the activities of my eyes.

Two villagers dropped their cutlasses on the side of the road and came to help pull the front tyres of our vehicle out of the furrow. They succeeded, and our vehicle resumed its irregular rocking along the route.

My father's homestead was not the only one wearing jackets of cobwebs and grass. Ba Ability's partially burnt house was next to our house and had suffered the same fate. He sat on the yanked shoulder of a kola nut tree, stretching forward his hand to weed grass that had coloured the walls of his house green.

As we approached, we saw many people around the Government Technical Bilingual High School Mbiame (GTBHSM). Hairy stems were growing on the roofs and walls of the school buildings. The football field across the schoolyard was a virtual hunting ground of tall, confused grass tangles. Excited boys and girls, wearing sky-blue jackets over royal-blue-shade hugging trousers and hugging skirts, respectively, were there. They stood, tilted forward like donkeys, and sang excitedly as they engaged the grass with cutlasses. The younger boys and girls were only playing in the trees across the yard. Some held the branches with their hands, screaming and shuffling their legs backward, forward, and side to side.

Our vehicle slowed down and halted briefly at the main entrance to the school. The Governor, accompanied by heavily armed state security forces, stood at the entrance. The Senior Divisional Officer, the mayor, the parliamentarian, Chief Fomu, Alhaji Kidado, and other dignitaries were also there. Women and men removed bags of cement and bundles of zinc from their high vehicles. Some items were relayed to the construction areas on the school grounds. Although they were now bent double due to age, Tav Kibari, Banadzem, Shey Lukong, Kinang and other men stood in another queue, passing buckets of water from one person to another, to the construction sites and to different sites on the school campus where blocks were being moulded.

I knew there would be reactions when all eyes suddenly turned towards the bricklaying women. The women had formed an additional relay line and were carrying dried red bricks to the top of the classroom buildings whose roofs and parts of the walls tottered threateningly. On top of the administrative buildings, others sang traditional songs with delight while weeding grass, trees and jackets of mould. Livinus popped out,

"Look over there!" He pointed at the women across the field, mouth open. They were smashing and mixing the mud. The plaited heads of the Mbiame-Kibang Women's Group jutted up from the large pit where red bricks were being moulded as they sang and smashed the mud. While some shuffled and smashed the mud, some scooped the dough-like paste and filled it into four-sided containers, pressing down on the surface with shovels and their palms and soles. They would then lift off the container from the moulded block. A relay group took the scooped mixture to mould bricks. Many of the men and young boys had died at the war front, which explains why it was mostly women moulding the blocks. The sight of women moulding bricks seemed to infuriate the men who did not hide their disgust.

"Women cannot mould bricks. Moulding of bricks is for men." Livinus protested.

"Since when did women become bricklayers? They can't make strong blocks! I can't live in a house whose blocks were moulded by a woman! Never! The breeze will blow it off!" Atang spoke rapidly from the top of the carriage, a look of surprise on his face. You could say that he was protesting. His finger kept waving in the air like the wagging tail of a mad dog.

"What's the problem with a woman moulding soil or making bricks? Girls are admitted and trained in technical schools just as boys are. They should be able to mould blocks and even build houses," I said.

"Those bricks cannot be strong! The sick building will even collapse the same day it is built!" Livinus argued. He was grumbling, and Atang seemed to agree with him, saying,

"I will never send my children to a school whose blocks were moulded by a woman! Never!" Most of the men flustered with laughter, corroborating Atang and Livinus. I turned my head away to cheer up the brick-making women. They were mostly members of my all-female group. So, I waved encouragingly and with delight, particularly at Berka, Beri and a few others. They waved back excitedly.

"Kila, when you arrive in the land of the White man, buy me a good telephone so that you can see the person you are talking with and the person also sees you, I beg. Don't forget to buy me that face powder that looks like red bricks. I don't like the one that is sold in our market. I used it one day, and my husband asked if someone smeared my face with mud…" One woman spoke, attracting a rainfall of laughter from the women.

Another echoed, "Kila, buy me a handbag and a big, beautiful jacket like the one you are wearing!"

Yet another said, "Kila, buy me human hair, oh; don't buy the type they sell here. Buy that one, which when you wear, someone would think bees settled on your hair, oh! I also like the one that looks like the hair of corn." "Buy me the hair that looks like a skirt of leaves dancing on tree tops," another pleaded.

I couldn't keep count of the relayed messages and could hardly distinguish between the voices. All I remember is that the voices of Berka, Jaika and others shouted out the things they wanted me to buy for them.

It took two hours from our take-off to reach the Berlem stretch, a distance that used to take about 20 minutes. It had become impassable due to grave-size cuts inflicted on the road by the farmers who protested the constant destruction of their crops by cattle. The plain, too, had lavish evergreen vegetation. One of the streams, Mairin, that tore through Mbiame had its source in Berlem. Cows could be seen shaving off and munching on leaves of breast-sized pumpkins and corn stems.

Everywhere we passed, different types of reconstruction activities were taking place. A tiny crowd of workers stood around a roadside market, where our driver stopped briefly to buy fuel and inflate the vehicle's tyres. A jumbled spread of homesteads, cobwebs, and confused grass on the walls and rooftops lay splayed on the left side of the road. On the premises of the Heaven Embassy, men and women were also weeding grass and detaching bird nests from the walls and windows of the church building. A man, the size and shape of a praying mantis sat on the shoulder of a nearby tree. He constantly stretched his hand to wrench off the grass from the top of a decaying electricity pole. Council workers walked around the market with cutlasses and shovels to clear and weed the grass that had grown in a spread, covering the tops of market shades and shops. Our driver stopped briefly to add fuel. All eyes fell on us with seeming admiration. We waved to them, and they waved back.

Since the start of the journey, I had noticed one familiar feeling or mood as our vehicle drove along. Happiness sprouted on our faces even when no one had heard good news worthy of attracting that blissful posture. Who could be travelling to Amerika, the plantation where money was harvested, without letting everyone around know?

The intentional actions of the travellers involved stunts to draw attention to our new attire and to trigger assumptions that we were travelling to America. An irritating display of attention-seeking smiles characterised us as we waved repeatedly to the council workers and vendors. It was the kind of smile that did not need a soothsayer to toss five pieces of cowries or kola nut shucks on the ground to interpret, using the sitting positions of the pieces, to read and with constant nods, decipher the news that we were travelling to Amerika. I was of the same make as all others.

I pushed the wavy edges of my hair to fall over my chest, where they lay in a twisted spread like a gathering of resisting intestines. All eyes trooped to my hair, and that strengthened the weight of superior uniqueness that I had already attached to my new attire. I received showers of praise for my wig and jacket. How could someone travelling to Amerika still dress like someone living in Kibaaka? My human hair, jacket, and long-neck heavy boots announced my destination to onlookers, and I ensured they did not miss it.

I lifted my fingers slightly above my nostrils. Onlooker eyes followed and saw my artificial nails. A voice said my fingers looked like the beaks or the claws of a duck tipping the webbed toes. Although my jacket was strangling my body with heated tightness, I made sure I tilted the conversation to it. I then swirled my head around and pushed the wig back over my neck with a quick head jerk. The clustering long hairs bounced up and fell back over my shoulders. This human hair is gorgeous. It looks like bees hanging down from the branch of a tree. Livinus said and shifted his stare to my high-heeled boots. The boots swallowed my feet and ankles right up to the knees. Although I had always been the shy type, my intention to invite assumptions that I was travelling abroad overcame the shy mood.

Little did I think of the boomerang effect of my displays. They reduced me to ridicule and a subject of laughter. The different reactions that trailed my attire from the travellers across the carriage spoke it out.

"Beautiful boots with a foundation," Livinus said, pointing to the heavy soles of my boots and remarking that they looked like a tiny coffin or, more considerately, like the concrete structure on which a house is raised.

"Kila, I used to think that only a house needed a foundation. Those big shoes you are wearing make you look like a house standing on a foundation, ha ha ha ha ha…" Laughter drizzled from lips to accompany his remark. He was not through with me yet. "Kila, if I now say that your big shoes look like the wheels of a caterpillar or tractor or trailer, that one that used to dig our road, you will say I insulted you," he added. From my boots, he turned to my jacket for ridicule.

"See how you are already sweating, ha ha ha ha ha. Kila is dressed like a night watchman," he added. "Have you seen the statue of Zint-graff in the city? Ki ki ki ki ki ki ki. Anybody watching you in that heavy jacket and on that story building that has swallowed your legs does not need to be told that you are travelling to the land of the Whiteman, to guard big shops, ha ha ha ha ha ha…" Laughter erupted from lips again.

Livinus had broken the dam. I was waking up to its effects as an avalanche followed. "Livinus is right; not even a security guard can defeat Kila in a dressing contest…" Atang joined what looked like a campaign to reduce me to a clown. This drew more attention to my heavy attire. Everyone was pulled in to comment, and they broke into convulsive laughter.

I felt downcast and embarrassed, robbed of the respect and admiration I had gunned for. They reminded me of what Yaya had also said the day I returned from the market and tried on my wig, shoes, and new jacket.

"You have roofed your head with bees! *Mbarang*! Kila, will people not call you juju when they see you wearing those bees? Only a juju wears a mask. Even that sweater makes you look like a gathering of plantain stems! Now, look; when you go to the land of the red-skinned man, do not close your eyes and ears. Learn their ways. If you see what is bad, turn your back and go away. If you see what is good, learn how to do it. That is how you will return home with much to teach the women of this land. But do not throw away the ways of our land. Your eyes will be your sieve. Take from them and join with yours to make it better. Do not dump your own ways into the rubbish heap. Continue where I ended."

What Yaya had told me had a positive focus. It was a hard lesson. Livinus and his crew were debasing me and generating negative feelings.

I wasn't the only traveller in the vehicle who wore a heavy jacket, and I wasn't the only traveller who felt superior and different for wearing the White man's attire, either.

Livinus threatened to get what he wanted when he would eventually obtain his documents. He said something which made me feel he was already enjoying that authority which only those who make it to Amerika wield over their communities and families back home.

"Atang, as soon as I grab my residence permit and load my valise with dollars and senior money, ha ha ha ha, I will spend the next Christmas feast in Mbiame. Old boy," Livinus tapped Atang on the shoulder, "let me see which girl in the village will again reject me or say I am short! As if short people should not enjoy life! Old boy, let me see how those university girls shall call me empty pockets again! They will suddenly forget all that and even quarrel and fight each other over me! Ha, ha, ha, ha. They will pour into my Mum's compound to make friends with her. They will even sweep her kitchen and clean the dishes, buy gifts for her, wash my sister's clothes, and ask if there is still more housework. They will form a queue behind me, fighting to pay my groom's price! Ha ha ha ha ha ha. Everywhere I step my feet, they will run after me, calling me sweet names: "Sweetheart, Honey, Baby, Soulmate, my King, how do you want your breakfast served? Ha ha ha ha ha," Livinus rhapsodised, staging an imaginary love scene with the supposed female admirers, attracting laughter. "Atang, Atang, Atang, let me see how Yaya will ever again pour a pot of water on me, twist her lips, shake her head, and tell me that Nyuydzesi is not for palm wine tappers like me! And let me see how my father will again tell me to sit quiet during family meetings," he went on. The travellers choked with laughter as he bragged, often intentionally arranging the oversized bracelet on his neck.

Livinus, who looked like a fifty-year-old man trapped in the skin of a mushroom, wore small round earrings and a thick pullover over jeans with butchered knees. A light, stretchy scarf with the colours of the Amerikan flag with cutaway edges was tied around his head to form a tail behind. His heavy pullover made him look like the Graffi masquerade often displayed at funerals or the 'Ngonso' festival. He was not happy when people called him by his name. He simply wanted to be called a 'bush faller'. He kept pulling the tail of his head scarf whenever he waved at someone he knew.

We were several then, seeking attention, attired strangely enough to invite laughter and speculations. And I wasn't the only one wearing what looked like a coat of leaves on a plantain tree either. Jawara, too, wore a long, heavy coat. Aboki looked like a comedian in his hairy jacket. Even my neighbour's hairstyle was eye-catching. Her long braids were piled high on her head in one compact bunch. It was as if a heavy bunch of bananas was sitting upright on her head.

Whoever was wearing or doing anything, the common thing was that the general mood was excitement. Livinus, Atang, Jawara, Aboki, Fola, Ntumfon, and others kept stretching out their necks and hands to wave unsolicited goodbyes to the vendors and women farming along the shoulders of the ring road. I knew, and we all certainly knew, the main reason behind our inflated enthusiasm.

A vehicle was already planted in Menda to smuggle us out of the country. But who would not be happy to travel to the world's financial capital as Kaba had described Amerika? He had convinced us to sell our family lands, take loans, and add to our rehabilitation package to enable him to process our travel documents and flight tickets. Back then in my village and even now, travelling abroad was known as the death of poverty, the birth of money, power, and authority. So, who could hear that people harvest basket-heaps of money from ordinary jobs like cleaning and babysitting or hair plaiting, being a sales agent or driving and make-up fashion agent, or attending to corpses or telephone assembling and mortuary security... who could hear that and still hesitate to sell their only family land to raise funds for travel papers? That's what happened to us and many of us who set out on the journey of no return to become breadwinners.

It wasn't just the prospects of making money, even from small jobs, and the exaggerated excitement about travelling abroad that was responsible for my decision. The thought of sitting somewhere and enjoying a meal or a conversation without moving my head or body quickly to one side and then back and forth like someone trying to dodge a punch was something I had missed for a long time. The thought of moving into an environment where I could walk freely along the streets without being forced to stay at home, or under the bed, by stray bullets and protracted ghost towns and lockdowns, without being threatened by exploring knives and the roaring rage of guns that coughed and charged confusedly across the neighbourhoods of Mbiame-Kibang and Gidang, was the reason for my self-inflicted journey. That same thought had taken away my attention from the pain I was subjected to, leaning in a squash, in the discomfort of the hard iron bars that girded the carriage. My enthusiasm never bowed to the roughness of the ride to Menda and its connecting Kibaaka Trans-African Highway, which was the transit route for those travelling to Dubai or Amerika through the backyard.

***

Mbiame-Kibang and Gidang were two major communities of Kibaaka headed by one central ruler. The two rival groups traced their roots to Rifem in Banyo. Mbiame-Kibang, or simply Kibang, referred to as the Graffi, were mainly farmers of Christian origin who had run away from Rifem. Constant attacks from the wandering Fulani cattle herders and a succession crisis had driven them to settle in the vast plains of Kibang, where they found fertile land for farming activities. Gidang, another extraction of the Rifem family tree, was called Bororo or Fulani. They were the brothers of the Graffi from another womb. They had migrated to Kibang and settled in empty areas with vegetation for their cattle. Theirs were the mountainous areas of Gidang. The positioning followed repeated cycles of land disputes with the Kibang branch of the Rifem family tree. Yaya had told me the story, insisting that the Fulani and the Graffi tribes came from the womb of the soil of Rifem.

The fertility of the soils of Mbiame-Kibang had attracted heavy colonial and government presence ever since colonial days. Mountain-size buildings that hosted administrative structures streamed across Kibang, especially in the capital city of Menda. Mbiame-Kibang lay in a humble and submissive sprawl at the foot of Gidang Mountain, a few of its neighbourhoods stretching across raised land areas. The entire land was well-girded at the far ends by surging hills that exuded meandering sheets and billows of clouds. A look across Mbiame-Kibang from a raised surface revealed flung settlements and a sustained spread of hugging houses springing up across the plains in endlessly deferred rungs. Some settlements sat comfortably in the confused cohabitation of houses, trees, cattle, and ravishing vegetation. The homesteads of the suburbs mostly bordered farm-lands, streams, and tiny forests. In the heart of Menda, the capital town of Kibang, buildings as tall as the Kibaaka Mountain hugged each other, contesting for space and attention. The houses seemed to be striving to be noticed or acknowledged as the most obese and tallest in the Region.

A river that looked like the body of a massive ash-brown snake meandered across Kibang. It gave birth to streams, some of which strayed and furrowed in the suburbs into rice and maize farms. I remember seeing people who looked like chicken drumsticks sitting on the edges of canoes, thrusting sticks and nets into the water and dragging the sticks repeatedly back and forth as their vessels glided across the water.

What attracted me first as our modified vehicle drove through the low-lying Ndop plains of Mbiame-Kibang was Gidang. Gidang was a mountainous settlement with barren, thirsty soils but had sprinkles of trees and grass across its villages. From the regional ring road that cut through the low-lying villages of Ndop, you could see a muscular mountain flanked by adjoining fleeing hills. The mountain was called Gidang Mountain or Mount Kibaaka. It had a cliff facing the plains of Ndop Kibang stretch. Locals called it the 'water-spewing mountain.' Others said the mountain vomited from its chest, a sign that the gods were angry with the people of Kibang and Gidang for refusing to live in peace. Their assumptions could be understood.

Water drooled out of the navel of the cliff, looking from a distance like a mountain urinating. Large stretches of land had been eaten up by Gidang Mountain, flanked by nipple-head hills that jutted into the sky in symmetrical rungs—only a few areas of flat land featured across villages. The obese mountain had super-endowed hips and a flabby tummy that descended right to its foot and formed a bumpy surface. Some believed that the bumpy surface linked the two communities. The intimidating posture of the mountain was accentuated by the drooping boulders growing out from the walls. The top edge of the mountain slightly leaned forward like someone bending to peer over a surface.

There were many other attractions across Gidang. Tiny settlements of flung homesteads of houses with rectangular walls were splayed all over. Some looked from afar like enlarged coffins on the shoulders of galloping hills and raised surfaces. The coffin-shaped buildings seemed to enjoy cohabitation with droopy boulders, staggered trees, and the cows on the hills. Nearest the visible houses were mostly sheep, cows and goats.

One thing could not miss my roaming eyes. As our vehicle danced across the long plains, files of cows and sheep weaved their way in and out of slim passages and drifted downhill towards the maize and cassava farms of Ndop Kibang border communities. The maize and cassava farms, the streams, rice farms and other gorgeous vegetation were unavoidable lures that stirred the storm of anger that threatened to burst forth from Atang.

"Our streams are not for *Come-no-gos*! Our grass is not for cows," he began.

"I support!" Livinus joined Atang, who was talking and pointing across the hills at the herd boys and the cows. Women and children also meandered through the slim passages between drooping boulders, carrying buckets and calabashes.

"Atang is right!" Livinus emphasized, shifting his confrontational stare from Jawara to Aboki. They were visibly unhappy that their relatives were called *Come-no-go*.

It was not the first time that Atang and Livinus had confronted the Fulani with provocative statements. Atang was always hurt that they allowed their cows to browse the fields in Kibang and drink water from Kibang streams. Like his father, Ability, Atang was one of those who had led a protracted campaign to stop Gidang people and their cattle from fetching or drinking water from Kibang streams, a decision the Fulani people had strongly resisted. The geography of

Gidang explains the reasons for this resistance.

Gidang land had barren soils and lacked water. The kind of gorgeous vegetation across the Kibang plains of Ndop was absent. Gidang herders often led their cattle to the grassy plains of Kibang. Besides, Gidang women and children usually trekked long distances to the valleys in Kibang to wash dirty clothes. They also would grope the banks of Lake Kibang and River Kibang for fish and tadpoles. However, these Gidang ladies and children would not risk going down to Kibang on such a mission if the herders did not accompany them. What a man like Atang would do to Gidang women, children, and their cows if he were to meet them fetching water from Kibang streams was unimaginable. He continued to hurl insults at the women and the cows across the hills.

"How many times will our people tell the Fulani people to stop fetching water from Kibang streams?" he thundered.

"Direct your question to these *Come-no-gos!*" said Livinus, pointing provocatively at Jawara and Aboki. Livinus then winked repeatedly at Atang, moving his head from left to right; vigorous chest jerks as if urging Atang to start a fight accompanied this action.

"Livinus and Atang, if you are hungry for a fight, we are ready...," Aboki glowered.

Jawara picked up the case. "The stream that flows through Kibang comes from the Gidang Mountain..."

"*Yowaaah, wuseko, madallah,*" Aboki applauded in the Fulani language before Jawara could finish speaking and continued, "If somebody should claim ownership of River Kibang, it should be the people of Gidang! You heard me well!"

"How can you own something that is found in another man's yard?" Livinus threw his hands apart. "Or, did our ancestors sell our land to sojourners and drifters?"

"Good question! Even the Bible says in Genesis..., no, no, Nicodemus, yes, Nicodemus, Chapter 10, Verse 50, that...," Livinus kept poking his head with his fingers while batting his eyelids as if he was trying to remember the quote, "you shall not desire your neighbour's land..."

"Livinus, so you know God!" Jawara questioned, shaking his head in disapproval.

The vehicle soon became rowdy with arguments, counter-arguments, and even insults tumbling from the lips of the different factions. Each side claimed ownership of the cattle routes and water resources in Kibang. You could say it was a mini congress despite its chaotic tone.

The dispute over the paternity of water sources and cattle routes in Kibang had raged among the Graffi and the Fulani-Bororo even before I was born. The differing views over the ownership of River Kibang had the singular fallacy at the base that its actual place of origin had never been traced.

The River Kibang, which gave birth to many streams as it widened its flow across Kibang, actually rose from a sweating surface that connected the communities of Kibang and Gidang. Gidang's belief that the River Kibang sprang from Gidang Mountain had its own justification.

From a distance, something like urine creeping out from the chest of Gidang Mountain drooled down, forming wet surfaces that stretched to the ridge at the foot of the mountain. The border ridge, as it was called, was the boundary line between Kibang and Gidang. Border spaces were generally no-man's land between ethnically unrelated groups. It was difficult to trace or determine the real ancestral homeland of the disputed water source.

So, the river birthed as a drool from a V-shaped surface on the border, flowed across the vast plains of Kibang, and widened its prowl, giving birth to smaller streams. The trunk of the river is what they call River Kibang. It flowed across the vast Kibang plains of Ndop and formed a massive bowl-shaped lake. The lake, in turn, gave birth to another stream that ambled backward to the outskirts of Mbiame, a village in Kibang. To this village, herd boys moved their cattle during the dry season.

The confusion about claims of ownership of the river remained a highly contested issue between the two neighbouring communities. Kibang people, believing River Kibang to be the property of Kibang, tried to bar those considered non-natives from using the water sources.

The controversy raged on, and I jumped into the argument. I had worked in the Mbiame-Kibang Council, whose administrative borders encompassed the two rival communities. I had visited all the villages across the two communities. I could not sit quietly and watch my brothers tearing themselves apart.

"It is from the sweating surface on the ridge that River Kibang was born," I announced and continued. "The books also say River Kibang is a communal property belonging to everybody. It is even the property of the Government of Kabaaka." Resentment welcomed my intervention, and 'black leg' was what Atang and Livinus called me.

"Those of you who were born yesterday should sit quietly when arguments concerning the ownership of River Kibang come up!" Atang barked out.

"Kila, you are a woman! You know nothing about land matters," Livinus enjoined.

"I once asked Yaya about the ownership of River Kibang. She said the umbilical cord of that river is the surface with beads of sweat at the foot of Gidang Mountain," I said.

"What does a woman know about rivers and land borders? Yaya is a woman! If you want to know anything about Kibang land and its rivers, go and ask people like my father, Ability, Shey Lukong; ask Baa Banadzem and Baa Kinang!" Atang was roaring like a storm. He and Livinus violently disagreed with Jawara and Aboki. A fight seemed close to eruption. The vehicle rocked and danced violently, causing everyone to grab the edges of the iron bars to avoid being hurled off. This went on for a while and dissipated the acrimonious feelings that had been mounting. But it was only a lull for the raging debate quickly resurrected. The venom was already taken out. I privately celebrated that my intervention had weakened the virulence. The memory of my horrifying childhood encounter with the herders on Gidang Mountain was raised as I watched cattle ambling in and out of slim passages.

9

Down Memory Tracks

Back then, I was a form one student at Government Secondary School Mbiame, which was later upgraded to a high school. We would climb up to the topmost ledge of Gidang Mountain and its shelving hills to chase Alhaji Kidado's cows. It was always fun to chase cows around. Mountain climbing had other advantages for us kids growing up in the village. We often returned home with snails, grasshoppers, or meat, a delicacy commonly only eaten in our home when Yaya attended a death celebration. From festive events, she brought back home part of the meal she was served, which, in some localities, is called 'should-in-case.' At times, we clambered up the mountain to dig crickets from cow dung. These we sold to raise capital to buy delicacies like sugar cane, sweets, bonbons, rice, and meat stew after the march past ceremony of the Kibaaka National Youth Day. Youth Day and National Unity Day were the only opportunities for some of us to eat delicious meals that only children from homes with financial muscles, like Jawara and Aboki, could afford at the time. The delicacy of meat stew and rice for us came when Livinus, Atang and the young boys in the neighbourhood crawled to the top of Gidang Mountain and chased Alhaji Kidado's cows onto the cliff. No cow that fell down that dangerous plunge could survive; not even Yaya's herbs could resurrect the cow with broken limbs that resulted from a tumble down the cliff. Atang and Livinus told us that Alhaji Kidado and his family would never eat beef from a cow that tumbled onto the cliff and died.

A few days before the National Youth Day celebrations in Kibang, cows decided to invade Ability's wife's maize farm just when Atang and Livinus were looking for an excuse to chase them into the ravine to die from broken limbs. The coincidence of this happening shortly after Livinus' reasoning in that direction is hard to explain.

The cows had invaded and destroyed crops on Ability's wife's farm. A Mediation Council Panel (MCP) delegation from among the council of elders, led by Tata, Tav Kibari, and Dr Jerry, visited the farmland to assess the damage and report to the council of elders. Their report did not implicate the herdsmen. The cows had just started browsing on grass that was growing on the shoulders of the cassava farm when they were found and chased back to the hills, the Mediation Panel stated in its report. So, Alhaji Kidado was not fined by the council of elders as requested by Ability. Ability stormed out of the Mediation Council Session, promising to make sure a heavy price was paid for the damage.

It is hard to know if Ability knew about Atang and Livinus' plan, and it is hard to see the relationship between the two events. I do, however, remember the benefits Atang and Livinus promised us if we followed them to the mountain for the cow chase.

With Youth Day just days away, we needed funds for it. There were entrance fees for the late afternoon musical show or 'teatime,' which we did not yet have. Mbarga used to organize it. We did not yet have money to purchase the niceties like sugar cane, rice, and stew, rare delicacies that pupils and junior students bought and ate after the march past. A confident smile smeared his lips as Atang whispered, "Baba Kidado is a Fulani man. If a Fulani man's cow falls from the top of the mountain, rolls down the cliff, and dies, he abandons it to the villagers. Fulani do not eat the meat of animals that are not properly slaughtered."

"Atang is right. A Fulani man would not eat the meat of animals that were not slaughtered by a Fulani man," Livinus supported, smiling.

Atang and Livinus then clarified our job descriptions. We simply had to climb up the mountain, and place corn cobs and fresh maize stems on the top of stones carefully positioned on the edges of the hanging cliff. Our role as girls was clearly defined. We had to hide in different locations and report the approach of the herd boys or any suspicious movement. We were to do so by coughing or hurling a stone to fall lightly in a specific location.

Meanwhile, the boys were to guide the cows to the trap and then withdraw into their hideouts. Livinus rehearsed how a cow would slip and tumble into the ravine while trying to eat the installed plants. The unfortunate cows would be confirmed dead at the foot of the mountain a reasonable distance down, which would roll over and over on the boulders. Alhaji Kidado or his herd boys would come down and confirm it dead and abandon it to the villagers. We would be the first to rush to the scene of the accident, dismember the cow and sell our own share. The proceeds would serve us for the National Youth Day celebrations; Livinus' explanation attracted repeated nods from Atang.

I was initially afraid and hesitant, but Atang and Livinus secured my loyalty with their juicy promises. A massive budget of three hundred francs CFA worth of sugar cane, Alaska, and rice and meat stew watered my mouth in anticipation. Collaboration with Livinus and Atang at the approach of the National Youth Day was, for me then, a job opportunity. Atang did not tell us that nobody ever killed a cow and returned home with his head still sitting on his neck.

The following morning was a Saturday, and we did not attend school. We were Beri, Berka, Jaika, Livinus, Fola, Atang, Awudu, Yurika, Nyuydze, Miranda, Savage, Verdzekov, Kitam and I. We immediately crawled up the bony walls of a conjoined cliff that emerged from the waist of Gidang Mountain. Our snare fresh corn cobs and stems were brought by Atang and Livinus. We carefully placed them on the boulders and treacherous surfaces at the top edge of the cliff. While the girls hid in specific locations, the boys sneaked around. One could think a thousand horses were galloping inside my chest cavity as I lowered myself behind a giant boulder, stretching out my neck in every direction, afraid of herd boys. The shudder tearing through my body was violent, especially when my eyes located stones and clubs chasing and hitting the confused cows escaping toward the cliff's edge, closely followed by Livinus, Atang, and other boys. The wild chase stopped as the animals reached the edge of the overhang fodder, and the boys retreated to hide behind the boulders. Immediately, two cows started fighting over the feed, knocking and tossing each other with horns; I knew our prayer had been answered.

"*Nka nkum, nka nkum, nka nkum nka nkum*," my gaze quickly shifted toward the crushing noise. Two cows had suddenly tripped, fallen down the cliff, and rolled right down to the foot of the mountain. Livinus swiftly sprang up from behind a nearby boulder and started winding his way down the walls of the hill. The message was clear. We took to our heels and wound our way down the narrow passageways. We had not gone far when a spear from nowhere hit Yurika on the arm. He stumbled forward and collapsed directly in front of me. The herd boys must have seen us; I screamed like a cricket as we tried to use all means to escape, leaping across boulders, crawling on our stomachs between narrow passageways, and trying to dodge charging spears.

News about our cow-chase escapades on Kibaaka Mountain that resulted in the murder of two cows and the transforming of many into cripples reached Kibang earlier than we expected. We resurfaced only later in the evening, having lingered in the bush to avoid the herd boys. The first thing that caught my attention immediately as we wriggled out of the narrow passages between boulders to the foot of the mountain was a vast crowd. You could tell from their gaze and different emotions that something was wrong. Could the herd boys have reached the village before us and reported us to the elders? Yaya would not cast such a stare of surprise at me and then shrug and shake her head for nothing. Someone had reported me to her, I imagined, stepping forward reluctantly. My gaze was fixed on the ground, pretending not to notice that Tav Kibari was snapping his fingers to beckon us over.

Two cows lay humbled at the foot of the mountain, their stares purposeless. Tav Kibari asked us to follow him. I knew our destination was the Palace.

The atmosphere in the Palace Hall was tense. Among those present for the emergency meeting was Fon Fomu, the Chief who happened to be the youngest ever crowned in the clan; he was at the threshold of thirty. The honourable member of parliament was there, as was the mayor of Gidang, Ability, and prominent members of the council of elders, including Tav Kibari, the high priest and adviser to the Chief, Tata, Dr Jerry, the retired medical practitioner, Kinang and Shey Lukong. Alhaji Kidado, or Baba Gidado, as he was alternatively referred to by the children, sat at one end with Wakilu and their children and the herd boys—Jawara, Aboki, Musa, Gado, and Yaaji. They were directly opposite the elders. The mayor and the MP sat between the two camps. All the faces were anxious when Fon Fomu cleared his throat to speak.

"Elders of our land, we greet you."

"*Mberrhhh*," the elders supported their chins with their hands and hummed like bees in the customary manner of greeting the Paramount Chief of the land.

"We are here because our brother Alhaji Kidado and his people have come with heavy hearts. Alhaji Kidado, we will hear from you first," the Fon said, ushering Alhaji to the floor.

"Fifur (people) of Kibang land, these are *kiriminals*," Alhaji Kidado pointed at us.

We cowered like fowls waiting to be slaughtered.

He went on, "They *klimbed* the hill and put *girass* and corn pilants on the head of the mountain, knowing that the trap would attract my cows to the head of the mountain to fall and roll down the hill and die. And that is what happened. My cows followed the feed and fell into the kiliff, rolled down the chest of the kiliff, and died."

Alhaji wiped his face.

Musa and Aboki nodded in approval as Alhaji Kidado went on. "It is not the first time your children have chased my cows into the chest of the kiliff to roll down and *bireak* their legs and die. They have killed two big-big cows. As I speak, eight of my cows are limping. I have come to ask you to pay 500,000frs for the damage."

"Yowaa," the herd boys applauded.

"Alhaji Kidado, you are making the claim to kill the matter that we all know!" Ability rushed forward, wagging his finger threateningly, but Alhaji Kidado dropped ten thick fibre ropes before the elders and returned to his seat.

Ability's wild protest did not surprise me.

To dissuade us from making friends with his son, Atang, whom many saw as a bad boy, Yaya had told my siblings and I a lot of things about Ability. He had only recently applied for the Red Feather title to qualify for a seat in the traditional cabinet of the council of elders. Pending approval and rites of initiation, Ability wielded self-imposed authority with no tolerance whenever a disagreement erupted between the farmers and the herdsmen or between Gidang and Kibang. He arrogated to himself the power to decide for all, allowing for no other views contrary to his own, an attitude Atang had also picked up. Ability would rather start a fight than sit and watch a divergent view germinate in his ideological territory. He was particularly provocative and uncompromising during community assemblies convened to resolve the conflict over land ownership, water sources and cattle routes between Graffi farmers and Gidang Fulani cattle breeders. He would hurl insults and divisive utterances at the herd boys and anybody who did not join his campaign to weed out the herders and their cattle from Kibang land. It was difficult to reason with Ability when the dispute involved the herders or Alhaji Kidado, reputedly the most prominent and respected cattle breeder in Kibang-Gidang. Even when the matter under discussion had nothing to do with open grazing or ownership of water resources and grazing routes, Ability managed to turn the discussion to the invasion of maize farms by cattle. He aimed to harvest the support of the farmers to push the herders out of the land.

Ability had developed a hatred for the Gidang people, whose leader was Alhaji Kidado, following the repeated invasion of farmlands and destruction of crops by their cattle. He had extended his hatred to government authorities, blaming them for not enacting a law to stop open grazing in Kibang. His colony of enemies rose and involved Alhaji Kidado when his son and only heir, Atang, lost his manhood through the traditional justice system of forced castration. The moment coincided with Ability's dismissal from the public service for inciting mass riots and violent protests against the appointment of a Fulani man as Senior Divisional Officer in Kibang. His entire household, therefore, was surviving on what his wife made from her *buyam sellam* business.

His chronic hatred for Alhaji Kidado took a great leap when his son, Atang, was dispossessed and replaced by Fomu as the Kibang Royal heir following the rape-induced foot-testing traditional trial. The trial had been presided over by Alhaji Kidado. Ability expressed his frustration; flames of hate fluttered in his words, looking for a target. When he got up to respond to Alhaji Kidado's request for compensation following our mountain-climb adventure that led to the killing of two cows and injuring of many, furious sparks flew in his words. The atmosphere soon changed from conflict resolution to chaos, where flaring tempers, intimidation, provocation and flinging of insults at one another took over the stage.

"Alhaji Kidado, you have come to collect a massive 500,000frs CFA from Gidang people as compensation for the cows that fell into the chest of the mountain and died on their way to Gidang to transform my maize and cassava farms into their dining tables as usual! I knew a day like this would come. Alhaji Kidado, let me remind you that last week, your cows invaded my wife's farm and destroyed crops. They ate up all the cassava, onions and maize on the farm. Did you pay for the damage? No! You oiled the SDO's lips, and the matter was swept under the carpet as usual!"

Kinang and Banadzem jumped with joy at Ability's rhetorical flair. To show their support for Ability, they hit their palms together, repeating this twice with the backs of their hands.

"Baba Bility, the cows ate *girass* when they entered your farm; they did not eat cassava and corn and onions," Alhaji Kidado countered.

"Is there grass in my wife's farm that she planted for your cows to come and eat?" Ability quipped, shaking his head. "Alhaji Kidado, you actually came here to collect 500,000 from who? Tell me. Is it from the same farmers your herd boys and cows have vowed never to see corn cobs spring up on the chests of maize plants right in their own farmlands…?"

Shey Lukong, Banadzem, and Kinang concurred by nodding.

"Alhaji Kidado, your cows and sheep have transformed our corn farms, fields, and streams into charity organisations. The rivers and streams flowing across Kibang look like mud each time your cows come down to drink there. It was not long before people's stomachs were grumbling, and the openings between their buttocks dislodged rivers of excreta. Many ended up dying because your cows spoiled the water they drank. Alhaji Kidado, how many times have you come down to Kibang to pay 500,000frs to the farmers for their crops, grass, and the streams your cattle ravaged? Hurh! Kidado, if you don't want the rest of your cows to walk on crutches, build a fence in Gidang and keep them inside! And if that is not done, your cows and sheep will sit on wheelchairs before browsing and drinking from our streams…"

"What did you just say?" Thundered Alhaji, his chest rising and falling.

"Our grass, streams, and crops are not for cows! You heard me! Alhaji Kidado! Do not say Ability did not warn you!" Ability smacked to end an insult that was not taken lightly by Alhaji Kidado and the herd boys.

"Baba Bility, one of us will silip (sleep) in the *girev* today while the other will silip in jail! You know very well that the person that will silip in the *girev* shall not be me!" Alhaji threatened, attracting nods from the herd boys.

"Come-no-go!" Ability insulted.

"*Giraffi* fifur are farming and building their houses on cattle routes where Fulani fifur first settled. Yet, you call me a 'Come-no-go? Baba Ability, who is the real 'Come-no-go' here? Is it the Fulani or the Giraffi man? *Stupis!*" Alhaji sneered.

"I am now convinced that this Come-no-go does not even know where he came from. Kidado, did you just say Graffi people are farming and building on cattle routes? Do Fulani people have cattle routes in Graffi land? Kidado, the hair on your head looks exactly like the hair of corn, and yet you say you have land in Kibang! How is that possible? Tell me, which Graffi man has hair on his head that looks pale, sick, and weak, like the hair of a newborn baby? This Come-no-go even went as far as calling Graffi people 'Come-no-gos! And these timid elders sitting here," Ability said, pointing to Fon Fomu and the elders one after another. "They see nothing wrong with swallowing the insults!" He shook his head repeatedly and then continued. "Well, Alhaji Kidado, you must know from today that referring to a Graffi man as a 'Come-no-go' is not only an insult to our kinsmen but one of great cultural consequence! It shows gross disrespect of Graffi history and the ways of Kibang land…"

"And who created the history and the ways of the land you are talking about? Is it not the same Giraffi people?" retorted Jawara, and Alhaji Kidado nodded.

"Alhaji Kidado, your cows will continue to fall onto the cliff and die. Nobody in Kibang will pay for any damage, no matter what happened. Mark my words," yelled Ability.

"Baba Bility, I am not surprised at your reaction. Your opportunity to eat meat is only when a cow falls into a kiliff and dies or when masqueraders are rewarded with fowls and goats during a funeral ceremony. So, after waiting and waiting and waiting, and no cow is dying, you sent children to kill cows." Alhaji Kidado deliberately shamed Ability.

"Come-no-go! Babysitters for cows! You rush your cows to the

Veterinary hospital for minor injuries. But you cannot replace the teeth you have lost from your mouth. Nonsense!" Ability insulted with a fixed stare at Alhaji Kidado.

"One more insult from ya mouth! Stupis Giraffi man! Giraffi pikin dem kill my *animus*, and destroy legs for eight big-big cows, na Fulani *fifur* you go come de insult? Baba Bility, if you are *hungiri* for a fight, we are ready," Musa threatened. He sprang to his feet, accompanied by the other herdsmen in a huddle.

"Yowaarrrrh," Wakilu and the herds boys, including Jawara, Aboki, Yaaji, and Gado, applauded, bending forward with fists clenched. Tav Kibari, Tata, the MP and the mayor stood between the two camps, telling them to calm down.

"Allow the Come-no-gos to dare a son of the soil! Musa and these other babysitters for cows," Ability pointed to Alhaji Kidado and the herd boys with his finger as he spoke. "I did not hide my mouth before saying that the Come-no-gos do not have any land in Kibang! What that means is that if I ever see you and your cows in Kibang again, I will not only give you the real reason to fight me! More cows will sit on wheelchairs before grazing on my crops!" he spat. If Fon Fomu had not intervened on time, war would have been sure to break out at that moment.

"Ability, it's enough! This is not what brought us here!" Chief Fomu shouted. But Ability remained standing, throwing insults at Alhaji Kidado.

"I have swallowed pilenty insults. And I will not sit here to be insulted by Bility again. Elders of our land, if Baba Bility is not kicked out from the gathering of the Elders of our land, I will tear myself out of this family, and you will never see me and my people here again," Alhaji Kidado threatened and got up to go out with his people, but Tav Kibari and Tata intervened to bring them back to their seats.

"Alhaji Kidado, we do not throw away our loincloth because it has a tear. No, no. If we find a hole in our garment, it is good that we patch it to make it useful. We will mend Ability. If we throw him away, who will teach him how to love? We are very sorry for the insults.

Sit down, please. Fon Fomu was talking when you got up to go away. Let us listen to the Fon," Tav Kibari said, waving a peace plant in the air before turning toward Ability. "Ability, our people say you must stop sowing the whirlwind if you are to avoid a gathering storm."

Tav Kibari's brief intervention paid off as Alhaji Kidado and his people returned to their seats. Applause was heard across the hall.

"Tav Kibari has spoken our minds," Fon Fomu said, looked around, and continued, "Ability, Kibang and Gidang or Graffi and Fulani are all children from the same source. We are a tree with many branches. We are a river flowing and giving birth to streams. Nobody is a Come-no-go here. I might be the youngest in the traditional council, but my father told me that. By the way, our children have not accepted or denied the accusation brought against them by Alhaji Kidado and his people. That is what brought us here. We need to hear their own side of the story."

"The Fon is right," said Dr Jerry, standing up.

Dr Jerry was one of those who hated disputes and conflict. He had lost his lone son and many family members during one of the confrontations between the farmers and the herd boys. Since then, he has dreaded conflict and all conflict alarm bells. He took to the floor, and the hall was calm again.

"Musa, Aboki, Yaaji, Gado, Ability, calm down and sit down. Ability, we need solutions and not insults. The cows Alhaji Kidado is talking about were not killed or destroyed on anybody's farm. They stumbled onto the cliff and died while trying to eat corn and grass that someone had deliberately kept at the edge of the precipice. The matter requires investigation by the police."

Fon Fomu, Tav Kibari and Tata nodded approvingly as Dr Jerry spoke.

But Ability spurted out, "What investigation are you talking about? Huh? Dr Jerry, if you find a childhood admirer staring at the buttocks of your wife at close range, would you wait until he takes away what belongs to you before you pull out a cutlass from its sheath?"

"*Wusai!*" Kinang and Shey Lukong quipped.

"Ability, we will not pull out any cutlass from the sheath. We should be correcting our past mistakes, not creating new ones," Dr Jerry rebutted. Kinang and Shey Lukong scowled, but the elders nodded approvingly, and Dr Jerry continued. "I don't just speak; I speak from experience, which people say provides knowledge the classroom does not offer. My people, I am a retired medical doctor. You all call me doctor, and you are right. My medical knife separated broken arms, legs, and limbs from bodies that were still breathing. I did that to save lives. My medical register will tell you we buried many legs, arms, and fingers during the last battle between the farmers and the herders. I am left with nobody to call me father, but I gave birth to children." He wiped his eyes as he spoke and stared at Ability, who ignored his anguish and immediately sprang to his feet.

"Dr Jerry, your father made a very fat mistake to send you to do medical training? When the White missionaries returned to Kibang to compensate your family for the land your great-grandfather had reduced to a gift for the construction of the Catholic Church, all the children of school age in your family were, unfortunately, girls. You were the only boy whose right hand went over the head and touched the left ear. That is how luck fell on you when the Whiteman decided to train a child from your family in their school to learn to treat people using their medicines. It was better for your father to have sent a girl child to be trained than to send someone who is blessed with an anthill between his legs and yet shrinks at the mention of a cutlass like a woman. Dr Jerry, this is not the first time you get up in an assembly of men to talk about the legs and arms your medical knife separated from breathing bodies! You do this to discourage us from going to war with the people whose cattle are why our barns are empty. Kibang people are dying of hunger. Your medical training should have been an opportunity to learn how to prepare powerful insecticides whose smell or taste would poison any cow that grazes on our plants and grass, but you didn't. What did you do instead? You went to the big school, and the only skill you learned was how to dig out babies from the lap of women, a job meant for women…"

The Fon, Tata, and other elders, including the visibly embarrassed Dr Jerry, looked away, shaking their heads.

Ability went on, "Dr Jerry, you cannot grow a beard on your chin, wield an anthill between your legs, and still have the mind of a woman…"

"Ability, you need to be evaluated by twenty psychiatrists to ascertain that there is still a connection between your heart and your mouth!" Doctor lost his temper.

"And Dr Jerry needs fifty psychiatrists to ascertain that there is still a connection between his umbilical cord and Kibang land!" Ability shot back.

Fon Fomu had to step in again to avert the degeneration the meeting was taking.

"Ability, you sound like someone quarrels with your love for Kibang. No, that is not what brought us here. I cannot let this to continue. You are in the traditional council, and this should be the last time we will tell you to talk only when necessary! I allowed this conversation to continue because I thought we could all learn from Dr Jerry's experiences and do the right thing. But it is turning to a different thing. It has to stop now! We need solutions and not insults. Alhaji Kidado, we are deeply sorry for this distraction. Elders of our land," Fon Fomu turned toward the elders as he spoke, "Alhaji Kidado has told us what brought him and his people to Kibang. Before we proceed, we will allow our children to tell their own side of the story." The Fon turned to face us. "All of you, step forward. One after the other, you will put your hand on this *Asho-h* and swear to your innocence or acknowledge your guilt before the gods of our land." As he spoke, he pointed to a carving made of wood on the floor. "If you lie on oath, *Asho-h* will strike you dead. He sees your mind and knows when you are lying."

"Kila, it is your turn. Tell us what happened." I was the last person to speak; like the others, I simply acknowledged our guilt.

"Elders of our land, our ears have heard from both parties; it is now your turn to speak," said Fomu. Wakilu was the first to react.

"*Ngomna*," Wakilu pointed to the mayor and the parliamentarian as he spoke," drag these children to *pirison*, dat is where *kiriminar* belong."

"Yowah!" the herdsmen hailed Wakilu when he called us criminals.

My heart raced at this labelling. Baba Wakilu had decided that our punishment for killing the cows was imprisonment.

Tav Kibari, a top member of the elders' council immediately took to the floor.

"Wakilu, elders of our land, our children have not denied the wrong they are being accused of. They intentionally broke our brother's calabash, and we must mend it."

"You have spoken our minds," Tata echoed Tav Kibari.

Yaya was the only woman allowed to participate in the decision-making assembly of the clan, perhaps because she had entered menopause. She said, "Until the injury on the legs of marriage is repaired, it will continue to limp." She said.

The turn of the mayor to speak had now arrived. "My people, I have listened to everybody. I am happy we chose dialogue and a peaceful negotiation in this matter. We need to love and tolerate each other. We need to teach our children the right manners. And to you, children, do not push cows onto the cliff again. If somebody tells you to do it, come to me and report the person to me. I will hide your identity." We nodded, and the mayor continued. "If you find cows in your farm, report to the council immediately. We will arrest and impound the animals. Do not take the laws into your hands. The council workers are working with the council of elders and the relevant government authorities to put an end to the problem between the farmers and the herdsmen." All nodded except Ability. The mayor sat down.

After the mayor's intervention, the elders led by Tav Kibari withdrew to the yard, spoke in low tones, and returned to their seats in the hall.

"People of Gidang land, we have accepted to pay compensation for the damage our children caused to your cattle," Fon Fomu said, collecting the ten ropes Alhaji Kidado had earlier dropped on the floor: "Alhaji Kidado; you will hear from us before the next *Wailun* market day. For the sake of the parents of these children, kindly take back five ropes. You are also a father. We give birth to the child and not to his character." Fon Fomu then turned to the children, "Our children, what you did was naughty and should never repeat itself!" We nodded consent, and the fon continued. "Now, listen to your punishment. Every morning, beginning tomorrow, you will all fetch water and firewood and take them to the homestead of Alhaji Kidado in Gidang. You will do that for two weeks..." Ability, Banadzem, Kinang, and Shey Lukong exchanged gazes and stood up. They grumbled as they stormed out of the hall. Alhaji Kidado stepped forward, picked up five ropes from the floor and returned to his seat, a gesture that attracted nods from the elders across the hall. Eyebrows were still raised at the apparent disrespect from the action of Ability and his supporters when Lankar, the hunter, began to stagger across the yard, screaming. Everybody stormed out of the hall, staring frightfully at Yurika dangling across Lankar's shoulders. Tav Kibari and two other men helped Lankar to lay his load on an extended bench made of bamboo. Lankar immediately offered an explanation. He found the girl lying somewhere on the Gidang Mountain. She was bleeding and writhing in pain. He had climbed up the hill to check his traps.

"She is breathing," Tav Kabari, who had placed his ears on Yurika's chest, suddenly screamed joyfully. Yurika was lifted into the mayor's car and rushed to the hospital. Meanwhile, Fon Fomu requested Tav Kibari to assist Kinang in reporting the incident to the police, promising justice for the victim's family.

Ability and the MP were the only two people who lingered behind when the crowd hurriedly rushed Yurika to the hospital, where her recovery took months. The MP muffled a response to something Ability had said as Yaya and I looked over the grass around a nearby eucalyptus tree farm where Yaya had smuggled me in to urinate. "Ability, the governorship election is around the corner, and you know my ambitions. My political rival is powerful. I need both the Gidang and Kibang people in order to succeed. The Alhaji will tell his people to vote for my opponent if I allow the herders to stay a night in the police cell. Ability, it is not as if I don't feel for this little girl who was stabbed in the stomach, probably by the herders. I must be cautious. This is not the moment to lose the political disciples I have worked hard to harvest for many years. As I told you, I promise you a big position in my cabinet if I become senator or even governor of this region. So, don't worry. I will visit the hospital and pay all the hospital bills for Yurika." They separated. Later, Yaya had me well beaten when we returned home from the palace.

10

Rugged Ways

I was lost in my thoughts when a loud bang from our vehicle awakened me. I was disoriented for a while before my senses returned after some minutes. Our vehicle had just swerved and planted its front wheels again. This time, it did it against a tree at the sharp edge of a dangerously steep incline along the road. There was another car in the valley.

The vehicle had been at full speed when the driver tried to avoid a collision with another car. We were at the death trap of a descent that separated Upper Kibang from Lower Kibang. I had always closed my eyes to avoid eye contact with the dark and yawning chasm each time I travelled that road. The chasm fitted the frightening description that our catechist once gave of it as the first chamber of hell. That was when we were preparing for Christian baptism. No car had ever stumbled into it and got repaired. Only Kibang fighters and the likes of Atang and Livinus were known to have successfully made it through rugged surfaces and narrow passageways to either hide weapons or recover abandoned cows that accidentally fell off the cliff and rolled into it.

It was thanks to the municipal council that planted eucalyptus trees along the top fringes of the descent. One of the trees had just stopped our vehicle from taking the tragic dive down to join other casualties. It took over thirty minutes to pull the vehicle back onto the road. My heart only stopped dancing wildly when we passed the shelving, bumpy hill and approached the vast plains of Kibang. But that was a false sense of security.

A squad of boys suddenly appeared in front of our vehicle. They were wielding guns and waving cutlasses in the air. Aboki spotted them first.

"Vigilante! Vigilante!" he muffled a scream and pointed to the bend about thirty metres ahead. The boys chained themselves across the road, stopping every passing car, questioning the passengers, and collecting money. They were known as the Vigilante Guards, created by Ability, Atang and Livinus at the request of Kibang farmers. They were expected to guard farms from cattle encroachment. Stray animals like cows, pigs, sheep, and goats had become regular farm visitors during farming seasons. They often destroyed crops and brought on the threat of hunger. During the dry seasons, when the fields would dry off from the effects of the roasting sun, cattle often strayed into farms to graze on grass and crops. Community groups were needed to guard entrances into the village, some of which were cattle routes to the streams and valleys where vegetation and farms were found. With time, the Vigilante Guards had stopped taking orders from Ability, Atang, and Livinus because they disagreed over the sharing formula for funds raised by the community for the purchase of raincoats, rain boots, and other security outfits. It was said that the original intention for creating the vigilante guards had been abused. Stories circulated about how the guards went from door to door or mounted roadblocks to collect money from poor villagers and travellers. They often arrested those who did not have and pretended to be raising funds for security outfits. This is precisely what happened to us when we drove into the group.

They had mounted a roadblock of large banana trunks across the road. Cars were lined in opposite directions. One needed much courage to look straight into the gnarled faces of Kibang guards. Tiny forests of hair sat on their heads. They were no source of reassurance. My heart was beating fast when one of them approached our vehicle, which had been carefully parked by the roadside. He ordered us to give them money.

"Na we de do *sikirity* work for Kibang. Na we de guard farm dem make cow no enter destroy corn and crops. Na we de guard this land so dat cows no go follow enter our streams again. We work na for make sure say dat cholera weh yi de kill we when we drink bad water weh cow don waka shit for inside no go deh again. Wuna give support for de *sikirity* work weh we de do. We need money to buy rain boots, raincoats, and cutlasses. We work na for protect wuna. Anybody weh yi no give support, na Big Faya and Harmattan go judge yi case for inside bush!" The short, beefy fellow had scars on his arms and forehead the size of a millipede. He threatened us and then stretched a deep basket to us.

The threat of being dragged into the bush to face the wrath of Harmattan and Big Faya instantly sent hearts dancing wildly. None could hesitate to release the support requested. I hurriedly dropped a thousand francs note into the basket and turned to talk to an old woman who was nudging my arm and mumbling some words. She wanted to know what the young man had said, for she only understood Lamnso, the native language of the Nso-Graffi people of Kibang.

I hurriedly summarised the boy's words and assisted the woman with a note of five hundred francs. From the tears welling up in her eyes, I deduced that she had no money to give out.

Long after we had driven past the cutlass-wielding guards, I was still in fright. Before I could settle into some peaceful calm, however, our vehicle was suddenly stopped at another bend by two men in uniform. We scurried down the walls of our vehicle and joined the long queue of travellers. Livinus and Atang were convulsing like shuddering hatchlings at the sight of a hovering hawk and withdrawing from the queue in reverse.

"*Bonjour, votre Carte d'Identité,*" a heavy voice descended on my ears. The officers were collecting and verifying IDs. Those without identification papers were asked to withdraw from the long queue and move into the hut by the roadside. As I looked, the uniform officer had a flat-top round navy-blue hat with a tight band around his head. His heavy stomach made me imagine an obese boulder sticking out from the waist of a tall mountain. The boulder-like stomach wobbled from the waist of the officer in a downward plunge and shaded his hips. One of the officers grabbed Kitam. Without a word, he clamped a heavy ring around Kitam's hands and hurled him into their vehicle before returning to us. He had simply arrested Kitam after looking at his National ID card. I was still in shock when thick, leafy elephant grass stems began to whisper vigorously behind me. I turned swiftly toward the swooshing grass. I could see a hedge of fleeing grass tearing furiously across the farm. The car suddenly honked, taking my eyes away from the two shapes burrowing through the leafy path.

When the officer was through with verifying my ID card, curiosity sent me peering into the roofless plank walls of the roadside hut where people were filing in and out of the hut. The sneaky fingers of the officer shuffled something from the middle of a page and then returned the car papers to our driver. He then turned to the next man and pulled something out of the man's partially closed fist. Those who did not have National Identity Cards then occupied his focus. From the outside, it looked as if he was shaking hands with them as he burrowed his middle fingers into their folded palms, one after another. I had seen enough and risked being noticed, so I sighed and returned to the vehicle.

Soon, our driver returned with the other passengers and ordered us back in the vehicle. When I did not see Atang and Livinus, the shapes that had burrowed violently through the bush instantly returned to my mind. Our vehicle drove across that stretch of road and slowed at a bend. Livinus and Atang surfaced out of the bush and joined in. It was not the first time Livinus was going to evade security officials. And it didn't surprise me, however, that he felt targeted at the mere sight of security officers.

Livinus was the kind of person whose presence was always viewed with suspicion. Like his friend, Atang, he would dash off into a bush or bend over the grass at the mere glimpse of a police officer. It was an attitude that made him look guilty even before a cow was reported missing, stabbed in the stomach or pushed off the cliff. He habitually changed his appearance by slipping into and out of different garments and headgear. When he didn't wrap his head around with a light headgear, leaving a tail to dangle behind, he wore a hat that swelled up slightly at the centre with a spreading, rounded edge. This made him look short and much like a mushroom plant. His general look was suspicious. It was the kind of look that did not need to remind a woman that her daughter was unsafe to hang around him. Each time you told someone in the village that you wanted to see Livinus, the next question you heard was, 'Whose cow do you want to kill?' Although the last time an alarm was raised that a cow was poisoned or pushed off a cliff from a height had faded from my memory, the presence of Livinus or Atang was still viewed with suspicion. Livinus once bumped into police officers on patrol and immediately started shivering, confessing that he would never again lure cows into falling off the cliff. My mind dredged up this incident as Livinus climbed up into the already moving car and stared at my wallet. I quickly hid it.

Our vehicle now drove through the community farms that straddled the road, not far from the checkpoint. The unexpected happened. A confused spread of frowning cows that looked like they had just graduated from a fattening-course institute and suffered from obesity was pouring into a farm. They stared at the plants with the kind of entitlement that only landlords are known to wield around their shivering tenants at the end of the month. As soon as my eyes fell on cows casting suspicious stares at plants like a man feasting his eyes on the wiggling waist of a lady who has had surgery to enhance her buttocks, I immediately knew that the ears of corn on the chests of maize stems would be casualties of cattle invasion.

My guess did not fail me. The cows grazed on corn, cassava leaves and bean sprouts. They trampled on young green pepper fruits, potato sprouts, and other young plants as they stretched up their necks to cut the stems of pumpkin plants that were creeping on cassava stems. You could think the farmland was a charity organisation. The sumptuous aroma of young plants wafting from roadside farms across the neighbourhood seemed to have invited other animals to join in the feast of the greenery. Sheep streamed into the farms, opening and closing their nostrils like a domestic servant sniffing the inviting scent of chicken soup drifting in from the master's table. For almost a ten-minute drive across the stretch, a confused battalion of pot-bellied cows with flabby hips kept ambling in and out of the farms. What surprised me is that the cattle robbed the farms of their greenery with immunity. Excreta riotously escaped from the gaping clefts on the buttocks of the animals and settled on the naked ridges like tiny mountains. You had the impression that you were watching addicts who frequently hosted episodes of anal encroachment but now suffered from chronic anal diarrhoea. Tears welled in my eyes as I watched beheaded stems of maize, pumpkins, pepper, and cassava plants that bled like the limbs of a fallen tree. Aboki soon distracted us from the pathetic sight when he observed, "Whenever cattle graze on corn, the procreation is high."

Aboki's statement was not taken lightly by Atang, judging from his reaction.

"Did any other person hear what this 'Come-no-go' just said?" asked Atang, pointing at Aboki. "I now understand why cattle will stop at nothing until they complete the job that monkey pox disease and the coronavirus started! And this level of damage to plants is the price the farmers must pay for refusing to tell strangers like Jawara and Aboki and their cows that they have overstayed their welcome in the backyard of Kibang land!" Atang's verbal attack invited a gale of laughter from the travellers.

I still remember how Jawara, who had before now sat with his hand supporting his chin like the man who has impregnated a neighbour's wife, reacted.

"Atang, if you dare refer to Aboki and I as 'Come-no-go' again, I will tell you what your ears will never want to hear!"

"Atang, you heard Jawara, well-well!" Aboki reminded.

Atang was still lamenting and flinging provocative insults at Jawara and Aboki when the rat-a-tat-tat sounds of gunshots began to rend the air across the vicinity, a little further ahead. All eyes shot off in the direction of the gunshots. I located a group of men tearing through the vicinity and advancing toward the invaded farms, wielding weapons.

"There's danger!" Livinus screamed, pointing a finger across the vicinity. Things happened so fast. Faces that looked like the boys we had met not too far behind were tearing out of a shortcut in the area and charging toward the cattle-besieged farms. Boys with dense chins sprang up from among the grazing animals, wielding thirsty guns and arrows pointing toward the boys charging into the farms. A closer look showed that both groups were wielding knives, cutlasses, spears, and guns as they charged into the spreading farms from every direction. I wasn't the only one that was afraid. Livinus squirmed with fright, gripping his amorphous trousers that seemed to have resulted from a quarrel with the tailor who had stitched it. In Kibang, the presence of maize farms was usually an invitation to a cattle feast and a potential battleground where farmers and herders tested the strength of the muscles of their cutlasses, knives, guns and spears.

Our driver must have perceived the looming danger, too. He quickly pulled to the side of the road and stopped. We all leapt to the road and lay flat on our stomachs behind the vehicle, whose mountain of luggage shielded us. The events of that encounter were not to be forgotten in a hurry.

The battlefield shifted to my heart and ears. Loud roaring and grumbling sounds met with screams and shrieks and rang continuously above our shivering heads. I slithered back and forth on my stomach, shuddering violently, quickly shifting my head forth and back in an attempt to dodge the confused flight of arrows that came in from every direction. It was soon apparent that it wasn't safe to stick around. I tried to crawl into the nearby farm, but a charging cow knocked me over. I didn't immediately notice that a stray spear had also torn off the skin on my arm as I tried to avoid the inevitable encounter with the charging beast. A sharp pain drew my attention to blood oozing from the scraped part. I still remember writhing in pain, frightened to the core, as I lay flat on the ground. I mustered just enough courage to wrap my shawl around the wounded arm.

I thought my world had come to an end. Then, from nowhere, as it were, a police car arrived at the battle scene. The police officers jumped out of their vehicle and sent sporadic shots into the air. The fighters started fleeing, but within about ten minutes, the police officers clamped heavy rings around the wrists of a handful of them. There was already a long queue of cars with people lying flat on their stomachs, all travellers.

As soon as the officers dragged some stiff bodies to the roadside, they ordered us to leave the scene. The bloody stretch of road could be mistaken for a slaughterhouse. Brutally severed headless bodies, bleeding heads, and limbs of humans and cows littered the area. The slightest rustle of grass and leaves terrorised my heart, dancing excessively. I felt it convulsing like treetops during the storm.

Far from the battle scene already, the dead bodies and body parts maintained shuddering presences in the corridors of my mind. They clustered like bees and gave it piercing nudges. I had always wanted to write a book on conflict and its resolution, using the hostilities between the farmers and the herd boys as the test case. The savagery of the scene immediately sprang up in my mind, the need to document the experience in a novel.

Like a man anxious to plant the first seed and seal the lips of impatient birthright contestants who had doubted his ability to father a child, my mind opened its lap to harvest the convulsive drizzles of memories of the just-ended battle, wafting into my mental hatchery. The mental intercourse conceived a brainchild—a narrative on the journey to Amerika. How to keep track of all the events on the long journey became my preoccupation. The memory of the mobile phone and its small power bank, which I had carefully buried in my underwear, joyously came up. I saw the need to videotape and take pictures of every event on the way. But before long, the phone battery ran low. Before it did, however, I took photos of some events and places.

A yawning divide meandered like a snake along the shoulder of the particular stretch of the Ring Road. In it lay a naked water pipe, vomiting water from the brutal cracks on its body. The water tore across the road, whose gutted bed swallowed it and left what looked like a tiny lake at a bend. The sticky pond swallowed wheels and held a few vehicles in temporary captivity. I could see the hind wheels of an overloaded truck in one of the branches of the pond, imaging like a dog urinating at a roadside. As the wheels of moving vehicles churned the mashed soil and danced wildly, trying to avoid gliding into the bowl-shaped mini-tiny lake, young boys stared impatiently from the pavements. They were ready with shovels, spades, and thickly interwoven ropes. Each time a passing car got clogged in the pond, they screamed with delight. Now, a queue of vehicles, including ours, was swallowed and held in the highway detention lake, awaiting bail payment for their release.

Cars lined along the road on both sides. Travellers' faces dripped with sweat as they leaned out their heads from the windows of vehicles stuck in mud. We were fortunate that our vehicle spent less time in detention. A few meters after the road checkpoint, I noticed a girl in the same car whose face reminded me of my childhood friend, Savage. I tried to engage her in a conversation. Suddenly, a rainfall of confused noises began to waft toward us. We were already approaching Menda, the heart of Kibang.

***

Driving through the streets of Menda in the early hours of the morning was like tearing through a thick forest of tangled stems and branches. We were still some kilometres away from the heart of the town but had to contend with hawkers, motorbikes, truck pushers, cars, interurban vehicles, and lorries converging into the main street from village roads. They obliged our vehicle to join the queue from the tail.

A tangle of imposing buildings connected by overhead ropes sprang up in rungs across the low-lying heart of chaos. Uproarious noises encased our vehicle in all directions. The air above my head erupted in erratic beeps of cars honking, beeping, and blaring frenziedly from behind and in front of us. Some arrived in the town from distant cities across Kibaaka while hustling around for short-distance travellers. Some shuttled in and out through different exit roads to villages and the neighbourhoods of Menda. The noise increased as we inched forward.

"Pim piiiiim! Pim piiiiiim! *Tweeeet! Voooom! Ntun ntun ntooooom.*" What a rainfall of noises! I mused. My ears hummed as if they were hiving an assembly of snoring bees. Menda was a town of beautiful disorder, I concluded, looking across the mix of shambles and exquisite buildings in the vicinity.

A heaving populace of motorbikes surging vigorously up the paths from side roads poured unceasingly into the streets. Particularly, the main street that tore through the town was heavy with jammed lanes of interlocked and confused vehicles. You could hardly tell which cars were heading forward and which were from the opposite direction. There were many things on the street. You saw humanity's jungle in the jumble of cars, dribbling motorbikes, pedestrians, hawkers, school children, and wheelbarrows manoeuvring through the jammed street. It was a confused spread of swaying backward, forward, and side-to-side swings. Moving files of persons shuffled and staggered between impatient bike riders with confrontational faces sitting on the necks of their smoking bikes. They were leaping like frogs, ready to jump. When they did, their motorbikes wriggled in and out of unbelievably narrow passages between the streaming cars like wounded worms. Each hastened to overtake the other. Faces studded with sweat peeped over broken brown windows of vehicles to display and introduce bread, jewellery and clothing items for sale. At one corner, muscular wheelbarrows and transportation agents sweated under mountains of luggage, mostly bloated bags. Timid school children in different kinds of beautiful uniforms, many of them accompanied by young women and teenage girls, meandered through this maze in all directions, trying to cross to the other side or to get to a loaded bike or taxi. Traders in national colours stood in the middle of traffic, and slipping their fingers into the pages of car documents, they smuggled out bank notes.

Traffic did not look tame, and the populace was scattered in the perspectives and directions they went. Road pavements were foundations for eateries and palm wine joints, or drums for roasting fresh fish, suya, yams, maize or plantains. Some of the drums exuded red tongues of flames and flared spreads of wood ash tossed around by the wind. Beer parlours and palm wine bars double-functioned as cafeterias and restaurants that stretched frontward with roofed planks and merged with the road.

People rushed from rectangular buses that looked like church buildings into bars. Craters of pounded yams held in yellow sauce were installed in plastic dishes and fenced with chunks of meat and cooked vegetables. They were like small fishponds. Behind every loaded dish sat its owner. Their middle and forefingers dived aggressively into the plates, cutting and scooping chunks from the bowl-shaped pastes to chuck into their ravenous mouths. Every table had food and drinks, and crowds of jubilant flies followed the aroma right to the moist lips of palm wine and beer bottles. Withered-looking young boys and girls stretched their necks over the open windows of these eateries, yawning, waving to the customers, begging for food, and trailing impatient fingers, lifting chunks of food into their mouths. On every stretch of the main street, women and young girls with babies strapped to their backs sat under umbrellas with spread-out edges, selling recharge cards or peeled oranges. Our driver's attempts to drive quickly through the confused spread of cars and charging motorbikes proved futile. The protracted swaying back and forth of the woven vehicles took almost two hours.

The strength of Kibang's financial muscles was visible in the number of bars and trash bins overrun by swarms of flies. Pulsating jangles of tangled Makossa, Njang, Gospel music, Bottle dance, Bensikin, and Bikutsi rhythms tumbled from the loudspeakers hanging down from beer parlours' eaves. My ears droned and murmured as if they were hosting thunderstorms. I could sift out my take even from this intermarriage of pulsating rhythms. And I wasn't the only one enjoying the soul-nourishing rhythms of the rich diversity of Kibaaka music. Livinus, who was huddled up with other passengers, raised and dropped his buttocks with fast, jerky motions that initiated the pulsating soul's enjoyment of the wafted rhythms. Half-closed eyes, he unconsciously smiled, his thick protruding lips widening to the shape of a millipede. I could guess from his motion that his pick was the melodious Douala-styled Makossa song of Salle John. His trousers had dropped below his buttocks, revealing three layers of different pants, red, brown, and blue in shades. Buried in the music, Livinus took no notice of any other thing. Across the road were continuous taverns that announced the heavy presence of drinkers in town.

Garbage collection containers stood at every stretch, overpowered by mountains of garbage with jubilant flies leaping back and forth in childish games they indulged heartily in. Plastic bottles were arranged in stacks along roadsides, apparently waiting for buyers who often were suppliers or hawkers of palm wine and oil. Mama Jumrika is the face I located among the cluster of women, children, and men digging the trash bins for discarded food crumbs. Mama and her ten children were among those displaced from Kibang village during the bloody conflict between the farmers and the herd boys. The fire had gutted homes, including hers, leaving only an orphanage of headless chests of buildings in the neighbourhood. The fire incident popped up in my mind as I watched the skinny body of Mama Jumrika bent over a big trash bin, the baby strapped on her back. She was sorting and lifting pieces of bread and plastic containers.

"Mama Jumrika," I shouted and tossed her a thousand francs CFA note. I still recall how she instantly leaped off the trash bin and fell on the banknote, dragging it from the hands of a bony young boy who had abandoned the bin he was rummaging and dived for the money.

"Nobi for you she give dat money! Na for me! I sabi dat woman. Na my neighbour for village." Mama Jumrika told the young man.

"Do you know the woman?" Savage asked, staring back at Mama Jumrika, who was still waving back at me and dancing.

"Yes, I do. She ran from the village during the confrontation between the farmers and the herdsmen. I am not sure her husband is aware she now lives in Menda. He has been looking for them."

"But she's carrying a baby on her back." Savage stretched the conversation further.

I was in the middle of a conversation with Savage when an uproar drew my attention to the swarming street. One of the bike riders with a forest of hair in the middle of his head had just hit a car from behind, shattering its rear lights. Instead of apologising, he started insulting the driver.

"Carry dat ya old thing comot for road make ma *bend skin* pass! From which driving school dis man collect driving license na? See how he de drive like woman! See yi head like grinding stone."

"*Ya mami pima! Regarde-moi un danger public! Toi-même, tu as appris à conduire* où ? *Est-ce que tu as même un permis de conduire* ? See how yi face wowo pass *kibaranko* yi own!" ("Your mother's backsides! Which Driving School did you attend? Do you even have a Driver's Licence? Your face resembles that of the most dreaded and ugly masquerade in Graffi land called Kibaranko"). The enraged driver switched between French and Pidgin English.

Two traffic police officers were struggling to control the traffic. One held his left hand high in the air, a whistle stuck firmly into his puckered lips, his right hand waving slowly back and forth. The confused lanes of cars were on hold so that the vehicles on the right lanes of the road could drive across the intersection. In the midst of all this came a crushing sound accompanied by a scream of agony. A young girl with a bloated sack slung over her shoulders was twirling at the road edge, some metres after the intersection. The *bend skin* (as motorbikes were called) rider who insulted a driver had carried five school children on the same bike, one in front and four behind him. He was dribbling off to avoid traffic police, undoubtedly conscious of violating traffic rules. He had knocked down the young girl but had not stopped. Blood oozed from the girl's nose. One of the police officers jumped on a motorbike and was tearing through the jammed street after the fleeing bike rider. Unable to escape with his bike and five-person load, the rider abandoned everything and disappeared behind the houses. The story of what eventually became of the children, the girl knocked down, or the offending bike rider is blank. I have no idea if the family of the victim ever got justice. It took another hour to drive to the Menda Express Agency, where we were transferred to another vehicle. Despite the pain in my arm, the excitement of travelling to Amerika again arose.

11

From Abakwa-Menda to the Borders

From Abakwa to Ekoka, I kept taking pictures and making short videos of the unfolding Trans-African Highway flanked by mountains at whose feet were flung, dotting scattered houses and thick forests. Some of the forested hills stretched and merged with distant sheets of clouds. The highway looked like an old man's bald head, but it was a tedious ride. Our driver constantly took shortcuts to evade the endless security checkpoints on the highway. He took narrow-twisting paths that tore through private yards and stretches of bushes. He would take a bush track and ripple over grass each time he faced an oncoming motorbike, taxi, or trans-urban bus. At times, he stopped the car and directed the passengers to walk past the next security post and wait for him somewhere ahead. Each time our car had to burrow through the bush, the yielding hair of tall grass would ruffle, slap, or poke my injured arm, sometimes teasing out blood from it.

The tiring meander compelled many of the travellers to fall asleep. I was taking pictures and forwarding them to Berka and Beri when the driver of an approaching car honked, pointing to the ground with his finger as he drove past.

"Immigration deh ahead. If dem ask where we de go, tell dem say na church rally for Ekoka we de go attend." Our driver announced and continued. At the next security post, our destination and the

reasons for the journey were the only questions we answered, followed by a thorough check of our national ID cards and luggage by
two security officers we met.

After driving through continuous villages, we turned off left of the
highway around the entrance into Mamfe town, entered a twisting
bend and pursued a minor track off the main road. This pathway
was lined with transparent plastic bottles and different-sized jugs
filled with liquid the colour of ripe palm nuts. Such a big market
with hordes of fuel flourished in this backyard. The two empty plastic
bottles tied to the arm of a tree at the entrance to the fuel market
were a veiled signal for the fuel business. Oil-filled jugs and plastics
with long necks and narrow mouths stood everywhere.

I followed our driver and the motor boy, as the bus conductor
was usually referred to, looking for food to buy a little further down
the path. After enjoying a combination of roasted corn and plums,
which I bought, I took some pictures. The backyard bustled with fuel
retailers, hustling into and out of the adjoining thickets, clutching
empty plastic jugs and plastic containers in their bent elbows. They
pestered our driver, who occasionally shrugged them off, describ-
ing their container sizes as 'cut and patch.' The measurements were
apparently faulty.

"Who get *funge* with colour for palm nuts? Na dat one I de buy,"
our driver told the hawkers the colour of petrol he wanted.

"Na me, sir. Na original *funge* I deh sell, I no de mix *funge*. Na
from Japan ma *funge* comot sir." The young boy, who looked like an
eight-year-old, answered, trying to seize the driver's attention. The
driver inspected the fuel before requesting the motor boy to drop the
plastic jugs to the vendor. My camera followed the vendor sucking
fuel with a rubber pipe from a slightly long-neck gallon that had
been buried in the soil and emptying the contents into jugs. I stood
there till the filled jugs were transported to our vehicle.

The motor boy had barely finished passing the last stretch of a
thick rubber cord around the saggy buttocks of our vehicle to hold
the five jugs of fuel they had just bought when the fuel retailers

stampeded into nearby bushes. The heavy thuds forced me to look in their direction immediately.

"Police! Police!" Livinus screamed.

Police officers were charging after the fleeing fuel retailers. The officers made several arrests and struggled to shove the fuel dealers into their vehicle. One of the officers who had caught and pinned a bolting fuel smuggler to the ground tried to lock the heavy metal ring around his protesting wrists.

Nobody needed to remind us that it wasn't safe to stick around any longer. We scrambled for the walls of our vehicle to get in. The signal of a message on my phone distracted me from the scene. The message was from Miranda, a friend and registered nurse in Amerika. I skimmed through it.

"Kila. What's up? Hope you doing good. I just turned on my Facebook page, and pictures of a truckload of *bushfallers* popped up with the caption *On the way to Amerika*. Livinus uploaded them online. The dude praised activist Kaba for preparing your travel documents. That caught my attention. I know how the nigga does things. He is a *doki* merchant. He collects heavy sums of money from unsuspecting victims to prepare their travel documents, including a passport and an invitation letter from a company. The company promises you a job and a huge salary. They claim to have agents everywhere to receive you on arrival. It is when you get to your destination that you know the truth. Their agents seize your passport and telephone on arrival. You live in hiding under hard conditions. You cannot be issued a residence permit. You cannot be issued a work permit. You work with a different identity if you manage to get a cleaning job. The owner of the papers you presented to apply for the job receives your salary in his or her bank account. The good ones collect the pay package and decide the sharing formula. You can't report any injustice to the police because you would be discovered and repatriated after serving jail. In the worst situations, you take a new name; you go into prostitution. You hawk your organs for a living; you sell one of your kidneys; you start doing drugs. You are caught and placed on death row. The niggas don't tell you this. They don't tell you that you gonna travel through the desert. You discover things when you are financially engaged and in transit. I am saying this so that you know what you gonna expect. Hide ya money, and ya telephone deep in your underwear, preferably between ya laps. You need enough biscuits and dry food, babe. Drop pictures on my WhatsApp. Tracking signals necessary. Welcome to Amerika."

Fear gripped me after I read the message, but I did not want to entertain any thoughts that I could have been scammed. I forwarded the pictures and videos already taken to Miranda and Berka and began to move my palm back and forth along the bleeding wound on my injured arm. Thoughts of the message seemed to have intensified my pain, which now simmered like a festering wound. Atang must have noticed my severe pain, judging from his prompt but provocative reaction.

"Until Kibang people understand the need to come together as one person and weed out the 'Come-no-gos' like Jawara and Aboki and their cows from our land, bullets and arrows will continue to chase and tear our arms. Read my lips. Not even magic from Oku would chase them out of our land," he said, pointing at my injured arm and casting an accusing stare at Jawara and Aboki.

"Did I not warn this Graffi woman who calls himself a man never to refer to Aboki and I as a Come no go?" asked Jawara, casting threatening stares at Atang, who suddenly carried his verbal threats to another level.

"Jawara, you cannot continue to enjoy a landlord status at a tenant's price!"

While the passengers convulsed with laughter, Jawara swung into verbal action.

"Atang, just one more insult from your mouth, and I will reveal your true identity!" Jawara's threat invited a nod from Aboki.

"A plaited rope does not cough in a gathering of sons of the soil. Jawara, that is what my father told me." Atang dared.

"*Reng reng!*" Exhorted Livinus. He quickly hung back and kicked out his right leg while prodding Atang on the leg with the edge of his shoe.

"I am sure your father equally remembered to tell you that a son of the soil must be a real man and not a carving!" Jawara snapped, staring fixedly at Atang and grinning. Atang's face suddenly developed red hives, stung by the embarrassment of his comparison to a piece of wood. "Are you surprised or offended that we know you as a piece of wood?" Jawara provoked, staring at Atang, who stood cold like a statue, open-mouthed, wide-eyed, and staring vacantly into the air.

Meanwhile, the other passengers continued to vibrate with laughter. Atang's visible embarrassment reminded me of his past.

He was known to be intolerant and provocative, an attitude noticed also in his father, Ability. Many people held that if Atang were a country, his courage would have the surface area of a raging region like the Middle East. Yet, it was said that, despite his violent courage, Atang was as harmless as a carving or a male statue. Atang's harmlessness had nothing to do with physical strength. He harboured a secret burden, which I assumed was the cause of his explosive anger and aggressive behaviour. I didn't know if Jawara was aware that it was his father, Alhaji Gidado, who denied Atang the privilege of growing up as the man he was born. We were all young when the castration incident occurred. I also didn't know if Jawara was aware that his father had transformed Atang into the semblance of a carving. The buried story of how castration rendered Atang as harmless as the naked statue of a man had been unravelled to me by my mother.

The paramount ruler of the then Kibang-Gidang had just joined his ancestors, and the battle for the throne had swung into action. The Ability branch of the Graffi family tree was the next in line to the throne, followed by the Fomu and the Fulani royal extractions, in that order. Ability's royal entitlement as the successor to the throne was refused endorsement by Njobdi, the then Senior Divisional Officer of Kibang-Gidang. Ability had triggered and sponsored massive riots across Kibang that led to the burning of tyres along the streets and the destruction of a giant bridge along the regional ring road. Ability had intended to stop the installation of Njobdi as the new SDO of Kibang-Kidang. He argued that Njobdi was a Fulani man and, therefore, a stranger in their land and that he had to be replaced by a son of the soil. The SDO's decision saw the younger Atang immediately groomed for the attendant enthronement ritual to the Royal throne to replace his father. Unfortunately, a rape incident implicated the young Atang and led to his disinheritance in favour of Fomu. The assault was reported to the council of elders. Three emissaries led by the then chairman of the council of elders-Alhaji Kidado, who also happened to be Jawara's father, were immediately dispatched to the crime scene for investigation and recommendations. Following their report, live footprints sat on the topsoil where the swoop had taken place. As it was the tradition and custom of the land, anyone found guilty of rape was punishable by castration for the male and banishment for the female. All the males were summoned to the scene of invasion for a foot-comparing test. The foot that corresponded with the surviving naked footprints on the soil would be the footprint or tracking signal for the culprit's identity. The young men took turns carefully putting their feet on the short-lived sandy soil footprints. Atang's right foot fitted one of the footsteps on the sand.

The match between the right foot of Atang and the footprints on the soil was taken as evidence of his participation in the violation of the girl in question. Atang had committed a crime against the land. The verdict of guilt was declared following the customs of the land. Because of the strength of the rights of supervision conferred on him by the council of elders, Alhaji Kidado immediately requested that Atang be castrated. The plea of innocence from Atang and Ability, his father, was not considered by the elders. The elders said that Kibang-Gidang was the land where nobody could step on the toes of tradition and remain the same. On the recommendation of the investigation team, the council of elders, led by Alhaji Kidado, insisted that the foot measuring test found Atang guilty. Tradition had to be repeated. Atang was dragged to the place where three roads met, and the two balls between his legs were brutally butchered. Jubilant birthright contestants immediately incited a battle to disinherit him because his castration was a mark of infertility and a threat of extinction to the royal name. That was how the young Fomu became the heir apparent to the throne of Kibang-Gidang, and, subsequently, the paramount ruler of the land.

The castration story still replayed in my mind when Atang's hatred for strangers mushroomed into threats.

"Fulani man! You called me a carving!" Atang clenched his fist and leaned back while Livinus furtively hit the air twice toward the right with his head. Livinus clearly wanted Atang to attack Jawara, who stood alert, observing Atang's body language.

"Atang, history remembers men and not carvings! Your name died the very day you lost your balls! I am ready to finish the job which tradition started!" Jawara quickly wrenched a knife from his waist and leaned back while threatening.

"Atang, Jawara, we have lost over two hundred people since the conflict started. Please stop it now! I beg you in the name of God," I intervened.

"So, the conflict has even killed up to two hundred people, and Jawara is not one of them!" Atang lamented. "Well, Jawara, I am also ready to finish the job that the conflict started," Atang fumed.

I couldn't miss Livinus' stealthy activities as a hedge of arms tried to build a fence between Jawara and Atang, who were now hurling insults at each other.

I had known Livinus from our early days in the village as someone who would voluntarily inherit enemies to serve his interest and switch sides as soon as he got what he wanted. I wasn't surprised then to see him flapping his eyebrows to prompt violence without necessarily giving verbal clues. His goading body language did the trick. He hung far back, shooting instigating glances at Atang, kicking out and hitting the air with his head toward the left from the right and toward the right from the left. It was as if he was trying to toss a ball with his head into the goalpost. His manipulative character, as clearly replicated in his body language, efficiently yielded the expected results. Before I could warn him to be very careful with his utterances and body language, it was too late, especially when the situation was volatile.

Atang suddenly hung over and released a punch at Jawara's nose. Aboki leapt across and struggled to tear through the hedge of arms blocking him and Jawara, who had been disarmed. Jawara managed to thrust a clenched hand across at Atang. He missed his target and hit my injured arm. Aboki swiftly smuggled himself through the legs and tried to uproot Atang from his inclined position, but Ntumfon and Savage held him down and out of the fray. Atang and Jawara tried in vain to shrug off the grip of Ntumfon, Savage, Yuka and other neighbouring hands. Wild screams attracted the attention of the driver. He stopped the car and threatened to throw the fighters out of his vehicle. That is how the fisticuffs ended, but the rowdy talk with differing views persisted. The argument moved from comparing the individual Atang to a carving to a revival of the issue of ownership of land and water sources in Kibang.

"Atang, I have nothing to lose if you and Jawara decide to fight and tear each other to pieces. Your lives are yours to do with as you please. My worry, and the reason I won't let it happen, is that you are brothers. And I am not ready to lose important brothers like you and Jawara in one day. You are destroying the bond you need to protect. If we hate and fight as we have been doing, our children will grow up to know nothing but hatred and violence." I said.

"Kila, Graffi and Fulani herdsmen will never be brothers," Atang countered.

"If truly we are brothers, why do we speak different languages? How can brothers speak different languages? Why do they look different?" Livinus asked.

"Atang, Livinus, read your history book," I said.

"Just how much were you paid to insult the history of Kibang?" Atang said. "Kila, are you sure the Fulani herdsmen did not write the history you are talking about to justify their illegal claims to ownership of our cattle routes and rivers?"

Atang's referring to Gidang people as strangers did not align with what Yaya had told me.

She had said that until the sprain on the legs of marriage is healed, they will continue to limp. Graffi and Fulani are like rivers that give birth to streams as they flow through the land. They have lived in Gidang-Kibang for as long as the length of a river.

Yaya was a herbalist. She long escaped from Upper Kibang to live in Mbiame village, close to the forest. She once told me why she left. She had a problem with her husband. Also, the constant confrontations between Kibang farmers and Gidang herders over ownership of grazing land, cattle routes, and water sources had caused her to leave. She had chosen to live near Kibang forest for several reasons, one being that the valley was far from the fighters and scantily populated. Its extensive and fertile land was suitable for cultivating crops, particularly herbs with which she cured minor diseases and disorders.

"We'll soon reach Ekoka," Barrister Kaba announced as we drove past a straddling forest. This land belongs to Kibaaka but has been neglected to suffer severe linguistic and physical encroachment from fishermen, farmers, and herders drifting in from the neighbouring country of Bamfada. Kaba was detailing much of this to travellers as our vehicle pulled to the side of the road and stopped. The driver had his scheme put in place to cut down on the harassment from immigration officials:

"Listen attentively! We will soon reach the border town. There are immigration officials on both sides of the Bridge. They will ask you about your name, country, where you are going, and why. Each of you has this to tell them:

"We are farmers from the villages of Kibang and Gidang. The herders are killing the farmers in our villages. They wanted to transform our farmlands into grazing lands. When we resisted, they started killing us. We have been living in the bushes. They will kill us if we go back to the village." We all nodded in acquiescence. Kaba looked at the crowd and continued. "Don't be afraid when you speak! I am an internationally acclaimed human rights activist. I will intervene. Look at this sheet of paper. It contains your names."

I raised a brow of surprise as he waved the sheet of paper containing our names in the air and continued:

"The names were compiled by my NGO. I will take the letter to the immigration officials myself for entry visas. They may or may not invite you for questioning. Don't be afraid. I am the lawyer representing you. Have I made myself clear?"

"Yes!" We chorused, relieved that we didn't need to respond to the sometimes-tricky immigration inquiries.

"Good! Look at me when I speak! Now, everybody, hand your passports and mobile phones to me!" As others obeyed Kaba, I saw Livinus hiding his. I tiptoed through the crowd to the rear and smuggled my mobile telephone into my lap.

Kaba had initially made it appear that the journey to the financial catchment called Amerika would be by air. He changed the itinerary without informing us. His voice no longer sounded as friendly and consoling as before. He was assertive and intrusive, sometimes shouting and threatening. He also invented different reasons for the journey. This sudden change of attitude, tone of voice, and language invited suspicion, fear, and even distrust from several passengers. I wondered why he would collect our passports, travel documents, and telephones. "Why was he inventing another reason for our travelling to Amerika? Can I still trust him? Are there things he is not telling us?"

I wasn't the only one who looked worried. Most of the faces around me spoke fear. Immediately, he collected the things and spoke to the driver, who drove slowly into the corridors of the border town. Men and women clustered on the windows of arriving vehicles, advertising various items and services.

"Benga, one chance! Agadez, one chance! Libya by night! Tripoli by night! Welcome, Sir, welcome, Ma. How family? How work? What of your *chuuren*? Which currency you want buy or sell? I get Dollars,

I get Shibe, Naira, CFA Francs, Euro, Dirham. I *gettam* all! Which currency you want? My exchange rate is very good, oh! My name na Alhaji Serikin. Na from my shop all man de buy or sell currency! Follow me to my shop. I no de cheat." Currency vendors and motor boys were advertising their services as our vehicle elbowed through the crowded road.

The queue of buildings at the borders hedged the right and left flanks of the administrative quarters, overlooking a heavily girded iron bridge down a slight bend.

The bridge and hugging buildings caught my attention. There was also the soaring signboard: "*Ekoka Border Immigration Service.*" The border was overlooking queues of people and vehicles heaped with mountains of goods.

Ekoka was a small town with confused or shuffled buildings, beer parlours, and huts squatted or staggered on the foot-heels of the road. The structures hugged each other. Squatting buildings ran across the area. Below the customs office lay the motor park, which was buzzing with people and cars. The town was linked to neighbouring Bamfada by a gigantic bridge. It was also the gateway to an adjoining desert.

I saw Kaba tear through the crowd of weary-looking travellers filing in and out of a long building. He disappeared into the building with the inscription "Immigration Post." Travellers slouched over the short iron bars that constituted the frontage of the gate. Some even slept, their gaping lips drooling with thick saliva.

I shifted attention to Alhaji Serikin buying and selling currencies, struck a bargain and followed him to a suffocating room buzzing with money-exchange agents. Some of the passengers from our vehicle were already in the room. I made the exchange, stepped behind the house and squeezed the money into the obscurity of my lap before quickly returning to our vehicle.

Kaba was not yet back. What was keeping him for that long? I wondered, staring across the road. When he eventually emerged, his face was furrowed. All was not well. He spoke briefly to our

driver and then ordered all to return to their seats in the vehicle.
Our driver reversed the vehicle and pulled into a twisting path. He
drove through the border village, an isolated settlement with scattered
houses sticking out of farmlands and palm trees. The wheels of our
vehicle would grab a surface, churning, lifting, and tossing off shreds
of sandy soil into our faces as we drove on. The rugged road led to
a deep plunge with a silent, grimacing river far down. Our driver
stopped and ordered us to step out of the car. We filed through a thin
passage between hanging rocks to the bottom of the plunge, where
we each paid transit fares to be ferried across the border river. When
we crossed the border that separated Kibaaka from Bamfada, we took
a vehicle that Kaba had arranged to smuggle us into the next border
for the next phase of the journey. We were happy being smuggled
successfully across the border without knowing what awaited us in
the desert and the subsequent journeys, especially across Bamfada's
continuous towns.

12

Across the Bamfada Continuous Towns

The journey across Bamfada's continuous towns was one of nervous calm and panic excitement. Although I wasn't sure of anything anymore and constantly reverted to fear and uncertainty, the road journey remained a friendly and attractive threat compared to the desert journey I recounted at the start of the novel.

The road had bony shreds of tar on many stretches, causing the vehicle to switch lanes suddenly, often subjecting the already exhausted travellers to swerve forth and back with the vehicle's movements. My impatient eyes kept staring curiously across the continuous towns along the highway. Herds of cows ambled along the fields and the roads in endless stretches, often straying into farmlands and robbing the ridges of their aromatic greenery that reminded me of my own country. I remember seeing women hunching over ridges in cultivated lands with large baskets slung over their shoulders. I saw men lying on mats under trees whose branches drooped heavily with fleshy mangoes, paw paw, lemons, oranges, or pear fruits. The presence of life did not, however, kill the fear and the uncertainty that the encounter with invaders and human traders had planted in me during the desert journey. I really needed some distraction from the menacing mental pictures of the desert experiences that kept popping up in my mind.

The thought of my mobile phone brought temporary relief. I

sneakily plugged the phone into the power bank to recharge. When it had harvested considerable streaks of battery, I pulled out my phone from the power bank and quickly forwarded the pictures and videos of my earlier encounters to Miranda, Berka, and Buri. I remember dropping a message of caution, requesting Berka not to share the information with anybody, including Jeff. I didn't want Jeff and Yaya to suffer a shock.

Memories of the desert journey, particularly my agonising encounter with the invaders, kept hovering before my eyes, and I needed to be distracted from them. I needed to take more pictures of places and experiences to send to Miranda, Buri, and Berka as tracking signals. That would at least distract my mind from the fear that had planted its seat there. So, I shot pictures of just about anything along the way.

A hill humbled by the forces of nature stared at us. A large mass of ground had collapsed from its side and covered most of the width of the road, leaving only a narrow lane that was enough only for the wheels of a small vehicle to pass. Water was welling up from a tiny gorge on the walls of the hill and gliding down to the road. Something had prompted the landslide, and water drizzled downward from the waist of the hill and had formed ponds on the road. Young boys sat holding spades and shovels, jubilating when a pond held the wheels of a passing car captive. One of them jumped onto the road and asked our driver if he needed help.

The water trail, which would have emptied itself directly into a ditch at the foot of the hill, now crept downward through a freshly curved conduit, straying into the main road and creating tiny lakes along the road. These settlements of ponds sat in the middle of the road, some bowl-shaped. They swallowed the wheels of vehicles and held many cars in detention. Our driver tried to balance the wheels of the vehicle in the left lane. I knew he wanted to force his way through. The impact of his accelerated bumps and swerves was to be expected, so I held the iron bar above my head to avoid being hurled off to the road.

Our driver drove madly, trying to go through the slippery-sticky ground with speed impulse, but his first and second attempts failed. He made a third and desperately wild attempt to smash his way through the sticky surface. Our vehicle danced agitatedly, ramming its front into one of the victims of mud arrest. Violent jerks and collisions of heads in the bus were the result. Something wobbled in my mouth like a small pebble, and I spat it on my palm. It was one of my teeth. I felt my tongue sweet with fresh blood. After a benumbing moment, I felt harrowing pain on my neck. What I had feared had just happened. Our vehicle now joined the confused queue of cars squatting on their hinds, some partially swallowed and held like captives in mud custody. You could think you were watching dogs urinating at the roadside.

The young boys who had stood watching from the roadside descended onto the road to liberate the trapped vehicles from incarceration. Despite the pain in my neck and mouth, I continued taking pictures. The young boys pushed, jerked, and towed the cars one after another and with the help of a long rope. The driver of one of the vehicles just freed from mud detention, squeezed some money into the impatient fingers of one of the boys, who stared at it with a smile of gratitude. The boys then shifted and placed their palms at the rear of our vehicle, huddled over. Our driver stopped quarrelling with the driver of the car he had rammed into, jumped in the car, and started the engine. The vehicle blared, raged, coughed repeatedly, and grumbled, dancing wildly, but the desired results didn't come. The group leader beckoned a few more boys to join their batch for reinforcement. The wheels of our vehicle churned convulsively in the pool, splashing muddy water high and on anyone or anything behind it. Sheets of sticky brown water spurted across the road. Unannounced, our vehicle danced and swerved riotously in the sticky pond, farting out a rolling mass of dark smoke and then took a sharp swerving glide across a gorge before heaving itself back onto the road. I ignored the pain on my neck in the joy that our vehicle had regained its freedom.

Our driver stretched his hand outside and squeezed something into the greedy fingers of the same boy who was collecting money from the drivers of the released cars. We drove slowly off while I videotaped the queue of vehicles still dancing on the muddy stretch. Tugging vehicles from ponds was a financially juicy business in that particular stretch. As we drove further away, more boys of school age could be seen loitering around that stretch of road. Some wore school uniforms. They had shovels, buckets, and other implements ready for the road-generated employment. About a kilometre after the mud catchment yard, our driver unexpectedly stopped the vehicle at a bend and asked everybody to step out.

"Police and immigration dem plenti for dis road. Make all man give me forty-forty *taasand*. Dat money na for settle all control for road. If na me de settle control, I go make good bargain. Person weh yi no get money, na yi sabi," he announced.

The message was understood. The driver needed the money to negotiate payment settlements at road checkpoints for those who didn't have valid travel documentation. The driver took the money from our outstretched hands and gave more instructions. We were to cut short sticks from fresh branches of nearby guava trees. Whenever we encountered immigration and police officers, we would start chewing or brushing our teeth with the sticks. When someone had cut the sticks and shared them with everybody, the driver jumped into the vehicle, and the journey continued. The motor boy, the bus conductor, must have noticed from the questions we kept asking that some of us did not understand the reason for chewing sticks.

Many native people in that area did not usually go to the market to buy toothbrushes. They brushed their teeth with sticks, chewing the edge of short-wet sticks to form bristles. With the bristles, they brush their teeth. The people held these sticks in their mouths, even in transport vehicles. The men usually had long beards. Some wore red caps with a round middle jutting up. The women usually wore long coverings over their heads and necks. To evade scrutiny of their travel documents and extortion of their money, travellers, especially non-indigenes, imitated the practices. The trick usually worked very well. Officers don't request national identity cards from travellers who chew sticks, wear red caps, wear thick beads around their necks, wear long beards, or wear long head and neck coverings. They assumed that those were natives from parts of Bamfada. The motor boy also taught us a few Pidgin English expressions typical of Bamfada. Holding a toothbrush in the mouth made from wet branches was thus a kind of citizenship test. The same was true for wearing long beards and long coverings over the face and neck or mixing Pidgin English with particular expressions from native languages across Bamfada.

When we further questioned, the motor boy explained what "Settling Control" meant. It was an illegal practice whereby irregular travellers and drivers bribed immigration and police officials to evade verifying their travel documents and national identification papers. The practice was so common, virtually normalised along highways. Security agents at checkpoints were bribed with money to evade the legal provisions subjecting a car or a traveller to possess and present valid proof of identity. In the case of illegal immigrants, passengers without valid travel documents gave money to the driver, who then acted as a mediator, retaining a juicy percentage for himself while giving the rest to the security agents on control along the highways. The immigrant thus avoided arrest, detention or repatriation. Passengers who refused to cooperate or had no money sold items like jewellery, clothing, or shoes to other passengers to raise the required funds. This is what some of the travellers in our vehicle did. If you didn't, you could be abandoned at security checkpoints. It was known that some passengers got themselves unsuspectingly betrayed by the drivers on the assumption of unwillingness to cooperate. Drivers whose vehicles did not have valid or complete documents often entered a lingering bargain, negotiating and paying settlements with the immigration and traffic officials. We experienced this throughout our journey; the officers usually refused to accept any downward review of their outrageous fee.

At the first security checkpoint, for example, you heard,

"Nothing for the boys?" The man in uniform asked while skimming our faces, one after another.

My eyes trailed the officer's hand, smuggling something out of the middle of the car documents he had just collected from our driver. Immediately after that, the officer returned the documents to our driver, and we left.

It was easier to tell that we were no longer driving along border communities. Houses with overhead ropes stretched endlessly. The streets were becoming increasingly crowded with hawkers, mostly women, young boys, and girls, selling fruits at the shoulders of the highway, especially near checkpoints. When our driver stopped a few metres from a road checkpoint and stepped on the road, two water vendors rushed to him.

"Mineral, mineral, mineral, pure water! Because of God, please buy mineral. I am hungry. Give me money make I buy food. God go bless you," one of the boys pleaded, holding out a see-through plastic bucket filled with water sachets. Our driver squeezed something into the vendor's cupped hand and returned to the car without collecting water. Our vehicle was in the protracted queue of cars driving indolently toward the checkpoint. A few metres down the road, two uniform officers were stopping all approaching vehicles and verifying documents. I watched passengers in transit filing in and out of what stood at the roadside like a tall coffin. Some sat on the ground, and some knelt before one of the officers inside the hut. When our driver approached the officer collecting and verifying documents, the water vendor who had just collected what I now understood to have been money from our driver a few metres to the checkpoint looked at the officer and then at our bus and nodded. The officer waved to our driver, smiling, and he drove past without stopping. The eye contact negotiation and exchange signalled that we had settled the control and were allowed to pass. Our vehicle was not stopped for document verification as we had expected.

We soon drove into a locality with cows ambling along the road and across the fields. There were no houses in that stretch. Settlements of cows and sheep sat across the widening fields. The place looked like a cattle colony. Cows and sheep strolled in and out of farmlands like landlords. When we reached a stretch of thick forest, the motor boy explained that the area had been a base for kidnappers and cattle rustlers. My heart missed a beat when we drove past a bend and plunged into logs of wood raised across the road like a ridge. Our driver instantly stopped to avoid a head-on collision.

An armed gang of about eight young men with tiny bushes of hair scrambling for spaces below their chins flustered out of the bush and surrounded our vehicle. From the missed heartbeat, a horse race started inside my chest cavity. Another car came into the scene from behind us and stopped. The tallest marauding gang members ordered the drivers to drive the vehicles into the bush.

"Driver, turn moto, drive follow this side for inside bush immediately!" The gang leader ordered, pointing to the left direction. "If person try for smart, we go waste tam!" The sternness in his voice smashed our ears and hearts with the callous weight of finality. The gun-wielding young man looked about sixteen years old.

The two drivers swiftly did as they were bidden. I thought my world had come to an end. The blast of the siren from a police mobile car on patrol approaching from the opposite far end changed our fate miraculously. The police dashed out of their Hilux car and charged after the young men, firing at them. The hoodlums fled, firing their guns into the air. The police returned shortly afterwards and spoke briefly with the drivers before clearing the hedge of logs from the road for us to drive off. We thanked them and drove off, but the blight of the fear that had almost consumed me festered on. The attempted kidnap scene lingered on in my mind until a spread of houses across the vicinity, way further ahead of us, redeemed the assurance of security from the human masses.

We were now in a big city, which was characterised by the increased number of pedestrians, hawkers, and vehicles on the road. Our vehicle wiggled its way between the heavily trafficked stretch and stopped on the heels of the road in front of a restaurant amidst buzzing bars: "I give wuna only tarty minutes for chop. After tarty minutes, moto no go wait for anybody," the driver said immediately he stepped on the road. We had thirty minutes to eat and return to the car.

While we ate, young boys and girls wielding plastic dishes kept weaving in and out between moving bikes and cars. They mainly targeted approaching vehicles. It was a settlement of child beggars who scrambled for the doors and windows of every slowing car. Some sat beside their parents on road pavements, singing and hitting plastic dishes with short sticks.

My gaze trailed one of the child beggars. She stood on her toes and stretched the upper part of her body over the bonnet of the slowing bus. She had a cleaning brush in her hand. She swished the brush back and forth over the windscreen and then moved to the driving mirrors. When she had finished, the driver squeezed money into her fingers. She ran across the road and dropped the money in a plastic dish in front of an old mother who sat on the ground with her eyes partially closed. My sympathetic admiration for the struggling girl turned into sadness when a passing motorbike hit her. The little girl had swiftly jumped back into the street to continue her cleaning job. A charging bike almost knocked her.

Meanwhile, children kept weaving in and out between stationed and speeding vehicles, selling or displaying drinks, bitter kola, mangoes of all shapes and sizes, peeled oranges, peanuts, grapes, and other food items. Flies flirted from carrots to oranges, boiled cassava and other food items on trays. We soon returned to our vehicle, and the journey continued, but one could not miss out on the generosity of some of the passengers. The prayer warrior who sat eating boiled cassava and slurping water from a sachet extended a piece of cassava to me. I was already full, however. After he had eaten his cassava, the young man switched to mangoes. He was still enjoying his fleshy mangoes when his stomach started grumbling, 'Gverrrhh! Gverrhhh', attracting looks from many. He soon started pressing in the lower part of his stomach with his fingers and screaming.

"Driver, stop the car! Driver, stop moto, please! I take God beg you, driver!" He pleaded, twisting his buttocks. The driver continued speeding despite all the efforts from the man who was now stamping his feet on the carriage floor. Mass protests from other passengers eventually obliged the driver to pull over to the side of the road. The young man scrambled down the vehicle's walls and crawled across the edge of the road, seemingly unaware of the baskets of oranges lined along the road. He quickly plucked off the jeans with the two or three layers of boxer shorts he wore. His buttocks hung directly above the baskets of oranges, creating a tragicomic scene. I peeked across the road from the corner of my eye.

An impatient exodus of sheets of stool darted out, spraying the buckets of fruits below his buttocks. What could have attracted sympathy soon evolved into a comedy. The attention of the orange seller, who had been busy selling oranges to the passengers and oblivious of the goings-on at the edge of the road, was quickly drawn to the excreta eviction episode by the laughter that tumbled from our lips. The lady's reaction created more drama. She ran across the road and grabbed the edge of the man's shirt with one hand, the other hand clamped over her nostrils, tugging, lamenting.

"Nobi na bad luck be dis! Na only ma orange, you see? Ma enemy dem send you? Dis man get shame?" She lamented, staring at the man whose face looked like he was readying to sneeze. "Who send dis man to come spoil ma market na? Which god I offend? Mr. Man! Ya bill na 10,000 oya, when you finish excrete come settle ya bill! Shameless thing! Na which woman open leg born dis man sef?" The angry orange seller insisted the fellow must pay for messing up her oranges and containers.

It now made sense to me why men like wearing double boxer shorts. The young man used one of his boxer shorts to clean the mess on his legs and buttocks. When he pulled up his trousers, he squeezed out something from his pocket and extended to the orange seller. She released his shirt and plucked the money from the man's fingers, avoiding direct contact with his hands. We, too, roofed our nostrils with our fingers when the young man climbed back into the car. Even long after the excreta scene, an offensive stench kept invading us from the young man's body.

Our vehicle later rattled to a stop, awakening me from deep sleep. It was a checkpoint where two police officers requested everybody to climb down. They started asking questions, perhaps after realizing that most travellers were foreigners trying to impersonate natives of Bamfada. He ignored our evasive tactics of brushing our teeth and spoke to us in the native languages before switching back to Pidgin and the English language.

"Which country wuna de come from? And where wuna de go? Make I see your National Identity cards! What is your name? What is the name of your father? Which Local Government area do you come from? What is the name of your village? Who is the Governor of your State? And who is your Local Government Chairman?" The officer asked all the travellers, one after the other, to switch from Pidgin to English and back to their native language. It was a citizenship test, and as the first candidate, I failed it. The driver, the motor boy, and a few others answered the questions and were asked to return to the car. No one else responded to the officer when he switched from Hausa to Fulfulde and other native languages.

"Can I see your Yellow Card?" the officer continued, shuffling his eyes from Savage to Livinus and then to Atang before eventually turning to me. I made a mental note of how the roadside immigration post had acquired the status of an international vaccination centre.

"Each person must pay 2000. And anybody who does not have a Yellow Card must pay an additional 25,000. Arrange yourselves and cooperate!" the officer roared, darting his eyes from one passenger to the other. The uncompromising frown on his face meant that his word carried the weight of the law. All attempts from the travellers to negotiate for a downward review of the fees charged only received threats of detention and eventual deportation, a thing dreaded by all. We eventually collaborated, and the journey continued, passing through settlements and houses stretching unendingly across the contiguous towns. I might have slept for long until a hand prodded me on the shoulder to wake up. What greeted my ears were confused, deep sounds that hummed and murmured continuously across the vicinity like droning bees.

"What's happening?" I asked, wiping my eyes with the back of my hand, trying to figure out what caused the uproar. Savage was pointing to a widening stretch of darkly lit, gigantic buildings across the neighbourhood. It must be a big city, I told Savage, who nodded. It was getting dark, but I could see the open facial view of the city through the drizzle of light that filtered reluctantly and sparsely from the continued flow of buildings in the town. Something attracted my attention.

Endless queues of vehicles lay on both the left and the right sides of the highway as we clambered down. Travellers on transit were getting out of their vehicles and drifting into tiny groups on the shoulders of the road. Road pavements swarmed with people of different moods with silent expressions on their faces. Some stood, their mouths wide open, their upper eyebrows lifted. Some were thrusting the flat palms of their hands into the air.

"Why are vehicles parked along the road?" I stretched my mouth close to the ears of a young man standing by and asked.

"Dis Goffmen no di work well at all, at all. Na petrol don finish again so. Driver dem go add price for transport now! Price for food go double, de go up de double! Man go well for dis kontri so?" The young man responded in a lament while staring across the lanes of vehicles and shaking his head. He said that there was fuel scarcity and blamed it on poor leadership. He projected that the drivers and businesses would take advantage of the situation to increase the prices of goods and transport fares.

It wasn't only the stream of vehicles that raised fear in my heart. My ears droned, snorted and raged like a howling storm. It was like the snore of a thousand bees. My ears were harassed by heavy, irritating, continuous snorts everywhere I turned my head. You needed to place your ears on the mouth of someone to be able to hear what they were saying. You needed to shout for someone to listen to what you were saying. Everybody looked confused.

"What is happening here?" I asked Savage, whose upper lip was lifted as she peered into the road. Savage seemed to have no answer. With the right hand holding the wing of her ear in a lifted position, Savage stretched her head over her neck. She was listening to something, although there was raging noise everywhere as if a thousand pigs were snorting across the vicinity.

"What is snorting in the air like pigs?" I asked again. The man who had assumed that the long-drawn-out queues of vehicles across the road were due to fuel scarcity heard me asking the same question repeatedly. He looked at me again, stretched his mouth close to my ear, and said:

"You be stranger for this Kontri, abi? No doubt. Light no dey. Dis kontri de share light na for small spoon. Na generator we de use to get power... How you open mouth de look me that way? You niva use generator before? Your kontri no sabi generator? Or you want talk say your small-small kontri dem get light pass ma kontri?"

"Sorry, Sir. Do you mean people rely on generators for their power?" I asked, and the young man nodded, shaking his head.

A tiny crowd ahead of us was staring at a big signboard. We trekked further up to the towering signboard, where other travellers in transit stood, asking questions about the snoring in the air and holdups of cars and transport vehicles. I could read different moods of anxiety in the faces around me.

"Why are people crowding here?" I asked, prodding one man on his shoulder.

"Young lady, did I eat your school fees? Your own eyes do not see? Look at what is written on the signboard and stop asking questions!" The tired-looking traveller with eyes the size of a small orange responded in anger as if I was the cause of the obstruction in circulation. The disgruntled traveller had large eyeglasses and was right to say the answer to my question was on the signboard.

'Benga' was the name on the towering board. A small crowd had clustered at a kiosk near the towering signboard and scrambled for space as they skimmed through the papers dangling from the walls of the sales booth. The headlines on the front page of the Daily Voice, as the newspaper was called, read: "Bamfada Government Declares 30 Days Lockdown across the National Territory. Air, Sea and Land Travels Temporarily Suspended. No Movement of Persons, Animals, Goods, or Vehicles. National Borders are Closed. Only Vessels, Vehicles, Airplanes and Persons on Essential Duties are Authorized to Work." Our mouths hung open.

What had happened to oblige the travel restrictions because of which many cars and vehicles were already offloading? I shifted from the pavement and managed to lower my buttocks to a stone. I wiped my drenched face repeatedly with the back of my left hand. My entire body was simmering in that scorching heat of uncertainty.

I did not quite understand the implications of the 'lockdown' message on the papers and the signboard until I joined the crowd at the side of the road. A man, the height of a mushroom, who looked as if he was kneeling until you came closer to him, was in the middle of the crowd, holding a newspaper in his hand and speaking to the visibly weary and curious crowd of travellers.

"White man sickness don carry foot enter dis kontri! The name for the sickness na, emmmrr, Corona, yes, yes, COVID-19. Dem say the disease de spread like smoke from a big fire."

"Hei," the crowd screamed.

"Na radio and television and newspaper dem carry the news come reach we, no be from me dat news comot," he continued, pointing to the headlines on the newspaper he held in his hand, "Na through the nose and the mouth corona de pass enter body. And once corona enter ya body, you go join your ancestors."

The swelling crowd screamed. The man had now gathered more attention, being the first to break the news about corona virus. He swerved back and forth as he lectured on the strange illness. "As I am talking to you now, if somebody cough or sneeze for here now, and the air carry spit from dat person mouth and nose put for ya face, na corona you don carry."

This additional information threw everybody into a panic. People quickly lifted their hands to cover their mouths and noses while some drifted backward and away before the man could finish talking about behaviours that could promote the spread of the strange disease.

"What is happening here? Why are cars not circulating here?" One man asked, pointing to the vehicles parked haphazardly along the road.

"Government don declare emmrr, emmrr 'lockdown', yes, 'lockdown', for one moon. It is written in this newspaper in my hand. Lockdown mean say ehhrr no movement. No going to the market or shop or church or mosque. No travelling. So, if you take moto cross dat bridge, na government you de fight," the man said, pointing at the crossover some five hundred metres away. "Eherr, eherr, nothing for me?" The narrator asked, stretching out his hand. He wanted a tip, some financial reward or entitlement for explaining the puzzle. Some people squeezed money into his hands. During my stay in Benga, I noticed that nothing went for nothing. If anyone offered you help of any kind, they expected a tip. And if you didn't give it, they asked for it. But he was the bearer of unsettling news. Everyone looked frustrated after the explanation of lockdown measures. I didn't immediately know what to do or think about. The driver may have something to say, so I suggested that Savage invite the driver to talk to us on the way forward.

The driver came with the canoe man, and both looked confused at first. They spoke in hushed tones, and then the driver asked us to return to the vehicle and be ready to pass the night there. I felt weakened, robbed of strength and hope at his mention of sleeping in the vehicle. I started to blame myself for everything I was going through, asking myself why I had left home. My mind and my heart were once again in a mental battle. My heart urged me to persevere and continue the journey, but my mind wanted me to return to my country.

Was that what people who travel abroad to look for jobs went

through? Was it not better to go back home? But how? I preferred
to go back home. Then, negative thoughts invaded my mind as I sat
in our vehicle in the heart of Benga City. Savage, Livinus, Jawara,
Aboki, Atang, and others were there, but I was alone with my dark
thoughts.

13

Benga City

Benga town, or Central Area, was in the heart of Benga and was one of the biggest cities in Bamfada. It was a bustling town with imposing buildings and large roads accommodating six lanes of moving vehicles at a time. Benga attracted people and youths from across Bamfada and neighbouring countries. Its location along the TransAfrican Highway made it both a lure and, at the same time, a gateway to the land of the Whiteman. The displaced, street children, beggars, and job seekers from within and outside the borders of Bamfada found refuge there. Large markets, business centres, hotels, training grounds, and refugee and IDP accommodations were some of the facilities that had made Benga famous, its greatest population concentration being the Central Area. Its outskirts had extensive uncultivated fields with lush vegetation suitable for farming and grazing activities. Crop cultivation and cattle rearing were major occupations of its inhabitants. Given the mass flow of immigrants, job seekers, street children, farmers, and cattle movements in Benga, the entire city was always battling insurgencies and insecurity. Its location and attractions made it home to migrants, displaced persons, beggars, gangs, and humanitarian activities. There, our journey was aborted.

One noticeable attraction of Benga Central Area was an imposing bridge that spiralled overhead. The road cut through the bridge from below like a big U-shaped door. Under the bridge, five major roads from different cities across the country merged with the TransAfrican Highway. It created an intersection that was like a large ring with exit branches. The bridge itself had shelving rungs and cascaded over the ring from the left edge of the road to the right edge, linking the two neighbourhoods by staircase railings. The overhead bridge had supporting bars on the edges of the stairs that served as barriers. From where I stood, the bridge looked precisely like two large ladders standing apart, joined at the top by a two-lane road with bars at the opposite edges that served as a pedestrian crossing stairway. It helped pedestrians to cross or trek over from the left-handed neighbourhood of the central area to the opposite vicinity without being constrained by the protocols of heavy traffic.

On the rungs of the spiralling stairways, we passed the first two nights after escaping police checks on arriving in Benga. We weren't the only ones; the bridge was like a hive for the homeless. At any time of the day, the overhead bridge droned with sojourners, stranded passengers in transit, street children, beggars, hawkers, and the homeless in general. Permanent street dwellers had secured their spaces on the staircases or rungs with folded cartoons picked from rubbish heaps around the town. Breastfeeding mothers and their children sat on other rungs, their backs leaning on the bars. They jolted and drooled occasionally, singing and begging for alms. I remember seeing some of them stretching out deep plastic dishes to solicit arms. They looked drained. Others walked up and down, stalking others. It wasn't easy to get a space on the bridge the day we crept out from our vehicle at the sight of the police and mingled with the buzzing crowd on the staircases. A young boy of about ten years, as could be judged from his looks, smuggled his hand into the left pocket of my jeans. He would have snatched my telephone if Savage hadn't grabbed his sneaky fingers on time. It took us a long time to tear through the swarming staircase, trying to avoid stepping on sleeping figures and squeezing ourselves into our narrow spaces. A stout fellow with intimidating looks sold his space to us.

My two days on the rungs of the bridge were like a year of burrowing in a tight squeeze. I could hardly sleep. Urination and excretion were in plastic papers bought from hawkers. They called the papers mobile toilets, which were mainly sold to the people sleeping on the rungs of the bridge. We descended the stairs early in the morning and dropped the sealed plastic bags in a large container. Many of such heavy containers with wide gaping mouths stood at garbage collection points along the streets of Benga. Some urinated or excreted on the stairs. Although some women passed very early every morning and swept the rungs on the bridge and emptied waste in garbage vessels, the stuffy and pungent smell of urine that had drizzled on the floor of the staircase rungs, attracting flies, soon became unbearable for me. I started throwing up with violent movements inside my stomach. The invading smell of urine and excrement kept in sealed plastic bags and bottles kept my fingers clinging to my nostrils for two days. I badly needed a fresh environment. This, I told Savage, and she thought so too, but where were we to go?

After our brief encounter with the man who broke the news about the eruption of the COVID-19 pandemic, we moved back to sleep in our vehicle and waited for instructions from our driver. I sat on my bag and leaned against the bars around the bus wall, trying to catch some sleep, when a hand prodded me in the back. I turned to find out what the matter was.

"Get up, pick your bag immediately!" a voice screamed. Although the canoe man simply mouthed his words by opening and closing his lips, pointing to the police officers leaning on the windows of the vehicles parked along the road and talking to the passengers, we understood that trouble was at hand.

"Police! They are requesting the stranded passengers to present their national identity cards. I overheard them. I heard everything they said. I watched them put a metal chain around the wrists of one guy after checking the papers he presented. We are in trouble. We need to leave this place immediately!" The canoe man's message came through his teeth as he panted. The driver and the motor boy soon resurfaced with the same message. On the instruction of the canoe man, we sneaked away and mingled with the crowd on the stairways of the overhead bridge. It was better we hid where he and the driver could quickly locate us, the canoe man added, pointing to the bridge. Savage, Jawara, Atang, Aboki, Livinus, I, and others tore through the crowd and climbed over the bridge.

After realizing that the security officers had extended their search to the bridge, the driver and the canoe man later made suggestions. There was a moderate guest house in the neighbourhood. There were also the IDP and the refugee facilities, very far away from the central area. It was safer to move to a guest house and then relocate the following day to the IDP or refugee facility in the suburbs. We could mingle with the IDPs, and refugee camps which were safer locations for illegal immigrants. We would infiltrate the IDPs and the refugees until the travel ban was lifted. The canoe man pointed to the guest house across the vicinity and left with the driver and the motor boy. We moved to the inn and contributed money for a single room. That night was another harrowing experience.

Thick heat hugged me in its roasting grip immediately we stepped into the darkly lit room heavy with a musty smell. Although there were no lights, thin rays from moonlight trickled into the room through the glass window and the glass door that separated the balcony from the room. I immediately lowered my painful buttocks to the bed, wishing I could pluck off the wet clothes that desperately hugged my body. Drizzles of sweat glided down my face, and I decided to leave the bed and sit on the floor, my back propped against the wall. The men pulled off their wet shirts. It was so hot inside. I needed a shower to cool off. A bruised brown three-winged dish hung from the middle of the ceiling. A telephone set on the table close to the bed had a number on it. I reached out to the receiver and dialled the telephone line. It was dead. I decided to grope for the bathroom.

"There is no water. Not even a drop. I have been there," Savage informed me.

"We need to talk to the receptionist," I suggested. Savage and I went downstairs to see the receptionist.

"Good evening, sir; our room has no water and no electricity; it is very hot inside," I told the jovial young man who sat behind the raised table in a well-protected area.

"Eiyeah, sorry Ma, sorry oh. No vex, Ma, no vex oh. Since the day before yesterday, electric light is coming and going and coming and going and coming and going. Sorry Ma, no vex, sorry oh. But we have a generator, Ma. We power it when we have many customers. I will go behind now and power the generator. Ma, sorry, Ma. Water will come tomorrow, Ma; we had water today, Ma; they just cut it, Ma," the young man told us effusively.

The receptionist was so friendly, jovial, and welcoming that we soon forgot his duty as a service provider, which was to ensure customer satisfaction and not to tender effusive apologies for inadequate services.

Back in the room, we contributed money for water and biscuits and sent Livinus, who left and returned a few minutes later with the items. I sat on my right buttock, eating the biscuits and observing the suffocating room.

The single room had an extension hemmed round by raised protective bars. The bed and table took up the entire width of the room, leaving only a tiny sleeping space to accommodate two people on the floor. A television was propped against the wall, and the other facilities included a chair, a fixed telephone set, a tiny bathroom and a menu sheet lying on the table near a Bible and a Koran. The bed was just enough for one person. I was still thinking of how to arrange the sleeping positions when the assailing heat chased me out of the room to join my roommates leaning on the balcony's protectors.

It wasn't better outside. The wind drifting into the balcony from the open air was hot. Mosquitoes buzzed around, biting my ears, arms, and cheeks. I lowered my buttocks to the floor of the balcony, hoping to catch a nap. It was the first time I had the opportunity to sleep in a house since the journey to Amerika began. I battled with mosquitoes and assaulting heat throughout the night but also battled with thoughts. My money was almost finished. I could not afford another day in the inn. What I had left was only enough for biscuits. The driver had said he would get back to us when the travel ban was lifted. But when? There was no more money for accommodation, food, or water.

"My money is almost finished. I can't afford to spend another night in the hotel. What do we do while waiting for the travel ban to be lifted?" I wailed to my roommates as we lay squashed on the floor of the balcony. I wasn't the only one in those straits of financial starvation. We all resolved to return to the bridge and live there until the COVID-19 travel restriction was eased.

Back on the bridge, there were a few idlers, mostly women and children. The atmosphere around the Benga Central Area was panic and uncertainty. Apart from the lanes of cars along the highway, only a few newspaper vendors and immigration officials were seen around. The bridge that buzzed like a beehive just two days back was almost deserted. Shops were closed. Newspapers displayed on the kiosk carried different frightening news variants: "Wear Face Masks to Protect Yourself and Others against the Killer COVID-19 Pandemic; Maintain Social Distancing; The Mass Presence of Illegal Immigrants Sleeping on Benga Bridge and Around Threatens to Escalate into Insecurity in Benga; Immigration Determined to Track Down Illegal Immigrants in Benga; COVID-19 is Real; Go to the nearest COVID-Centre and Get Vaccinated."

On the first page of one of the newspapers, I read that an arrest of all the strangers and undocumented people in Benga had been launched. Security operatives had sprung into action, picking up and detaining people without proper identification papers. Those who couldn't speak any of their native languages and couldn't identify their states and local government areas were prime suspects.

The newspaper headlines and accompanying details made it clear that it was unsafe for us to nose around any longer. We decided to slip back into the neighbourhood to plan the next step. We were about one hundred metres into the quarter when we sighted immigration officials storming the premises of the guest house where we had spent the night. The entire neighbourhood was under siege. Immigration and police officers trickled into every side road in the quarter to fish out people without proper documentation.

In our attempt to escape, we stumbled on our driver and the motor boy. They had been looking for us everywhere. We had to escape straight to the facilities for the displaced; it was safer there. The driver, who spoke through his teeth to mask his words, said and led the way.

14

Benga Internally Displaced Persons' Camp

It took us a full day of trekking to get to the facility for the internally displaced persons. The canoe man led the way. Many of those with whom we had travelled were also fleeing in the same direction. You could tell from the panicking stares on our faces and the suspicious manner in which we weaved our way between jamming buildings that we were evading immigration officials. After meandering between buildings across the continuous neighbourhoods, we eventually emerged into a spreading bush of shrubs and grass scattered here and there.

The journey through the thickets was even more tedious. It felt as if we had been travelling for a week. We tore through hedges of tangled stems, falling and getting up. The soles of my feet developed raised, painful spots. I started feeling intense heat. Pain ripped through my lower stomach. Then, something started moving wildly inside my stomach, sending the pain roaming within me and multiplying its territories of incursion. Before I knew it, water broke loose from my lap, and my legs and fingers trembled violently. My feet suddenly became heavy, and I couldn't move a step any longer. I lowered my buttocks to the ground and saw trees spinning around with me.

Savage retreated and bent over me.

"Kila, is everything okay?" Asked Savage, begging the canoe

man not to flog me.

"I can't walk anymore. Allow me to die and be free from pain. Don't risk your life." I said, shooting surprised glances at the canoe man and wondering why it took him so long to flog me. Everyone looked surprised when the canoe man did not use his whip on me.

Savage lowered herself to the ground in front of me, too. I knew she wanted to carry me on her back. Atang ran back and lifted me to his back, helped by Livinus, Jawara and Aboki.

Lumps of blood ran down my legs immediately Atang lowered me to the grass in the IDP camp. I did not immediately understand that the content being smuggled out of my lap was the most cherished male seed Jeff had planted while we were still back in my country. I tried hard to open my eyes but saw nothing except an expanse of brown darkness. What happened to me immediately thereafter, I couldn't know. I blacked out and woke up later in an IDP settlement.

The flung settlement stood on a level land overlooking a flung village where the refugee camp was located on the outskirts of Benga. The spanning neighbourhood from Benga IDP camp revealed large stretches of farmlands and dotted houses across fields with a heavy presence of cattle that filed sluggishly, sometimes sitting in clusters like settlements of trees. The Benga IDP facility had two living quarters. The environment looked starved of attention. It was littered around and within the living quarters with dwarf mango trees whose stretched-out arms had retained the flair of a reddened skin disease. The men, young boys, and girls often escaped their tents and slept across the branches of trees during the sweltering heat and periods of floods.

The camp entrance was a towering iron gateway with an adjoining short building. A rectangular pigeon-hole on the wall permitted Dumi, the chief security officer, as he liked to be called, to attend to visitors and control movements in and out of the camp.

The entire settlement was a confused straddle of mainly humbling buildings and dust-coated canopies that squatted inside the high-walled fence. The canopies or tents were mainly made of heavy cloth shaped like huge anthills and served as shelters. The lower edges of the canopies were firmly pinned to the ground with cane stems and metal props.

The lower section of the yard served as the living quarters for the IDPs. Shy-looking tents and rectangular buildings resembling long coffins huddled across this area of the yard. A tent was a bloated, umbrella-shaped shelter firmly pitched into the ground with the aid of iron bars, its roof supported by poles. The interior walls were held upright and secure with interwoven ropes. Stones with flat surfaces, mainly used as chairs, were leaned against the corners in most tents. Each tent featured an open door so low that it compelled every tall person entering to adopt a hunching posture. About twenty IDPs lived in each tent, equipped with flat mattresses for beds. Three stones were placed in every corner of each tent for cooking activities. Cooking was often done with firewood outside the crowded tents, particularly during the dry season. Short sticks made from raffia bamboo were frequently tied to the inner walls of the tents using woven raffia ropes, intended for hanging dresses and bags. A large area, nearly the size of a football field, dotted with mango trees, separated the IDPs' living quarters from the Administrative Block.

The Administrative Block stood on a slightly raised surface overlooking the IDP living quarters. It had well-furnished empty apartments whose occupants were the Director General of the camp, or Chief, as he was often called, and his dog, Jimmy. Jimmy lived in a cage in a well-furnished room and was always released from his cage at night when everybody had slept. There was a kitchen to prepare Jimmy's food.

Adjacent to the IDP living quarters was a hall of cane sticks planted firmly into the earth, tacked around its plaited chest with raffia threads to hold them firmly together. It was roofed with cane stems and zinc. Inside the hall were long bamboo benches arranged in two rows. Here, all activities took place. Here, too, nurses or women would assist pregnant girls in delivering their babies. Volunteers from Benga came to distribute clothing items, food, vitamins, paracetamol, tablets, biscuits, sardines, bonbons, and other candies to pregnant girls. There were many women and girls in the camp, perhaps. It gave the impression of being a human incubator.

Representatives of government, international agencies, NGOs, individuals of goodwill, and voluntary instructors occasionally came from the city to share relief aid with the IDPs. Routinely, Dumi collected the visitors' identification papers and issued them badges to distinguish strangers or visitors from the IDPs. He only withdrew the badge and returned the identity card to the owner at the end of the visit.

There were conditions to fulfil to become an IDP. First, you registered as an IDP and received an identification number. Only then would you be free from being stalked and arrested by immigration officers. The most stringent condition to be raised to the envious rank of the IDP was proof of citizenship. You needed to prove you were a native of Benga or its neighbouring villages. This required the possession of a valid national identity card from Bamfada. Usually, the fingerprints and photographs of the new arrivals were collected and processed by assigned security agents. The ID cards were then processed and issued to the IDPs with identification numbers. This strict registration formality was intended to check people who committed crimes in the cities and took refuge in the camp, posing as IDPs.

I was unconscious when we arrived at the camp. I later learned that Dumi collected money to smuggle us into the camp, thanks to the intervention of the canoe man. I was told that we agreed to pay Dumi and the canoe man to get agents to fabricate IDP registration numbers for us.

I woke up from a hard-bony mattress in a crowded room where girls and women sat on mattresses across the floor. Immediately I opened my eyes, all eyes were on me. I felt strange and different, somewhat like a plant violently plucked by rainstorms from the burrowing arms of a moulded ridge and hurled into the bush to wither and die. Then, my eyes fell on Savage, and I knew I would have answers to some of the questions in my mind.

"Where am I?" I asked Savage, who was seated beside me.

"Kila can talk! Thank you, Jesus," Savage screamed with delight, a reaction that attracted the attention of many others inside and outside the hall.

"What happened to me? How-how-how did I get here?" I asked again, confused and a little frightened at the sight of a woman and young girls who were staring at me from adjoining urine-laden brown mattresses. They were rather convulsive as they scratched their armpits and bushy heads. I was still awaiting an answer to my question when Atang, Livinus, Jawara, Aboki, the canoe man, the driver, the motor boy, Dumi, and another man whom I later knew as Paapa, ran into the room and stood gazing at me.

"You were very sick and unconscious when we brought you here. Atang had to carry you on his back. You could not walk..."

Savage was still talking when Livinus impatiently cut in.

"Kila, you lost your baby..."

"W-w-w-w-w-what! How? Where? W-w-w-w-what happened...? What will I tell my husband?" I screamed, anguished and touched my flat stomach. I felt gnawing pain below my navel. I panicked.

"I want to see his grave; take me there," I said passionately, tears gushing from my eyes.

"You can't see him again. We buried him in the bush already. He was not breathing when Big Mami dug and pulled him out from your lap," Savage said, pointing to an elderly woman staring at me from a nearby bed space. "It wasn't easy."

"How will I break this rotten news to Jeff and Yaya? They think I am now in Amerika, working," I lamented inconsolably.

"Kila, stop crying, please. Jeff will understand. Be strong. You lost a lot of blood. Big Mami said you should not do any hard work when you get up. You need to take a long rest. Savage tried to console me, wiping the tears on my cheeks with the back of her hand. She then narrated the events before and after my miscarriage.

Tears kept rolling down my cheeks as I lamented in a muffled, weak voice. "My family sacrificed everything for me to travel to Amerika. We gave all the money we received, all our compensation package for Kaba to prepare my travel documents. We sold our only parcel of land, too. My family thinks I am now in Amerika working. My children are at home, waiting for money to return to school. How will Jeff survive the shock of my miscarriage? How will he even feel if he hears I am still on the way, hiding in another country in frustration with nothing certain now?"

Savage bent over and whispered in my ears.

"Kila, you don't have to do anything to attract attention. You shouldn't be seen or noticed. You shouldn't do anything that will make Chief notice you. We do not yet have the IDP Identification Cards. You will expose us if you continue to cry. If they know that we are not from here, they will inform Chief. And Chief will inform the police, and the police will arrest us. Herrh, before I forget, their Pidgin English is different from ours. If you speak in Pidgin, they will easily know you are not one of them. That is what Paapa said." Savage pointed to a tall, grey-haired man with a stomach the size of a large watermelon. He was leaning on a tree across the yard, flanked by the canoe man, the driver, Dumi, and the motor boy.

"Who's he?" I asked, staring at Paapa from the tent.

"We met him here. Maybe he is the caretaker or head boy; I don't really know. They call him Paapa or Boss, and he seems to wield incredible power. Everybody fears him and the other guy called Dumi. They say you must know Paapa and Dumi if you want to live here. Paapa, Dumi and the canoe man are always together. The canoe man told us that Paapa would arrange for our IDP and refugee identity cards to be made. Each person will have two different identity cards. But we will have to pay. This information must not go out. Chief should not know about our plans. Paapa said we will have a meeting later. I believe he has something to tell us," said Savage in a calm voice, at the same time stealing glances at Paapa across the yard.

Paapa exuded nothing but fear with his unmelodious or disproportionately red-brick skin colour. The skin on his face and his legs glowed like burning charcoals. It was as if he always rubbed his face and legs with red palm oil. The knuckles of his fingers looked like the skin on a roasted overripe plantain. Greenish stretch marks the size of ginger roots lay on his fleshy arms around the upper part of the limb. He would pull forward his face cap to cover his forehead. Different kinds of tattoos and symbols, such as the scorpion and the millipede, smeared his arms and the neck and earrings dangled from his ears. The jeans trousers he wore hung below his buttocks with see-through, threadbare patches on the knees and the lap areas.

What Savage had just said about Paapa was evident in his physical appearance. I resolved to stop crying and keep my emotions in check. I was not sure of what to expect. I was like an uprooted forest tree that began a new life in a farmland where the passing floods deposited it.

Hunger soon swayed my attention from Paapa, the pain of losing an advanced pregnancy, and my fear of the immigration police to a pot that sat on three stones at one corner of the tent. "What are they cooking?" I wondered, fixated on the pot, which I could see through a reek of ashes rising and falling everywhere in the room.

A tiny girl with a mushroom-shaped head resembling a tangled tree top squatted on her heels close to the fireside. She scratched her head with her entire body dancing to the rhythm while trying to sprinkle some white powder on the green mangoes inside the pot. The pot gurgled like quiet waters flowing over rocks. "How could someone be boiling mangoes? Do people eat boiled mangoes?" I asked, my eyes travelling back and forth from the pot to Savage.

Big Mami definitely conjectured from my looks and questions that I wasn't used to the habit of boiling fruits.

"When you cook mango, she de ripe quick. Go collect mango from Baki give ya sista make she chop." Big Mami explained and requested Savage to help collect some mangoes from the girl by the fireside. Savage returned with two boiled mangoes.

Not only was I hungry, but my throat was also too dry. I murmured a 'thank you' to Big Mami and Savage and ate the huge mangoes with their skins as I saw others doing. It had no taste, just sticky-soft in my mouth, but it was something.

Another lanky girl, looking much younger than Baki and wearing a see-through short gown that revealed bloodstains on her fatigued buttocks, joined Baki and the other girls at the hearth. Her eyes trailed Baki's fingers to the beetles wiggling on the glowing coal. From Big Mami, I learned that her name was Kaki. A scar the size of a millipede was on her forehead. The girls soon moved over to sit on the floor. Big Mami introduced Baki and Kaki as her daughters.

15

The Lice-Hunting Expedition

I didn't know the human body could be a fertile ground for breeding lice until I met Baki, Kaki, Big Mami, and the other IDPs. Baki and Kaki, along with a group of girls, joined us on the floor. Five other skinny young girls, later identified as Kuta, Kaka, Tapu, and Bida — the first three with babies strapped to their backs — became part of the heap of lice hunters, bending over one another like a cluster of plantain stems. The girls took several postures: some stood bent over, some were seated, and some squatted on their heels. I had never before witnessed such a lice-hunting expedition. Their fingers clawed tirelessly through the tiny bushes of hair that resembled treetops, weeding out and crushing the predators between their nails. My ears tingled continuously at the short, sharp snaps of fingers as the lice hunters harvested and crushed the pests. Big Mami staggered to her feet and drooped toward the ground like a bent stick on an animal track that holds the trap for catching 'giant rats.' She scratched her back and neckline with the edge of a short stick, stretched the stick along with a shredded cloth to Kaki, pulled her bra from a short stick jutting from the see-through wall, and sat down on the adjacent mat.

I could see tiny ridges of misery and frustration mapped on Big Mami's forehead as she stared at flies taking off and landing on Kaki's backside.

"Poor thing!" I mused, staring at the area on Kaki's backside with the shape of the map of Africa. Kaki looked shy as she scratched her bushy hair, armpits, and the region below her navel with the claws of her nails, twitching in feverishly thrusting gestures. Then she shifted her buttocks and rested her bushy head across the lap of Big Mami. Big Mami was weeding lice from her brown bra, which looked like the intestines of a fowl, and crushing noisily between her blood-stained fingernails. Once in a while, she sprinkled water on the forehead of a baby lying by, hissing like a snake.

"Dada," said Kaki softly to Big Mami, lifting the woman's hand to her head. Nobody needed to tell me it was an invitation to weed lice from the forest of hair on her head. The top edges of Kaki's hair were clustered with tiny white eggs as if white powder obtained by grinding dried corn had been poured on them. Big Mami instantly abandoned her bra to pay attention to Kaki. From time to time, she turned and patted the baby and sprinkled more water on its forehead.

Everybody was busy with their different prey-hunting specializations. One girl was skimming the dresses' armpits, meshed like a lice hive. Another lady was digging out jiggers from the skins and feet of younger ones. Within a few minutes, the floor was teeming with jiggers and lice hunters. One after the other, my eyes fell on their bloody nails, as long as duck beaks, crushing lice. You could tell from the collective hunt that the hunters were passing the message, 'trespassers would be persecuted,' to other potential predators.

Kaki's head and pubic regions seemed to be the most heavily invaded by lice-breeding hatcheries, making me wonder whether her blood was more delicious to the assailants than that of others. The cry of the baby she had just strapped to her back did not distract her or her mother from tearing through the tangled hairs to harvest those healthy ash-coloured insects hiving in the hairlines. Kaki's feet, too, were heavily colonised by jiggers, leaving no empty spaces. Jiggers had burrowed on her soles and looked inside the skin like seeds growing on corn cobs. Kaki wiped the sweat from her cheeks as she dug out jiggers from the soles of her feet with a sharpened stick. Once in a while, she slotted her fingers into her lap or armpits and scrubbed noisily like someone grating cassava. I remember seeing lice slithering back and forth on her neckline.

Kaki's head was not the only succulent part of her body that had suffered dense invasion and occupation by settlements of lice, as her armpits and soles were also victims of unwarranted annexation. Each time she lifted her arm, I saw fledglings of lice clutching desperately at the tiny bush under her armpit. It was pathetic to watch her vigorously scratching her armpits and hairlines, jerking her body but partially closing her eyes as if she were enjoying the tingle act. My sympathy shifted to Baki rummaging for lice in her bra. The breast pads looked exactly like mauled fresh beef recovered from the fangs of a hungry dog. My mouth drooled with bitterness as I watched the lice-rummaging expedition on the human body.

Everything around me seemed strange. Big Mami suddenly carried the hissing baby lying on the mattress and asked Kaki, whom I was told was the baby's mother, to go out to the bush and dig beetles and crickets. Her action was unexpected and invited questions.

"Why did Big Mami suddenly ask Kaki to withdraw?" I pondered, staring at the baby crying, its chest rising and falling.

Big Mami pulled up the lower part of the loose blouse she was wearing and stuffed the edges under her armpit, leaving exposed, withered, shy breasts plunging reluctantly from the walls of her chest. She then tried to squeeze the nipple of her breast into the baby's gaping lips. Nothing came out from the breasts, not even a drop after several attempts. Then, she sat back and stared emptily across the room.

I was concerned about the baby's sudden restlessness. My eyes rolled from the brown hair scattered over the baby's massive head to its stomach, which looked like a gigantic pumpkin fruit pushing up from a creeping stem. A deep furrow separated his chest in the middle. Big Mami noticed I was stealing sympathetic glances at the baby's eyes, which were turning white.

"Pikin for ma pikin get plenti sick for *sikin*," she lamented about her grandson's deteriorating condition, adding that she had informed

Dumi to send word to Chief. Chief had called a medical doctor from town to attend to the sick child. The distant look on her face told of how Big Mami was worried and frustrated by the child's declining health.

"Big Mami, take heart; your grandson will be fine very soon," I consoled her, not knowing what else to say or do.

Big Mami was determined to save her baby. She went out and returned with some fresh leaves, which she rubbed between her palms and squeezed into the child's mouth. The liquid drooled from the edges of the child's gaping mouth.

"Pfeeeeeeeeee! Pfeeeee!" The liquid waste exited in hurls from the boy's anus. Big Mami sat back, shook her head repeatedly and sighed. My eyes trailed her stretched-out hand to the corner of the hut, where it dug a chunk of soil. She then sprinkled the ground on the slimy excrement.

A massive hairy beetle clothed in a light cocoon jacket darted from where Big Mami had dug the ground. It had already shed off its old skin and was now growing a new one. The transforming beetle was partly wounded on its fluffy tail, which could be seen shedding tiny drops of creepy liquid. I shrugged when Baki, noticing the crawly, immediately dived across the floor and grabbed it from ending in the hands of another girl who had also made for the grabs. I watched the poor girl run to the fireside to roast the beetle before my attention returned to Big Mami and her sick baby. I was sorry and worried that I couldn't help.

"Is there a hospital here? What do people do when they fall sick?" I asked.

"I was told that they have a visiting doctor," Savage said.

As we sat waiting for the doctor, I had the opportunity to learn more about Big Mami by listening to her pathetic story.

What had Big Mami not seen? Which season had come and gone without her burying a child? Which of the gods did she offend? She was the oldest of the IDPs lifted from the streets by the government and brought to the refugee camp from where she later moved to the

Benga IDP settlement because of its rehabilitation facilities.

"Big Mami, where is your house? Where is the father of your children?" I interrupted. Big Mami's response was heartrending.

She was only seven years old when she was wrenched from her mother's arms and brought to Benga to babysit for Big Madame and make money for her school needs. When they arrived in Benga, Big Madame changed her name. She was kept in a house surrounded by high walls. They were prohibited from going out, making friends, or speaking to anybody. It was a home where children who had lost their parents were adopted and raised, Big Madame told her. She shared a room the size of a courtyard with many young girls, aged between ten and fifteen years. There were about twenty young girls and two men whose job was to sleep with the girls and impregnate them. Big Madame had wild dogs. They would attack and maul anybody who attempted to escape.

She slept with men every night. She felt as if pepper had been smeared into her private parts. Her underbelly had been hurting ever since she started sleeping with the men. She had to do what they said to avoid being beaten and starved to death by Big Madame. She had her first child when she was just twelve. She gave birth to four children, but her Madame sold them. She became sick and tired of sleeping with men. She made friends with the gateman, who was also caring for Big Madame's dogs. It was a strategy. She would offer to wash his clothes and to also sleep with him. The gate man trusted her and allowed her to give the dogs food and play with them. One night, it rained heavily. It was so dark and stormy that one could not see anything. She sneaked out of the room, chained up the dogs in the backyard, climbed the high wall, hurled herself over the iron bars, and ran as far as her legs could carry her. She started sleeping in an unfinished building and eating from dump sites. One day, officers chased a thief into the building, stumbled on her, and rescued her. She told them her story and everything she knew about Big Madame, and they promised to arrest her. As Big Mami told me, she had lived in the camp since she was picked up from the streets.

She was named Big Mami because she started helping women and young girls during delivery. She gave birth to thirteen children in the camp. Four of her children were once kidnapped alongside many others by unidentified gunmen while they played across the field in the neighbourhood. Some individuals and groups that parade themselves as 'the voice of the voiceless' have since been urging the government to bring back Big Mami's children. The same 'voice of the voiceless' had been using her misfortune to source funds from big groups. She had since vowed to remain in the IDP camp until her children were rescued and brought back to her.

Big Mami wept profusely as she narrated her story, causing Savage and I to shed tears.

"Baki and Kaki told me that Madame Nurse offered to take them to her house so that they can live with her and attend school and you refused. Big Mami, kindly allow the woman to help your daughters, they need a better life." Savage suggested. Big Mami stared vacantly across the room and answered.

"Na home we need, nobi house."

She needed a home and not a house. Big Mami boldly reiterated, apparently unapologetic.

"Would you like to go back to your country and reunite with your family if given the opportunity?" I asked Big Mami, and she nodded. She consented but tried to explain the reason she had kept the same thought in temporary detention.

Who would willingly abandon the bed to sleep under the bed? Who would leave their compound to burrow into tracks and holes like a cricket that heard the scream of a hawk? Big Mami had always felt like a plant pulled up by the roots and hurled to the bush by floods. She needed to go back to her motherland. She needed to identify with someone. She needed to know her family tree. Her children, too, needed to know where their mother came from. They had been asking questions about their grandmother and grandfather. Her failure to answer those questions left them feeling that she was a ghost in its afterlife. She needed someone to love her and her children.

Nobody deserves to grow up without a father figure, mother, and family. But tracing her roots was like tracing the source of a river. She left her single mother when she was only seven or eight years old and she had now grown grey hair. She would not know the way back to her country. She would miss her way to her mother's village. Nobody would even recognise her, and she wouldn't recognise anybody. The only thing she remembered about her mother and her last moments with her was that she bought her a new dress and asked her to follow Big Madame to a distant land to babysit her children and make big money from her babysitting job. Besides, she couldn't afford the transport fare to her country.

My eyes wobbled with tears as we listened to the pathetic story. Big Mami was still lamenting, weeping and sprinkling water on the sick child when suddenly, Dumi rushed in, accompanied by a man and a lady in white garments. The man asked everyone, except Big Mami and his companion, to step outside. It must be the doctor, I judged.

"Big Mami, what is happening with your child? How the sick start, and when?" I could hear the doctor's voice right from the yard. He wanted to know the symptoms and duration.

"Since the day before yesterday, him body de burn like fire. If small food manage enter for him belly, shit go de rush like tap water. You go think say somebody de chase de shit."

I could hear Big Mami explaining the duration of the illness and the frequent evacuation of watery stools each time she fed the baby. I was still peering into the hut and hoping that the doctor would save the sick child when a prolonged scream rose from the hut. It was the voice of Big Mami. I immediately knew she had lost the baby even before the doctor and his companion came out of the tent, carrying him, well-wrapped in a loincloth. They handed the parcel to Dumi, who, holding a shovel, immediately burrowed into the bush in the vicinity.

Kaki, Baki and Big Mami were inconsolable, screaming, lamenting and rolling across the floor. Kaki had lost another son again;

Big Mami kept lamenting. We gathered around Big Mami and her daughters, crying and offering consoling words. I later asked who fathered the deceased child, and Kaki whispered that it was both Paapa and Dumi.

Immediately after the doctor distributed tablets to the IDPs, which he said were anti-cholera drugs, and left, Madame Nurse came around.

16

Madame Nurse

I had heard many stories about Madame Nurse even before I met her. She was a human rights activist and founder of the NGO 'Feed the Needy' whose activities included philanthropy and the empowerment of women and girl children. It was said that the beneficiaries of her charity project were the IDPs and the refugees who lived in tents across the fields bordering the IDP camp, as well as those in the government primary school in the neighbouring village.

I still remember the day Auntie, as she loved to be called, visited the IDPs with food items. She came with a man called Gari, who was holding a big camera. Auntie and Gari wore face masks, hand gloves, rain boots and thick, long trousers. In the twinkle of an eye, a jubilant crowd had gathered around Auntie and her car even before Dumi was directed to offload bags of food items from the car. Savage and I had discussed the security implications of being seen around or being identified as undocumented migrants, and so we lowered our heads and bodies down in the crowd to avoid being noticed.

The visit started with a photo shoot, the yard swarming with visibly excited IDPs. Savage, Jawara, Aboki, Atang, the driver, the motor boy, and I swiftly squatted in the crowd so that the cameraman would not capture our faces when taking photos of the IDPs. From this position, I followed the event with keen attention.

A tiny mountain of food items flanked with empty crates and

cartoons was erected in the middle of the yard, and a basket stuffed with wads of bulging brown envelopes stood before it. The IDPs stood behind the gifts. Standing in the front row, Auntie stretched out her hand, holding wads of money from the edge. Following her instructions, Dumi, Sariki, Kaki, and Baki held the cash from the opposite edges.

"Laugh! Lift up your hands! Smile! I need to see your 32 teeth! Picture!" Gari took different positions as he took pictures of the IPDs clustering around Auntie, smiling and reaching out to touch the money. Big Mami, however, hid her face from the camera as she lifted her hands to her face and bent her head over.

"Kila, they have started sharing rice," said Savage, pointing to Auntie. She was scooping rice from a bag with a small round plastic dish and distributing it while posing for pictures.

"We need to collect our own share," I said.

"We can't go there. We shouldn't be seen around. We don't have IDP identity cards." Savage reminded, with frustration on her face. Atang, Livinus, Jawara, Aboki, the driver, canoe man, motor boy and a few others had wriggled through the swarming crowd, stretching up their necks, each like a snake emerging and disappearing into a hole. I could see the frustration in their pale faces each time our peeps bumped into each other.

"This is the second time food is shared, and we can't even get crumbs. We need to do something," Livinus lamented. He was right. I felt frustrated watching others collect food but unable to go for mine. I felt like a prisoner, the only difference being I wasn't in chains.

My eyes left Livinus, who was now making suggestions for a meeting, and trailed Auntie and Gari, tearing through the swelling crowd across the yard, taking photos with the same wads of money and the sealed envelopes. My intestines grumbled repeatedly. I was starving, but going to ask for food was like declaring myself a thief before the magistrate. At the end of the visit, the visitors sprayed what looked like hand sanitisers from a small bottle into their palms and all over their bodies and left.

Savage and I picked a few grains of rice that spilled out during the sharing and returned to the hut. Questions kept ringing in my mind:

"Why had Big Mami been hiding her face from the camera? What was inside the heavy envelopes? And why was the money the visitors held out not shared with the IDPs at the end of the photo-taking session?" I resolved to dig out the truth from Big Mami.

"Big Mami, you hid your face from the camera; you covered your face with your hands. Don't you like your face to appear in the picture?"

"Kila, na we *futu* Auntie de use de collect big-big money from *gomen* and Whiteman. But na for she pocket dat money de enter. Na we be the farm where she de harvest money," Big Mami whispered and pouted her lips. I understood her and felt bad when she disclosed that Auntie was using their photos to beg for money and humanitarian assistance from the government, international donors and prominent associations, which often ended up in her pockets. After going round and round, I finally gathered the courage to beg for food.

"Big Mami, Savage and I are very hungry. Please, give us rice to cook."

"Kila, Auntie just share rice na, why you never collect you own?" She asked, surprised.

"Savage and I…, emmrr, we came late," I struggled to fabricate a response.

"Kila, which kontri you come from? Which kontri dem born you?" Big Mami pried, throwing a suspicious stare at me.

Whatever prompted the question of my nationality, I did not know. It came as a surprise to us, causing Savage and I to exchange cautionary glances. I was actually shocked when she asked about my country of origin. "How does Big Mami know I am not from here?" I mused. I wanted to answer her question, but what Savage had said about the need to keep my identity a secret instantly rang in my head. "Kila, you don't have to do anything to attract attention… If they know that we are not from here, they will inform Chief. And Chief will inform the police, and the police will arrest us."

"Na only name for ya kontri you de still *find am* so?" Asked Big Mami this time, shaking her head. "You de answer Kila. You don't speak like us. Which one be your kontri? Na river you be?" Big Mami dug on, singling out my name and accent for analysis as unfamiliar and strange to the ways of her host country. Baki instantly confirmed this observation with repeated nods.

"Weti be the meaning of Kila?" Asked Baki after concurring with Big Mami and her sister that I spoke English with an unfamiliar accent. Savage must have noticed from how I was blushing, that I was going to fail the citizenship test as she snappishly cut in to answer some of the questions.

"We went to school in the city, emmr, the English that city people speak is different from the English that is spoken in the village..."

I nodded as Savage tried to justify our unfamiliar accent.

"People who grow up in the city speak differently."

Savage's explanation that exposure was the reason for our unfamiliar accent did not stop Big Mami and Baki from further embarrassing questions.

"If na for city school them train you, and if na city English you de speak, then weti bring you for this bush? Nobi gomen talk say when you go school learn book, you go get better job? No be Chief join mop with gomen tell we say na people weh go school go get job? How man go go school turn beggar like we where we never go school?" Big Mami shakes her head and continues. "Weti you carry city book come dey do for village? Nobi for city them di find work? Or your *satifiket* and city English no reach level for find work for city?" Big Mami was unstoppable, her stares shuffling from Savage to my humbled face. You could infer from her questioning stares and gestures that Big Mami was suspicious, as she pouted and then raised and lowered her shoulders.

I stared shyly across the room, feeling humiliated by Big Mami's critical questions.

Despite the pressure and the fear now rising in me following this somewhat disguised citizenship test, it all ended well. We cooked the little rice Big Mami gave us from her limited stock and ate before thick darkness covered the room.

The night turned out to be the longest ever for me. The thoughts of living in hiding, begging, uncertain, with no food and no idea what would happen next, crawled in and ruffled my mind as I stared at the moonlight streaking across the room through the gaping door. At this point of desperation, my mind recalled my family. I started thinking about my children. Then, a strange feeling visited me. My nipples suddenly tightened up and stood straight. I could feel beads of tears slithering down the walls of my chest. I pulled up my blouse to examine my breasts. They were teary, with water dripping from the teats as if they were weeping. I immediately recalled what Yaya had told me about the language of the breasts. I was missing my children. What was I to do now? I pondered as tears ran down my cheeks. An idea suddenly came to my mind.

"I need to recharge my telephone. It is in my bag. I need to upload pictures from my telephone and send to Jeff. I can't do this anymore! My children need to see me. My family is worried the same way that I am worried. My children will be calm if they see my pictures. But, but ... would it not break their hearts if they saw me in this present condition, looking shabby? Jeff will ask about the baby. What do I do now?" I was still knee-deep in thoughts when birds began to chirp from the trees across the yard.

The following day was meeting day. We had been told the IDPs would meet with Chief at nine in the morning. It was unsafe to nose around when Chief's car was parked in the yard. Savage and I decided to withdraw from our room before the arrival of Chief. We moved to sit under the trees across the field until Chief could be seen driving out of the camp. Livinus, Atang, Jawara, and Aboki were already there before we arrived. Familiar faces with whom we had travelled across the desert were also hanging around.

It was an opportunity for Livinus, Atang, Jawara, Aboki, Savage and I to hold our own meeting. The issue of identification cards was the main menu on our discussion table. We could not continue begging for food from people who didn't even have enough. We needed the IDP identification cards to move about freely and collect our food whenever it was brought to the camp.

"We are finished!" Atang, who had been skimming through the headlines of *The Voice of the Voiceless* newspaper, open-mouthed, suddenly screamed, sweating.

After reading it, Chief had dropped the newspaper on the table in front of the administrative block. Atang had found it when he, Livinus, and the motor boy crept into the administrative area the previous night to steal the dog's food. After luring the dog off the yard and strangling it, they wrapped the food in the newspaper and took it away. They didn't know its content until now. After explaining how he found the newspaper, Atang read us the headlines on the paper's front page.

"COVID-19 on a rampage: Respect safety measures; Illegal Immigrants Infiltrate Benga IDP and refugee facilities; police launch mass manhunt for travellers on transit and all other undocumented persons in Benga; Travel Ban imposed in Benga for three months; Benga inhabitants urged to inform police of any strange persons or suspicious movements in their community; A hoard of arms and ammunitions discovered inside a coffin in a vehicle apparently abandoned in the heart of Benga City by Travellers on Transit; Arm dealers and masterminds behind the recent Farmers-Herders violence infiltrate Benga community; A handsome financial reward awaits anyone with relevant information that can lead to the arrest of the suspected killer gunmen and undocumented persons in Benga City; Bamfada Government bans Inter-State travels and orders border-closure for three months…"

The legs of my heart galloped in a loud stampede at three particular headlines: "Illegal Immigrants Infiltrate Benga IDP and Refugee Facilities," "Bamfada Government Bans Inter-State Travels and Orders border-closure for Three Months," "Police launch mass manhunt for Travellers on Transit and all other undocumented persons in Benga."

For almost five minutes, none of us uttered a word. Only the pounding of hearts inside our chest cavities could be heard. It was as if a building was collapsing nearby. We gawked expressionlessly across the fields.

"What do we do?" Savage asked, breaking the protracted silence.

"We need the IDP identification cards. That's the only way we can evade arrest," I said, and others nodded their consent.

"Kila is right. We need to meet urgently with Paapa, Dumi, Sarikin, and the canoe man. There's nothing we can do without them." Atang completed our thoughts.

17

The Meeting with Paapa

Chief had just concluded the meeting with the IDPs to discuss the COVID-19 safety measures; however, because we lacked IDP identification cards, we did not attend. Dumi served as our eyes and ears at the meeting. As usual, we had retreated into the heart of the bush whenever we wanted to avoid being seen by Chief or other visitors to the camp.

We were still yawning and hiding in the bush, awaiting nightfall to return to the camp. We had agreed to hold an urgent meeting at night. News had leaked that the police were searching and arresting illegal occupants in the camp, so we urgently wanted to arrange for our IDP identification cards.

Jawara came up with a suggestion which replicated our thoughts. Given the ease and flexibility with which he skilfully controlled his mushroom-size body and would fold it into any crippled shape or weave in and out of a gathering unnoticed, Livinus was assigned to run undercover errands for us. He would sneak into the huts to inform Paapa, Dumi, and the canoe man that we were in the bush and would only join them for an urgent meeting at night. Livinus met them on the way, and they had urgent information for us. They soon joined us under the mango tree where we sat.

Everybody was quiet when Dumi, Paapa, and the canoe man drifted in a group, spoke in hushed tones and then returned to join us under the tree. Paapa pulled a lighter from his pocket and lit one end of the wrap, about the length and size of a healthy thumb, and began to smoke, releasing sheets of snaking smoke into the air. Dumi was the first to speak, and all eyes turned to him as he dipped a hand into the hollow pocket of his long brown robe, looked around as if to be sure he had everybody's attention and started.

"This talk weh I bring am na for travellers without papers, wuna get doki?"

"No o, gate man," we chorused.

"My nim is not gate man! Na my sekwond, Sarikin and Gimba Musa, de answer gate man. I am the Chief Sikiriti Officer Dumi. After Chief na me. So, if you have problem, na me you go see first, before I go see Chief. So, you must join Chief Sikiriti or Sir to my nim before you talk to me!" Dumi wore a stern look as he spoke.

"Sorry, Sir," I apologised.

After bragging about his position in the administrative command ladder and additionally introducing Paapa, whom he called boss, and the canoe man as the key persons we needed to work with, Dumi reminded us of just what we didn't want to hear.

"This message is coming from the mouth of Chief, and she deh important. So, open your ears. The White man sickness has visited our land. And the nim of dat sickness is COVID-19. If COVID-19 catch you, na your nose and your mouth she de first enter. But you can hide from COVID-19 if you follow order from gofmen. If person *sinees mchia, mchia* for your face," (he tried to imitate the sneezing sound as he spoke,) "COVID-19 will come out from dat *person* nose and enter your own nose and mouth. After two weeks, you go sleep for grave. But if you lock your nose and mouth with face mask, COVID-19 no go see road for take enter your body." He held out a sample face mask which Chief had given him for demonstration. "Man weh de hear word no go die like fly weh follow die body enter grave! This one now na sweet news. Chief go share rice the day after tomorrow."

The most heart-shredding part of the report was when Dumi

confirmed that the government had issued a travel ban for three months, adding that there would be an extension, depending on the rate of the spread and the response to the thousands of COVID-19 cases already recorded across the country. My feet went cold, and my heart missed several beats when he said immigration police had planned to search the Benga IDP camp following reports about the massive presence of criminals and also foreigners whose journeys were stalled by COVID-19 in the camp. Silence followed Dumi's speech, which reminded us of what we hated to hear at that moment. With the wrapped bundle still stuffed into his mouth and his eyes partially closed, Paapa released billows of smoke and turned to speak to us.

"You have heard the message from Chief. You can now tell us why you sent Livinus to us."

"We want IDP cards. We cannot collect food without the cards. We have been picking snails from the bushes around and digging crickets from cow dung, but the snails and crickets are getting scarce now. The grass is drying up, and cows are moving to places with feed."

Everybody quickly nodded in consent immediately I mentioned the disturbing issues of identity cards, security, and scarcity of snails and crickets.

The canoe man looked worried. He was always lamenting about his goods. He had invested a lot in the business and was afraid he would not be able to recover the money he had put in. His boss was expecting the goods, he had said, urging us to hurry and get identity cards.

"Paapa, my boss is waiting for me with his goods intact," the canoe man said, looking worried.

Whatever the canoe man meant, I didn't understand, but he had always talked about his goods as he just did now, staring at Paapa, who immediately responded.

"You need food. You need identity cards. You have clothes and shoes. You have beautiful babes. You have what I like. I have what you like. You know what to do." Paapa paused and continued.

"The registration cards are paid with cash. Food can be negoti-ated. But not the identity cards. The identity cards need stamps and signatures. The cost of a single identity card is 50k," he finalised, staring at us.

"Paapa, we are ready to do anything to get the IDP cards," Atang said, and we nodded assent.

"When am I expecting the money?" Asked Paapa.

Paapa might have noticed that our facial expressions suddenly changed, and he immediately asked for the money to be paid as a precondition to establish our IDP identity cards.

"I am a good rider. I can creep. I climb mountains," he said, lifting and lowering his buttocks, an indecent body language sign that immediately suggested the meaning symbolised by the action. "I also accept other forms of payment. Anything apart from money would just be considered as part payment." Stares of disappointment shrouded our faces. I immediately knew I wasn't safe around Paapa. Not knowing what to say and afraid to say anything that may be construed as a willingness to collaborate in matters relating to the hunger of the loins, I simply dropped my head. I sat thinking about how we would raise the money for our identity cards. A thought suddenly came to my mind.

"Paapa, we are willing to do farming work in the neighbour-hoods to raise the money; we can farm. I can mould bricks, yes, yes, we used to do it when we were in primary school." Savage, Jawara, Aboki, Atang and Livinus swiftly moved their heads up and down with excitement as I suggested the options to Paapa. Dumi and Musa agreed they would contact some women in neighbouring villages to negotiate farm work for us, and Paapa continued.

"Now, listen very well. Before I do the identity cards, you need to take new names. The police can easily know your country of origin and even repatriate you if you keep your real name. But you must be smart. Don't wait until you are caught before you start looking for answers. Stock your head with ready-made answers, *ohh*! Speculate the police and get your answers in stock before they surprise you! If you are caught with a different name, tell them that your mother is from here and your father is from another country. If you can learn to speak through your nose, you are safe. You can even say you are a Black Amerikan and would want to be sent back to Amerika. This lecture costs 500k!" Paapa said, adding that his services had yet to be costed out. We nodded consent. It was now our turn to react.

Savage reminded everyone that we had no food, and we made an urgent decision about it. Dumi rushed to the camp and brought our bags. I gave my shoes, wig and a few clothes to Paapa and Dumi in exchange for rice, which I collected later. My friends did the same, parting with their jeans trousers, jackets and some shirts. Atang had lost his luggage in the sea when our boat capsized. He wasn't really bothered as we agreed to share our food with him.

The canoe man seemed to be more familiar with issues relating to living as a refugee. On his suggestions, triggered by news about the police search, Paapa agreed we needed a Plan B.

"You need refugee cards too. I prefer we also do refugee cards for you. It is easier to get it done than to do the IDP card. Once you get your refugee card, you can go anywhere, and the police will not harass you. You can collect food whenever they share it. You just need to show your card. I can do the card for you once your money is ready. That's my job. I have been doing that for years. I don't work alone. That's what you need to know. And as I am talking to you now, somebody has asked me to bring strangers for registration even if they are not refugees. Once the cards are ready, you can move to the refugee camp. That place is safer for you." This is the option we adopted.

No service was rendered for free. Whenever somebody advised you on how to evade the police, they stared into your face, expecting a reward. We gave Dumi extra clothes, but that was for a reason. Dumi would inform us whenever the police came to the IDP camp so that we could take refuge in the bush. He was from the same village as the Chief, and they spoke the same language. Chief trusted him most, and he would always inform him about the camp's programme of events well ahead of time.

The face of the sun had drifted past the middle of the sky, staring down at my right shoulder, in the process, becoming too hot. Even the dress I wore clutched desperately onto my skin and dripped from the edges with water. Paapa closed the meeting and left alongside Dumi, the canoe man, and the motor boy. We sat back when the others got up and started walking away towards the camp.

"Chief is returning to town," Savage suddenly said, pointing to Chief's car across the field, driving off. At that, we got up with excitement and returned to the camp.

18

The Invasion of Baki

It was far too hot, the sun positioned directly overhead in the sky. Savage and I climbed up and straddled the branches of a mango tree. The relentless heat made me feel as though a thousand needles were pricking my skin. The trees had shed many of their leaves, allowing sun rays to penetrate our shelter and sting our skin. The scorching heat seemed to have driven almost everyone from their homes, with many people clustering beneath the mango trees. Savage and I descended and sat under one of the mango trees where Big Mami and her children were. Baki and Kaki rushed over from the opposite end to join us as soon as they spotted me. However, they immediately swerved and cowered behind Big Mami upon seeing Paapa and Dumi seated opposite us. No one needed to inform any observant eyes that Baki and her sister did not feel safe around Dumi and Paapa. Kaki held tightly to her mother's dress, virtually trembling with teary glances cast at the men. Like a creeping pumpkin stem, Baki crawled to the back of the tent, perhaps trying to escape the intimidating presence of the big boys. She did this, unaware of what awaited her there. I observed Dumi's furtive movements as he kept an eye on the poor girl across the yard. This was not the first time Baki and Kaki had changed direction or fled when Dumi and Paapa were near. But something else was occurring.

The yard was busy, and the younger boys were playing football made of straw. Others were leaping over and across the branches of mango trees, swaying their legs in unison and inviting applause from the spectators. They would scurry up the tree, clamber across the branches, swiftly spin, and land on the ground with their feet. They would leap across and grab a branch on a neighbouring tree, swing or walk on the branch with skilful control of their footsteps. Little boys with hair that looked like bushes were hopping about, lifting mango fruits with their toes and hurling about in every direction.

I had never seen such a crowd in this camp since I came there.

"Why are there many women and children in the camp? Why did this crowd abandon their villages and homes to come and live here?" I asked Big Mami. She had lived long in the camp to know many things, I imagined, staring at her for an answer.

Some of them had escaped their villages following floods, killings and violent confrontations between the farmers and the herders.

"Why did you abandon your wife and children to come and live in this place?" I mobilised courage and asked Paapa.

He told me that he had worked in the Ministry of Finance as General Manager of Salaries but lost his job when he was arrested and imprisoned on money laundering and corruption allegations. He escaped from prison and changed his name from Josua Likiba to Paapa. He had lied to Chief upon arrival in the IDP camp that he lost all his family members during the violent clash between the herders and the farmers, lost his house and property to fire and had nothing in the village to keep life going. That is how he came to be living in the IDP camp for many years.

We had chatted for long before Big Mami suddenly stopped talking and tilted her head to the left from where a muffled scream was coming a little to the rear of the yard. It was a familiar voice, the voice of Baki. Big Mami and Paapa sprang up and followed the direction of the noise. Savage and I trailed them and found Baki twisting like a crawling millipede in severe pain. Dumi was busy zipping up his trousers, which he hurriedly wore inside out. Musa stood at the rear of the pit toilet, his mouth ajar, like a dog waiting for its turn.

An argument erupted between Paapa and Dumi over ownership of Baki, who was now being assisted by her mother to stand up.

"Dumi, how many times have I told you to stay away from my territory?"

"Paapa, which one be your territri? Herr? How much I rent Baki from you? And for how many day? No bi day before today I give you 2K to occupy Baki for one week? My turn never even finish you come de worry. You de Kiris? You de mad? Why you wan end contract when my turn never expire? Since I pay rent for Baki head, na only two time we come join! My rent never even expire, you come de chase me away de open eye! Why you go even rent Baki to me and Musa at the same time? See how we come de fight on top Baki! No be even the first time you de cheat me. When Baki born girl, you go say na me give am belly. But when she born boy, you go say na you give am belly. So, all fine-fine thing na you get abi?" Dumi paused and continued. "Paapa, if you kiross boundary again, I go comot knife! I go even tell Chief who you be..."

"Do not forget to tell Chief about the missing children," Paapa interrupted, and Dumi dropped his head.

"Dumi, I told you yesterday that I have decided to keep Baki for myself. What that meant is that your period of occupation came to an end yesterday! And you, Musa, did I not tell you that I have ended your contract? Why are you still loitering around Baki? Dumi, Musa, you will not like my reaction if you go near Baki again!" barked Paapa.

"I beg, shift! Na you be Papa for Baki?" Musa responded.

"I first discovered Baki. So, she is mine," Paapa bragged, hitting his chest.

"You no fit build house for my compound," Musa retorted.

The argument degenerated into fiery obscenities, insults, and threats to life. Their argument was pitched in shameless greed. Dumi was not happy about his aborted occupation of Baki, who, to him, was like empty land waiting to be occupied. Dumi had hired Baki from Paapa for one week, but Paapa had also rented the same Baki to Musa for the same week before Dumi's occupation period had ended. The invasion and occupation of the little girl had been going on for some time, the two invaders taking turns in the abusive incursion. Baki was still under the intimate occupation of Musa when Dumi, who felt it was his turn because of his one-week contract with Paapa, took over possession by force, brutally ending Musa's control. Paapa's shameless greed was also reflected in his claims to ownership of male children.

Baki had earlier told me that Paapa, Dumi, Musa, and some young boys in the camp were the biological fathers of her children. A similar earlier argument between Paapa and Dumi over the paternity of Baki's three-year-old son came back to my mind as I stood still, looking at my little friend, Baki, in pain. Paapa had maintained an exclusive right of access and ownership of Baki, and also her sons, considering Baki his wife. He insisted that no other person would mine or feast on his domestic territory without paying a levy to him.

Paapa, Dumi, and Musa always fought over ownership of Baki and her son despite the village of children in the camp who looked like them. A particular case was the boy with a smooth, fair complexion, curly black hair, and long legs. He had retained Baki's startling beauty, which was almost obscured by the scars that had smeared her withered skin. Among the stories told about the boy was the one that some seven months after his delivery, unlike other babies born in Benga camp, he started walking, often drawing the attention of everyone around to his exceptional attractiveness that was emphasised by his long face, pointed nose and chin, and ripe-mango complexion. Apparently, Baki hardly knew her son's biological father, going by what occurred behind the hut.

While Musa walked away quietly in apparent defeat like the coloniser who packed his bags and left because he lost his territory to another intruder during the war of occupation, Dumi did not seem happy. The prolonged argument over ownership of Baki led to a full-fledged fight between him and Paapa. The shameless disputants kicked, pushed, lifted, tossed, and hurled each other around. Many people, including young boys and girls, gathered around, and no attempt to separate the fight yielded any fruit. The fighters rolled over each other, got up, kicked, and fell. Only the collective intervention of the canoe man, the driver, the motor boy, Atang, Jawara, and Aboki succeeded in tearing the two apart from each other's grip. Even then, the two continued to hurl insults and obscenities at each other.

Back in the yard, there was another scene. The young boys and girls were booing Baki and peering from behind her at the blood that was gliding down her legs. So, it wasn't just the invasion that made her cry but also the boos from children between five and fifteen. They roofed their nostrils with their hands and peered at the stained spots on her dress directly below her buttocks, chuckling. One of the giggling boys was pointing to streaks of fresh blood gliding sluggishly down her legs. I pulled off the scarf on my head and tied it around her waist to cover her buttocks to save her from further embarrassment. Then, I held her by the hand and asked her to follow me to the hut where her mother sat sobbing. She simply dropped her head when I asked whether she had sanitary pads. I had to judge whether her action meant that she didn't understand the meaning of hygienic pads or that she didn't have any.

"Do you have the thing that women put where their legs meet when blood is coming out of the place where they urinate?" I tried to simplify my question, pointing to her thing down there.

"Na condemn I de use. I get condemn," she said shyly, bringing down from the nail on the wall the medium-sized bag known as 'Ghana must Go.' The bag had mainly tattered dresses, some looking like a cow's innards. She tugged a threadbare bath towel from the bag and tore it into two halves. Then, she lifted the bag, tied its handle to a short stick that stuck out of the wall, and disappeared behind the hut with the shreds. I understood what she meant by 'condemn.' She used the worn-out towel as a pad during her menstrual flow. I followed her to the rear of the yard. She would never marry, she said abruptly, and she burst into tears. Although it was getting dark, she seemed less concerned about returning to the hut.

"Baki, why are you crying, and why did you say you will never get married?" I asked.

Paapa, Dumi, and other big boys in the camp had been sleeping with her since she was six. They dragged her into the bush and forced her to open her legs. They beat her whenever she complained or attempted to resist. She always felt severe pains where her legs meet. She didn't want to be pregnant again. She didn't want to sleep with a man. She was tired. It was better to be single. She hated men. She wanted to die and end it all. She wanted to escape to the city. She would live in abandoned vehicles and buildings and beg for alms to buy food. It was better living on the street. She had done it once but was picked up by the police and returned to the camp.

"If the big boys want to do it again, go and report them to Chief," I tried to advise in a hushed voice, staring around me.

"Dem go beat me well-well if I report dem. Dem get power, I get nothing." Baki protested, weeping profusely. She wanted to be single. She didn't want a man in her life because the presence of a man around her made her tremble with fear, she told me, wiping tears from her eyes.

"Stop crying. I love you so much. I will always protect you from the bad boys. I will go with you everywhere I go. I will help you," I said, not knowing what else to say. Thereafter, she never stopped begging me to run away with her and wanted us to live together in the streets.

19

The Season of Rains

It rained heavily for almost a week, leaving pools of standing water across the yard. Water began to seep into the huts, soaking the mattresses strewn across the floors. The straw mat that Savage and I had woven from raffia fibres and placed on the floor for our sleeping area became damp and started to smell. We had to lie on the bare, hard floor for several days. Only individuals with a legal identity or IDP registration gained access to protection, food, and resources, including mattresses. Another option was for us to climb and sleep in the treetops, which we opted for on the day it rained heavily, as the floods inundated the entire area, toppling some of the tents and submerging others.

The floods stood above neck level, forcing us to climb and sit on treetops. Both trees and the shoulders of shrubs were more reliable open-air sleeping beds. The fields were covered with water, and you could see treetops jutting up from the surfaces of water across the neighbourhood. Bodies of cows and sheep floated on the surface of the water. Big Mami and the young children who could not climb the trees looked for raised surfaces and stones to sit on, and some were swept away. Yet even the treetops did not provide the much-needed comfort.

Savage, Baki, Kaki, and I had to battle with soldier ants, wasps, and spiders. The creatures were evidently protesting our encroachment on their territory. We were continually smacking our cheeks and ears, making dodging motions to drive off the creatures. All night, I leaned against the tree trunk, unable to sleep due to the mosquitoes and other protesters. When I finally felt dizzy and sank knee-deep into sleep, I fell but came to no harm, thanks to the pool of water beneath the mango tree. I woke up confused, contemplating whether it was a dream until I heard Savage and Baki screaming from the tree. Savage proposed a solution that worked. To avoid another fall, we used our fabrics to strap and secure our legs and arms to the branches of the trees. However, it was nearly dawn because, before long, I heard a cock crowing from a small village across the hills, closest to our camp. Nobody needed to remind the unregistered IDPs that it was time to descend from the trees and withdraw into the bushes. It had become routine to take refuge in the nearby bushes to evade attention.

Newspapers carried different opinions of people on the causes of the floods. People had built residential estates on the plains, blocking drainage channels. The gods of River Kijaro were angry that people had transformed their habitat into residential areas. It was due to climate change.

***

It was not only the standing pools of water that had chased us out to take refuge on treetops. Some people suspected to be immigration officers had sneaked into the camp and made arrests that targeted mostly unregistered persons, people with no legal proof of nationality, prison escapees, as well as those who had committed crimes in villages and cities and ran to the camp to evade arrests. The arrest of the prayer warrior intensified our fear because he could give information about us under duress. We had earlier been warned by the canoe man, Paapa and Dumi about the consequences of declaring legal ties to our country. We would be deported.

Dumi was now our only hope. He was our eyes and ears in the

camp, a service for which he was paid. He knew when the security operatives would arrive because he always eavesdropped on the Chief's telephone conversations. If he were told by the Chief that the police would search the camp, he would signal us to hide. That's what happened.

Following the tip-off from Dumi, Savage and I left the camp very early and strayed into the bush, further than we were wont to. The bush was thick with overhead lean, hairy stems and stretched-out branches, some of which were shaped like human hands. A tiny lane led us to the heart of the bush, where we sat below a mango tree. A particular raised area below the tree had naked ground and looked like the surface of a fresh grave, although no roads led to the area.

Atang, Livinus, Jawara, Aboki, the canoe man, the driver and the motor boy were also in the bush in different locations. We lived this way for three days or more, mainly eating yams and cassava tubers stolen from distant farms during the day. We would give Dumi to roast them for us. Otherwise, we ate mostly raw beetles and crickets dug from tiny hills of cow dung. We sometimes made a fire and roasted yams and the crawlies before eating, thanks to the matchboxes from Dumi, which we enfolded in nylon bags to avoid contact with water. We ate ripe or unripe fruits and sour berries as well. These, we harvested from the vicinity.

The first day we slept out, thick darkness had covered the entire vicinity when I woke up late at night. I was reeking like a bag of crayfish, having gone for days without cleaning even my pubic regions. I wanted to take a bath, but I was gripped by fear. I groped around, hoping to locate Savage. I stretched out my hands and legs, trying to touch the surfaces in front and behind me. The space where Savage was supposed to be lying was empty. Where could she be? I panicked, but I had shifted away from her before falling asleep. She had constantly been rubbing her chest on me, although I felt embarrassed. I lifted my head to peer through the pitch darkness of the neighbourhood and got no sound apart from the shrieks of insects.

"Savage! Savage, where are you?" I screamed with fright.

"I am right down here. I will join you soon," she answered. I remember hearing the leaves rustling toward where she had left me sleeping.

"Where have you been? It's risky moving in the night," I cautioned.

"My throat is too dry, and my armpits were already smelling of sweat. I couldn't sleep at all. I went looking for water," she said.

"Your dress is too wet," I observed when she sat leaning on me.

"I have gone four days without cleaning myself. I had to pour water on my body; I had to clean my armpits," she answered, adding that she felt fresh after pouring water on her body and scrubbing herself with wet grass.

"Why didn't you inform me when you discovered the stream? I am stinking with sweat. I need to clean myself, too," I complained.

I was not surprised, however, that Savage went to have a bath alone. She had never stripped herself naked before me, although we were both women. She was always the last person to go behind the yard to clean herself. She would go to the stream for a bath when every other person had done so and returned to the room. Whenever she felt the urge to urinate, she went further away into the bush. She never took off her dress in my presence. I had never seen her urinating or bathing. The following morning, Savage led me to the brook down the path and sat watching. I protested, undressing naked before her. I insisted on being left alone when she tried cuddling the palm of my hand. When she drifted into the bush, I had a cold bath before locating her up the path.

We returned to the camp the following day after Dumi informed us that the immigration officials had returned to the city. Our excitement was, however, short-lived. Savage and I were still contemplating survival strategies when Dumi approached us to tell us the bad news.

"Big problem dey for road de come. Police will come here again next tomorrow to catch all the trinjers. As I deh wash floor for Chief day before yesterday, I come de hear as Chief de talk for telephone with big man for immigration. As I pretend de sing song, I come hear as Chief de tell am say many trinjers still de hide for inside camp de do bad things. After the telephone talk, Chief come say make I find out if trinjer dem de hide for here, inform them."

Dumi's message was clear. Chief had been informed that out-siders and strangers had infiltrated the IDPs and were hiding in the camp, causing havoc. He had then informed immigration through a telephone call. Dumi added that the police would also search the nearby bushes when they came.

We held an urgent meeting to devise evasive strategies. As usual, it was safer in the bush, we all agreed. We knew what to do, as it was not the first time we had taken refuge in the bush or on treetops. Everything happened as planned.

The day programmed for the search, my friends and I crept into the heart of the bush at the first cock crow. The guys decided to go bird hunting as usual. Savage and I were asked to stay under the same mango tree, our favourite spot for many reasons. It had a slightly raised surface with no grass to suggest and engineer the fear of snakes and other prey. The treetop had umbrella-like spreading branches whose leaves provided a comfortable shade. The camp was visible from there as its rooftops jutted into the sky. Watching any action there or across the fields from our spot was easy. We sat discussing under the shade.

"The police and immigration officers can't see us even if they climb and stand on the top of the tallest tree in the camp," Savage observed, smiling. It was the first time I saw such a smile on her face. I walked around the area and returned to join Savage.

"Someone has visited this place before. I am quite sure. Some-one cleared off the grass from this surface," I noted, pointing to the ground area with two slightly raised naked mounds.

"It should be the herd boys. That should be where they rest when they get tired. I can see cow dung around," Savage replied.

"Why is the ground on this surface fresh and slightly raised? It looks as if something is inside the ground," I said, pointing to what looked like the buttocks of the ridges jutting up from beneath.

"Why don't we talk about important things? Savage said, a smile spreading across her face.

"Is there anything more important than our security? Well, go on," I encouraged, anxious to find out what Savage had to say.

"Kila, there's something I have always wanted to tell you, but there was no opportunity to do so. I..., I..., I love you," Savage said, leaning over, and, at the same time, trying to tickle my left jaw with her finger as she called me mango face.

Although the touch seemed inappropriate, I had no clue what she meant until she closed her eyes partially and stuck out her tongue, moving it up and down like a dog wagging its tail at the sight of its favourite meal. My first reaction was shock. I was embarrassed.

"A woman cannot touch another woman in that manner," I protested and violently pushed her away as she tried kissing my lips.

She was a woman like me. Why would she touch me like that? Why would she want us to lock lips? The memory of my brutal invasion at the desert hung over me, and I hated it.

"I don't like what you're trying to do," I said.

"Something is rioting within me. I just want to find out if you have the same feeling," she said, boldly staring into my eyes and trying to prod me again on the jaw.

"Stop it now! Don't you ever do that again! You are a woman. I am a woman. It is forbidden for a woman to sleep with another woman," I protested in anger.

She was saying something when we heard grass whispering furiously a little further down the yard. Our eyes turned toward the noise of a moving hedge of grass from where the swooshing movement was coming.

"Something is moving in the grass," I whispered in panic, pointing to the faltering leaves down the path.

"We are finished!" Savage said in a hushed voice, causing my body to rattle.

"That should be Immigration," I corroborated. The legs of my heart started kicking aggressively inside my chest cavity, and I was instantly bathed in hot sweat. We stood up simultaneously and were about to start running away when Paapa pulled out in front of us, accompanied by two skinny young boys holding two empty bags. I took a deep breath as we sat back on the ground. A stare of surprise smeared Paapa's face. He must have noticed the fright and distress in our looks.

"What are you doing here? How did you find this place…? Have you seen anything?" asked Paapa, staring fixedly at the raised ridge below the mango tree.

"No, boss," Savage and I answered simultaneously.

Paapa asked us to drift further across the yard and wait for him. We were told not to look behind us, and we obliged.

"I think they buried something inside that raised area, which they want to dig out," I whispered as we sat down, stealing glances across the field from behind the shrubs. My guess was correct. My prying eyes located the two boys lifting what looked like sugar cane stems.

"Guns!" I whispered, shaking, and Savage nodded.

So, they have guns! Where are they taking them? I pondered, the corner of my eye trailing the guys as they trudged through the bush.

We stared at each other in disbelief when Paapa's deep voice wafted across the stretch, asking us to join him under the mango tree. Paapa was not smiling when we joined him.

"This bush is too big, and there are many other places where you can hide. I don't ever want to see you around this mango tree again!" Paapa warned and then shifted his stare to Savage.

"Remove that thing and open those legs," he ordered, tugging Savage's trousers with the tip of his left foot. Without wasting time, he pulled her legs apart and pulled off her underwear, which he held together with her jeans. Just as he was about to descend on Savage, Paapa pulled himself back with a surprised look. He shook his head repeatedly as he stared at her naked lap.

"Why is he staring at her lap in that manner?" I pondered, trying to avoid direct eye contact with him. My heart danced wildly in its chest cavity when Paapa shifted his gaze to my waist. His look was not innocent, and I immediately knew I would be invaded again.

Memories of what happened in the desert hung before me when Paapa stood above me like a big tree, staring at its shadow lying across its foot. I started begging him to spare me, but his response left me helpless.

"Immigration officers are in the camp arresting strangers. Choose between prison and sleeping with me!" His words disarmed me. He kicked my legs apart and yanked the trousers from my waist, tearing my pants in the process.

What looked like an obese tuber of yam, fenced by a confused hair growth hung down from his waist. He then descended on me like a hawk. It was another episode of brutal invasion. I was still wriggling in pain when Dumi started charging across the field, screaming as if being chased by a hungry lion.

"They are kpoming! They are kpoming, they are kpoming ohrr!"

Our reactions were wild. Paapa grabbed his trousers and staggered to his feet. Savage and I picked up our dresses and ran falteringly after Paapa as he tried to tear through the undergrowth, stumbling to the ground and getting up. In that confusion, we bumped into Dumi, who was gasping and pointing across the field. Dumi stopped screaming immediately he bumped into us.

"Paapa, so, you send me make I go collect information come give you, then, you come de de enjoy!" Dumi fumed, shifting his gaping mouth and wide-open eyes from the breasts drooping from my chest like sheets of water plunging from a rocky cliff to the balls hanging down from Paapa's lap like a criminal that has committed suicide.

"They are coming; they are coming! Who is coming?" Paapa asked, ignoring Dumi's embarrassing stares.

Dumi managed to explain that the police were everywhere, searching and arresting strangers in the camp. They had extended their search into the bushes around the IDP camp.

Savage and I quickly wore our dresses. The confusion Dumi had caused did not only affect us, for Jawara, Atang, Aboki, Livinus, the driver, the canoe man and the motor boy must have heard him. There was running, stumbling, and falling in every direction of the vicinity.

On noticing the confusion he had caused, Dumi squeaked three times continuously. We knew the signal. We understood the sound and its meaning. They followed the direction it was coming from. It was an invitation to gather together. It was one of the sounds we had been taught to recognise when locating each other in a difficult situation. As soon as they had joined us, we all moved up the bumpy surface.

Paapa did not hesitate to express his discontent with Dumi's announcement of the presence of immigration hunters in the camp.

"What was that drama for? Did you have to run and shout like a lunatic? Dumi, I work with men and not women! Next time, if you interrupt me again, you will know why I am the king of the jungle!" He raged, staring at Dumi.

"Paapa, you no go klimb for my back again!" Dumi said, staring at Paapa.

Paapa was still ranting when Livinus tapped his leg and pointed to his manhood, which had just leaked out of his trousers through the open zipper. I knew what had happened, what led to the degrading unveiling of Paapa's staff of authority. I was scared. Paapa quickly arranged himself, pelting blame at Dumi.

"What is happening? Are we safe?" Livinus asked, and Dumi tried to justify his dramatic action.

"Na immigration *wahala* come make me I de run like wind. As I de talk to you now, *sikiriti* don arrest my *sekwond (second)*..." We shivered, and Dumi continued. "Yes. Sikirity has arrest my sekwond. Them say me and Musa savi everybody in the camp. As my wife see as them join Musa hands put chain, she come tell me. And as me too I see sikiriti de enter for bush like hunters de bend down, de stand up, de look left, look right, look far, look near, arrest seven fifur throw inside moto, my heart come de dance de make kum, kum, kum. The sense weh full my head tell me say make I run quick come tell wuna."

Dumi's message drove spears into my flesh. The immigration officials had launched an aggressive manhunt in the bushes for strangers suspected to be hiding in the IDP camp. They had arrested Musa, whom they felt, or had been told, had relevant information about all the strangers in the camp. They suspected Dumi of hiding information, too. That was the content of Dumi's explanation.

We were at the mercy of our predators for solutions, I mused, looking at Paapa and Dumi.

"If Musa is truly arrested, then we are finished! Our secrets are not safe in his hands," lamented Paapa. "Musa will leak our plans to them, and they would arrest Dumi and I. That's my fear."

"Na exactly my fear be that," Dumi interjected and crossed his hands over his head.

"What do we do now?" cried the canoe man. "My job is gone! I will lose my job and even my life if I fail to deliver the goods to my boss! I know my boss very well. His eyes and ears are everywhere, and he takes no excuses. Paapa, Dumi, do something. I am nothing without this job. And I don't want to die. Do something. I have paid you. You have to fulfil your own part of the bargain." The canoe man was whispering as he shifted and leaned on Paapa's right ear. It was not the first time the canoe man was referring to us as his goods. Whatever that meant, I didn't know, and I didn't even care to know. All eyes had maintained a fixed stare at Paapa and Dumi, whom we all looked up to for solutions from police arrest. Paapa, the canoe man and Dumi shifted aside, spoke in hushed voices, and then returned to us.

After staring across the field for a while as if expecting answers from the passing wind, Paapa coughed and began.

"We have to change our game plan now!"

"*Gwam!*" the canoe man commended and said, "Paapa, whatever it takes to save my goods, do it. I promise you a big commission if they arrive Amerika intact!"

"Consider it done, but on one condition."

"What is it again? I thought the deal was concluded!" asked the canoe man.

"Taiga," Paapa said, staring at the canoe man as he spoke. "You are not new in this business. I don't accept crumbs for big jobs. Nothing is done for nothing! We still have a real deal to strike. Everything is business! You know the rules." The canoe man dropped his head.

Paapa and Dumi repeatedly exchanged silent stares and nods. Spending a moment with them was like watching a movie about becoming a criminal. They were adept at cooking stories, manipulating, and taking risks, including survival strategies. And that's precisely what happened.

Paapa wore a bullying face as he stood tall before us, assuring us that he would move us to the refugee camp and would also get both the IDP and the refugee registration cards for us through his agents on the principle of 'nothing goes for nothing.' His terms of contract were clear.

"Listen very well. Now that Musa is arrested, we must act fast before he informs the police that you are hiding in the bush. There are two things we need to do urgently. Number one, you need to take on new names. Number two, we will make the camp ungovernable. It is risky but not impossible."

Paapa peered into our eyes, one after the other, and continued.

"Our food is finished. We do not have water. Most of the tents were destroyed by the floods and the remaining buildings are overcrowded. There is cholera in the camp now, children are dying, and Government is doing nothing about it. We will use the miserable conditions of the IDPs as an excuse to incite trouble. And once we cause big trouble, the government and immigration will stop whatever they are doing in the IDP camp to concentrate on calming us down. The only vocabulary that will pour from the lips of NGOs, human rights activists, lawyers, and everybody once our fire starts burning is: "Government must start dialogue with the protesters…""

"Unconditionally," added Livinus with a smile across his lips.

"Gwam!" Dumi cheered Paapa as he spoke.

"Government must look into the matter immediately…!"

"Na so!" Dumi hailed as we cheered joyfully. Paapa nodded and continued.

"Nobody will know peace in the camp. Now, this is what we are going to do, and it must not go out."

Paapa pulled a razor blade from his pocket, which he used to cut and spill blood from everyone's finger into the ground. He mixed the drops of blood with soil and asked us to scoop portions and swallow. It was a ritual of sealed lips, a collective agreement that the participants in the oath, even at gunpoint, would not spill out the secret of our planned protest in the camp, he warned. "We will set fire to the Chief's house and the tents in the night. Once you hear fire! Fire! Fire! Run for your dear life. Everybody will run into the bushes, and news will spread like fake news. Of course, we know what social media can do. The streets and walls of Facebook, Instagram, TikTok, and WhatsApp will be crowded with the news. Auntie Nurse, politicians, religious leaders, lawyers, NGOs, human rights groups, journalists, reporters, comedians, and other news hawkers will storm this place and ask Dumi and I to explain what happened. And we will tell them what we want their ears to hear."

"Sense full Paapa head!" Dumi cheered, we nodded and Paapa continued.

"As we speak, the cameraman will record everything. You can predict what the next move will be. Auntie and the other news dealers will storm the streets of social media platforms with pictures of IDPs sleeping in bushes, complaining of hunger and neglence from the government. The newspapers, journalists, religious leaders, political activists like Auntie and other NGOs will gladly join her in blaming the government for negligence, the riots, and insecurity in the IDP camp. Once they tell the whole world about insecurity, hunger, fire, neglect, and disease in Benga IDP camp and how the government has abandoned the IDPs, government will receive verbal attacks, condemnation, and even threats from Amerika and big groups. Ha, ha, ha, ha, ha, guess what?"

"Everybody will become soldier ants for government body," Dumi answered, shuddering with laughter. We, too, trembled with laughter.

"Dumi is right. As government will not want to carry shame, they will bring us food and drugs immediately. They will organise meetings and invite the IDPs and Auntie for dialogue. During this period of deliberate distraction, the immigration will not come around to arrest you," Paapa clarified, eliciting various emotions from us.

In jubilation, Taiga, Paapa, and Dumi repeatedly hit the back of their hands in the air. "Government will pump big money into the bank account of Auntie to shut her up. Big groups will flood Auntie's account with dollars. They call it humanitarian assistance, ha ha ha ha ha! Not just ordinary money! Senior cash! And we will have our own share", Paapa, Dumi and the canoe man celebrated.

"Oh yes, Dumi and I are not new in this business. When we make the IDP and the refugee camps ungovernable, immigration will not come around to make arrests. Within that period, you will do farming jobs in the neighbouring villages and make money for your registration cards. That is how we make money from the comfort of our bedrooms. As it stands, if we allow peace to pour in this camp like rainwater, we will cease to be relevant. And you will not be free from the hands of immigration, even Dumi and I too," Paapa concluded and charged us to pay for the strategy, nothing going for nothing.

We hungrily agreed to pay and adopt Paapa's distraction strategies. I could not voice my thoughts for fear of the unknown. I was uncomfortable with the idea of inciting chaos to make the camp ungovernable. Although I wanted to be free of Immigration harassment, I disagreed strongly with this method.

After the meeting, I became restive as I ruminated on Paapa's strategies to evade arrest.

So, we would foment trouble to give the impression of rising insecurity, hunger, health challenges, and neglect in the camp. That would distract the attention of immigration from arresting the unregistered IDPs and foreigners. We would then be temporarily free from police harassment and arrests as the government, big groups, and NGOs would step in to try to engage in dialogue and restore peace. While attention will be diverted to activities to restore peace and order in the camp, we would do farm work to raise money for our registration cards. The matter was preoccupying.

As I pondered, I imagined the punishment we would receive if we were arrested. Deportation! Imprisonment! Did Paapa even consider that possibility? I thought of how much my family depended on me.

I resolved to pull back from the plan, but how was I to communicate my intention to Savage and Jawara, whom I knew would exercise discretion, in order to make them reason with me? How was I to tell the others that we risked plunging into more problems if we tried to cause disturbance in the camp? We all wanted registration cards, but was it possible to get them by such a risky take? Were we not going to worsen our plight? I resolved to convince Savage and the friends I trusted to escape with me to the refugee camp. No participation in the riot, I resolved.

"My dream is to get to Amerika, work and earn money, and lift my family from poverty and suffering. I can't go back with empty hands. I will be rich and happy one day. But I will not join the demonstrations..."

"You are lost in thought," Savage observed, staring at me.

"Savage, Paapa said we will incite a rebellion. That does not seem to be a good idea if you think of the possible consequences. For one thing, we may lose our lives and cause the death of other people. We may get arrested for causing disorder. If they arrest us, then I am finished. For one thing, we would not travel to Amerika for sure, implying that I will never be able to help my family and clear my debts. Let us try another option. Let's do farm work indeed to raise the money for the registration cards and move to live in the refugee camp instead. It's just over there, across the field, not far from here," I said.

"I have also been thinking about the dangers of staging the riots. It is easy to start a fire, but you cannot control its outcome," Savage corroborated. We agreed to convince our brothers not to join the riot.

20

Survival Strategies

During the prolonged period of illegal immigrant arrests, we adopted new names, typical of the tribes in Bamfada. Paapa suggested them. I became Ayakila Liza Paapa, the name my registration cards would bear. Ayakila was a typical Benga native name, Paapa said, and he went on to assign new names to the others. He named us as if we were his children, I mused humorously. Taking on a new name felt like being a fruit from a grafted plant or like a young butterfly shedding its old skin to develop a new one. My new name and identity did not signify a complete separation from my tribal roots, as the name was a blend of different cultures. I retained my old self within the new. It was a shift from one identity to another, with the roots of the old remaining untouched.

Impersonating someone or taking on a different identity was common in the Benga IDP camp. Many reasons were advanced for this. The likes of Paapa and Musa had been prison runaways; others were wanted criminals, escapees from their communities after criminal activities. A few, like us, were foreigners trapped by cycles of travel bans or financial constraints while on transit routes to other destinations. The spate of advancement in the business town of Benga, favoured by massive government presence and infrastructural development, also made the city an unavoidable breeding ground for such furtive adventures. The refugee and IDP camps mainly served as enabling hideouts.

Identity shifting to evade arrest was not just about adopting new names. Accents could tell. So, taking on the accent of the host native community was another common strategy. It took us almost an entire season to learn to speak both Pidgin English and the native language of the host community. Strangers did this not just to survive but also to gain acceptance. Another reason was to avoid being charged extra amounts of money when buying food in local markets and shops. So, among our daily practices, we learnt and imitated the linguistic habits and manners of the host community. Paapa and Dumi taught us Bamfada Pidgin English, but Paapa was a better language teacher than Dumi. The Bamfada accent was characterised by sonorous and pulsating drawls, inflexions and exclamations, Paapa began.

"How that one take concern me?" (That is none of my business)

"Which name you de answer?" (What is your name?)

"Na she be ma Mama?" (Is she my mother?)

"You de mad?" (Have you lost your mind?)

The interactive lessons involved listening and repeating words and phrases in their proper order and pronunciation. Examples and a question-and-answer session followed every explanation. Paapa's positive quality was his ability to teach the local accent.

It was very easy to pass for an indigene of Benga if you spoke the English Language or Pidgin English with their native accent. One only needed to imitate the ethnic accent of the natives as well as their word placement. Benga Pidgin English was energetic and yet had modulating, melodious inflexions. Even the English Language had to be spoken with a Bamfada accent. The police usually quickly identified non-natives from their unfamiliar English accent. After a series of classes and drills, I could speak English and Pidgin English with an acceptable Bamfada native accent.

Paapa also taught us the manners and habits of thought typical of Benga natives. "You must spice Bamfada spoken English or Pidgin English with native expressions such as *ba, eryaa, abi, shaa, erwoo, nkwo, shebi, haba,* and *gbwam.* Women and girls bend forward and genuflect deeply when they answer greetings from an elderly or wealthy person," he added.

During the time for questions and answers, I asked the first question.

"Why do you speak English and Pidgin English with a lot of force in your voice?"

"Government serves electricity in teaspoon. We live in darkness always. You cannot even sleep well in the night because the heat is too much. So, people prefer using generators to light up their homes, markets, and business centres. If you are a big man, you need an air conditioner in your office, and you will also need a generator to power it. *Wahala* too much, ohh. If you go to any market in Benga, your ears will be singing 'huuuuuuum; huuuuuum; huuuuum; ghooooooooorrrrr, as if ten thousand bees are snoring inside. In the market, you only hear the cough and snore of generators: Khooorrr! Khorrrrrrr! If you don't shout when you speak to someone, how will they hear what you are saying?" Paapa asked. From his explanation, I understood why they kept screaming as if arguing among themselves.

The first time we drove into Benga City, we heard generators coughing, snoring and grumbling. The power supply was always epileptic, so everybody preferred using generators to power their homes, business centres, and other needs. Whenever the generators were turned on, they rumbled like a passing storm. In a market or busy business centre, you hardly hear what someone is saying without bringing your ear closer to the speaker's lips.

Paapa always demanded payment for any service he rendered, no matter how small. Despite our familiarity, he did not twist his tongue before requesting payment for his lesson and answering my question.

Imitating the Bamfada Pidgin accent to comply with their tribal or ethnic linguistic manners wasn't a charity service. Paapa insisted that we would pay for the lessons in cash and kind. Of course, we had to teach him some of the basics of the French Language.

The following day, we had a brief exercise in the French

language—brief because I started feeling pains below my navel. We started with greetings. Although in an informal context, this was my first time teaching French to a foreign learner. I still recall the content of our first lecture.

"Bonjour" (Good morning)

"Bon après-midi" (Good afternoon)

"Bonsoir" (Good evening)

"Comment t'appel tu?" (What is your name?)

"Tu viens d'où ?" (Where do you come from?) etc.

Our lessons also included conjugations, and we gave them along with their English equivalents:

"I am" (Je suis); 'tu es' (you are); il/elle est (he/she is), etc.

"How do you insult somebody in French?" asked Paapa, a curious choice of interest that aligned with his mindset.

"Ta mère' (your Mami); 'Idiot!' (idiot); 'Chien' (dog); 'Regarde moi un sorcier' (look at this Witch!'; 'Regarde moi un marabout' (Look at this Native Doctor!); 'Regarde comme elle est laide' (see how ugly she is!" the insults with their English meanings, poured like diarrhoea-induced human waste from the lips of Livinus who reacted impatiently as if he knew a question on insults would be asked. Paapa and Dumi seemed more interested and excited about the lesson on insults.

"Kila," you have been twisting your waist. I hope all is well?" Savage asked.

"I have been feeling some pecking pain below my navel; it comes and goes," I told her, and she said I needed some rest.

The language lesson inspired some feelings in me. For the first time, I felt proud and superior to Paapa who regretted that his country had only English as its official language. I felt proud that my country had some linguistic advantages over other countries. I even boasted that my country was the 'Linguistic Big Brother' of Africa due to its bilingual nature and heritage, a claim that appeared to humble Paapa. I could deduce this from his looks. I bragged further about the advantages of speaking and writing English and French.

"In my country, we speak both English and the French languages; we also have over three hundred native languages. You enjoy many advantages when you can speak and write in the two official languages. You are relevant both at the national and international levels. You don't suffer to look for a job. Jobs look for you," I joked, knowing that I was merely being flowery, but I got the direct hit immediately.

"What are you doing here then...?"

"Gbwam!"

"Why didn't you stay in your bilingual country and wait for jobs to look for you?" Paapa quizzed while Dumi mocked.

"Kaba told me that in Amerika, you earn more money even from cleaning jobs, washing corpses, taking care of babies and old people, selling in shops or restaurants, making beds in hotels or even from plaiting hairs. If you do a babysitting job in my country, you will get very little pay at the end of the month. Some people don't even pay at all. Some frame up a story implicating you in theft just to avoid paying you. Some chase you away empty-handed despite the years you spent caring for their children, washing their napkins and changing diapers, cooking, cleaning, washing, ironing dresses, and taking their children to school and back. Even when they pay, it is not encouraging at all. And it is not only about the little pay you get from humbling jobs; people laugh at you if they hear you are cleaning dishes, looking after babies, or working at the mortuary," I elaborated.

Yet Paapa became even more hungry to learn French and join us on the trip to Amerika. He acknowledged that the pay package for menial jobs was also very discouraging in his own country.

"I like to speak the French Language so much. I would like to visit your country when I leave the camp. I don't want to go back to my village. There is no job to do there. We need to have more lessons in French so as I teach you our Pidgin English, you will teach me French."

I agreed to teach Paapa French in exchange for free lessons in their Pidgin English. As we discussed this, Paapa revealed more survival strategies.

"Something just came to my mind. We need not only plans A and B but also plan C. Now that Musa has been arrested, police will torture him to tap information from him. Musa cannot be trusted not to tell the police where to find you people. I am suggesting that we learn how to speak English like Obama. If the officers arrest you and you tell them that you were born in Amerika, they will believe you and deport you to Amerika. They respect Amerikan citizens more than their own citizens. You need to let the words glide over your tongue and come out through your nose, and you need to see how they will respect you like treetops bowing to the passing wind. They will greet you with a smile even if they see only the back of your head. Our people behave towards Amerikans and whites the way prayer warriors behave in the presence of their spiritual leader," Paapa continued.

The suggestion to imitate Obama's English accent was received with jubilation. Atang, Livinus, Jawara, Aboki, the canoe man, the driver, and the motor boy, who had remained silent since they joined the language lesson, hurriedly stood up and staged different dance steps. The next day, we had a rehearsal on Amerikan English. Livinus opted to lead the class.

In preparation for the lesson, Livinus wrapped a scarf, the fabric cloth usually worn by women, around his head, leaving a tail dangling directly below his neckline. He then insisted that we call him 'Amerikana'. He was not a bad teacher, perhaps because he could rap well. He started by teaching us how to fold in our tongues before pronouncing words. We did as he directed, trying hard to imitate Obama's accent, speak through our nostrils, and drag the words and drawl. We tried to let the words glide out of our tongues in rhythmic drawls, repeating each word after Livinus, trying to move back and forth. I would fold in my tongue and try to speak through my nostrils, gurgling the words in a slow, lengthened tone or speaking slowly with vowels intentionally prolonged. We had to sluggishly pronounce all vowel sounds with a degree of laziness, dragging them out to give rising and falling rhythmic endings. We did this in a staged conversation with an immigration official, conceived and directed by Livinus.

Officer: What is your name?

Migrant: Yeah, yeah, ama Jimmy Ebilidy, mehn. You look geud, mehn! What's up dude?

Officer: Where do you come from?

Migrant: I come from Emerika, mehn. I was born in Chicargo. My Maama lives in Kalifornai, mehn. I came here for a research project on witchcraft, but gat kidnapped mehn. I lost everything to the kidnappers, mehn. I wanna go back to Amerika, Mehn, ama need you to help me, dude. I wanna see ma Maama, you know.

We repeatedly rehearsed this conversation in pairs during the simulated rehearsal, with Livinus as stage director. Livinus swayed back and forth, dribbled past us, limping from side to side, and then lifted and lowered his buttocks with corresponding jerks, jolts, and nods, answering citizenship-related questions from an imaginary investigating officer. We were tasked to do the same in pairs. Playing the role of the officer, Paapa roared, his mouth and face twisted, revealing ridges and furrows across his forehead: "What is your name?" staring at Atang, who acted the role of the migrant.

"Ama Jordan Ortn, Mehn," Atang answered, patting Paapa's shoulder as he spoke.

We all took turns in pairs, the supposed migrant rocking back and forth, lifting and lowering their buttocks with jerks when answering a question from the assumed officer. Imitating Amerikan manners was the way for us to get into another skin to hide our real identity, Livinus said in an echo of Paapa, who gave birth to the idea.

We had a lot of fun with Livinus, who perfectly mimicked the Amerikana and spoke through his nostrils. It was not a difficult rehearsal anyway. After many practice sessions, we learnt the tricks of speaking through our nostrils and letting words slide along the tongue in a drawl. I could also talk through my nostrils and combine the English sounds with the Benga native accent and expressions when speaking English.

By speaking Amerikan English or the Pidgin of our host community and adopting their manners, we gained self-confidence and the officers' confidence. We could pass for native inhabitants of the host community or gain acceptance otherwise. This was the way to ward off the suspicions often associated with infiltrators.

On the evening of the day we had the simulated citizenship test, the neighbourhood was moonlit. Savage and I had gone out to pick snails from the bush and spotted Paapa and Atang across the yard. We squatted, afraid Paapa would harass us on assumptions that we were stalking them. Not only were they spotted together like a couple, but their lips were joined together. Paapa's arms were wrapped around Atang's shoulders. It was like a fowl spreading its jacket of feathers over its chicks. A strange intimacy was brewing in the pot of their peculiar affection. So absorbed were they that they didn't notice anything. Atang had a tight-fitting shirt and clinging blue jeans shorts that reached below his knees. I couldn't believe what happened next. Atang kneeled on the ground, and Paapa planted his waist onto his buttocks like a man riding a horse. I ventured that it was due to this intimacy that Paapa collaborated with us to keep our identity secret, pending our raising enough money for our registration cards. Savage and I exchanged glances and walked in the opposite direction.

Paapa had programmed another class the following day. Everyone awaited the class with excitement. Paapa had said he would teach us greetings and some basics in Benga native language. When he came in to teach, I started feeling uncomfortable again, something pecking my intestines and the entire area below my navel. I held my lower abdomen in a squash, wriggling in agony.

"Kila, you are not fine," Savage observed, ever the first to notice my malaise. I couldn't talk. She held my hand and led me away to lie on the mat. Blood again glided down my legs. Big Mami stood up and came to help, pressing in my stomach. The baby was threatening to come out. I needed bed rest, she said and sat down. At first,

I thought that it was part of the complications of the miscarriage I had suffered, until it became obvious that it was another pregnancy from my encounter in the bush with Paapa. I hated seeing Paapa.

21

The Protest

After chewing herbs Big Mami harvested for me, I recovered from the pain and eventually felt lighter. The wisdom of the saying that you cannot fall very far if you are already down applied to me. I could now trek to distant places to do much work without fear of losing my baby. Paapa, however, spoiled my joy of recovery by suddenly distributing sheets of paper with the message that the planned demonstration would occur sooner than expected. In a brief meeting, he explained that Dumi had told him officers would return to search for illegal persons in the bushes around.

That day, the IDPs poured into the neighbourhood to cause disorder and attract attention. The riots did not happen by chance. The chief had a predictable weekly schedule. Knowing when he would be around or absent from the camp was easy. Despite the ongoing national confinement measures to avert the spread of the COVID-19 virus, he usually visited his family in the city every working week, returning three days later. That day, Paapa had a meeting with us in the field.

"My shadow has fallen at the side of my left foot. That means Chief has left the camp. He should be on his way to town now. Let's get up and be ready!" he shouted, tapping Atang on the back. We stood up from the grass where we passed the night in the bush after learning that there could be surprise arrests.

Paapa was right. My eyes fell on Chief's car driving off along the twisting path that wound its long brown lane out like a snake. When we reached the camp, Paapa and Dumi assembled the IDPs in the courtyard and gave directives.

"Mami dem, Papa dem, my brothers, my sisters and my pikin dem, wuna don wake up from sleep?" Paapa asked if we had spent the night and woken up, the customary way of saying "good morning."

"Yeeees Paapa, we don wake up," the voices confirmed.

"We de face four big-big problem and wuna know already. Number one, dem de open legs sleep with woman and girl pikin dem everyday, give them belly. Number two, dem de kidnap wuna children everyday. Number 3, hungry de kill we but we no get food. We no get good water. Electricity no dey. Sick de catch we every day. Even when dem bring chop, ee no di last for one week sep. We don gather here to agree say we go turn karangwa, ants and bees for Ngomna body until dem go sit down talk with we…!"

"Yeeeeeeeeeeeeeees!" Voices of approval chorused across the yard at Paapa's suggested metaphor of lice and bees releasing stings on government, and the need to make the camp ungovernable to attract government attention to their problems. The problems he identified were rape, unwanted pregnancies, babies making babies, children dealing with adult situations, lack of attention, scarcity of food and water, disease, and lack of electricity.

"My dear people, another problem be say Whiteman don send big-big money make Ngomna give we. But Ngomna don carry that money go give politicians make then usam buy votes."

"Na true talk be dat," Dumi corroborated. The IDPs around me opened their mouths wide when Paapa said the money meant for them had been diverted and shared with politicians.

"Ma Mami and ma Papa dem, my brother and my sister dem, if you don't fight for your rights, nobody will fight for you, na lie I de talk?

"Noooooooooooo!"

"The time to fight is now…!"

"Yeeeeeeeeeees!"

"The time to take back your money from Ngomna is now!"

"Yeeeeeeeessssss!"

"The time to stop sleeping with our women and girls and planting babies in their lap is now…!"

"Yeeeeeeeeeeeeeeeessss!"

"The time to stop kidnapping our children is now…!"

"Yeeeeeeeeeeeeeeeessssssss!"

Big Mami made dance steps.

"Listen very well. Chief has gone to town! The time for action is now! We go set fire on all the buildings inside this camp now…!"

Paapa pointed to two gallons of petrol and two boxes of matches on the ground in front of Dumi and continued, "We go block road with stones and branches of trees. Na for bush we go de sleep. When Auntie Nurse go hear say camp don burn and na for bush IDPs de sleep, she go write for inform Amerika. She go put fire under Ngomna chair. When journalists, politicians and lawyers dem go hear say na for bush IDPs de sleep, dem go join Auntie and pour into the streets for make sure say the news go spread like bush fire, ha ha ha ha ha. And when the matter go enter for Amerika ear, dem go start chuck eye. And when Amerika go put hand for the matter, Ngomna go carry bags of rice and beans and cooking oil and water and mattresses enter camp and we no go lack anything again. We no go hear about rape and kidnapping again because Ngomna go send soldier dem for come guard we."

I could see nods of approval as Paapa repeated the strategies to get their attention. The IDPs had to set fire on the buildings in the camp, and then block the main entrance into the camp. They would then move over to the bush across the neighbourhood. Auntie, the activist, would draw the attention of the media, the press, and, particularly, Amerika to the plight of the IDPs. The lawyers, politicians and journalists would join Auntie to pour into the streets. They would inform Amerika and pressure the government to find an immediate solution. Government would quickly bring bags of food to the camp.

Security measures would be put in place to prevent rape and kidnapping in the camp. A whirlwind of excited voices tore across the courtyard as Paapa poured out his well-cooked strategies to convince them and get the support he wanted from the IDPs.

Things happened faster than I expected. Everything was filmed by the two guys with whom Paapa had exhumed a hoard of guns from beneath the mango tree. He had apparently brought them from the city, and it was my third time seeing them.

The demonstrations started with a protest march inside the IDP camp. Banners carrying different inscriptions like 'Bring Back our Food'; 'Bring Back our Children!' 'End Hunger and Disease Now!'; End Rape Now!' were erected at the entrance into the camp. The friends of Paapa and Dumi must have brought the banners from the city.

Savage, Jawara, Aboki, Atang, and I watched the young boys and girls tearing in and out of the bush with heavy branches of trees, which they used to erect a barrier at the entrance. Before long, the irate protesters had blocked the main entrance into the camp with a mountain of stones interspersed with branches of trees they had cut. Then, suddenly, we heard exploding sounds from the direction of the buildings. Brown sheets of furious smoke started escaping into the sky from every direction. Dogs barked furiously from inside as the buildings continued to vomit thick brown sheets of smoke into the air. Chief had brought the two dogs from town the previous week. The dogs could not have survived. I was happy that we all moved to the nearby bush without losing a life. We sat on the grass, looking miserable, placards held up in the air, reciting the inscriptions on the placards.

No matter how organised a fire starts, the starting differs from the end. Before long, things went out of hand just two hours after the fire started. Vehicles charged across the hill in the direction of the camp. People from the neighbouring village had seen the sheets of smoke rolling upward and wafting across the fields. They had quickly informed the fire brigade. The vehicles galloped continuously across the field. Paapa saw them, too, and was the first person who reacted.

"Look over there! That's Chief's car right in front! That one looks like the police vehicle! There's another one behind it, with a long pregnant stomach! That should be the water extinguisher! Ha ha ha ha ha ha ha! Our strategy is working…"

"Gwam!" Dumi exclaimed in jubilation.

"No dialogue, no peace! No money, no peace!"

"Gwam!" Dumi cut in again as Paapa spoke.

"Our bank accounts will soon be pregnant with senior cash again! Ha ha ha ha ha!" added Paapa, swaying from side to side in a dance mime.

We watched the vehicles enter the far end of the vicinity, expecting things to happen as Paapa and Dumi had assumed. They didn't.

Two heavily loaded police vehicles, accompanied by a water tanker trailed Chief's car toward the camp and stopped abruptly in front of the erected barrier. The water tanker lifted a long-drawn-out rubber pipe over the fence and hurled sheets of water across the yard. The 'firefighters' dragged open the door of the main entrance to get in.

"Is there anybody inside the buildings?" one of them shouted out.

I had speculated that there would be trouble because the men in navy attire were jumping off the road, staring at the smoke and then at the barrier and asking questions.

"Who brought these branches and stones here? Speak! Who brought them? Who raised this barrier? Who did it? Who did it? Who set fire to those houses? Who did it? Speak! OK, since you are not talking, I go use force now. Thud! Thud! Thud! Pah! Pah! Pah! All of you, climb into that vehicle now! Very fast! Na who set fire on the buildings! Talk!"

The police unleashed heavy kicks and slaps on the IDPs, directing them to climb into their vehicle at the same time, asking questions.

"Who set fire to those buildings? And where is Dumi?"

"Officer, I beg, no beat me, I beg! I beg, Officer! No be me burn house."

"Who burnt the houses then? Speak!"

"I go talk, I go talk, na Paapa and Dumi come talk say make we burn the houses so that Ngomna go bring pilenty food and pay the money weh Big-Big pipi for Mirika send make dem gif we," the young boy stammered, turning around with a finger lifted and peering through the smoke drifting in every direction. I knew the young man was trying to locate Paapa and Dumi, who sat wedged between Atang and Livinus, a little further into the bush while the smoke continued to waft across the yard. It was impossible to see well through the smoke that looked like drizzles of wood ash. Through the hedge of smoke, I could make out the young boy shading his eyes and still trying to peer through the field in search of Paapa and Dumi.

I soon heard a continued rustle of grass from behind me. I turned my head sharply to find out what was causing the noise. A moving mass of grass was fleeing off across the field.

Paapa, Dumi, Livinus, the canoe man, the motor boy and their friends who came from town were no longer where they had been sitting before. Suddenly, the wind changed direction to waft sheets of thick smoke across the entire neighbourhood, causing us to cough violently. There was confusion everywhere. People were bumping into each other and stumbling to the ground as they tried to escape. Heavy footsteps pounded the earth and the grass in every direction. Savage and I got up to run away but got confronted with the sheets of smoke stinging our eyes. Before we knew it, we had been fenced by the officers, who waited for the wind to change direction again before guiding us into their vehicle.

The vehicle that whisked us off to town was high. A huge rectangular compartment of iron walls sat on the four wheels. It was roofed with a thick wooden cloth. When the vehicle eventually stopped, the thick cloth over our heads was lifted, and we were asked to get down and led into dusty and smelly rooms with brown walls. The police cell had a pigeon-hole on the front part of its high walls. The hole served as a window and had two healthy rows of iron bars. You could hear heavy feet passing along the corridor and voices in the courtyard, but you couldn't see anybody because the tiny window was high up the wall. We were about thirty in the sweltering room. Others had been kept in the adjoining rooms. We sat wedged on the cold floor, our backs on the wall. We were not allowed to go out. Two buckets with large mouths stood at one corner of the room. On the back of one was written "For Urine"; on another, it was written "For Excreta".

The only consolation was that Savage, Atang, Jawara, Aboki, and I were in the same cell, perhaps because we sat together in the vehicle that brought us to the Immigration Service.

22

At the Immigration Centre

The following day, we were given slices of bread to eat. I asked for water to drink, but the officer who brought the bread asked me to give him money to buy water for me. Thereafter, we were led, one after another, into a room in a three-storey building across the yard.

I was the last person to be led to the big man's office for questioning. The big man, whose name I have forgotten, introduced himself and from his double high-back swivel chair, stared at me when a warder hustled me into his office. An air conditioner whispering from the top edge of the ceiling breathed fresh air into the room. A massive flat screen, propped against the gorgeously tiled walls, blossomed with images of men and women appearing and opening and closing their lips. As I guessed, a family picture with a beautiful woman and three children on the glossily framed colossal photograph sat on his table. A set of bright, soft leather chairs and a central table occupied the left flank of the office, where another officer sat, taking down notes.

The big man lifted his eyebrows as he spoke to me.

"What is your name?" he started. The rehearsed lesson on Amerikan English immediately popped up in my head.

"Yeuh Mehn, ama Liza Ayakila. Em from Chicago in the *Unaided* States of Emerika, mehn. Your office looks fantastic and amazing, mehn." I bent my tongue inward, trying hard to speak through my throat and nose while staring fixedly into the big man's eyes. His eyes were locked into mine. He had a look of surprise and embarrassment. I became more nervous than courageous now as the big man stared directly into my eyes; without uttering a single word or blinking, his lips squashed.

Did he notice that I was faking the Amerikan accent? What was he thinking about? Why wouldn't he say a word? Just one word. Anything. Just anything. Perhaps I had behaved childishly, I thought. My heart started pounding inside my chest. Standing like a military officer performing military honours to the superior officer, I tried to stifle my fear. Unable to sustain that theatrical posture any longer, I released a long breath.

The big man shook his head and opened his lips to speak.

"Did somebody tell you that my office is auditioning comedians for movie roles?" he asked. "Young lady, I'm sure you are quite aware that this is an office and not a stage for theatrical activities. And if you are here to act a script, I do not intend to constitute your audience! Have I made myself clear?" he thundered.

Not knowing what to say in self-defence and feeling somewhat humiliated and guilty, my quivering lips managed to tender an apology.

"I am so sorry, officer, I am really sorry," I muttered, looking at my feet and biting my lower lip.

"I have been doing this work for twenty years and know your kind when I see one. You are surely not from here. So, tell me what I need to know. You don't speak like us. Where do you come from?" Fear tore my heart when the big man asked the question.

"I was born in Benga. My parents moved to Chicago, United States when I was 10," I squeezed my fingers as I spoke.

"What is the name of your Local Government Area in Benga?" asked the big man with a suspicious stare. I bit my lower lip and looked at my feet as if the answer was lying somewhere on my feet.

"What is the name of your father's village?" the big man continued.

"Benga," I stammered.

"What is the name of the Governor of Benga? ... What is the name of your local government chairman? ... Which primary school did you attend in Benga? ..."

"How did you find yourself in the IDP camp?" the big man continued.

One could think ten women were concurrently pounding yams in a mortar inside my chest cavity as the man queried further, skimming my eyes as if to find traces of guilt.

"Can I see your identity card...?"

"Young woman, I have been very patient with you. We will take you to prison now if you don't speak the truth! This is the last opportunity we are giving you to defend yourself. And if you don't speak the truth, you will rot in jail!" The officer threatened, peering into my eyes with his red eyes.

"Which country do you come from?"

"I am a citizen of Kibaaka."

"How did you find yourself in the IDP camp?"

"We were in transit to Amerika. There were many of us. When we got to Benga City, we met a queue of vehicles parked along the road. We were told that we could not continue. We asked why. We were told that the government of Bamfada had placed a travel ban on movements to contain the spread of a new disease called COVID-19. We had no place to go. We could not return to our country. We passed the night on the staircases on the overhead bridge. The following day, the police surrounded the area, arresting people. We managed to escape. We needed help. Someone advised us to go to the IDP camp."

Tears welled up in my eyes as I narrated, giving the names of my group members. I denied involvement in the burning of the camp when he asked.

"So far, we have profiled four citizens who confessed to coming from Kibaaka. Kibaaka has an Embassy in Benga. We will speak with your ambassador. Take her to the Special Department for further inquiry. She should join the other five," the big man instructed his colleague, who immediately led me out of the office to another cell where I joined Savage, Jawara, Aboki, and Atang seated on the floor.

Two days later, a member of the staff of the Embassy of Kibaaka in Bamfada visited us. After questioning us and collecting vital information, a photographer took passport-size pictures of us. The conversation between the immigration officer and our embassy staff member introduced the proceedings.

"Your Excellency, you are welcome! These are your citizens! We arrested them at the IDP camp. They were part of the violent demonstrators in the camp. Many of them took advantage of the smoke and escaped. These five claimed their international passports got burnt in the fire. We are still investigating the cause of the fire. We have profiled them, and so far, we have interrogated them twice. All of them confessed to having infiltrated the IDPs on their passage to Amerika. They claim they were held here by movement restrictions due to the outbreak of COVID-19. We cannot ascertain the veracity of their claims because we have many illegal immigrants causing problems in our country. Some are cattle rustlers, some terrorists, some part of armed gangs, some belong to drug syndicates, some sell human parts, some are kidnappers, and others, scammers. We cannot take what they say at face value. They don't even have any international passports. They don't have any national identity cards. We have, therefore, decided to take them to prison for illegal immigration into Bamfada."

"If I may ask you, sir, why would you lock my compatriots in your prison on grounds of mere suspicion? Are the citizens of Kibaaka not allowed to move freely in Bamfada? Kibaaka and Bamfada have a convention on free entry and free movement of goods and persons. Why would you take them to prison even after they have explained the circumstances that kept them here?"

"They infiltrated the IDPs. They are not IDPs."

"They are not criminals as well. What provisions did you make for travellers on transit, blocked in your country due to travel restrictions determined by your country?"

"Our regulation provides for the arrest and deportation of illegal immigrants."

"Send them back to their country of origin then."

"My office does not have deportation logistics."

"The same regulation that allows for the deportation of illegal immigrants is supposed to make provisions for logistics, I believe so." It was a heated argument.

We could hear them arguing from the big man's office as we stood on the veranda, leaning on the window to eavesdrop on the conversation from outside. We quickly drifted away when we heard the door of the next office opening to let someone out. The face was familiar. I had seen the boy in the IDP camp. He was one of those who was arrested with us. They must have brought him in for investigation, I thought, as they led him away and brought in a girl.

The following day, the same diplomat from the embassy of Kibaaka in Bamfada came to see us again. We were happy when our cell door opened, and a warder walked him in. The diplomat was such a nice person. He asked us many citizenship-related questions. He said many things. He came on behalf of the ambassador. He wanted to know about our welfare in general. He wanted to know how we found ourselves in Benga, where we were heading and why. He wanted to know if we were given enough food and water. He pulled out 50,000 Shibe from his chest pocket and handed it to us, adding that it was to assist us in buying our food. He had also brought documents he called 'Laissez-passer,' established in our names. He had given the papers to the Bamfada immigration chief to facilitate our deportation; he would revisit us to finalise deportation formalities, he told us.

"Thank you so much for the Laissez-passer, sir. Thank you so much for the money. We appreciate your kindness," I said on our behalf.

"This is the only consular assistance we can offer a Kibaakan citizen in this type of situation," the diplomat said. Before leaving, he told us that discussions were ongoing to ensure our safe return to Kibaaka.

Immediately the diplomat left the following day, his last words about facilitating our deportation to Kibaaka kept ringing in my ears. How could I go back home empty-handed? We lost our only house to flames. The entire family is counting on me. Would Jeff survive the shock of finding me in front of him, so pale, telling him that I have been deported? What about Yaya? What will people say? What about my children? Where will I get the money from to sponsor their education? There was another complication. I hadn't had my monthly flow since Paapa invaded me. I am not sure of anything now. Will Jeff accept me carrying another man's baby in my womb? Will his family not ask my people to return the bride price and take me away? And then, the whole village will hate me, call me a prostitute, and point fingers at me everywhere I go. Nobody would ever respect me there at home. I am not returning to Kibaaka empty-handed. I will die while fighting."

"Kila, you are always thinking. What's it again?" Savage asked, wrapping her hand around my shoulder.

"The diplomat said they will deport us but we can't go back the way we came. I have a suggestion. We will cross over to Amerika when the travel ban is lifted. We cannot go back to Kibaaka now. I can't return empty-handed. My husband and I lost everything. My family depends entirely on me. We have endured a lot. We cannot give up now!" I whispered, trying to convince the others to accept my escape strategy when we would be left alone in our cell.

"I think Kila is right. I can't go back empty-handed," Savage said in her throat.

"My father will make life miserable for me if I return with nothing to show. He sacrificed everything to make sure I travelled to Amerika. Those university girls will laugh at us. They will reject us; they will even transform us into a subject of ridicule," added Atang, and Livinus nodded.

"We cannot return empty-handed. My father will be disappointed. People will mock us. Paapa and the others must have escaped to the refugee facility. We already know the bush very well. We can find our way to the refugee camp. Now that they allow us to go out and buy food, it is easier to escape and join them to continue planning our trip to Amerika," whispered Jawara, smiling. He seemed to have spoken our minds as we all nodded.

The escape was easy. We took advantage of the heavy rains and the fact that we were now allowed to move freely, pending when our embassy would conclude discussions with the Bamfada immigration for our return.

23

Escape to the Refugee Camp

My story of becoming a refugee is as long and twisted as the River Kibang. It started with my harrowing escape from jail and the tedious trek through the bush.

We knew the security officer would not stop us from leaving through the gate. He had seen the big man allow us to go out and buy roasted maize and food. He had seen a big car with a diplomatic plate number come in and a cold, composed, straight-faced guy step out to see us. He had seen the guy talking with us across the yard on two occasions and had rushed over to prostrate in front of the diplomat. He knew we were now free to move about freely. He knew our embassy would come and take us away. We approached him seated inside an adjoining compartment at the gate.

"I saw somebody eating maize. We are hungry. Where can we buy some? You can buy yours with this token," I said, squeezing a 2000 into the hand of the security officer. The guy opened his hand, looked at the money, opened his mouth, and prostrated.

"God go bless you. Na only God go bless you. You will see the children of your children! Your husband no go suffer waist pain." We smiled.

He danced excitedly before pointing to two women roasting maize at a roadside bend.

When we got to the bend, we bought maize and branched off into a path. My heart leapt with joy when my eyes fell on the overhead bridge across the neighbourhood.

"Look at that overhead bridge over there. Can you recognise that bridge?" I asked with a smile.

"That looks like the place where we spent the night during our first day in Benga!" Atang said, peering across the area to confirm.

"I was already wondering how we were going to locate the refugee camp from this town," I said as we meandered between houses to avoid being noticed in case the immigration officials were tracking us.

"Let us cross over to the bridge. From there, we can trace our way to the IDP neighbourhood and the refugee camp," suggested Jawara.

We excitedly agreed. It wasn't easy reaching the bridge, which had seemingly stood at close range until we started trudging towards it. We weaved through the continued buildings until we sighted the bridge at a stone's throw away.

Jawara led the way, and we followed, most often missing our way, retreating, and following any direction we determined could take us to the spreading fields, which stretched right to the IDP facility. After trekking for many tedious hours at night, we entered the village that bounded the IDP facility. We sat down, rested and continued trekking until we sighted the walls of the IDP facility across the far end. We started hearing the cocks crowing across the village we just passed through.

"The cocks have started crowing. Very soon, it will be morning. The immigration officers may hunt us to this place; who knows?" I expressed my fears.

"What do we do now?" asked Jawara.

"We could be arrested around the IDP camp. We need to proceed to the refugee camp over there. That's the only place where we can hide for now. But we cannot take a straight path to that location. Let us go very far into the bush. We can rest under the mango trees where we used to fetch snails and beetles. Nobody will know that we are there. We will stay there until nightfall." We were familiar with the bushes and neighbourhoods around the area. "From there, we will figure out how to locate and find our way into the refugee home," Jawara suggested. It was the only thing to do at that moment. We left immediately and trudged into the heart of the bush. There we stayed until twilight.

"I am afraid the immigration may come looking for us in the refugee camp. Let us go to the far end of the bush and spend another night there. We can then find our way back to the refugee camp from the other far end of the vicinity," Jawara said, and we left.

Thick darkness had swallowed us. We moved, lifting our legs forward, kicking out, trying to feel the pathway with our toes. We moved, stretching our hands before us, feeling the grass and shrubs with our hands and toes, trying to locate any obstacle on our way to avoid physical confrontation and injuries. One time, I rammed into Savage and fell on her as we both tripped and tumbled to the ground before struggling to get up. We faltered on and on till we got to a tiny forest where we almost bumped into cows tied to trees. All the cows wore shoes facing backwards.

"Do cows wear shoes?" I asked, peering at the sleeping cows, thanks to the moonlight.

"Who must have tied cows to trees in this distant place?" asked Savage.

"Shwwwwwp!" Jawara hissed, his finger placed vertically on his lips.

"Let's go away from here! Very fast!" Jawara said in a whisper, dragging my hand and that of Savage.

We limped off hurriedly as if something were chasing us. I panted when we were further up the path, asking, "Why did you say we should move away from the cows very fast?"

"That should be the work of cattle rustlers. They wear shoes on the feet of stolen cows before moving the cows away. The foot marks on the ground are meant to distract trackers and send them in the wrong direction while the cows are taken to another location. They always do that when they steal my father's cows. At times, they hide the stolen cows in the bush and go around to look for buyers. The guys are smart but very wicked. They could kill us if they found us around the cows. They are violent when they find a strange face around their stolen cows," Jawara explained, and Aboki nodded.

Jawara's explanation was a warning that we were not far from danger. We trudged further and further until my legs could no longer carry me. I started feeling biting pains below my navel again and complained. Savage suggested that we sit down to rest. We were surrounded by trees and no sign of human presence, even from a distance. My friends immediately fell asleep. I was restless when others were sleeping. I was also bleeding from the deep cuts on my arms and legs. I cut a few blades of fresh grass and wiped off the streaks of blood oozing from my lap, arms and cheeks. I felt grating pains in my stomach and on my skin as I struggled to clean blood from these wounds. Savage was the first to get up the following morning and knew I wasn't feeling fine at night. The others soon awoke from sleep. The gnawing pain in my stomach grew worse, so severe that we stayed on that spot longer. The sun started smiling from the sky, but my legs were numb. My entire body was in pain. I felt sick.

Something terrible happened. Shredded lumps of blood suddenly started crawling down my lap. Within a short time, the contents of my stomach lay between my shaky legs. She kept pressing on my stomach with her fingers until it became flat. The whole day, I was throwing up, but there was no water to drink. I wasn't hungry, though. My mouth was bitter as if I had chewed bitter leaf. Aboki and Jawara returned from the bush later in the day and gave me some herbs to chew. The vomiting ceased immediately I chewed the herbs and swallowed the juice. They also brought green berries. I had lost my appetite and didn't eat the berries. We spent another day in the bush as my body was still weak and heavy. Throughout the night, I had kept staring into the sky, unable to sleep. The following day, I felt better, however. We spent another day in the bush, eating guavas and berries until I could get up and walk.

The following day, we started retreating and trying to find directions to the refugee camp. After trekking for several hours, we finally sighted the roofs of the school buildings hosting the refugees. Paapa was the first person we saw when we hustled up from the bush and sneaked into the camp. He jumped on me, screaming with joy and asking questions.

"I was afraid I would never see you again. Where did they take you people to?" The canoe man began. "Atang, what happened?"

"After we escaped from detention......hurh, hurh, we were locked up…, in a cell…, hurh, hurh, at the immigration centre. Hurh. They-they- took our names… hurh, hurh, they asked questions… and took pictures of us. A diplomat… came from…our embassy…to see us. Hurh, hurh. He…he told us…that… they were working with the Bamfada immigration… to facilitate our return to Kibaaka since we had no international passports and no national identity cards. Hurh, hurh. We managed to escape." Atang bent forward and held his stomach, breathing quickly and heavily as he managed to speak. Savage, Jawara, Aboki and I had immediately sat down, our chests rising and falling as we sat breathing in and out loudly, our mouths open.

Before we knew it, a small crowd had gathered around us. Among them were Paapa, Dumi, the canoe man, driver and motor boy. They were staring at us, their mouths agape, surprised. We took the time to recount our experiences in jail and eventual escape.

"We are thirsty…," I said, and Savage, Jawara, Atang, and Aboki nodded simultaneously before I could finish speaking. "Is there anything we can eat? Is there water to drink?" Paapa led us to their space in one of the classrooms, where they offered us half-cooked, saltless white rice and we ate like dogs fighting over bones. We lay on the floor to sleep and continued the next day. We spent the first two weeks resting and the next two seasons or more, sleeping, getting up and combing nearby bushes for snails.

24

Benga Refugee Camp

Benga refugee camp had a larger population than the IDP camp. The refugees resided in some of the classrooms within the buildings that housed Benga primary school. One of the longest-serving refugees mentioned that the governor of Benga City relocated the school to a different area two years ago to make room for the influx of refugees arriving from neighbouring countries facing security challenges. Tents were set up behind the classrooms for cooking. The camp was situated at the foot of the village, facilitating interaction between the refugees and the indigenes of Dibaba and beyond. Unlike the IDPs, the refugees were not restricted, which granted them the freedom to enjoy the open village boundaries.

We met people from Chada, Benim, Mageria, Kibaaka, and Nijer, all speaking their national and ethnic languages. Some locals had also moved into the camp, pretending to be refugees. I met people speaking English and French, some of whom told me they were from some parts of Kibaaka. They had escaped their communities and wandered right to Benga, away from the violent gangs and kidnappers that drove into their neighbourhoods and schools to forcefully whisk off young boys and girls to their hideouts. Others had escaped their villages during the bloody clashes between farmers and herders. It was like a country, with women and children constituting the majority. Identifying somebody you have met just an hour before was even more difficult. We cooked in the open air, using firewood, and the women and girls prepared pap to eat or sell. We harvested cassava or yams from farms to cook and eat. Various countries sent their refugees food items, mattresses and health care facilities through their diplomatic representations. Once in a while, some representatives of the United Nations brought food, clothing items and medications and distributed them to us.

Problems started during my first day in the refugee camp. Savage and I went to bed early. We lay on the bare floor beside Livinus, Paapa and Dumi. I was scared of lying close to Paapa, but I had no choice. Each time I heard a noise, I jumped up in fright, thinking it was Paapa trying to touch me. But it wasn't just the fear of Paapa that gripped me that night. I felt my intestines constantly turning and grumbling. At some point, I felt the urge to expel human waste that was revolting in my stomach for the first time in four days. Savage accompanied me outside, off the yard, as she was used to when we were in the IDP facility. Livinus had told us that there were bushes around, adding that there were farms behind the classroom. Thank God we could see well because the moon was shining brightly. We were still approaching the rear when a crowd of buzzing flies lifted from the excrement mounds that sat everywhere as if to welcome us. I plugged my nostrils to avoid the stench that hovered in the air. I had to do it standing up, my legs apart. Savage shifted further away to urinate. She had always isolated herself when she wanted to pass out waste, and I simply considered her the shy type. I cut some fresh leaves to clean my anal track, and when Savage eventually joined me, we returned to our room and lay down to sleep.

We woke up the following day smelling of sweat and needed to bathe. We were led to a river across that was also the source of our drinking water. I washed myself, washed my dress and underpants, and squeezed out water thoroughly before wearing them. Savage had again gone further up the river to clean herself. She also washed her dress and undies and wore them before joining me.

The first person we met on our way back from the river was Baki.

Kaki ran down the path and also bumped into us. We stood staring at one another for a while, our mouths open. I wasn't expecting to see them, I said, excitedly holding their hands. Baki did the explanation. They had escaped to the refugee camp during the arrests that followed the demonstrations. Their mother and siblings were in one of the buildings. They had once eavesdropped on our conversation and knew we would move over to the refugee camp at any given opportunity, she added, giggling.

We turned and accompanied Baki and Kaki down the river to fetch water. When we returned to the camp, we were joined by Livinus, Atang, Jawara, and Aboki, who had come looking for us. I started asking Baki, Kaki and others, who had been there before us, questions. I wanted to know if they had refugee identity cards. The canoe man told us a lot of things.

Officers had visited them and taken their names to prepare their identity cards. From every indication, one could lie about his origin. You could lie that you were a refugee and call the name of any country. They had been asked to bring more community members to give their names for the cards to be made. Livinus added that the officers apparently wanted to swell the list of refugees in Benga camp. They were going to come again. The information was delicious to our ears.

I still remember the day representatives from the Kibaaka embassy in Bamfada visited the refugees from Kibaaka. The diplomat who came to see us at the immigration detention centre when we were arrested led the delegation. Immediately after they arrived, they assembled us for a meeting. Savage and I hid behind the crowd to avoid being noticed, although we could hear everything he said.

They were sent by the government of Kibaaka to see us. They had come with relief items to give us. They brought us rice, groundnut oil, garri, corn, beans, salt, seasoning cubes, and more mattresses. They wanted to know how we were faring. The travel ban had just been lifted and the borders were opened. The government of Kibaaka was working with the government of Bamfada to ensure conducive conditions for the safe return of refugees to Kibaaka. When the diplomat had finished addressing us, he and his collaborators shared food items and mattresses. People were presenting their refugee cards to collect the food and mattresses. They also distributed nylon plastics, with springy ropes strewn into the mouths to serve as toilet bags.

Paapa wasted no time explaining to Savage and I how to use the mobile toilet bags.

"They call it 'mobile toilet.' You simply open the mouth and excrete in the bag. Hold the lips together and use this small string to tie the neck of the bag. You can throw the contents off the yard. You can throw it in the river or the farm."

Savage, Atang, Jawara, Aboki and I did not join the queue to collect the relief items.

"You haven't collected food," Paapa remarked, staring at us after returning from the room where he had rushed to keep his own items. "They are still sharing. Go and collect your food. There is no food here," he urged.

"That man sharing food over there is a diplomat from the Kibaaka embassy in Benga. He is the man who came to see us at the immigration centre when we were arrested and kept in detention. He will recognise us if he sees us," I explained in a whisper, adding that Dumi should get a mattress for Savage and I. He succeeded in doing so, lying that his mattress had been stolen.

After distributing the relief items, my eyes trailed the vehicles that brought the Kibaaka diplomatic representations out of the yard. Atang, Livinus, Jawara, Aboki, Savage, the canoe man, the driver, the motor boy and I retreated to the classroom where we had our bed spaces. I collected rice from Livinus and cooked it in a small pot. We all ate and decided to sit outside.

I knew the issue of identity cards and travelling to Amerika would be the subject of our discussion.

"Now that the government of Bamfada has lifted the travel ban, what is the next step?" I asked, avoiding the eyes of Paapa, whose sight was becoming my source of anguish and hurt.

"I wanted to ask the same question," said the canoe man.

"We don't need to raise money for refugee cards any longer. They are doing them for free. One man even came asking me to go to the University of Benga over there and look for students from my country studying there to come and register for their cards. He said he was going to make refugee cards for them which they could present anywhere they want to avoid police harassment," said Livinus, attracting screams of joy from all of us except Paapa, who did not seem happy, perhaps because Livinus' revelation had frustrated his extortion plan.

"In that case, we still need money, not for the refugee cards but to facilitate our onward journey to Amerika. Our vehicle is no longer where we parked it," said the canoe man, shaking his head and twisting his lips.

"Really?" I asked.

"Yes. We asked Paapa's boys to check, but they returned and told us that there was no vehicle with the description we had given around Benga Bridge."

When the canoe man announced that our vehicle was missing, I could see the others' frustration.

"How do we raise money here?" I asked, frustrated.

"This is my territory. I know all the villages and neighbourhoods around. Dumi and I will go around looking for farming jobs," Paapa, who had been silent all this while, said, attracting smiles again.

"And when we have made sufficient money to take us to the next borders, we will cross the forest and enter Mexico. I will call my big boss to explain everything. His telephone number is in my head," the canoe man added.

"I am also travelling to Amerika," Paapa said.

"Me too," Dumi added his voice and said some of the IDPs who were interrogated after the fire incident said it was he and Paapa that burnt the camp.

Just then, a wild scream from the yard drew our attention to a man chasing Baki and Kaki into the courtyard. He was wielding a cutlass in the air and carrying two tubers of cassava in one hand.

"He-lep me, he-lep, he-e-p me ooohhh, he-lep me, he go kill us ohhhh," screamed Baki as she staggered to the ground along with her sister who had just tripped and fallen on her. Jawara, Aboki, and Savage leapt over in time to grab the cutlass-wielding man from the back, disarming him immediately. We all joined them to beg the man to spare the lives of the two girls.

"They are not thieves, please. They just wanted something to eat, sir. Sir, we do not have food to eat, so please don't harm them. Please, please, spare their lives!" I went down on my knees, begging the man who was still struggling to tear out of the grip of Savage, Jawara, and Aboki.

"I catch dem inside my farm digging cassava! Now I know who de come tif my cassava and my yams every day for night! Them go pay!" the man insisted. A crowd had gathered around, booing Baki and Kaki.

"No vex ohh, no vex, we take God beg you, sir. Pity them. Na hungry push dem to steal. They will not steal from your farm again, Big Mami joined Jawara and other voices to plead on behalf of the two girls. The farmer refused to let go of the matter, threatening to take the case to their quarter-head. Big Mami went to the classroom, brought out her mattress, and gave it to the farmer. He collected the mattress and his tubers of yams and left, promising to do his worst if he found anybody around his farmland again.

That day was another bad day in my life. At night, Paapa moved over to my bed space and forced himself on me again. I begged him to stop it, but he threatened to beat me. Nobody could help me as Savage and the others pretended to sleep out of fear. I knew I could be pregnant again because it was during my unsafe period when the invasion happened.

25

A Month Later

The grass was still wet with dew when Paapa and Dumi led us to a neighbouring village where they had negotiated a farming job for us to do. I started vomiting and feeling feverish. My mouth was bitter as if I had chewed bitter weed. I knew what the signs meant. Paapa had done it again. My morale went down, but I managed to follow the others.

We met Baki, Kaki, and many other refugees chasing farm owners everywhere for farming jobs. Many women and girls were also on their way to their own farms with shovels, hoes, and deep baskets with large mouths slung over their shoulders. The men carried cutlasses, a few carrying guns slung by ropes across their chests. Many farms along the pathway had women bent over and doing different farming activities. The men on those farms mostly cleared the grass while some women weeded it. Some, particularly the young ones, were scooping and gathering grass in heaps. Mostly, grown-ups were digging and forming long ridges with earth, piling earth on heaps of grass and setting fire to old heaps that looked already dried due to exposure to the sun. Small, rounded, slightly raised earth, looking like burial mounds and precisely the shape of small, rounded hills, jutted up in many of the farms we passed. Yam shoots were growing up from some of the mounds. Other women were planting cassava stems on the ridges. Some farms grew vegetables with large, flat green palms, which I had not seen in my country. I recognised growing cabbage, maize, beans, tomatoes, onions, and other veggies. But mostly, we passed through stretches of yam and cassava farms in many vicinities.

On the shoulders of one farm, a crowd of cows had invaded the farm, grazing on cassava stems and plants. Two herd boys stood by, watching. We had not gone far away from the farm when we heard frenzied screams and ran back. Big Mami, Baki, and Kaki had been stalking us from behind, hoping they would also get a job where we were heading.

"What's happening?" I asked as the two herd boys and a few villagers were seen chasing each other with knives and guns in every direction—Baki explained.

Apparently, the owner of the farm and another young man had stalked the cows grazing on their crops and thrust an arrow into the stomach of one of them. The distressed cry and wild reaction of the injured cow had drawn the attention of the herd boys to the scene, who, in retaliation, had chased and shot the two men dead. We quickly ran back and away from the scene to the next village, where a job awaited us.

The elderly farm owner was already on her farm when we arrived. She showed us a large portion of land, the size of four football fields joined together, and issued stringent instructions.

We had to clear the grass, gather in heaps and pile fresh earth on the heaps. We had to raise ridges of earth on another section of the farm and plant cassava on the ridges. We had to raise rounded mounds of earth in another portion where yams would be planted. She had brought cutlasses and shovels for us to hire and use. She would deduct the hire money from our pay package. Nothing went for nothing in this setting. Paapa was the contractor through whom we would be paid. We were expected to finish the work and plant cassava stems and yam tubers, which she showed us in a small farmhouse built with thatch. So many refugees were drifting back and forth, looking for farming jobs. The lady concluded that we could start immediately if we agreed to her terms.

"How much will you pay us, Ma?" I genuflected as I asked.

"Na with contractor you go discuss dat one ohhh! Na him I know," the lady said, pointing to Paapa, who nodded and smiled broadly.

We agreed to do the work and started immediately. Paapa allowed Big Mami, Baki and Kaki to join us. We finished the backbreaking work in about eight days. It had taken too long to complete the job because we had to take a different path to that village. We had to avoid the direct pathway, which had become the scene of continued violence between the villagers and the herdsmen. The villagers were not on their farms when we went for planting, which frightened us. Why are the farms deserted? We nonetheless bent over ridges, planting cassava and yam tubers. But even the farm owner didn't come around on the planting day. When we had finished doing the job, Paapa went and collected the pay. He paid us 1000 Shibe each, including Dumi. But to Big Mami, Baki and Kaki, he only gave 500 Shibe each. We were dissatisfied, and our furrowed and ridged foreheads told us this as we collected the pay.

When we were about to leave the farm, the village youths stormed the farmland and dragged us to the quarter-head.

The village head was flanked by the elders, who were all elderly men, frowning, accompanied by angry youths. Before the trial began, he ordered us to kneel, and we obeyed.

"Today is called Akaba Day in Batam village. We do not do farming activities on Akaba day, a day set aside for sacrifices to the gods of our land. You have desecrated our land by working on the farm on Akaba day."

To this accusation, the village head announced that we would be taken to the shrine of Akaba, where our punishment would be decided. We prostrated and began to plead that we did not know about the ways of the land since we were all strangers. After concerting with the elders, all men, in low tones, the village head coughed and asked us to each pay 500 Shibe. We did with grateful relief. We were taken to the river for a cleansing ritual.

Doing farming jobs in neighbourhoods soon became our regular activity. We chased all over neighbouring villages looking for farming jobs and goods to carry to or back from the market. Any other activity that could fetch us money was a boon. The only conversation on our lips was about raising money to buy food, to travel to Amerika. Despite the fluctuating high to cold temperatures and vomiting, including general body weakness imposed on me by the pregnancy, I followed the job caravan out almost everyday. We combed the neighbouring villages for farming jobs. We looked for building sites where we could mould blocks, carry blocks, or get water to the sites. Paapa was always the contractor for every job we did. We were always paid through him. You could work for three to four days and earn some 500 to 700 Shibe, as their currency was called. It was better than doing nothing.

Problems in the camp kept rising as days went by. I particularly hate to remember the day the herders stormed our neighbourhood because some farmers had stabbed and killed cows grazing on their crops. We were sleeping at night when we heard gunshots coming from every direction. The neighbourhood became a battlefield with the herders chasing, catching and slaughtering anybody they could lay hands on. Villagers ran into classrooms, walking over our bodies, trying to infiltrate the confused refugees who were now jumping up from the floor and running into the neighbourhood. Savage and I bumped into a hedge of smoke as we tried to escape the danger. Fire was everywhere, and desperate cries rose from some houses as if people were trapped in the flames. Savage and I ran behind Baki and Kaki, who knew the setup better, tumbling and getting up until we came face to face with a tall man in a long white gown, Imam Abaka, who stood before a mosque. He directed the fleeing inhabitants into the mosque and some to his compound nearby. He asked people who ran up in that direction to get inside and lie on the floor. He locked us inside the mosque and remained outside. There, we met familiar faces, including our friends, who were already on the floor. Bullet sounds coughed and whistled, tearing through the air in every direction. Then heavy footsteps stumped outside and stopped in front of the mosque. They were speaking a language I didn't understand. The hinges of the door squeaked, and the voices became louder. My heart was pounding and changing gears.

"What's happening outside? What are they saying?" I whispered to Baki. I had heard her and her sister speak the same language I heard now. Baki whispered that the herders were trying to force themselves into the mosque but that the imam was resisting. They asked if the imam had seen where the fleeing villagers had run to, but the Imam said no. After a while, the heavy footsteps trooped off the yard.

When the imam released us the following day, he asked his wife to prepare a meal of pap and *moi moi* for us. After we had eaten, he asked for our names and where we lived. When we told him we were refugees, he called his two sons, who accompanied us back to the camp. He sure did the same for the villagers; it was such a demonstration of practical love.

That week was a week of trouble. The lifeless body of Big Mami was found behind the classroom with stab wounds. We had also finished the food, and I wasn't sure if the refugee identity cards Paapa's friends had hurriedly brought from town were valid. Savage and I were always afraid we would be accused of fraud and arrested if we presented the identity cards to collect food. There were many other challenges, like no bushes to comb for signs of fruits, mushrooms and water. Food and water crises, besides the lack of healthcare facilities, were menacing challenges. Stealing was rampant, and younger refugees faced a lot of brutality from the older ones. Big boys slept in bushes with whoever they wanted and whenever they wanted. The number of pregnancies, births and deaths surpassed that in the IDP camp. We were no longer afraid of the villagers again. We harvested crops, including cassava, yams, cabbage, and potatoes, to eat or sell. We had problems with villagers from communities bordering the camp.

It was within that same week of horrors that the vigilante group stormed the camp and started to beat the refugees at random. They were protesting against the frequent theft, rape, and unwanted pregnancies, whose authors they claimed were mostly refugees. Complaints of girls and boys disappearing, with kidnappers asking the poor parents for ransom, were on the rise. The poverty, misery, and insecurity around did not make the refugee camp a better place than the IDP settlement as we had imagined. We had to work hard to increase the little money we had raised from farm work to leave, although finding a job wasn't easy.

26

The New Church

We did not earn as much money from farming jobs as we had anticipated. We needed alternative sources of income. Livinus suggested that we start a church at the camp. People would join gradually. He explained that the money we would raise from offerings would facilitate our trip to Amerika. The idea of running a church business was warmly embraced. At a meeting, we decided who would be the pastor and what the name of the congregation would be. Livinus chose to pastor the congregation. However, he had to study the Bible and prepare himself with the word of God. He would use the Bible that the reverend sisters gave him when they distributed Bibles to the refugees.

Paapa suggested using one of the classrooms as the worship venue. Livinus suggested naming the congregation "Our Way to God."

The problem came with who would be in charge of the finances.

"I brought the idea of starting the church. I will be the treasurer," Livinus argued.

"You can't be pastor and treasurer at the same time! I am the treasurer of the church! Nobody tells me what to do! I tell my subjects what to do! This topic is closed!" Paapa, with an intimidating stare on his face, thundered.

Livinus spent much time studying the Bible and attending weekly worship services at the Fountain of Glory church in the neighbourhood.

When our church started, Paapa, Atang, Dumi, Livinus, Savage, Aboki, Jawara, Baki, Kaki, the canoe man, the driver, the motor boy, and I were members. A month later, the congregation increased; other refugees and the natives of the village joined us every Sunday for worship service.

On our first Sunday service with Pastor Livinus, we contributed money and bought a black suit, a red tie, a black pair of socks, and a pair of black shoes our pastor wore that morning. He was the last person to walk into the church. Everybody arose from the benches as the pastor walked slowly to the raised platform. He held his hands together as he walked past with a straight face. He was more coherent and cautious on the stage than I thought. During the fourth Sunday, his sermon centred on giving.

"Praise the Lord!" the Pastor began.

"Alleluia" chorused the congregation.

"Praise the Living Go...d!"

"Alleluia!"

"You may be seated. As I was praying, the Holy Spirit administered to me, and I want to share the word with you," he announced.

"Give to the poor, and you will see the Kingdom of Heaven. Plant a seed. Pay your tithes. I slept, and God spoke to me! Somebody say amen!"

"Amen!" we chorused.

"If you are in trouble, plant a seed! If you want to be rich, plant a seed! If you are looking for the fruit of the womb, drop your offerings in that basket, and you will see miracles," the Pastor pointed to a basket near him as he spoke. "If you need a visa to travel to Amerika, Dubai, and the embassies have denied issuing the visa, drop your offerings in that basket today! And next week, a miracle will happen! You will receive a telephone call from the Amerikan embassy to come and collect your visa, Amen...!"

"Amen!" we chorused cheerfully.

"It is now time for offertory. Remember that God answers only the prayers of those who give to his anointed," the pastor warned.

People stood up one after another. The pastor led the song, and we sang and danced graciously as we dropped Sunday offerings in the basket. So many refugees standing outside soon joined us when we started singing and dancing. When the worship service ended, Paapa carried the basket and hurriedly left the hall.

The following Sunday service had more people than the previous ones. The worship service started with a prayer of confession and acknowledgement that one is now a new creation, which Pastor Livinus recited, and the congregation repeated after him, as instructed. The prayer session followed a lengthy discussion on why we should pay tithes. The preaching focused on giving in expectation of heavenly rewards. Offertory immediately followed. We were still in the middle of the service when a big car drove into the yard and parked in front of the classroom where we were having our service. A tall man, accompanied by two police officers walked in, attracting all the eyes to them. The tension in me immediately dropped when the tall man in a long green gown started dancing as he walked to the front of the congregation. He asked the others standing outside to come in. Everybody was silent when he coughed and explained why he visited the refugees.

He was the governor of the State. He had received complaints from the community about the refugees. He had been told that we were stealing from farms around and raping girls and women. Therefore, he decided to meet with the community and the refugees. He was pleased that he met us, very organised, and praying. He decided to encourage and support the congregation. He hoped that moving closer to God in prayers would transform us and change mindsets, and many refugees would stop stealing and avoid crime. He wanted us to live in peace and harmony with the host community. When the governor had finished speaking, he spoke to one of the police officers. The officer went to where their car was parked and returned with a massive brown envelope. The governor stretched his hand and dropped the envelope in the basket, adding that he was supporting the congregation with 50,000 to buy drums and other instruments for the church choir. The congregation went wild with jubilation as the pastor prostrated to thank the governor.

When the governor left, we decided to hold a meeting. But Paapa refused, saying that the money was in safe hands.

27

Mediation Meeting with the Host Community

The town hall was crowded. Just before the meeting commenced, two of the dignitaries brought in a fresh peace plant, a bunch of plantains, a plantain trunk with suckers protruding from its chest like a baby suckling from its mother's breast, and a bundle of brooms. They carefully arranged the items on one of the tables.

The governor was the last person to walk in, accompanied by two police officers and two others. He and his close aides sat facing the crowd. The refugees sat behind the crowd. The MC made the introductory remarks, mentioning the names and titles of people: The Governor of Benga, the United Nations Regional Representative for the IDPs and Refugees (UNRRIR), the Chief of the Immigration Department, the Local Chairman, representatives of Civil Society Organisations, religious and traditional authorities, representatives of women groups, representative of the Vigilante Group, representatives of the farmers and herders, the youth and community leaders. Among the dignitaries was the imam, who had helped us during the communal clash. The MC handed the microphone to the governor after reading the agenda from a sheet of paper.

The national anthem of the host country was rendered. Prayers were led first by Bishop Peters Babangida Baitama, followed by Imam Abaka. They all called on God and Allah to inspire the participants with wisdom, productive ideas and strategies to build love and constitute solutions to the killings, hate speech, conflict, and crime in the communities.

The governor began by stating that the meeting's purpose was to end the protracted conflict between the farmers and the herders and advise the refugees to avoid crime and live in harmony with their host community.

"We are like a broom; we are like a millipede which carries all its one thousand legs along wherever it goes; we are like a cluster of plantains; we are a tree with branches sucking from the breasts of its trunk", the governor said, insisting that the message was meant for the farmers and the herdsmen.

"I am privileged to represent the President of Bamfada in this important dialogue, which aims to promote unity, living together, acceptance, love, tolerance, solidarity, understanding, and peace amongst the communities invited to this meeting. We initiated this dialogue in concert and consensus with all the representatives of the community and the groups here present. I want to recognise the presence of our regional partners and diplomatic representations working with our communities to create an enabling environment for conflict resolution and peace. You may wonder why this dialogue needed a regional approach. We have recently witnessed the encroachment of extreme heat that is killing grass and even forests everywhere in the West and sub-Saharan Africa, plunging cattle into starvation. Our cattle now go everywhere looking for feed. You can't tell whose cattle it is that goes about destroying your crops in Benga. The crisis between the herders and the farmers is a common phenomenon in West and Central Africa and requires a collective or inclusive approach. That is why a regional approach to the farmers-herders crisis is necessary."

He said many other things including how he believed that the meeting would provide another platform for continuous engagement with dialogue amongst the concerned and that the platform was an occasion to harness views and make suggestions that would usher in lasting solutions to the tension created by the protracted herders-farmers crises, Boko Haram insurgence, rape in the IDP and refugee facilities, kidnapping, human trafficking, general rise in crime wave, and challenges faced by the IDPs and the refugees. Everybody was affected by the general insecurity in Benga and should collaborate with state security to identify and report early warning conflict signals. The State had provided assistance and programmes to facilitate communication networks among the stakeholders and the communities. In the last part of the governor's speech, he said,

"Whether you are a farmer, a grazer, a cattle owner or just a community member, we are all victims and culprits in one way or another. We are here because we are directly or indirectly affected by insecurity in our community and neighbouring communities. We are here to solve problems and not to create problems. We discourage the use of hate speech, insults or words that may incite hatred and violence. We discourage using offensive labels to refer to people from one culture, religion, political party, or part of the country. We can express our frustrations more politely. Before we say anything, keep the following in mind: There is another person who will receive your message. There is someone who can be affected by your words and actions. The receiver of your message is also a human being. Your words can light a fire. I want to assure you that we are here to listen to all the parties concerned. There will be fair intervention by the government and mediators." He gulped some water and continued. "I want to add that this forum is very democratic. So, feel free to speak your mind. The members of my delegation will faithfully convey your recommendations to H.E., the President of Bamfada, for attention and solutions. There will be continuous consultations at many levels involving everybody who is concerned or affected. We will make provisions for incentives and policy, and we want to assure you that the decisions, proposals, and recommendations from this meeting will be considered in order to make way for peace. I also want to add that suggestions, strategies, and hazards may be included in your recommendations."

Mr. Daiga Kidado's translator did not finish translating the last sentence when one elderly man, whose name we later got as Papa Kosimas, sprang to his feet.

"How many times government go carry investigation into the killings before herdsmen dem go stop killing my remaining children now living in bushes and abandoned vehicles? Errhh? Tell me!" "Government has ordered an investigation into the killings. We will bring the culprits to book," he mimicked and then continued ranting: "No be the same story we de hear every day from radio and television when herdsmen de enter village slaughter people...." Before he could end the sentence, another elderly person, Adamu, sprang to his feet in defence.

"Walahi. Dis farmer dem hate Fulani fifur well-well. Na farmer dem de kill our cow and goat. Farmer dem de put gun for inside anus for cow shootam. Dem de put iron inside anus for cow pull intestine comot. Dem say Fulani must carry their cow go back to their land. Dem say cow must not drink their water. Dem say cow must not chop their girass. Dem say Fulani must park kaya go. Dem say Fulani no get native blood. Dem say Fulani no get land. Fulani get another country somewhere? Nobi Fulani fifur first settle for this land before other fifur come join them? Tell me!"

When calm eventually resumed after heated debates and appeals, the governor spoke:

"The problem between farmers and herdsmen did not start today. It is as old as a river. This is not the first time we have come together to talk and seek lasting solutions to the problem. But we must evolve. We are all aware that the two sides have suffered heavy casualties. We are aware that hospitals and the IDP and refugee settlements keep swelling with women, children, and old people due to the conflict between the farmers and herders. The displaced people die of cholera, starvation, rape-related diseases and complications, and other dangerous diseases. So, this gathering is not about who did what to who or who settled here first. It is about the way forward. It is about how to live together in peace and harmony. It is about keeping and sustaining the peace we know is possible. It is about deciding that tolerance, love, and living together must replace anger and hostilities. It is about deciding that we are tired of internal displacements, of burying our children, parents, friends and neighbours. It is about deciding that we no longer want to lose lives, property and cattle. It is also about consoling the families of everybody displaced or killed in the recent ethnic clash between the farmers and the herders. It is about collaborative rehabilitation. This is the time to tell opposing groups to drop their anger and guns and embrace dialogue."

As usual, the interpreter waited for hand claps and voices of applause to die before intervening. The meeting continued, with the governor also addressing the refugees, the IDPs, who he said had recently joined the refugees, and reminding them about the need to stop crime and live in harmony with the host community.

Many others, including representatives of the different groups, spoke one after the other, principally repeating some of the governor's previous statements, such as the need for tolerance, acceptance, love, and harmony.

The UNR representative said the previous speakers had spoken their minds. He expressed the readiness of his association to continue sharing information with relevant stakeholders on their analysis of the different forms of threats and innovative and long-lasting solutions to conflicts. He added that their mission was to facilitate communication channels, provide material and medical assistance to IDPs and refugees, and build partnership and trust among the various groups working to promote peace and development in the communities affected by insurgency and communal clashes.

Before the interpreter could continue his job, the village head was up to speak.

"The viper must be crushed with its eggs lest the hatchery produce descendants that will grow up and continue to bite!"

"Iseeeerrrrrh!" The intervention of the village head was greeted with applause and enthusiastic exclamations of approval.

"For a long time, the villages around the refugee and the IDP camps have suffered diverse forms of assaults. We have had reports that some of the kidnappers, human traffickers, drug dealers, and rapists live among IDPs and refugees. Some of the refugees and IDPs sneak into homes at night. They rape widows and young girls and steal our fowls, goats, dogs, as well as firewood, yams, and cassava from our farms. Some people who pose as IDPs and refugees do not respect our ways. They farm on sacred days. They take our jobs and our women. For a long time, the villagers knew no peace. We don't want them again..."

"Something must be done by the government, now! Or we will be forced to use our own methods!" another man added.

Taking the floor, Bishop Peters Babangida began with a proverb: "Thank you all for your contributions. We have come together to build bridges and not count the costs and heads we have lost. This inclusive meeting is the only way to ensure peaceful coexistence between the farmers and the herdsmen, Christians and Muslims, as well as the refugees, IDPs, and the host community. We need to practice what we preach. Let us start by eliminating from our preaching, symbols, vocabulary, and all forms of portrayals of our brothers and sisters of other religions, tribes and ethnic origins as the 'stranger', the 'infidels', while considering ourselves 'believers', 'holy', and 'sons of the soil'. The decision to form an all-inclusive group to mobilise people for dialogue when there is need is a good one..." Bishop Peters waited for roaring voices rending the air to die before he continued. "It is necessary for every village to have a serious vigilante team whose needs will be provided by the neighbourhoods they are serving. They are doing a good job. We will do as we have been doing. I am using this platform to call on political contractors, human rights activists, and political activists to stop fuelling the conflicts between farmers and herders for their political gains and instead work in the people's interest. There is a need for an end to divisive rhetoric and hate speech. Let us learn to tolerate one another. We should grumble but stay together like ants that fight over crumbs and come back to live together rather than grumble and tear ourselves apart. Everybody is the same before God. No religion is above another. No tribe is superior to another. We should tolerate and respect each other's religion and customs. We need peace and not war."

"Useko! Useko! Iseeerrrrh!" Bishop Peters waited for vigorous voices and exclamations of approval rending the air to die before he continued. He also sent a message to the refugees and the IDPs. They should cooperate with the host community to end rape, abductions and criminal behaviour in the camp. Nobody should go out and steal from people's farms again. Nobody should take what does not belong to them. God will punish the sinners. That is what the Bible says. Girls and women should report cases of rape and sexual harassment. The vigilante should also take note and report suspicious movements in and out of the neighbourhoods, he added and sat down.

The youth leader discussed the need to assist the Vigilante Group with more money for materials, adding that they needed raincoats, boots, a salary increment, rainproof gowns, cutlasses, spears, and weapons.

The hall went dead when Imam Abaka stood up to speak. The MC had introduced him as another advocate of the gospel of "peaceful coexistence" between the Muslim community and the Christians, between the farmers and the herdsmen, and between the refugees and their host communities. He reiterated the need for love and tolerance, advising the herders, farmers, and religious groups to respect each other's religions and customs. Voices of applause arose and fell as he spoke. Misunderstanding and misinterpretation of the Bible and Koran by preachers with little education and experience, he said, was largely responsible for the religious and ethnic divides, in addition to the hate that was fast transforming tribes, religions, friends, and groups into enemies. He called on religious leaders to stop all half-educated persons from sharing or preaching the Holy words in homes, schools, groups, roadsides, market grounds, and places of worship. He added that they could render other services in their places of worship apart from serving as messengers of Allah, God. The imam reiterated that half-baked religious leaders and preachers were responsible for misinterpretations of the holy books, adding that some of them not only mislead their followers but also mask as messengers of the Almighty to lure unsuspecting followers to places of worship to be slaughtered and buried in the backyards and wombs of holy grounds for ritual purposes. The recruitment of young girls and boys into terrorist groups that send them out to bomb mosques, markets, and churches was primarily facilitated by the misreading of the holy books, he said. The imam's message attracted nods and applause across the hall.

All eyes turned toward the traditional ruler when he cleared his throat to speak.

"Who will marry our daughters whom these homeless young adults are impregnating in palm bushes? Who will marry a woman with twelve children who may never know their fathers? Tell me! If this is the way they have chosen to pay us for opening the doors of Benga land to receive them, then these refugees must be sent back to their various countries! Now…!' Voices of applause greeted the suggestion from the traditional leader.

The Chief of Immigration Service, whose face I immediately recognised and buried my face between my palms, stood up to calm the inflamed traditional leader. He said that the matter was already on the table of the government of Bamfada. The government worked with the ambassadors of the countries concerned and the Regional High Commission for refugees to ensure the return of refugees to their respective countries.

The governor invited the farmers and cattle breeder community leaders to stand up and answer questions.

"What kind of things do the farmers want the cattle breeders and the herdsmen to do or avoid so that the two communities can live in peace?"

"What kind of things do the cattle breeders want the farmers to do or avoid so that the two communities can enjoy everlasting peace?"

The two leaders were asked to write their answers on sheets of paper and give them to the governor, and they did as directed after a brief consultation with their representatives.

The next phase of the meeting was reserved for suggestions and recommendations. Many tips and recommendations were agreed on. The vigilante boys were to be placed on a monthly salary of 14,000 Shibe each. Every household would contribute towards their community security. Except for students, every man from the age of 22 would pay 1000 Shibe, while every woman from the age of 20 would contribute 500 Shibe. Every quarter head or community leader would coordinate the contributions in their various vicinities and ensure the payment of the vigilant guards. Any refugee, IDP, or anybody caught stealing or involved in any act of crime would be reported to the quarter head or the nearest police station. Any suspicious movement or activity in the neighbourhood, including fabrication and arms sales, should be reported to the police or community leaders through special security telephone numbers, which will be distributed in the hall. The government would continue consultation meetings with the farmers, the herders, and the stakeholders to seek lasting solutions to the root causes of their persistent clashes. The work of the vigilante guards was going to be evaluated by the community leaders for necessary action.

The use of words, signs, codes, symbols, images, or actions that may incite or draw attention to religious prejudice, bigotry or division, ethnic, racial or gender bias, as well as hate speech, would be prosecuted under the justice system according to the Constitution of the Republic of Bamfada. Any action, behaviour or utterance considered a violation of law, customs, morals, and religious standards shall not be tried in any religious or traditional platform. Only the competent court with legal jurisdiction or authority can try a case of crime or violation of customary norms. The farmers' and cattle breeders' leadership was to preach peaceful coexistence to their respective communities and people. All sacrifice and collaboration were needed to curb the crime rate and conflicts in the Benga Region. The vigilante group and traditional leaders had to collaborate with the forces of law and order to ensure peace returned to their communities. They were to report all suspicious movements and all unknown and suspected persons to the forces of law and order for investigation and possible action. They could call 999 to report any cases of alleged movements and suspected persons. Leaders of religious groups were to ensure that the interpretation and preaching of the holy word to any congregation or group of persons would be made EXCLUSIVELY by experienced and well-educated clerics with a history of moral rectitude, integrity and tolerance. The government of the Republic of Bamfada was to continue regional collaboration with the governments of other neighbouring countries to ensure the safe return of their citizens living in Benga refugee camp. An undisclosed network was already set up to follow up and report infiltrations in the IDP and refugee camps as a further measure to curb rape and other criminal activities in the Benga region as a whole.

The leaders of the cattle breeders' association and the farmers hugged, with the two traditional rulers holding up the peace plant, the bunch of brooms and the bunch of plantains that the governor had handed them. While this happened, the town crier ran around, hitting the gong. Bishop Peters and the imam hugged each other, and the meeting was closed.

Back in the refugee camp, my group and I met briefly at a corner. Our focus was far removed from the peace plan. We cared more about our narrow interests.

"They are planning to return the refugees to their countries. They have also sent undercover agents into the camp to collect information about people pretending to be refugees. Even if our refugee cards save us, we will still be repatriated. But we can't return home the way we came! Nothing to show! What are we to do now?" I also started thinking about the pregnancy and the treatment I would receive for carrying another man's child.

"We have already made some money from the church business. Let us share the money," suggested Livinus, attracting repeated and outwardly impatient nods from all of us.

"Paapa, kindly tell us what we have raised so far so that we can start planning our trip to Amerika, the canoe man added, and we nodded.

As if suddenly stung by a bee, Paapa lifted the fringe of hair growing along the top of his upper eyelids and stared at us with intimidating eyes as he spoke.

"We should share the money I am keeping! Herh, herh, herh! I see! There is one thing you guys are forgetting. Before we escaped from the IDP camp, I had arranged with my boys to make the refugee Identity cards for you. My boys did their job already. And whether or not the identity cards are now free, as I heard some of you saying, that does not affect my contract! By the way, you all know how you became IDPs! You know how you became refugees! The only reason you are still enjoying fresh air and not sitting on the floor and sweating in jail is because I allowed it. If you don't know, the fact that yams and grass grow on the same farm does not mean they have the same weight! Secondly, the fact that cassava and pumpkins have blisters on their leaves does not mean they are suffering from the same disease! I am a son of the soil and not a stranger like some of you! Try anything stupid at your own risk! You have ears…! Remember that we are just coming from a meeting! Do I need to remind you about what the governor said concerning secret agents that the government has set up to catch strangers and criminals living in the camp?" Paapa was all threats.

"By the way, how much did you pay my boys to take photographs of yourselves during the demonstrations in the camp which you will need to seek asylum in Amerika? My boys took photographs and mounted everything together with the photoshopped pictures which will help you to seek asylum in Amerika! That's not all! You sneaked into the IDP camp from another country! I asked Dumi not to inform Chief! You have enjoyed a free stay and free accommodation for a long time! I am still expecting the balance of my generosity from you for these services I have for you! You are asking me to give your share of the money we have raised and nodding like lizards. Stupid!"

299

Paapa grumbled and stood up to leave, threatening to set us up for arrest if we ever asked him for our own share of the money again.

"Paapa, it cannot end like that, gif my own share!" Dumi stood up as he spoke. Paapa dropped a chunk of squashed Shibe notes he had just pulled from his pockets into the palm of Dumi's right hand.

"Church givam money pfilenti! Ngomna givam money pfilenti! Na only *fiptin* Shibe I go collect? No!" Dumi counted the bank notes and threw back the money at Paapa, threatening. It was because of him that Paapa became an IDP.

"Paapa, you forget say na because of me you become IDP?" Their friendship was over, declared the enraged Dumi.

"I am no longer comfortable in low-class friends and environments!" retorted Paapa, a response that seemed to light more flames of anger in Dumi. Dumi rose to his feet, threatening to sell Paapa's secrets. He would betray Paapa by hawking Paapa's secrets to the authorities.

"Paapa…, Paapa…, Chief go soon hear from me! Chief go soon know who carry hand put fire for IDP camp, burn big house, burn dog, burn house for dog!" said Dumi.

"Dumi, my father used to tell me that it is only the person that throws ashes that the ashes follow. By the way, I can't sleep in that stinking cell. Auntie and my boys will release me the same day I am arrested," Paapa warned and again turned to go away.

"Paapa, do you know who I be? My Mama na *simul sitter* for Chief! Na Chief employ me make I work *sikiriti* work for IDP camp! We go see for who ashes go follow!" Dumi said, reminding the confident Paapa that he was the nephew of Chief, that he was employed as a security officer in the IDP camp by Chief; he was employed to gather intelligence about everything happening in the IDP and refugee camps, and would unquestionably have the support of Chief. Paapa might not have heard the last statement from Dumi; he was already about a stone's throw away from us and was also babbling something we could hardly hear.

For almost ten minutes, we sat, our mouths and eyes wide open.

Nobody said a word. The canoe man eventually broke the silence.

"Dumi, don't say anything to Chief for now. We are the ones that would suffer."

He had spoken our thoughts. Everybody quickly joined him to beg Dumi not to betray Paapa for the sake of our security.

28

Savage Blossom's True Identity

The sour relationship between Paapa and Dumi affected us. We formed strategic alliances. Atang and Livinus clutched at Paapa and tried to persuade us to believe he was more powerful and tactical than Dumi, whom they labelled as highly connected but irrelevant. The canoe man, the driver, the motor boy, Jawara and Aboki drifted towards Dumi, whom they saw as their shield. At first, I was confused about which of the snakes to hang on. I had long understood that Dumi had a barren mind regarding survival strategies. My pregnancy constantly reminded me of Paapa, who I now saw as a relevant danger. At last, Savage and I decided to form our own faction and watch how things would turn out. We wanted to be independent. We knew the community already. We wanted to go out on our own and look for farming jobs and do. We wanted to be the authors of our decisions and our money. The men had failed us, and for about a week, we stayed away from them, only joining them briefly. At my suggestion, Baki and her sister took us to local markets, which we started visiting on their weekly market days. We shuffled around the section where food items like beans, rice, corn, wheat, oranges, mangoes and different grains were retailed in buckets, baskets, and bags. We selected good oranges from the discarded heaps, washed and peeled off the skins, and sold them. Some days, we picked grains like corn, beans, and rice that had spilt to the ground. We sold some and cooked some as meals. There were days we did farm jobs and earned some money as well. Fluctuating between the local markets and the farms, combing places for farming jobs, or picking and selling grains and oranges soon became our life pattern. For two months or so, we raised a substantial amount of money. But Savage started behaving almost like a savage. I still remember one of the encounters I had with Savage.

I had gone to bed late in the night and dreamt that I was behind the classroom, urinating. In the dream, I saw Paapa standing behind me. He had come to invade me again, I thought. I was afraid and screamed, trying to run away.

"Kila, why you de cry?" asked Baki, prodding me awake on the leg with her toes. "It was just a dream," I said, lying on the floor and feeling embarrassed. My lap was warm; I wondered what was happening. I felt the warmth again and decided Savage should not know about it. I shifted my buttocks away, and on turning my head slightly to steal a glance at Savage, I found her space empty.

Where could she possibly be? Had she gone out to urinate? Thank God she wasn't in bed. Something was impatiently rioting along the road to my domestic hatchery. It was the remaining dregs of urine, and I quickly ran outside. Something was gliding down my legs even before I could reach the rear of the building. As the moon was shining brightly, my eyes fell on the figure of Savage a little further away.

She stood like a man, her upper body bending forward, her legs wide apart, almost wide enough for a small horse to pass between them. Urine darted out from where her legs met, leaping across the grass and heavily hitting a mango tree's trunk. It was like the noise you hear when rain falls heavily on a building's roof.

Wasn't that Savage? I wondered, staring from the bend where I stood. She suddenly pushed her buttocks behind, shaking her fingers as if she was ringing a bell. Then she lifted her jeans trouser to her waist.

Although shocked at what I saw, I didn't want Savage to read my feelings. I didn't also want her to discover that my dress was wet with pee. I tiptoed in reverse and stood in the yard, hoping the wind would dry off my damp dress before returning to my space. It was late. Savage had monitored my moves. She knew that I had seen everything. I knew it. I could see her body language when she approached me from behind and stopped. However, I was still in shock and didn't know what to say. She now looked strange, not the Savage I knew. The thoughts of the many times she had wrapped her hand around me in an inappropriate manner came to my mind, but I quickly shoved it aside as I tried figuring out how to dismiss her from my side so she would not get the smell of my urine.

"Savage, don't bother yourself waiting for me. I will join you later," I said, not knowing what else to do. She, however, broke into tears and attracted my sympathy for her.

"I'm sorry, I'm really sorry. I didn't intend to hurt you… I."

"Kila, even you! Are you going to avoid me, too?" asked Savage.

"No, no. You got it wrong." I said, somewhat confused.

"You just asked me to leave," she said. "You stood at the rear of the building staring at me… Is that why you asked me to leave?"

"Savage, I am sorry. But it's not what you are thinking. Perhaps we didn't just understand each other…"

"Understand what? What is it I didn't understand? You asked me to go away from you! Kila, I didn't create myself. But I have no regrets at all. I like myself the way I am," she said, aggrieved.

Savage had just indirectly confirmed my thoughts. I stood mute, arrested by both sympathy and shock.

"Everybody hates me when they know me. Nobody wants me around. I was hated and rejected by the people I trusted. Nobody wanted to eat from the same dish with me. My sister wouldn't accept the trousers I sent her simply because I had worn them in one of the pictures I had sent her. She simply returned it to me. They don't want me anywhere around the village. They said I was a curse…!"

"Savage, what are you talking about?" I asked.

"Nobody likes me when they know me," she repeated.

"Savage, I don't hate you. I'll do anything to make you happy.

Stop crying, please." I had no idea what else to do or say, even though I felt her pain.

"Are you sure?" she asked, her voice becoming relaxed.

"Yes, I will not do anything that can tear us apart," I pleaded, and she smiled. "What makes you think your parents hate you? What did they do to you?" I asked, my voice cautious.

"Promise me you won't tell anybody," Savage requested.

"Your secret is safe with me. We are in another country, suffering. We only have each other. This is the moment we need each other most. I would not want to do anything that can tear us apart. I will not tell anybody whatever it is," I said.

"I am Blossom…"

"What!" I screamed and stared at her. It was similar to the same absent-minded look that Blossom wore some decades back when she stormed out of the inspection hall the day the nurses came for inspection. We had just been admitted to the then Government Secondary College, Mbiame-Kibang. The school had lost two girls to abortion during the first semester, and measures were then taken to control the rate of teenage pregnancies. Pregnancy inspection and dismissal of victims happened to be one such measure. That day, two female nurses visited our school for inspection. All the girls were taken to one room, where they stood in a queue. When it was her turn, Blossom reluctantly left Miranda and I and walked in, her head hanging heavily over her shoulder. The door slammed behind her. After a while, the two nurses ran outside, screaming wildly. They stood on the long corridor of the building, their mouths and eyes open, staring silently at each other, raising and lowering their shoulders. At first, we were scared and confused. Then, we gathered the courage to go in and find out what had happened to warrant the dramatic reaction from the nurses. Just then, Blossom came out, looking at her feet as she walked past us. That was the last time she was seen in GSS, Mbiame-Kibang, and Mbiame.

"Could the reaction of the female nurses be connected with what I saw when I went behind the classroom to urinate? Could it be what I am thinking?" I was lost in thoughts, trying to establish a connection between the pregnancy inspection incident and what I saw and what Savage was trying to tell me when she spoke.

"I know where your mind is," she observed.

"Yeah, I was really trying to recall the incident at GSS Mbiame-Kibang when the nurses came for a pregnancy inspection. I have always wanted to ask if you are Blossom," I said. "You left school and never returned," I said.

"I didn't like the behaviour of the nurses. When I pulled off my uniform, the nurses ran away when they saw it. I knew they would tell everybody that I was different."

"What do you mean?" I asked.

"I have a furrow and an anthill down there," Savage confirmed my fears.

"Did your parents consult the native doctor for herbs that could stop the growth of the long one?" My voice trembled as I asked.

"My mother told me that they took me to hospitals and every native doctor in the land, but nothing changed."

"You didn't have to stop attending the village school. You didn't create yourself." I said, not knowing what else to say. I knew it was taboo in Mbiame land to give birth to a child with male and female genitals.

"You don't know what it means to feel hated and rejected. Memories of the reaction of the nurses tortured me. My mother asked me to get ready for school the following day. I refused. I hated school since that day. I still have bad memories of my little time in the village. I didn't like how I was treated when the villagers learned I had two. Nobody drank from the same cup I had used. My grandmother said I should not eat from the same dish as my sister to avoid spreading the curse. They said I was a witch. The villagers stopped coming to our compound. The native doctor advised my family to throw me in a river. My mother took me to Mawunde to live with my uncle. My uncle registered me in another school. His wife rejected me. I never revisited the village. I hated the village. After my university education, I remained in the city. I had known Evelda during my days at the university. We were good friends and decided to live together, but our neighbours hated our union and informed my family. One evening, one man visited Evelda and I. He presented himself as a relation from my father's family. It was a pathetic story listening to him. He was stranded. He came from our village to claim his salary arrears from the finance ministry. The procedure took a long time, and he ran out of money. He could not afford accommodation in the hotel any longer. He wanted to spend a few days in our house before travelling back to the village, as he was expecting his wife to send him money. He pretended he was sick. When Evelda wanted us to go and buy foodstuffs in the market the following day, he pretended that his situation was worsening. He needed attention, so I stayed behind, and Evelda left. When I entered the bathroom to have a bath, he locked the door and forced himself into me." Savage wept as she narrated the story. "The man hurriedly left before Evelda came back."

"Did you inform the police?" I asked.

"The police were looking for Evelda and I to arrest us," she said.

"Why?"

"A woman cannot love a woman. It is forbidden for a woman to marry a woman. A man cannot marry a man. A curse will visit the family if a woman marries a woman." Savage mimicked the villagers and continued. "That was the new song on every lip. They called us names. They said we were climbers and riders. They called us 'bend sikin' or 'bend over.' Everybody hated us." Savage broke down as she spoke.

She was right. It was believed that a curse would visit the land if same-sex marriage or relations were allowed. The clergy said it was a sin.

"Did you inform your family about what someone disguised as your uncle did to you?" There was hesitation and sympathy in my voice as I asked.

"What happened was a set-up, as I later learned. It was a set-up with the knowledge of my father. When I was born, my mother decided I should grow up as a woman. They didn't allow me to grow up and decide for myself. I grew up dressing in skirts and gowns. My family wanted me to marry a man and not a woman. Nobody thought about my happiness. I started feeling like a man when I was 16. When I informed them in writing that I was engaged to marry a lady, they replied that it would never work. My grandmother said I was initiated into a satanic cult and needed deliverance. They took counsel from a native doctor to pay a man to get me pregnant to divert my feelings toward the man. That's what the herbalist told them, and my father paid a bike rider to violate me. Savage wept as she narrated her pathetic story.

We yawned repeatedly as the cocks started crowing, and she again tried to lock lips with me, but I pushed her away, again embarrassed.

29

Arrest and Deportation

"Na de kiriminar dis! Officer, arrest him!" Savage and I were inside, resting on the mat, when confused noises woke me from a deep sleep, followed by heavy footsteps across the yard. We ran outside but rammed into police officers. There was a crowd in the yard and two high vehicles. Dumi still pointed at Paapa, whom he had described as the criminal. He was also lowering and lifting his head as if trying to locate another person in the crowd. Madame Nurse, Atang, Livinus, the canoe man, the driver and the motor boy stood shivering. Their wrists were joined together and clamped firmly with heavy metal rings. I knew it was the end of the road for us before the searching eyes of one of the officers who had profiled us at the immigration office landed on me.

"That's one of them! That's another! Arrest her! Arrest them!" the officer shouted, pointing at Savage and I in the crowd with the noose of his gun. My left hand was clicked to Savage's own with a metal ring locked around our wrists.

"Officer, arrest Dumi. Dumi hands no clean at all, at all," said Musa, pointing at Dumi from one of the vehicles with his mouth because his wrists were also handcuffed.

"Get inside that car! Immediately!" The police officer said, hurling us into the back seats of one of their vehicles. Four police officers climbed in, their guns pointing at us. Like a storm, they whisked us to the Immigration Service, and one after the other, we were taken into one office and questioned.

"How did you find yourself in Bamfada?"

I could not lie and there was even no point in lying. It was the same officer who had questioned me before. I recounted my journey from my country through the desert on my way to Amerika, citing the transit journey through Bamfada and the travel ban that stopped the journey at Benga.

"How did you know about the refugee camp?"

I recounted the details of our escape from immigration custody.

"You were present when the IDP facility was burnt. Tell us the role played by Dumi, Paapa, Musa, and others! What else do you know about Dumi, Paapa, and any other person or activity you think we should know? Remember that we have asked Musa and members of your travel team the same questions. You will rot in jail if you try to lie or to say something contrary to what they already told us," the officer threatened.

I was a very faithful reporter of the events I suffered or witnessed in both the IDP and the refugee facilities. I spoke out about the rape incidents and the activities of Madame Nurse or Auntie. I said everything I knew about Dumi and Paapa. I did not forget to disclose that I was carrying Paapa's pregnancy. There were other victims of the lecherous escapades of Paapa and Dumi, I added, citing the Baki and the Kaki factor.

After we had been so probed, Savage, Atang, Livinus, Jawara, Aboki, and I were taken to a dark, filthy, sweltering cell. There, we passed the night. The following day, we were informed that we would be repatriated to our country with the assistance of our embassy.

A few hours later, officials from the embassy of Kibaaka in Bamfada came to see us. It was the same official who visited us when we were locked up in immigration custody and told us that the Kibaaka embassy would provide consular assistance in the form of a 'Laissez-passer' to ease our return journey. The official had a lengthy discussion with us, advising us to get ready to return home.

***

The worst page of my life began the day we were repatriated to Kibaaka. We were taken to Kutaka International Airport as early as 7:00 a.m. by three officials, one from the Bamfada Immigration Service and the others from the Kibaaka embassy. After going through the formalities involving checking in and profiling, we were led to a counter. The lady who sat behind a large screen, printed tickets and distributed them to us. From there, two police officers led us through a long and winding way to a large space where we sat for a few hours. Soon, we heard an announcement requesting passengers to proceed on board, and we were led to a large aeroplane. It was my first air travel and the first time I saw an aircraft at close range. It was like a gigantic bird. It had a long-pointed nose with wings and a tail. We climbed the stairways and went in. My seat was close to the window. A lady, a flight attendant, asked us to fasten our seatbelts. She did a demonstration on how to use the life jacket. A few moments later, we heard a voiceover telling the passengers the airplane was about to take off.

Soon, the airplane taxied along the runway, and my heart almost leapt out of my chest when its speed suddenly accelerated, and then it skipped, inclining upward and plunging downward, repeating the action several times. It was not a smooth flight. The plane started mounting upward and heaving about noisily in the air, roaring like a car driving over gravel. I slept shortly after we were served snacks and drinks. During my waking hours throughout the flight, thoughts of how I would face Jeff and the villagers harassed me intensely.

I blamed myself for not telling my family the truth while away. I had allowed pride to decide for me rather than return to my country to try other survival strategies when it became apparent that I had been defrauded. I now questioned why I hadn't escaped after the dreadful desert journey. Why hadn't I informed Jeff and my family that I had been scammed and never reached the desired destination? Why hadn't I called to tell my husband that I lost our baby, that I was a victim of foreign invasion and occupation resulting in a pregnancy? What had I done to myself? Would Jeff accept me with another man's child? What about the village people? Would Jeff's family accept me? Was a woman invaded by foreigners and left with a seed different from soils contaminated by plastic waste from a nation of insatiable appetite totters? Is that not what they always said? I looked at my skin, desperately hugging its bones.

"Dear passengers on board, we are about to descend to the Buwala International Airport. The descent interval is approximately 25 minutes. Fasten your seatbelts." The sonorous voice woke me up from my thoughts. Soon, we were flying lower, and I could see houses streaming past. Then came a loud bang, a blast that left my heart galloping in fright.

"The flight has landed," the voice said. I prayed and thanked God for returning us safely, although my mind was not at rest. I returned home with nothing but my dead telephone, which had survived only because it was always in my underwear.

Fresh trouble started after our flight touched down at Buwala International Airport, one of Kibaaka's biggest cities. Immediately after we descended from the plane, sticky heat swooped on me, biting my skin. A policeman isolated us from the crowd and led us through a meandering path to a bus outside the enclosed airport buildings. We were sweating, frail like stems growing on marshland. The only person who spoke was Livinus.

"Do not tell anybody that we came back with nothing. They will use it to insult us. When people come to greet you, just say our cars and things are in a ship coming. If my father hears that I came back with nothing, the next thing you will hear is, "Livinus, your mates are driving big cars, raising grandchildren, and you are still eating from your mother's kitchen. I told you that nothing good can ever come out of you." He coughed and continued. "Atang, we need to plan what we will tell university girls. You know them, na. If the discussion is not about the size of your bank account, forget, forget, they will not even listen." Livinus had barely finished talking and arranging the Amerikan flag headscarf on his head when a heavy voice descended on us.

"Entréz vit dans le bus ci," the policeman shouted. We scrambled onto the bus, and it took us through thick traffic to the police station, where we were subjected to questioning. The Bamfada immigration officials must have informed their Kibaaka counterparts about our activities in the IDP and refugee camps. The security agents identified us and kept us in a facility for two days, trying to reach out to our families through the telephone numbers we had provided. There was anxiety, joy and mixed feelings when the officer opened the door of our cell and led us to their office to wait for our families.

A painful smile smeared my cheeks as I watched my husband walk towards the door, accompanied by two handsome grown-up boys, turning their heads and peering at the faces along the corridor. A gleaming, unhealthy, threadbare ash-colour cap with an extended frontal that looked like a bicycle seat grabbed Jeff's head. His wobbly suit had frowning surfaces. His chin and cheeks, including the edges of his headline, looked like he had poured corn flour on them. I moved my pathetic stare from Jeff to my children, who had changed significantly. A tiny bush of hair that looked like a fleshy crest on the head of the domestic chicken stood in the middle of Mbiame's head. I wasn't surprised at the curiosity on their faces when they walked in.

"Daddy, where's mum?" the boys asked simultaneously, shifting stares from Jeff to I and back, a question that left my eyes welling up with tears as I staggered forward to hug them.

They didn't recognise me but I hugged them, and then Jeff, crying. None of us spoke a word for a while. They looked at me, their eyes and mouths wide open. Then they looked at my face, my arms, and my feet. In their stares was a mixture of sympathy and confusion. Jeff stared fixedly at my bulging stomach and then broke the silence,

"Kila, is this really you?"

"Jeff, I'm s-so sorry. It's a long story." I managed to stammer.

"Where is my son? Or, you haven't given birth yet?" Jeff looked confused.

"W-w-we lost him...,"

"Lost him..., so where's this pregnancy from?"

"It wasn't my fault. It's a long story. I will explain," I stuttered. Jeff looked away, his body language a message of rejection.

"Mum, are you sick...?" Asked Bernsah, staring at me.

"Mum, where are your bags? Where are the things you brought for us from Amerika?" Mbiame interrupted.

"Mum, you didn't call to greet us. Why? We were worried and afraid when we hadn't heard from you for many years. Daddy was worried, and Yaya was, too," Bernsah said.

"Mum, you are not saying anything! Mum, are you tired? Mum, is there no water in Amerika? Do they grow food? Are there no nice clothes and shoes in Amerika?" The chain of questions kept pouring from my children's mouths as they stared at my fingers and toenails, which looked like ginger. I felt ashamed and embarrassed. But I managed to speak.

"What level of studies are you now?" I asked my children.

"I left school in form three. Bernsah left in form five. Daddy was very sick and had no money for our school needs any more. He suggested we learned a trade."

A sticky smell of cigarette gushed out of Mbiame's mouth as he spoke, causing my heart to burn inside as if it were engulfed by flames.

I went after money and lost my family. Was the journey necessary? The thoughts tore through my chest, causing my eyes to tear up. Bernsah wiped his teary eyes. In addition to Jeff's pitiful look, the smell of cigarettes from Mbiame's mouth and the shocking revelation that my children had dropped out of school rocked my body. My legs trembled, and then my body. I felt terribly guilty knowing how much pain I had caused my family. My legs could not carry me any longer. I sat on the bare floor, feeling empty.

"Mr Jeff, come over and sign here, and take your family home," said the policeman, shuffling his eyes from me to Bernsah, who was also sobbing.

Jeff turned and walked out without uttering a word. I went and signed the paper and joined him in the corridor. We followed him to the road and took a taxi to drop us somewhere. He found a bus loading for our region and paid to secure our seats. Ten tedious hours took us to our village, passing through major cities, towns and other villages and stopping briefly for people to eat before taking off. I was determined to give my telephone to Jeff, and I did.

"The answer to all your questions is in this telephone," I said, giving my dead phone to Bernsah, who pressed a few buttons with disappointment. Nobody was talking. My children understood that I was in anguish and stopped asking questions.

When we got to my village, Mbiame, there were many tall and beautiful houses. Even the road to my village had been tarred. Jeff took me straight to my father's compound. When we walked in, my father had been chatting with Ability and Taa Gheh in front of his door. Their beards and heads were completely streaming grey. Judging from their reactions and questions, my father did not recognise me, nor did they recognise me when I greeted them.

"Jeffiri, did they tell you that my compound has become a maternity?" asked my father, peering at my watermelon-size stomach from his seat with his starved eyes and sipping palm wine from his horn.

"Who is she?" asked Ability, his scrutinising, frail eyes searching my face and moving to my stomach, down to my legs, and then my feet, where they settled for a while before he lifted his head again to look into my eyes.

"Jeffiri, this compound is not a psychiatric centre. We don't have facilities for mental patients. Can't you see that this woman's body, from the face right down to her legs and feet, is wearing twisted, frowning, thin lines on the surface of her skin? Her legs look like the bark of a tree. Take her to a herbalist! Did you come with a coffin?" Ability observed.

"Why is she not talking?" Asked Ta Gheh.

"This is the time it always starts. Whenever you start seeing cracks on the surface of the soil, cases like this would be brought from the coast for treatment," Ability assumed.

"Why is this one not accompanied?" Ta Gheh wondered.

"Take her to Yaya. She is a specialist in the treatment of madness," said Ability.

"Why don't you give her food before taking her to Yaya?" my father suggested. "Kilara, Kilara…," he called.

"Father of children," answered my stepmother from her kitchen. She soon walked in and bent forward.

"Look for something and give to this mad woman to eat before they take to the herbalist," said my father.

"Is this not Kila? Mami Kilara asked, looking surprised.

All eyes turned toward me when Mami Kilara called my name. Their stares carried an air of disbelief that was hard to ignore. For almost three minutes, nobody uttered a word. My father staggered toward the courtyard and returned with a chunk of soil, which he threw at my feet as if to confirm that I wasn't a ghost. Then, he leaned back on his chair.

"Kila, is this you? This is what happens when you travel to far-off lands without your father's blessings," my father said, and Taa Gheh nodded.

"Kila, I hope you know that Jeff paid your bride price and you cannot be pregnant with another man's baby again." Ability's eyes shifted to my bulging stomach as he spoke.

"Whose name will that child carry?" My father asked.

"Jeffirri, is this why *ngomna* summoned you to Buwala?" Taa Gheh asked.

"Our people say that when marriage is broken, the bride price is returned," Ability said.

"Let us hear her own side of the story," suggested Buri, who was among the tiny crowd that had started to trickle into my father's compound.

"Even if she explains from Genesis to Malakai, what will change the fact that our daughter travelled to the land of plenty and the only thing she brought back home was the fruit of an animal trail affair? I will not sit here to listen to the story of shame! Never!" Ability fumed.

Ability's words stung my heart. The heat of shame consumed me. My dress was dripping with sweat. Warm urine scurried down my legs, attracting attention. My body reeled continuously. I hesitated momentarily, not knowing what to say, and then wiped the tears slithering down my cheeks. I felt embarrassed and rejected, wondering whether my unborn baby and I would be forgiven and accepted when they would have heard my own side of the story. Jeff, who had been watching the reactions, quietly turned and walked away.

The news about my return had spread like the dry-season fires, and more and more people were trooping into my father's compound, stretching their necks forward to have a glimpse of my ghost as I heard some saying in whispers.

"She is mad," I recall one woman near me confirming.

As I scanned the faces across the yard from the corners of my eyes, hoping to see Yaya, they, too, scanned me from head to toe. Everybody had something to say. Some believed I had lost my sanity. Others asked why I got pregnant by another man while still married. One man said someone had told him that I was retailing my waist in Amerika. Within an hour, the entire village had gathered in our compound, hurling deriding comments at me and asking for the gifts I had brought from Amerika. The embarrassing reception and reactions might have hastened my breakdown.

"Kila, is that really you, or my eyes are deceiving me?" a voice asked from across the door.

"Kila, I have come to collect my own share of the things you brought from the land of the white man," requested another, her twisted lips pointing at my gnarled arms.

"Kila, that place you are coming from, is it a barren land? Don't they grow food there? Or, were the people eating and wiping hands on your legs?"

Mami Regular staggered across the yard and twisted her lips while staring at my skin that was desperately clutching my bones. Then she lifted and dropped her shoulders. She compared my feet to the gnarled roots of an old mango tree growing above the earth and wondered aloud if it was the same Amerika from where Miranda kept sending cars and things to her family.

"The longest-serving prisoner in Kondengi has more flesh to cover his bones than Kila", added Ability, attracting a rainfall of laughter from lips.

Another woman said, "Kila, what is inside that stomach? You will soon hear from the elders if it is what I am thinking."

All this while, I sat staring at the cracks and ribs on my bony feet, sobbing, trying to avoid direct eye contact with the village of people, staring at me wide-eyed, open-mouthed, and farting out sarcastic comments which I didn't need at the time. While the flurry of insults kept stabbing me on all sides, specifically targeting my agony-wrinkled skin, I was fighting a silent battle, too. As my thoughts wound their way through the pain-laden memories of the journey, from the sea through the desert to the IDP and the refugee camps and then to the detention facility, I suddenly felt the heat of frustration consuming the last speck of strength I was holding onto. I couldn't bear it anymore. It would be better in the other world. I mused and started blaming myself, wishing I had not travelled out at all. I went out for greener pastures but returned more frustrated than I left, I said to myself, feeling empty, ashamed and guilty. I wished I could see Yaya and talk to her. She was the only one I needed at that moment. She would understand me, I mused.

Just then, Yaya tore through the forest of people across the yard, supporting herself with a stick. Jeff and his father came with her. As I later learned, she had been living with them in the two-room apartment Jeff had built in my absence. Yaya lifted her eyes and fixed a long stare at me without answering my greetings. Then, she wiped the tears streaming down her cheeks with the edge of her loincloth and began lamenting.

"Kila, is this you? Did they have to wait until she becomes ruins before returning her to me? Kila, is that not another man's seed you are carrying? Mbarang! Who did I offend? Who did I offend?"

Yaya was still lamenting when Jeff's father and two elders flustered through the crowd and stopped over me. When Jeff's father stepped forward, peered at my big stomach and coughed repeatedly to attract attention, I knew immediately that what he was about to say would rip my heart to shreds.

"Our people say that when the marriage is broken, we return the palm wine. I have returned your daughter to you. Return the bride price we paid for her. My people will come back after ten *ngoilum* market days to collect it." The words stung my heart. My body whirled repeatedly, and I saw the crowd streaming past in continuous motion.

Jeff's father then turned and held Bernsah and Mbiame by the hands, saying, "Let us go back home." I requested to talk to Jeff and his father, who were still at the door, insisting on taking Mbiame and Bernsah away, but they ignored me. Mbiame turned to go with his father and grandfather but hesitated when he realised that Bernsah was leaning on me, weeping profusely. I noticed a cigarette stick jutting from Mbiame's brown chest pocket when he lowered his buttocks and sat beside Bernsah. My heart almost crumbled at the sight of the cigarette.

The reactions of Jeff, his father, and Bernsah brought more pain and tears to me. The pain of hearing that my children abandoned school because of me was still tearing through my heart. The humiliating reception was weighing down on me. The decision by my husband's family to take back the bride price they paid on my head descended on me like a mountain collapsing and crushing everything on its path. I felt the instant heat of cultural sanctions in that rejection. The weight of insults, ridicule and threats of facing the sting of tradition simmered in my mind. The embarrassment inside me swelled with each passing minute. My mind was consumed with the heat of humiliation. The thoughts of rejection gnawed my intestines. The claws of fear tore through my chest cavity. Fire burned in me.

I felt the need to apologise to everybody who felt hurt by me, hoping I could get relief from tendering the apology. I opened my mouth to speak, but my lips only quivered. Numbing anxiety aligned with nervousness to make my legs heavy. My hair stood up to echo the burning sensations all over my body. It was as if I was stung by bees on every part. Then, I felt water gliding down my legs and thought I was dying. I became blurry, unable to see well. It was as if someone had hurled wood ash across the room. Whatever happened, I only awoke and found myself lying in a small bed. The room had the smell of drugs greeting you when you approach a hospital.

"W-w-where am I?" I managed to ask.

"Doctor! Doctor! Doctor! My sister can speak! She can speak! Thank you, Jesus," shouted Nyuydzesi. Buri also stood up, dancing and thanking God as the doctor walked in to examine me.

"She will be fine. Give her enough food and water to drink. She can now start taking her drugs. Check the leaflet for the prescription I already gave. If there is a problem, get back to me," the doctor said, adjusting the drip on my hand. He also adjusted the oxygen pipe in my nose. When he left, Buri and Nyuydzesi sat at the bottom edge of the bed, telling me what actually happened.

As I was told, I collapsed when my father was asked to refund the bride price Jeff's family paid on my head. I was unconscious when I was rushed to the hospital. I had been like that for almost a week, surviving on drips and oxygen. I gave birth to a boy immediately we got to the hospital. The baby was kept in the incubator. Yaya named my baby Fomunyuy Kila, which respectively means 'gift from God and 'who knows?' I didn't immediately know I had a baby. Nyuydzesi and Buri gave me new clothes. They also provided for the baby. My siblings contributed the money required for my hospital bills. Buri obtained a loan from the Women's Cooperative Group, and added to the money my siblings had contributed. I would refund when I could. These were the revelations Nyuydzesi and Buri made, sitting on the slim edges of my hospital bed, some moments after I started recovering. The doctor confirmed that I would be fine, Nyuydzesi added.

I managed to eat the food they had prepared for me, the first meal since my return home. But I wasn't hungry.

My situation soon worsened. I was moved to another unit in the hospital. I couldn't sleep. The patients were chained to their beds and were loudly aggressive, always talking with themselves, always quarrelling with themselves. My situation involved memory lapses, too. I constantly forgot what I wanted to say, even in the middle of a conversation. One day, I went out to bask myself under the sun and forgot my way back to the ward. I was later found wandering in the neighbourhood and brought back to the ward. I did not remember everything for a long time as I constantly glided in and out of awareness.

The doctor advised me to get busy and do something in order to hasten my healing. He said it the day I was discharged from the psychiatric ward. It was thereafter that I started remembering things and talking logically. I was taken back to my father's compound.

Yaya was now assisted in almost everything, and so was my father. Buri and Nyuydzesi by me were my joy, and I took care of my baby, cooking for us both. Buri came to see us thrice weekly, ensuring we chatted often.

"Kila, the Doctor said you need to be doing something to speed up your healing. If you continue to sit in the room like this, the illness may return after improvement; it may get worse. That is what the Doctor said." Nyuydzesi was reminding me.

"That thing will come back if you are not active. You need to start going out, maybe doing something. That is what the Doctor said," added Buri.

"I don't want to be seen anywhere around. I want to stay at home and take care of my children. Mbiame needs to stop smoking. I just want to be around them," I said.

"Then, the forgetfulness will return and send you back to the hospital again," warned Nyuydzesi, looking straight at me.

My recovery was slow but steady. My greatest fear was not being able to stop my children from straying. I wanted my children to regain their dignity, to succeed where I failed. I decided to counsel Mbiame about the health and other challenges that come with smoking and gambling. Thereafter, I sat, feeding my baby sweet palm wine and thinking. "I need to stay strong to care for my children and family. The doctor said I need to be active. How would I keep myself active? I have no money to start a trade." Then, I realised I could cook food and sell it. I had learned food processing and online marketing earlier in the IDP camp. It was time to use the skills I acquired. I asked Nyuydzesi, Bernsah and Buri to customise and promote my brand on Facebook and their WhatsApp platforms. I would take a loan from the women's cooperative to start the food business. I was still a member of the group. People would place orders online, and I would supply them in their homes. Bernsah and Mbiame could help with home delivery, too, especially as poverty had chased them out of school. Bernsah was learning fashion design at the Women's Centre while his brother was learning how to repair vehicles at a local car garage. I felt an urgent need to make them relevant. They had to join my business while doing their training.

All this while, Jeff never left my thoughts. I strongly needed to write a novel about my journey to Amerika. I needed to write to Jeff so he could know what actually happened. He needed to know that I never betrayed our marriage vows.

"I am happy to see that smile on your face. It's been a long time since I've seen you smile. What is it? Did you dream that you reunited with Jeff? Share the good news with me, na," said Buri, who had come to give me food.

I told her and my sister, Nyuydzesi, about my plans to start a food business with my children. They were happy and helped with ideas. Everything went as planned.

Bernsah took my telephone to a phone repairer. The phone was broken, but the SIM card was retrieved. All the recordings and pictures I took were recovered, and Bernsah transferred them to his telephone. The contents of my SIM card were later forwarded to Jeff's phone, thanks to Bernsah and Buri. I badly wanted Jeff to know that I was the victim of rape. I had heard that he had found a wife immediately after I had returned carrying another man's baby. I held no grudge against him but blamed what happened on my silence. The phone information was not enough. I wrote him a letter, a summary of my experiences during the aborted journey. The only thing I kept to myself was that the place where my legs met was leaking water, something like drool.

I also wanted to keep memories of the journey and use the power of the pen to talk on behalf of those who cannot fight for their rights. I tried to expose scammers like Kaba and also human traffickers. So, I started writing the novel, the subject matter being my experiences. At my request, Bernsah uploaded the videos, pictures, and voice recordings of my experiences from my SIM card to Facebook. I was writing and selling food at the same time. What Bernsah uploaded on Facebook soon caught the media's attention, and I was invited to grant radio and television interviews about my experience. Newspaper headlines screamed with excerpts from my interviews.

Everything went as planned. I scribbled with delight what I assumed would be read by many. My integrity would be restored. The novel would teach the lessons the classroom hardly provides. It would expose Kaba. Although my life was fast ebbing, my joy germinated as the novel took shape and my business grew. I no longer thought of my existence with regret. I was happy that I came back home. The business was slow but rewarding, and the novel was in progress.

Nyuydzesi, Buri, Bernsah, Mbiame, and I sat down one day to count the proceeds from the food business. I wanted to start refunding my loan and send my boys back to school to further their education, but Mbiame rejected the idea of returning to school. Mbiame insisted that he wanted to learn a trade and hustle. Nyuydzesi and Buri were incorporated into my food business. Before long, we rented a shed in the market. We were making little money from the food business, hoping it would grow. On our daily menu were rice and stew, kahti kahti and vegetables, beans and rice, achu, fufu and eru, okra soup and fufu/garri, yams and sauce, goat-meat pepper soup, mbongo chobi, ekwang, ndole and plantains, grilled fish and bobolo, and koki. We varied the meals depending on demand. Generally, the going was manageable, and I learnt that goodness tugs in greater good. My only worry was Mbiame and Bernsah. They had escaped their father's house and joined me in my father's compound because their stepmother hated them, gave them food only when Jeff was around, and constantly beat them and asked them to leave her house. They were now assisting me in my food business, but that was not what I wanted for them. They were too young to stay at home, selling food. They needed to do something sustainable. They deserved a better future.

Despite the profit I was making, something was lacking. The food business didn't restore what I had lost. The pain of watching my children, my pride, my only source of joy, reduced to delivery agents with no school certificate, no skilled training, and no proper upbringing, became more intense with each passing day. Jeff's attitude towards me had intensified my agony. It also affected Bernsah and Mbiame, who were out of school and straying. I decided to meet Jeff to discuss how to raise our children. I shared the idea with Buri and Yaya and they promised to arrange and facilitate a meeting between Jeff and I.

One evening, Buri, Yaya and I went to see Jeff. We were accompanied by Nyuydzesi and a few members of the women's association. We met in a bar because he had warned me not to come anywhere near his house. He was with Baa Ability, his father, Taa Gheh, and other village elders, and they were drinking and talking about my son. His father sat two tables away from us. That was the first time I discussed with Jeff face-to-face since my deportation. My first attempt to discuss with him had been several months before when I went with Buri to tell him what happened to me. I was denied entry into his compound then. I was happy that Jeff and the elders finally agreed to listen to me and that we had fixed a meeting venue. There, I narrated my story, Buri and Yaya making desperate attempts to persuade Jeff and the elders to lay down their anger and forgive me.

"Elders of our land, father of my children, kindly find a place in your hearts to forgive me. My pregnancy resulted from sexual assault." The women nodded in support, and I continued. "Jeff, for the sake of our children, we need collaboration. Our boys are out of school, straying, taking life lessons from the wrong people. They need both mother and father figures to tell them what is right and wrong," I pleaded.

"Jeff, the man we paid to prepare my travel documents is the cause of everything I went through. We should never have trusted Kaba. He took us through back roads and desert pathways. We passed through thick forests. We crossed empty sandy lands and big rivers, some fifty times the size of River Mairin, River Wouri and River Sanaga combined. Many travellers fell into the big river and drowned. We met bad men everywhere. We shared sleeping spaces with them. They kicked my legs apart and descended on me. They had guns. They threatened to kill us if we didn't cooperate. They threatened to inform the police that we were strangers if we didn't open our legs or bend over to let them in through the back door. We slept in the bushes. We ate tree bark and ground and tree leaves to survive. We urinated and drank." Tears gushed from my eyes, and the women wiped their cheeks as I narrated my ordeals. Jeff's eyes were also red.

"Kila, you brought this upon yourself. I read passages from your texts, your interviews, and other details about your journey in the newspapers, Facebook, and the letter you sent me. Well, Kaba has been arrested by the police." Jeff said, stretching a newspaper forward and pointing to the headlines.

"That's good news! He will not get away with it," I screamed joyfully, feeling somewhat vindicated and excited that I would get justice. The women were also excited.

"People are not always what you take them for, and there is indeed no art to read the mind's construction in the face," Jeff lamented, and the women nodded in agreement.

Jeff peered into my eyes, and our eyes met. Then, he bent over the table and gently held my hand. Yaya, Buri and Nyuydzesi leaned forward, exchanging glances. Their repeated winks and nods told me they were trying to goad Jeff into a compromise. My heart danced joyfully, and my eyes brimmed with tears as Jeff prodded my palm. It was like the fingers of the breeze caressing one's dry cheeks on a sunny, windy afternoon. I felt the weight of rejection and guilt falling off the shoulders of my conscience. I was inwardly happy watching Jeff's half-closed, teary eyes peering into mine and reminding me of the same stare that disarmed me of the capacity to resist his marriage proposal many years back. It was what I wanted. Craving and joy welled up in my breasts. I felt it. I felt the communion of hearts I had been starved of for many years. I felt his anger melting away. I knew he was ready to forgive me. I just wanted him to tell his family and the villagers my story so they would stop blaming me and calling me names.

The other women wasted no time to join the emotional feast of victory. You could not miss the feeling of victory in their body language as they winked at Jeff, nodding to themselves like the tortoise that outsmarted the dog and delivered the message of immortality. They sprang to their feet, lifting their legs slowly and rhythmically back and forth, moving their heads like nodding trees or flowers on long stems swaying in the direction of a passing wind. Yaya looked at me, smiling like a man expecting a male child. Nobody needed to be told we were basking in the warmth of victory. Nyuydzesi could not hide her excitement and kept saying, 'Thank you, Jesus! Thank you, Jesus!'

Just then, Jeff uttered the words I wanted to hear. "Kila, you had a mobile phone and could have called or texted me about your situation. Well, I acted in ignorance. I should have listened to your side of the story before acting like I did."

Jeff was still talking and brushing my hand when Ability stood up and frantically protested against his compromising body language. Ability was the first to stir a protest against Jeff's assuaging body language.

"Is that not Jeffiri holding Kila's hand? Is he trying to disgrace his family and our land? How can a man with balls go back to the same woman who went sleeping with tassel smokers as if she had no other business with her waist and brought home the product of animal trail affair?" The elders threw their hands in the air, their squashed lips pushed forward, and Ability continued. "Will a curse not visit us if we change the ways of our land? Is Jeffiri going to reunite with a woman who is now leaking like the fountain-head of a river?" I dropped my head, embarrassed.

"Whose name will you give to the tree whose seed was deposited in my farmland by the passing flood? Jeffiri, I hope you are not planning to put my family name on the stranger's birth certificate." Jeff's father's tone carried a feeling of rejection.

Jeff leaned back in his seat, staring, confused. My heart was pounding and galloping.

"Elders of our land, our people say when the penis is reckless, the vagina pays the price. Our daughter did not walk into the trap with her eyes open. Somebody forced himself into her. Lay down your anger and forgive her." Yaya pleaded, and the women nodded, kneeling. Ability shook his head in protest.

"What was the mortar doing near a reckless pestle? Don't we run away from fire when we see smoke? Why would Kila position herself where she would be located and invaded? If the farmland owner puts a fence around the waist of his land, would the land-grabber cross the boundary and steal crops? Tell me! Was Kila the only daughter of Mbiame land that travelled to Mirika? Was Miranda not there before her? While Miranda and others were making money and buying cars for their families, Kila was retailing her waist. We cannot continue to litter our streets with plaited ropes." The drunks erupted with laughter.

"Stop it now! I will not sit here and watch you insult my daughter and her son for a crime they did not commit! Bility, the boy you call plaited rope, has our blood in his body. That boy calls my daughter mother; he is a son of the soil," Yaya argued.

"If you put a cricket in the sky with birds, it will grow up and ask for wings to fly, thinking it belongs there," Ability countered, and the elders nodded approval.

"That boy bears my daughter's name. A curse will visit us if we reject the innocent child." Yaya insisted.

"Our people say a guava tree whose seed came from the droppings of a flying bird cannot attend the meeting of trees of the land," Ability maintained, and the elders nodded.

"A river that opens its legs and gives birth to a stream as it flows across the land will always call the stream the seed of its womb. We cannot throw away our own blood," Yaya continued.

"A plaited rope will always remain a plaited rope," Ability raged on, attracting nods of approval from the elders.

"Elders of our land, your head should be bigger than your heart. Let us grow what is good and throw away what is bad," Yaya was unstoppable.

"Two bloods in one skin! Two lives in one blood! *Mbarang*! No! No!" Ability protested, his tone condescending and assertive.

"This child did not choose to be born, nor did he choose who should bring him to the world! The village should be raising him, not rejecting him. We all have to accept and love him more than tradition hates him. Every child deserves a home and a father figure." Yaya made another desperate attempt to appeal to the conscience of the elders.

"We cannot live with that shame," barked Ability.

"Bility, do not be too quick to sing the dirge when your neighbour falls from a tree. Someone might be singing the same song in your compound sooner than you know," Yaya cautioned, but Ability took it far.

"Jeffiri, the woman whose bride price your family paid in full, has a son for another man. Who does that human graft resemble in your family? Tell me. Can he point to his father's compound? I wonder what his blood looks like! That boy calls nobody father. Nobody calls him son. He has no family name. A child conceived in an animal trail is a plaited rope. A child who does not know the name of his father's village will become a man with no example. Where will he perform his paternal rituals and libations? Will the gods of our land accept his initiation kola nuts and palm wine? Can the naming ceremony of initiation be organised for him? The answer is no! So, who is he? To whose ancestors would someone without roots offer sacrifices? Whose palm bush will he inherit when he grows up? In whose compound will he be buried? What would you do if the fruit of animal trail affair grows up in your compound and starts fighting over ownership of family land with men properly conceived under the roof? Tell the elders. How does it feel if one day there is a fight in your house and your wife tells you, 'Father of children, your children and my children are fighting our children?' It is not even an issue when a man brings a half-blood into the family. It is taboo and a scar on the family name when the woman brings foreign blood into her husband's house. . . Jeffiri, a child conceived in the animal trail is a plaited rope! A graft does not grow on the family tree! It has never happened in our land!"

"Jeffiri, Bility has spoken our minds. The pumpkin seed that falls from the droppings of a flying bird grows along the roadside. That is how it has always been. Jeffiri, do you want to change the ways of our land? Are you planning to accept a woman who has slept with another man?" Jeff's father asked and left.

"I cannot eat good food from a dirty dish!" Jeff said and left, followed by the elders.

For almost ten minutes, nobody uttered a word. The heat of shame and rejection consumed me like dry season fires as I sat, staring at my feet. My mind grappled with questions and worries. What I feared had happened. My dream died in shame. Was it not better to end it all and be free from silent pain? Why was my son rejected? How were the circumstances of his birth his fault? Why should he pay for my sins? I had to be strong for my son. I had to be the father that he never had. I resolved, my legs heavy, my heart simmering with peppery sensations.

When I managed to reach home, I called Bernsah and Mbiame and spoke to them.

"Illegal migration is not good. Greener pastures are not as green as they seem from afar. There is no place like home, even if it has its challenges."

About the Author

Photo credit: author

Associate Professor of English Literary and Cultural Studies, Pepertua K. Nkamanyang Lola, has dedicated over 25 years to various roles, including Research and Documentation Officer at the Giessen Graduate Centre for the Study of Culture at Justus Liebig University in Germany. She has also lectured at the Universities of Douala, Dschang, and Bamenda, served as Head of Service for Extra-African Cooperation at the University of Bamenda, and held the positions of First Deputy Mayor and Cultural Attaché at the High Commission of Cameroon in Nigeria. An award-winning playwright (2015) and nominee for the 2024 Aidoo-Snyder Book Prize for her work *The Lock on my Lips*, she is also a literary critic, poet, and novelist with publications in both national and international journals. Some of her notable works include *The Lock on My Lips* (drama), *Rustles on Naked Trees* (fiction), *Healing Stings* (poetry), *Fictions of Memory: An Intercultural Study*, and *Representing Fictional Minds and Consciousness: Analysis of Some Cameroon (African) English Narratives*.